To Tame
a Wild
Cowboy

By Lori Wilde

Lori Wilde

To Tame a Wild Cowboy

A CUPID, TEXAS NOVEL

AVONBOOKS

An Imprint of HarperCollinsPublishers

Excerpt from *The Christmas Dare* copyright © 2019 by Laurie Vanzura.

First Avon Books mass market printing: June 2019
First Avon Books special mass market printing: June 2019
First Avon Books hardcover printing: May 2019

Print Edition ISBN: 978-0-06-291296-1
Digital Edition ISBN: 978-0-06-246830-7

FIRST EDITION

19 20 21 22 23 LSC 10 9 8 7 6 5 4 3 2 1

To all the NICU nurses out there. Bless you. You make a huge difference in the lives of those preemies and their families.

Acknowledgments

MAJOR thanks to attorney-at-law Marcy Mailman Freeman, who specializes in family law and child custody cases. Your help was invaluable. Namaste, my yoga sister.

Note: Any mistakes in the research are totally my own. Because this book is a work of fiction, where story trumps the nitty-gritty details of real life, I claim literary license. No one should infer any sort of legal advice from the details of this fictional plot.

To Tame a Wild Cowboy

Chapter 1

COWBOY UP: Get mentally ready.

"It takes a village."

Huh?

Rhett Lockhart opened one eye and studied the shapely blonde in the bed next to him. Pouty red lips, which last night had tasted like strawberry gloss, glistened in the bright sunshine pushing against the edges of the light-blocking curtains.

Big smoky brown eyes, circled by smeared mascara, blinked at him. Full perky breasts, which tasted just as delicious in real life as they'd looked in last year's Rodeo Queens of New Mexico pinup calendar, thrust against his arm.

Miss September.

On the calendar, she'd worn spangles, bangles, a pink cowgirl hat, and little else. Much like she was dressed now, minus the hat. She was cute and perky and just the right kind of wrong.

Too bad his head throbbed like a sonofagun.

The culprit, an empty bottle of cinnamon whiskey, lay wedged between his pillow and the headboard. The celebratory hooch she'd brought with her because, as she'd said, he was *red-hot*.

"To get you up, cowboy." She glanced down at his crotch with a knowing smile. "Some bozo's been hammering on your door for a solid five minutes, and I've been calling your name . . ."

Nausea jiggled his stomach. It took him a second to remember where they were. Oh yeah, inside his Featherlite, a horse trailer with living quarters, currently parked on the rodeo fairground's back lot in Albuquerque.

Last night, he'd come in first place, blistering his biggest rival, Brazilian hotshot Claudio Limon. Claiming a solid ninety-two-point ride on Smooth Operator, one of the orneriest bulls bucking. Life didn't get much sweeter than that.

It was only May, but he was jockeying a hot streak. Burning through the circuit, racking up points left and right. This was *his* year. He was on the cusp of earning his lifetime goal and landing the dream he'd been dreaming since he was old enough to strap on chaps.

Come November in Las Vegas, he was finally going to shove Claudio off his lofty perch as a two-time winner of the Professional Bull Riders World Finals Championship and collect the title for himself.

"Rhett?" The blonde snapped her fingers in front of his face. "You with me, hon?"

Quick, what was her name? Carrie . . . Corrie . . . Chrissy . . . no . . . Cassie? Yes, Cassie. That was it. Right? Did he risk calling her Cassie, or just use his old standby?

He flashed her a big smile, winced against the added pressure in his aching temples, and drawled, "Mornin', sweet cheeks."

"It's Carla," she said, her voice flat, and her smile as fragile as iced lace.

Oops, not Cassie after all. But hey, her name started with a C. He was in the ballpark. Although the look in her eyes told him she wouldn't find that a plus.

Carla was on her side facing him, hands stacked underneath her cheek, watching him like he was a bug doing the backstroke in her soup.

"I know that," he lied through his teeth. "But those sweet cheeks of yours are drivin' me crazy." He reached to palm her butt.

"You've got a bit of the devil running through your veins, Rhett Lockhart," she breathed out on a wistful sigh. "You ooze temptation with that sexy walk and charmin' talk. How's an honest girl supposed to resist?"

She was right. He couldn't deny it, much as he might want to; he was Duke Lockhart's son. That ornery sonofabitch.

Bam, bam, bam. A firm and urgent knock on his trailer door.

"Shh." Rhett brought a finger to his lips. "Let's pretend we're not here. Maybe they'll leave."

She scooted away, nodded at his mobile phone on the bedside table beside a half-empty box of condoms. "Your cell's been pinging too."

"Ignore it." Rhett walked his fingers up her bare thigh, which was poking out from underneath the covers.

"What if it's an emergency?"

"It's not."

"How do you know?"

"Don't you want to spend the day in bed with me?" he wheedled.

"It's not me. It's the rude dude at the door."

"Maybe it's TMZ wanting an interview." He gave her another wink and a tickle. "I *was* pretty spectacular last night."

Carla laughed. "Yeah, right."

"Pardon me? Are you making fun of my bedroom prowess?"

"Oh, I have no complaints in *that* department," she purred.

Bam, bam, bam.

"It might not be an emergency, but whoever is out there isn't going away. For once in your life, face the music, Lockhart." Carla got out of bed.

Face the music? Not his strong suit.

"Rhett!" his lawyer, Lamar Johnston, called out. "Open the damn door. I know you're in there."

"Want me to get that?" Carla found his black PBR T-shirt draped over the footboard. Pulled the tee down over her head, covering those beautiful boobs.

Darn it.

"It's just Lamar." He reached for her arm and hauled her back onto the mattress beside him. "Ignore him, and he'll leave."

"Who is Lamar?"

"My Texas lawyer."

"Why is your Texas lawyer in New Mexico?"

"I might have been avoiding his calls."

"What have you gotten yourself messed up in?"

"It's nothing." Rhett waved a hand. "People like to sue you when you're in the public eye."

"It doesn't sound like nothing."

Bam, bam, bam.

"Rhett, I'm not going anywhere," Lamar confirmed. His attorney had crap timing. "You might as well let me the hell in."

Carla rolled out of his arms. Grabbed for the tiny scrap of pink silk that passed for panties lying on the floor and wriggled into them.

Rhett sat up. Shook his head. Wished he had another hour with her. But maybe this was better. Short and sweet.

"This wasn't how I anticipated the day going," she muttered. "I had plans for you."

Yikes, both intriguing and a little frightening.

"Me either," Rhett said as way of an apology. "I'd intended on taking you out to IHOP for breakfast."

"You mean lunch." She nodded at the digital clock on the faux panel walls. One p.m. Was it really that late?

"Rain check?" he asked to be polite.

"If I knew you meant it, I'd say yes." Carla stepped into faded skinny jeans that fit like a second skin. Wriggled and jiggled to get the zipper up.

Rhett licked his lips. He remembered why he'd brought her back to his trailer last night. Besides the pretty face and hot bod, she was an easygoing, no-strings-attached woman.

Just his type.

"But we both know this isn't headed anywhere." She came around to his side of the bed. Kissed him. A light brush of her lips. "I knew you were a good-time Charlie when I crawled into the sack with you. I had no foolish dreams that I was the one girl who could tie you down."

"No?" He gave her his best morning-after grin, relief breaking out all over him. "Giving up that easily? I wouldn't mind if you tried a little harder to lasso me."

She laughed a soft shame-on-you sound. "Do I look stupid? You're a fun guy, Rhett. But let's face it, you're not cut out for the long haul."

"That's it?" he asked, disappointed, and surprised at his disappointment. He liked Carla for sure, but the last thing he wanted was a relationship.

Not now. Not ever.

He wasn't like most people, hell-bent on finding The One, tying the knot, having a passel of kids, growing old, dying . . .

Just the thought of it made him twitchy.

And that spurred another thought. What would his life have been like if he hadn't been born to one of the wealthiest men in the Trans-Pecos, who'd swung through women, leaving a trail of broken hearts in his wake?

He recalled a time when he was seven years old and out to dinner with the family. His mother, that gentle soul, his brothers—two half, one full—and his father. They were at the Barbecue King in Alpine. He recalled the smoky smell of mesquite and the taste of mustard potato salad. One of the waitresses had taken one look at his father, let out a cry of shock, and dropped her tray with a clatter. She'd rushed over to slap Duke hard across the face. Rhett's mother, Lucy, had burst into tears. Duke laughed and rubbed his cheek, which had turned bright red in the shape of a handprint. The restaurant diners gaped. The owner rushed over, fired the waitress, and comped their meal. Ridge punched the old man in the gut. Ranger picked up a book and started reading. Remington threw his arm around their mother and glared at Duke. Rhett crawled underneath the table, stuck his fingers in his ears, and started humming "I Wanna Be a Cowboy."

Ah, family memories. Good times.

"Some people are born to roam the earth alone. That's you to a

T." Carla's eyes gentled. She was a kind woman. "Not everyone is meant to find true love and have a family . . . and there's nothing wrong with that."

He agreed. So how come he felt oddly put down?

And a tiny bit sad?

She plunked onto the end of the mattress, tugging on pink rhinestone ankle boots. Stood. Headed for the door. "By the way," she said, her voice as cheerful as Saturday night, "I'm keeping the T-shirt."

"You're welcome to it."

She brought the neckline of the tee up to her nose, inhaled. Sighed. "God, you *do* smell good." Her voice was wistful, but not in a fatalistic way. More like she'd missed out on a sweet deal on a used car.

She picked her cell phone up off the tiny shelf on her side of the bed. Glanced at her messages. "Ah," she said. "It's just as well that we didn't get to spend the day together."

"What is?" Rhett scratched his chest, yawned.

"My ex just texted. He got called into work and I have to go pick up my daughter."

"I didn't know you had a daughter."

"Ivy. She's four." Carla's face was ringed with sudden happiness. "Light of my life. Wanna see a picture?"

He held up a palm. "That's okay. You have to get on the road."

A new look crossed her face, as if she'd dodged a bullet on that used car that turned out to be a clunker.

Yikes.

Carla was the fourth woman he'd dated this past year that had a child. When did everyone start having kids? Goose bumps sprang up his arms, and his throat tightened. Kids gave him the heebie-jeebies. He had no idea how to relate to them.

She wriggled her fingers and squeezed out of the cramped bedroom loft. He watched her step down to the next level of the trailer, could see only her top half now. She opened the door. "Morning."

"Um . . . hello." Lamar's booming voice filled the trailer.

"Bye," she said.

Rhett heard them pass on the steps, Carla going out, Lamar coming in. The door closed, and he got the oddest feeling. As if something irrevocable had just happened.

Lamar's thick head of curly black hair poked into his doorway. "You're a scoundrel, you know that, right?"

Yawning again, Rhett interlaced his fingers, stretched his arms over his head. "What can I say? I love the ladies, and the ladies love me."

"Have you no shame?"

"Shame? What for? I have rules."

"Like what?"

"No one under twenty-one, and no married women, ever."

Maybe he should start adding "no mothers" to that list too. Kids complicated things. A lot. Last week, he'd spent the night at a woman's house and woke up to find a little boy in Superman Underoos staring at him. Acting as if it were no big deal to find a strange man in Mom's bed, the boy took Rhett by the hand, led him to the kitchen, and asked him to make "boo-berry" Pop-Tarts. Rhett threw Pop-Tarts in the toaster, poured the kid some chocolate milk, and got the hell out of there ASAP. That was the extent of his brush with anything remotely like fatherhood. He barely even saw his brother Ridge's two kids or his eighteen-month-old twin brothers his sixty-year-old father had sired with his third wife, Vivi.

"Oh, what a code of honor." Sarcasm was Lamar's touchstone.

"Hey, I don't make them any promises. The women know right up front where they stand with me."

"And you go through them like Kleenex."

"Why are you here?" Rhett lowered his arms. His mouth was as dry as the Chihuahuan Desert he called home. He needed a gallon of water and a fistful of aspirins for his hangover. But the bed was soft, and he was feeling lazy, so he lazed.

"Get dressed." Lamar turned and moved to the compact

kitchenette at the back of the living quarters. Pots and pans clanked. The coffeemaker gurgled to life.

There was something about his lawyer's tone of voice that grabbed Rhett by the short hairs. He threw back the covers.

"Are you fixin' my breakfast?" Rhett called, whisking his Wrangler's from the floor and pulling them on. An uneasy tingling tugged his belly. Something strange was afoot.

Bare-chested, he dropped down off the bedroom platform, landed on the laminate wood flooring with a flat-footed *plop*, and strolled the short space to the kitchen area.

Lamar stood at the gas stove whisking eggs in a bowl. He pointed at a chair with his elbow. "Sit."

Bumfuzzled, Rhett slouched at the table.

Lamar plunked a mug down in front of him. Coffeepot in hand, he leaned over to fill Rhett's mug. "Drink."

"You can cook?"

Fifteen years ago, Lamar had been the star of the Cupid basketball team; now, he was one of the top civil law attorneys in the Trans-Pecos. Lamar, as always, was impeccably dressed, wearing a tailor-made navy blue pinstripe suit, gold cuff links, a red pocket square, and a big diamond stud in his left ear. "There's a lot you don't know about me."

"Yeah, like why you're here cooking me breakfast at one o'clock in the afternoon?"

"Someone has to make sure you're taken care of since you seem incapable of doing it yourself." Lamar tsked, and tossed pepper, salt, and onion powder into the eggs. Scrambled them with a spatula.

"Hey!"

"Don't act offended. You're the superstar who leaves the grunt work to us mere mortals." The microwave dinged. Lamar removed a paper plate with two breakfast sausages on it. He added the eggs to the plate, sprinkled cheddar cheese on top, and passed the food to Rhett. "Eat."

"What's your problem?"

"You got bigger issues than me, buddy."

"Yeah, I don't have a fork."

Lamar rummaged around in a drawer, found a fork, and shoved it at him, tines first. Nimbly, he sank into the chair across from Rhett. He looked like a sleek panther that could easily snap Rhett's neck if he wanted. "We have to talk."

"What about?"

Lamar reached over for his brown leather briefcase, took out some legal papers stapled together, and dropped them in the middle of the table.

"What's this?" Rhett asked.

"Got the test results back."

Rhett stared at the papers in front of him. It was an incomprehensible list of letters and numbers. Oh shit. From the look on Lamar's face, he knew he was in big trouble. The eggs he'd swallowed hung in his throat. He couldn't get them to go either up or down. There they sat, making a giant knot, choking him.

"At last." Lamar chuckled. "You've got nothing to say."

Rhett spat the eggs out into a napkin. "Oh, I got plenty to say. One of these days, you're gonna walk in here and deliver some happy news. General Mills wants to feature me on a box of Wheaties. Claudio is quitting the PBR for good and returning to Brazil. Hollywood is paying big bucks for my life stor—"

"Surprise!" Lamar interrupted. "This time you won the paternity lottery." Lamar thumped the paperwork with a thumb. "Congratulations! You're a father."

The words didn't sink in. Father? Him? No way. He'd been sued for paternity three other times, which was why he had Lamar on retainer, and had always come up in the clear.

"I *can't* be the father." Rhett hopped up and paced the tiny trailer, hand on his forehead. "There has to be some kind of mistake."

"DNA is ninety-nine percent accurate."

"But I never ride bareback." Rhett whacked his hip into the counter, barely even noticed. "*Nev*-er."

"Accidents happen." Lamar shrugged as if he'd been expecting such news for a long time. "The only perfect birth control is abstinence, and the whole world knows you're incapable of that." He pointed to Carla's pink bra hanging from the doorknob. "Case in point."

"I was only with her once."

"Who? The owner of the pink bra or Rhona White?"

"Both."

"Once is enough."

Rhett muttered a curse. "Rhona set me up. She got pregnant on purpose. She just wants money."

"Takes two to tango. Besides, it's not Rhona who's after you, she seems to have disappeared. It's the state of Texas."

No. No. This could *not* be happening. Not at this point in his career. Not when everything was on the line. He shoved his fingers through his hair.

A sharp pinprick of memory pierced the base of his skull. The summer he was seventeen, Brittany Fant, the girl who'd shattered his heart, had ended any stupid beliefs he'd ever had about romantic love. He flashed back to a positive pregnancy test, a rush of intense joy at the thought of being a dad . . . and then the calm announcement by Brittany's mother that she was taking her daughter to a clinic and putting an end to this nonsense. "Is this what you really want?" Rhett had asked, pleading. A pale-faced Brittany nodded in silent agreement. And that had been that.

"I don't know why you're so shocked." Lamar propped his Gucci loafers on the Yeti cooler parked underneath the table. "It's been six weeks since CPS showed up with the swab. You think you'd have braced yourself for the possibility of this outcome."

"I was one of four potential dads. What were the odds it'd be me?"

"Um, twenty-five percent or better."

"How did this happen? It shouldn't have happened."

"You think you're special?" Lamar shot him a look of disdain. "That the laws of nature don't apply to you? You keep having sex with random women, even protected sex, and eventually it's going to catch up with you. Stay away from the casinos when you're in Vegas. Your luck has run out."

"Har, har." Rhett kneaded his brow, felt his stomach flip over. He picked up the papers, reread the part confirming that he was indeed the father of Rhona White's baby.

"Sorry to be the bearer of bad news, but it's time to accept responsibility for your actions, buckaroo."

Panic was a noose around his neck, growing tighter with each breath he took. Rhona had vowed she was on birth control. Assured him that he didn't need to use a condom. He'd insisted anyway. He wasn't dumb. She wouldn't have been the first buckle bunny to get pregnant in order to lasso herself a rodeo hero.

The thing was, he'd liked Rhona. She was cute and had a bubbly personality, and she looked at him as if he'd hung the moon. That was always a nice combo. Although she'd been younger than he liked, just turned twenty-one.

Still, he wished like hell he'd shut the door that night she'd shown up at his trailer, after they'd spent the evening playing darts together at a nearby bar. She'd been holding a bottle of champagne, wearing those hot pink short-shorts and an I-wanna-share-your-bed smile. They'd both gotten drunk, and one thing had led to another . . .

God, he should have known better. Rhett whacked his forehead with the heel of his hand—*stupid, stupid, stupid.*

"There's one major thing you forget in your selfish wallow," Lamar said.

Rhett blinked. "Who? Rhona?"

"The baby, you jackass."

Baby.

Rhett stopped moving, stopped thinking, stopped breathing. *Baby.*

The word rolled through him, a freight train of energy. Blasting hot and indigo up his spine. He clenched his teeth and his fist, but his heart loosened, floppy and soft inside his chest.

There was a *real* baby.

He was a dad. He slumped back down into the chair. His jaw dropped, his mouth falling right open of its own accord. "I have a son?"

"No, you have a daughter."

"What?"

Lamar tapped the paper with his index finger. "It's a girl."

"I have a da-da-daughter," Rhett tripped over the word. "Daughter" was so big, carried so many implications. It was too much to absorb. Feelings shot through him like lasers from a ray gun: fear, awe, inadequacy, helplessness, bravery, sheer terror, and, oddly enough, the most prominent feeling of all— joy. Followed by one prevailing thought, *I am not worthy.*

"You do indeed have a daughter."

"Where is she? Do you know?" Rhett gripped the table with his fingers, fear tearing at the seams of his heart. Good God, he was a father. How was he supposed to act? Certainly not like his own father. Oh shit, oh damn, oh hell.

"There were . . . complications," Lamar said.

"Complications?" His heart squeezed down to the size of a pecan. "What do you mean?"

"Your daughter was born four months premature."

"What?" He felt all the blood drain from his face. Cold, sick fear slapped him. He didn't even know the kid and here he was feeling sorry for her. "How is that possible? Can you be born four months early and still live?"

"She was very sick."

Was? His heart popped like a slipping clutch. "What? What? Did she die?" An ugly part of him was secretly relieved that maybe she hadn't made it, but the noble part of him was horrified that he could even think such a thing.

"Relax, she is alive, and finally out of the hospital."

"Oh, thank God." Rhett clasped a hand to his chest, dizzy and disoriented. "Is she okay now? How's Rhona?"

Lamar shook his head as if Rhett was a hopeless case. "No one knows where Rhona is. She abandoned the baby after giving birth at the hospital. She gave the hospital staff the names of potential fathers while she was in labor for fourteen hours. That's why CPS came looking for the dad. To find out if you want the baby. I explained all this when CPS first showed up."

Yeah, he hadn't really been listening, certain that the baby couldn't have been his.

A feeling unlike anything he'd ever experienced crushed Rhett in a powerful grip, flooded his entire system. Big and bad and scary feelings, especially for a man who avoided entanglements.

He had a daughter. A piece of him was out there in the world. Alone.

Thirty minutes ago, he was a cowboy without a worry in the world except winning the PBR championship. Now he was a father, and in one sharp moment, everything had changed.

"Where is my little girl? If Rhona took off, who's looking after her?"

"Relax. She's in good hands. Your daughter is living in El Paso with her foster mother, who, by the way, was also her neonatal nurse."

Whew, well, that was good. Someone competent was looking after her. For a second there, he'd had a crazy image of a little baby tucked in a wicker basket, swaddled in pink, left on a doorstep, coyotes howling in the distance. In much the same way that his older brother Ridge ended up dumped by his mother on their father's doorstep when he was three.

The Lockhart men had complicated histories with women and abandoned babies.

It was going to be okay, he told himself. He could have a kid. Lots of the guys on the circuit did. Yes, many of them were married, but having kids didn't seem to cramp their style. He'd provide for his daughter financially. Of course, that was a given, but it didn't mean he would have to give up his life. It's not like he had to change diapers or anything.

"What's the next step?" he asked his lawyer.

Lamar lifted his shoulders. "That's up to you."

"Meaning?"

"You can file for custody, or . . ." Lamar took a form from his briefcase, spread it on the kitchen table. "Sign over all parental rights so the foster mother can adopt her, and you can walk away with a clear conscience."

$$Chapter\ 2$$

RANK: A bull that is difficult to ride is considered "rank."

Meanwhile in El Paso, Texas . . .

"Have you heard from Child Protective Services?"

Tara Alzate, RN, shook her head. Her mother, Bridgette, sat in a rocking chair, feeding the sweet baby girl that Tara yearned to call her own.

Two days ago, on May 2, four months after Julie had been born, Tara brought her home from the neonatal unit at El Paso Children's Hospital. She'd been Julie's NICU nurse. The baby had been abandoned by her young mother, who'd taken off in the middle of the night.

The next day, Tara had started the process of becoming a foster parent with a single-minded goal. *Adopt Julie.*

From the moment she'd touched that tiny flicker of life, she'd known in her heart of hearts they were fated. Julie was Tara's second chance to become a mother. Two years ago, a month before her wedding to Kit Fedderson, her fiancé had contracted a virulent strain of viral meningitis and ended up in the hospital on a ventilator.

Four days later, he was dead.

In the shock of Kit's sudden demise, Tara miscarried their baby eight weeks into her pregnancy. Following the loss of both her husband-to-be and her unborn child, Tara's gynecologist had delivered more devastating news. Most likely, she would never be able to carry a pregnancy to term. A long struggle with endometriosis had permanently scarred her reproductive organs. Surgery was a remote possibility, but the doctor couldn't promise it would resolve her infertility issues. Since she had no romantic partner, and wasn't interested in anyone, she hadn't yet bothered with the surgery. Although she'd had her eggs collected and frozen. Just in case.

Tara rested her hand on her lower abdomen, felt the old pain surge up as if it were fresh.

But now, here was Julie, ready-made and heaven-sent. The baby needed a mom just as much as Tara needed a baby to love.

Julie had been an extreme preemie, born at twenty-seven weeks' gestation, and weighing only two pounds at birth. She'd been so tiny, so vulnerable, unable to breathe on her own. No one in the NICU had thought Julie would make it, and they warned Tara not to get attached.

But Tara believed. And for four long, arduous months, she'd prayed hard, and fought with all her heart, soul, and nursing skills.

She was taking a gamble. Years might pass before she could legally call Julie her daughter . . . if ever . . . but she couldn't regret giving it a shot.

"Tea?" Her mother called her by her childhood nickname, drawing Tara's thoughts back to the here and now. "Have you heard from CPS? Have they found Julie's father?"

"Paternity tests aren't like on TV, Mom. No results in an hour. First, CPS had to track down the men who could possibly be Julie's father. Then they administered the tests and we're waiting for the results."

"Frustrating."

"It was not an easy task from what the caseworker, Ms. Bean, told me. There were several potential candidates."

"I see." The expression on her mother's face told Tara she'd been lecturing again. The downside of being a nurse and a part-time child care educator.

"Sorry," Tara mumbled, and pressed her fingers to her mouth. "I didn't mean to sound like a know-it-all."

"You *do* know a lot. You've got a master's degree in nursing. It's something to crow about." Mom stroked Julie's head.

"I shouldn't talk down to you."

Mom's smile forgave everything. "You weren't. Do you have any idea who these men are?"

"That's confidential information. They won't give me the father's name until they've confirmed paternity. Privacy laws."

"Maybe he won't want this little munchkin." Mom tickled Julie's cheek and the baby grinned at her.

Tara's heart fluttered. Julie was still so small, barely five pounds. One tiny foot poked from the blanket; the yellow baby sock that was too big for her tiny foot dangled from the end of her toes.

"Although I have no idea how that's possible," her mother went on. "Look at that face! What kind of woman leaves a baby when she needs her the most?"

"Julie's mom was young. The responsibilities of caring for a preemie overwhelmed her."

"You're too kind."

"I don't want to get into the habit of bashing Julie's mom." Tara squatted beside the rocking chair, readjusted Julie's sock. "It's easy to judge when you haven't walked a mile in someone else's shoes."

Her mother cleared her throat. Loudly. "I'm proud of you for taking the high road, sweetheart, but I've had five babies, and I can't imagine any circumstances where it would be okay to walk away."

"Mom . . ." Tara chided, unable to stop herself. She shifted to sit down on the arm of the couch beside the rocker. "Rhona White came from an abusive home. She had no help from anyone. No parenting skills." Tara wasn't making excuses for the woman abandoning her baby. She simply tried to understand. One day, if she got to adopt Julie, she'd have to explain about her biological mother.

"I'm just saying, *I* couldn't have left her."

"Julie has me now. *Us*. Our family. She'll never be alone."

Her mother stilled, her face pensive. She opened her mouth, shut it, then opened it again. "Are you . . . absolutely sure this is the right thing?"

Puzzled, Tara cocked her head. "What are you talking about?"

"Adopting Julie."

"Of course I'm sure. You were just telling me how you can't imagine anyone abandoning her. She's helpless and alone."

"I meant her own mother abandoning her."

"You're worried I'm going to get hurt. Don't." Tara fiddled with the end of her braid, noticed she had split ends. Past time for a trim, but she'd been too busy to schedule a haircut. "I understand exactly what I'm getting into."

"I know, it's just . . ." Mom bit her bottom lip, her face filled with concern. "I'm worried that your desire to raise this child is rooted in your own tragedy."

Tara cradled her abdomen again. Yes, of course it was. How could it not be? Because she'd learned the hard way how fragile life was. But having her impulses guided by the past didn't mean she was living in the past. Even if Kit and their baby hadn't died, she would still want Julie. Life was precious. Julie was precious.

"I fear you're trying to replace the baby you lost. And while I completely understand that impulse, it's a pretty heavy burden to put on an infant."

"No," Tara said. "That's not it at all. I don't expect Julie to meet my emotional needs. I understand that she is a little person in her own right. I know she's not the child I lost." Tara clenched her jaw, fought off tears. "I'm not taking her on to salve my own grief. It's been two years. I've had therapy. I've come to terms with what happened . . . and my infertility. I want Julie for Julie. My motive is love and nothing more."

Mom leaned over to cup Tara's cheek, her eyes shiny with unshed tears. "Okay, I just wanted to make sure."

"Don't cry, Mom. If you cry, I'm going to cry."

"No tears." Mom sniffled. "I'm just so proud of you. You've been through hell and back, but you've done an amazing job of healing yourself."

"You and our family helped heal me. I couldn't have done it without you guys."

"Of course, darling. Nothing is more important than family, and it truly does take a village to raise a child. My big fear is what if Rhona comes back—"

"What if she doesn't? CPS has already started the involuntary termination of Rhona's parental rights."

"But that will be months down the road before it's finalized. Rhona could still return to claim her."

"Yes," Tara murmured. She thought about that all the time. "I can't help it, Mom. I love this baby with all my heart. Even if I have to give her up to Rhona, or the dad when they locate him, and he wants her, I've got to try."

"Your heart is so big, my darling. You always were my most compassionate child, but you're usually the most cautious as well. You're not the type to go out on a limb."

"Julie is worth it."

"Then there's the father too. What if he—"

"Let's stay positive."

"He could take her away from you."

"Trouble. Borrow. Don't."

"Court battles. Legal fees. Are you ready for that?"

"Stop worrying, Mom. If Julie's dad wants her and is able to care for her, then in a perfect world, isn't that the best scenario?"

"So you'll be able to let her go if it comes to that?"

"I can accept it."

"Are you sure?"

Was she? Letting go was not her strong suit, which made her

good at her job of saving preemie babies' lives, but had caused her quite a few problems in life.

Tara talked a big game. She hoped, if it came down to it, she could gracefully bow out. "Mom . . ."

"Yes?"

"She's stopped feeding."

"Oh, so she has." Her mother set the bottle down. Julie yawned, lowered her lashes, curled her small fists beneath her chin. Mom examined the bottle. Frowned. "She only took two ounces of formula."

"That's not unusual. She takes small amounts more often than a typical baby. It's quite common in preemies."

"How often do you feed her?"

Tara shrugged. "Every hour and a half."

"Goodness. When do you sleep?"

"Whenever I can," Tara said, reluctant to admit she worried about her abilities to mother a preemie with numerous health issues.

"Spoken like a true mom." Bridgette's eyes softened as she met Tara's gaze.

Tara reached for the sleeping baby. "I can take her now."

Mom tucked the blanket more securely around Julie. "Why don't you leave her to me and you go grab a nap?"

The idea was luxurious. She hadn't slept much in the last two days. Tara hesitated, conflicted.

"I know you want to do everything for her," Mom said. "But you've got to pace yourself. Motherhood is a marathon, not a sprint."

"It's okay, I'm fine."

Mom shot her a look. Tara knew that look.

She had a very clear memory of being five years old with her family in a crowded store. Tara needed to go to the bathroom, but she didn't say anything because her mother was so busy with the other kids, juggling Kaia on her hip, Aria in a papoose pouch on her back, hollering at Ember to stop climbing on shelves and at Archer to put back the toy truck he'd tucked under his arm. Tara hadn't wanted to be a burden. Inevitably, of course, she'd wet herself right there in the Wal-Mart, and burst into tears of shame. Mom had thrown her the same look then that she was giving her now, one of extreme exaspera-tion for her solicitous middle child. "Tara," Mom had scolded. "When you have needs, please make them known. It's much more trouble for me to clean up pee than to take you to the bathroom in the first place." Even at five, she'd been mortally mortified. Shame burning deep.

"You've got to learn to relax," her mother said. "It was a hard lesson for me to learn too, but when raising kids, it's better to lighten up, throw away the rule book, and just listen to your gut. And my gut is telling me that *my* child needs some sleep."

"Maybe just for fifteen minutes," Tara said. "It's a three-hour drive back to Cupid, and I don't want you out on the road after dark."

"I wish you lived closer." Mom shifted Julie to her shoulder. "Your sisters and I could help out more if you were home in Cupid."

"You know I love my job here."

"But you've got Julie to think about now, and I'm sure they'd love to have you back at Cupid General. I also heard there is an opening for an RN at the WIC clinic in Pecos. Those state jobs pay well with great benefits."

The Women, Infants and Children's Services of Texas might be something she'd consider down the road when she'd had her fill of the NICU stress. But as far as Cupid General went, return-ing to the well-baby nursery seemed like a step backward. Besides, her time as Julie's guardian wasn't guaranteed to last. She couldn't make a major life change regarding residences or jobs until she knew that the baby's mother and father had relinquished their parental rights.

Mom made a good point though. She didn't have any family support in El Paso.

"It's something I'll have to think about if the adoption goes through. Until then . . ." Tara lifted one shoulder. "I'll find a way to make it work. Luckily, the hospital offers child care for employees."

"Still . . ." Mom clucked her tongue. "It's not the same as family."

"As if you don't already have your hands full, helping Kaia and Casey with their little ones," she said, referring to her younger sister and her brother Archer's wife, who both had two small children.

"There's always room for another baby," Mom said, gently patting Julie's back. "Now go crawl into bed."

Tara kicked off her shoes and slipped into the bedroom of the small duplex she rented, an upgrade from the efficiency apartment she'd stayed in when she first came to El Paso. She'd moved in last month in preparation for fostering Julie. The duplex was close to the hospital and a park. A grandmotherly type lived on the other side of her. It wasn't a detached home, but it was a nice enough environment for raising a child.

Her head hit the pillow, and she'd just shut her eyes when the doorbell rang.

Talk about rotten timing.

"I'll get it, Mom," she called, and headed for the front door.

Through the peephole, she saw Julie's CPS caseworker, Mariah Bean, standing on the front porch. The younger woman was fresh from her master's degree in social work. She was a petite little thing. Barely five foot. She wore her hair, dyed flamingo pink, in a short razor cut. In a camo-colored wrap dress and incongruous purple cowgirl boots with elevated heels, she looked like a kid playing dress up, but Ms. Bean had grown up in the foster care system herself, had gone to school on the GI Bill after serving four years in the army, and fought for her young charges with dedication and verve. She was as bright and cheerful as cherry blossoms in the spring, and just looking at her made Tara feel joyful.

But what was the CPS caseworker doing here on a Saturday afternoon without calling or texting first?

Trying not to imagine the worst, Tara steeled her spine, forced a TV-commercial smile, and opened the door. "Ms. Bean, come in, come in," she invited, her pulse spiky against her veins.

"I hope you don't mind me dropping in unannounced." Ms. Bean shifted her oversized tote bag to the opposite shoulder. "I was at the hospital when I got the news, and since you were so close, I thought I'd drop by. Is now a good time?"

"Now is fine." What news? Tara barely managed to rein in her anxiety and waved the young woman into the living room. "Would you like something to drink?" What she wanted to do was grab the social worker by the shoulders, shake her solidly, and yell at her to spill it. "Coffee? Tea? Water?"

"No thank you, I can't stay long."

She introduced Ms. Bean to her mother. All three of them oohed and aahed over Julie, who was awake now and staring at them with wide-eyed curiosity.

Finally, Ms. Bean straightened and met Tara's gaze. The look said more than words, and Tara felt her stomach slosh into her socks.

"What is it?" Tara cracked her knuckles.

Ms. Bean's blue eyes dimmed, and her smile faded. "They found Julie's father."

"Oh," Tara said, and then, because she didn't know what else to say, repeated, "Oh."

"He didn't even know Julie existed until we contacted him a few weeks ago and asked him to take the paternity test. Rhona got around, if you know what I mean."

Yes, yes, Tara already knew all that. What she did not know was if the father was going to try and take Julie away from her.

"What did the dad say?" she asked.

"His people are delivering the results to him today."

His *people*. What did that mean? Did he have a legal team at his disposal ready to spring into action? All the air left her body in one whoosh, and it was only then Tara realized she'd been holding her breath. "I see."

"Don't look so distressed." The caseworker's voice carried a soothing tone. "This is a good thing."

"He wants to voluntarily terminate parental rights?" Tara asked. Her hope was a brittle sound, thin and crackly in the silence of the room. *Please let him not want her, please let him not want her . . .*

"I don't know that yet. As I said, he's being informed at the same time you are."

"Where is he?" Tara had visions of some big roughneck cowboy bursting into her house and demanding custody of his baby daughter. Her knees turned to water, and she had to put a hand against the wall to keep from losing her balance.

"Albuquerque, New Mexico."

Whew. Okay, he wouldn't be busting in her door immediately.

"But he is from Rhona's hometown, *your* hometown."

"Julie's father is from Cupid?" Tara whispered.

What were the odds? Cupid was a town of less than two thousand. Then again, many women from small towns in the Trans-Pecos came to the city to have their babies. Not such ridiculous odds in that context since El Paso was the nearest NICU.

Ms. Bean nodded, clutched her tote bag with both hands. "He is."

Tara could feel the woman's gaze slide up and down her body, as if she feared Tara was about to topple over. Mom too was watching her with narrowed pupils and pursed lips. Did she look that fragile?

Her skin felt cool and dry, but inside her blood pulsed hot and sticky. Dear Lord, did she know Julie's father? Most everyone in Jeff Davis County knew most everyone else. Odds were very good that she *did* know him.

"Who . . ." Her voice trembled. She cleared her throat, tried again. "Who is he?"

"He's a professional bull rider, as were all the men on our list of possibles. Rhona seems to have an affinity for rodeo cowboys," Ms. Bean said.

Why was the woman dragging this out? Tara squeezed her nails so hard into her palms that bites of pain shot into her wrists. In her gut she already knew the answer to her question before she repeated it. "Who is he?"

"Do you think you might know him?"

"Would knowing him help my chances of adopting Julie or hurt them?" Anxiety was a brick, clobbering every corner of her body.

"That would depend."

"On what?"

"If he's reasonable or not."

"Who is he?" Tara's voice was a thin wire, high and stiff. From the look on her mother's face, Bridgette had a shrewd guess of her own. Tara knew of only one professional bull rider in Cupid.

"His name . . ." Ms. Bean paused as if waiting for a drum roll.

Outside, a squirrel scampered across the gutter, clanking metal against the eaves. Tara sucked in a hard breath.

". . . is Rhett Lockhart."

Rhett Lockhart.

That scoundrel. She gave a little laugh, half amusement, half scoff.

Just as Tara had suspected, Julie's father was the most irresponsible man in Jeff Davis County. A man who'd once dated, and dumped, her youngest sister, Aria. A man with a reputation for blowing through buckle bunnies with the whirlwind blast of a hot desert sandstorm.

What juicy local gossip.

What controversy.

And what luck.

Rhett was a charming bad boy who cared about nothing but himself. No way was he going to want a kid.

She knew Rhett through and through. The Lockharts and Alzates were forever intertwined. All nine of the kids grew up as one big family, a pack of exuberant children who doubled as a softball team for family holiday gatherings and reunions. Her father, Armand, had been the Lockharts' ranch foreman; her mother, their housekeeper and surrogate mom.

Her brother, Archer, was the eldest of the five Alzate siblings. He had taken over as foreman of the Silver Feather once her father retired. Archer and his wife, Casey, were now rearing their two sons in the same rambling farmhouse where the Alzate children had grown up.

The next eldest, Ember, had married Ranger, the second-born Lockhart brother. They were currently living in southern Ontario, Canada, where Ranger worked as an astrobiologist and Ember had her own real estate company. They were expecting their first baby in June.

Tara was the middle child, halfway between Archer and Ember on one side, Kaia and Aria on the other. She'd long considered herself the family fulcrum, the grounding balance. Her practical, logical nature drew people to her. Particularly folks in crisis.

Kaia had married Ridge, the oldest Lockhart brother. Kaia, a veterinarian, was now a stay-at-home mom, while Ridge ran the Silver Feather.

"Rhett Lockhart," Tara whispered. "You old dog, you."

She and her mother shared triumphant glances, and Tara almost laughed out loud with relief. This was the best news ever. No way would the likes of Rhett want custody of a sickly newborn.

She was home free.

Chapter 3

MULEY: A term used to describe a hornless bull.

RHETT stared down at the form on the kitchen table.

At the top of the paper, in bold dark lettering, it read: VOLUNTARY RELINQUISHMENT OF PARENTAL RIGHTS.

"Sign the affidavit and your troubles are over."

"Really?" His hopes bobbled.

"We'll need to get a witness and a notary, but that's easily solvable. Clerk in the fairground's office has a notary sign on the wall. We can just walk on over to the office."

Rhett bent over the form, too leery to even pick it up. He rubbed his palms down the tops of his thighs all the way to his knees, read it over. Two times. "Do I have to sign it today?"

Lamar looked surprised. "No. I just figured you would want to. It's why I went ahead and flew out here. That and I had some other business in Santa Fe tomorrow."

"What does it mean if I relinquish my parental rights?"

"It means your daughter can be adopted out. The foster mother is eager to have her."

"What about the foster father?"

"Ms. Alzate is single."

Alzate?

Rhett froze. He straightened and met Lamar's gaze. He knew of only one Alzate who was a NICU nurse. The same Alzate who'd babysat him when he was a kid. The very same Alzate who was also his sister-in-law. Twice. Her sisters Kaia and Ember had married his half brothers Ridge and Ranger.

"Tara? *She's* my daughter's foster mother?"

Lamar nodded, confirming.

Oh wow. Tara made him uncomfortable because she saw through him like a windowpane. The one Alzate he'd never been able to charm. She'd always known when he was up to mischief.

He hadn't seen her since she'd moved to El Paso almost two years ago. Not that he'd ever really hung out with her. Just bumped into her at family functions where the Lockharts and Alzates mingled. He dredged up polite chitchat when he had to, but he'd always gotten the feeling she disapproved of him. Not that she'd ever said anything to that effect. Typically, she simply avoided him.

Her attitude bothered him. He liked women, and for the most part, they returned the feeling and then some. Tara's distaste for him had taken a stronger track since he'd briefly dated her youngest sister, Aria.

Rhett and Aria were a lot alike, both fun-loving and frisky, easygoing and expressive. They'd had a ball together. They'd both gone into the relationship knowing it was nothing but a fling. He hadn't hurt Aria. Aria hadn't hurt him. They were cool.

But Tara had disapproved. Throwing around her holier-than-thou frown.

A couple of summers ago, she'd backed him into a corner of the kitchen at his brother Ridge's house on his family's Silver Feather Ranch. It was during a party following the christening of their niece, Ingrid. Tara had shaken a chiding finger in his face and told him in no uncertain terms to leave Aria alone. Rhett explained that Aria was a grown woman who could make her own decisions. Tara countered by threatening his private parts if he didn't back off her sister.

Hmm. So Tara wanted to adopt his daughter. He wasn't sure how he felt about this.

"Does she know the baby is mine?" he asked.

"The caseworker is informing her today."

Was this a bit of good news or not? Rhett stroked his chin, unable to decide. If he signed away his parental rights and Tara adopted the baby, he'd still get to see his daughter from time to time when their two clans got together. On the surface it seemed like a win-win.

As if reading his mind, Lamar said, "Signing away your parental rights means you will no longer have any say in how the baby is raised. Not her religious affiliations, not how she's educated, not where she lives. Nothing. Even if Tara happens to let you see the baby once the adoption is final, you are not guaranteed that right by law."

Rhett rapped his fingers against the table repeatedly, feeling keyed up. He hadn't had time to absorb all this. "What about Rhona?"

Lamar put out a hand to stop the tapping. "The state has already moved to terminate Rhona's rights involuntarily since she abandoned the baby. Problem is, she's in the wind."

"Let me get this straight. Even if I were to sign this form right now, Tara can't move forward with the adoption until Rhona's parental rights have been terminated by the state."

"That's right. Or Rhona could come back and voluntarily relinquish her rights, allowing Tara to adopt her," Lamar said.

"Conversely, she could show up and want the child back before her rights have been terminated." Rhett toyed with the cow and bull salt and pepper shakers on the table, moving them around like chess pieces.

"That is a possibility."

"What if I sign over my rights, and Rhona wants the baby back?"

"Then, unless the judge concludes there's a good reason why not, Rhona *will* get custody."

"And I'll be left without a say in it."

"That's right."

"But neither will Tara."

"Yes."

"No one knows where Rhona is?"

"Do you have any idea?" Lamar asked.

Rhett shook his head as vigorously as if he were trying to dislodge hay from his shaggy curls. "I hardly knew her."

"I get the feeling you need more time." Lamar reached for the paper.

Rhett held on to it. Why was he hesitating? Sign the form. Get it over and done with and get back to his life. Did it really matter whether the baby went to Tara or Rhona? He was never going to be father of the year. The kid deserved better than the likes of him. It wasn't as if Rhett had had some great role model to pattern himself after.

Ridge didn't have a great model and he's an awesome dad, the thought rose up in his mind. Yeah, well, Ridge had always been the responsible type. The parenting gig for his older half brother had been like taking a duck to water.

But Rhett? He simply didn't have what it took to be a good dad. He wasn't cut out for it. A guy had to honor who he was at his core, right? Yes, he could provide for the baby financially, and he would. Even if he terminated his parental rights, he'd still make sure the baby was taken good care of . . . monetarily, that was. That, he could do. But the day-to-day? C'mon, let's be honest, he had absolutely nothing to offer.

Perhaps if the child were a boy, he could teach him how to ride horses and tame a bull, but what did he know about tea parties and hair bows? He'd lost his mother when he was eight. He knew nothing about what was in the hearts and minds of women. To be truthful, he'd never really wanted to know.

Women, in Rhett's world, were pretty playthings to be savored and admired, at least until it was time to move on to the next town.

For the first time ever, it occurred to him that the women he'd dated were someone else's daughters. One day, *his* daughter would be old enough to hang around the rodeo circuit and pick herself up a cowboy.

Yikes! Rhett yanked a palm down his face, snorted. *That* was a scary thought.

"You've got more depth than I thought."

"What does that mean?"

"I figured you'd be raring to sign away those rights at the drop of a Stetson."

"Shouldn't I at least see the baby first?"

"Personally, if it were me, I would. But I'm not you." Lamar futzed with his pocket square.

Rhett sat back down, anchored his elbow to the table, plunked his chin in his upturned palm. Cogitated. Sign the form and he was free as a bird. Or go see the baby first and risk losing his heart.

"What should I do?" He blinked at Lamar.

"You've spent your life keeping your heart out of the fray. Why change now?" Lamar asked.

"Because this is a baby. *My* baby."

Lamar spread his hands like goalposts. "And there you have it."

Oh shit, oh damn, he was screwed. "How can I be a single dad and stay in the PBR?"

"That's the same question a judge is going to ask if you file for custody."

"Nope." Rhett shook his head again as fear seized his stomach. "Can't do it. Can't give up the PBR."

Lamar pushed back his chair. "Let's go talk to that notary."

Rhett raised his palms, stop-sign style. "Not yet."

"You're vacillating."

"I know."

"I get it. It's a big decision, either way."

Rhett jammed his hand through his hair, his fingers getting caught up in the tangles. Maybe he should shave his head. Just for the hell of it. Change might be good. But women loved running their fingers through his curls. It's why he kept his hair just a little too long.

"You've got kids, right?" he asked Lamar.

"Two daughters, twelve and five, lights of my life." Lamar paused, let that sink in. "But it's hard, man, raising kids, and I've got a great wife. If you're thinking about raising a baby alone . . ."

"Think again?"

Lamar shrugged.

"I can hire nannies."

"Is that fair to the baby? Especially when someone like Tara wants to adopt her."

"Tara's single too."

"But Tara is a neonatal nurse, and she has a huge, supportive family."

"I got family."

"That you see a few times a year."

Rhett sank his face into his hands. Truly, he was surprised to find himself in this situation. After Brittany, he'd always been so careful. Sometimes he even wore two condoms, just in case. He'd heard of women poking holes in rubbers to lasso a guy. Had Rhona done that?

But if she'd gotten pregnant on purpose, why hadn't she told him? Why hadn't she shown up demanding marriage or money?

Well, he wasn't the kind of guy to sit around and think. He was, by nature, a doer. He acted. Right now, he had two choices. Sign the paper and forget about it. Or go see the baby and then decide.

That meant facing Tara.

Ugh. He wasn't looking forward to that.

It also meant skipping the next PBR event. Not that he couldn't spare the time away. He was the current point leader. But it wouldn't take much for his nemesis, Claudio Limon, to dethrone him. One week away was enough to lose the lead.

Almost on autopilot, he got up and went to his closet for a clean Western shirt, did up the snaps. Grabbed his boots near the front door, jammed his feet into them.

"Where are you going?"

Rhett chuffed out a long breath. "Guess I'm headed to El Paso."

"To file for custody?"

"Hell man, that's one giant step. Don't push. I'm just going to check out the situation." Rhett plucked his Stetson off the hat rack.

"Don't be surprised if you fall in love and can't walk away."

He paused with the Stetson halfway to his head. "Are you saying going to El Paso is a bad idea?"

"I'm saying that seeing your baby could change everything. If you don't want your life to change, don't go."

Well, that was a fine howdy-do. "And I pay you to give me this advice?"

"Just fair warning, that's all."

Rhett let loose with a string of curses. "Now I don't know whether to go or not."

"Ask yourself this, which will you regret more? Never seeing her and letting her go for good, or seeing her and having your life turned upside down?"

"This sucks."

"Think about the baby. She's already started life with several strikes against her. Born premature. Mama abandoned her . . ."

"All right, all right." Rhett settled the Stetson firmly on his head, feeling like a man being led to the gallows. "I'm going, I'm going."

He went outside to get his trailer ready to travel, heard the door click closed behind him. His boots kicking up fairground dust as he rounded the front of the trailer and out of nowhere . . . *bam.*

An angry fist plowed into his face.

The blow blindsided him, and he fell back on his ass in the dirt. Squinting, he peered up at Claudio Limon, who was cradling his knuckles and glaring at Rhett as if he were Satan himself.

"*Idiota!*" Claudio cursed in Portuguese.

"Whoa, whoa." Rhett raised both arms to cover up his face.

His head felt as if it had been slammed against a concrete wall. Hangover + finding out he had a kid he didn't know about + pissed-off fist = wallop of hurt.

"What the hell, man?" he asked Claudio.

His rival's nostrils flared like Riptide's, the meanest bull on the circuit, whenever he charged a bullfighter. "You sleep with my girl, Rhona!" Claudio added a few more Portuguese curse words.

"You didn't put a ring on it," Rhett pointed out, but gallantly he didn't mention that Rhona was just about everybody's girl on the rodeo circuit. "Face facts."

"You make her pregnant." Claudio's pupils narrowed to pin pricks.

"How did you know it was my baby?"

"The CPS call and tell me I not father. I see your lawyer coming to your trailer, I know you on list of possible fathers. Two and two, I can put together." Claudio surged forward.

Rhett bounced to his feet, took a boxer's stance. Plowed his right fist into Claudio's breadbasket just as the man grabbed him.

Stetsons flew.

They grunted and punched.

Cursed and kicked.

Knocked each other into the dirt. Rolled around.

Slugged and hammered.

Thrashed and crashed.

Eyes swelled. Noses bled. Lips split.

It had been a long time since he'd been in a down-and-dirty brawl with something other than a wild bovine. Rhett was a lover, not a fighter, but if someone took a swing at him, he sure as hell was going to defend himself.

A small crowd gathered. Lamar with his arms crossed over his chest, fairground folk, rodeo cowboys, a buckle bunny or two. They watched the altercation as if they had ringside seats to a cage match.

Which, Rhett supposed, they did. Two of the biggest PBR

rivals going at each other over a woman. Wait until TMZ heard about this.

"Hey, hey," Rhett grunted, running out of steam. "This ain't getting us nowhere."

"Makes me feel better." Claudio kept whaling on him, fists flailing.

"Does it? Does it really?" Rhett dodged him.

Claudio pounced.

Rhett clamped him in a headlock. "Calm the hell down."

Claudio struggled against him. Swore. Bucked. "She my girl."

"Not really."

"Supposed to be *my* baby!" Claudio stopped fighting.

Rhett let him go. His entire body throbbed with pain. Claudio dragged himself over to Rhett's trailer, propped his shoulders up against a tire.

They lay on the ground panting and glaring at each other.

It hit him all at once, why Rhona had shown up on his doorstep that night last summer. He'd thought at the time it was because of his win and she wanted to rub up against his glory. Now he remembered that it was the same night Claudio had gone off with a young, pretty barrel racer. Rhona had slept with him to make her boyfriend jealous. He knew for sure now, she hadn't gotten pregnant on purpose.

Rhett groaned. "Would that I could, I'd turn back the clock."

"I love her." Tears sprang to Claudio's eyes, which were both rapidly swelling shut.

"Aw, man. I'm sorry."

Claudio doubled up his fist, shook it at Rhett. "You stole everything."

"By the by, do you know where Rhona is?" Rhett asked.

Claudio raised one shoulder in a halfhearted shrug. "I have not seen her since last summer."

"You didn't know she was pregnant?"

"Not until the CPS came to . . ." Claudio made a motion of swabbing out his mouth.

"We weren't the only ones she slept with," Rhett pointed out. "They swabbed two other guys."

Claudio growled and tried to lever himself off the ground.

Rhett put up both palms. "Whoa, whoa. No more fighting. It solves nothing. She's done with us both and she abandoned my baby at the hospital. Consider yourself lucky."

Apparently, that was *not* what the Brazilian wanted to hear. He launched himself at Rhett and they went back at it again.

Lamar disappeared, then reappeared with a metal bucket, fastidiously holding it away from his suit, and doused them with cold water. "Knock it off, you two."

They broke apart, sputtering.

Exhausted, Rhett collapsed onto his back. Claudio fell right beside him. His entire world had imploded, and it was his own damn fault.

No denying it. He was one of those scoundrel Lockharts through and through, and he had an illegitimate child to prove it.

Chapter 4

SET YOU UP: The act of a bull that drops a shoulder like it is going to spin in one direction, and then immediately does the exact opposite.

Three days later . . .

MARIAH Bean's space alien green Kia Soul pulled up outside the duplex. Followed shortly by a familiar bronze Ford King Ranch one-ton dually pickup truck.

Distressed, Tara stood at the living room window, arms wrapped securely around Julie. Her heart skipping crazily.

This was it. The moment she'd been dreading since she'd learned who the baby's father was. Mom, Kaia, and Aria had offered to be here for the showdown, but this was Tara's battle. She needed to fight it alone.

At least for now.

Afterward, her family could help her pick up the pieces.

There she went again, preparing for the worst. Cheer up. It was Rhett, the rolling stone. A baby would seriously cramp his style.

Always a good hostess, she had set out a teapot and coffee carafe on the coffee table, along with finger sandwiches and scones. At the last minute, she'd bought pink strawberry wafer cookies because she remembered that they were Rhett's favorite. Catch more flies with sugar, right?

The plucky Ms. Bean got out of her Kia. Today she wore a raspberry beret over her pink hair, an orange paisley jumpsuit, black high-top Converse sneakers, and a peace sign necklace. She looked as if she'd raided the wardrobe closet of *That '70s Show.*

But it was the man stepping from the expensive pickup truck that drew Tara's attention.

His hair was the color of aged whiskey, private select, and on the sexy side of shaggy. He wore a straw Stetson cocked rakishly to the left. His heavily starched jeans clung tightly to his muscular thighs, and a gold rodeo belt buckle glistened in the afternoon sun like the Holy Grail.

Transfixed, she watched him walk with a lanky roll, his hips lean and loose. A leisurely lilt that said, *I've got all the time in the world for you, babe.* Tara understood why women fell over themselves to get next to Rhett Lockhart. He possessed that undeniable *something.*

Tara steeled herself. Denying it. Denying him.

And yet, her womb gave a strange, uncharacteristic squeeze. Cramps, she told herself, because that bowl-'em-over charm didn't work on her. She knew all his roguish tricks. She'd been the babysitter standing outside his bedroom window, fourteen to his ten. Arms crossed over her chest, catching her impish charge as he slipped to the ground, incorrigible and unrepentant. Even then. Now, eighteen years later, she was caring for his infant daughter.

Fate was a fickle wench.

The resolute Ms. Bean crossed over the lawn to speak to him, held out her palm, tote bag hoisted up on her shoulder. He shook her hand, but his eyes stayed trained on Tara's front door. He was coming in.

Instinctively, Tara clutched Julie closer.

Rhett and Ms. Bean turned and moved up the sidewalk in lockstep. They cut an uneven picture. Five-foot Ms. Bean in her kooky duds, placing a hand on her beret to hold it in place against the wind. Five-eleven-inch Rhett, sporting designer boots, sweeping off his Stetson and resting it against his chest.

The closer they drew, the harder Tara's heart pounded.

Julie squirmed, made a soft mewling sound. Tara hitched her higher, kissed the baby's cheek. "It's going to be okay, sweetheart. You're about to meet your daddy."

This was a good thing, Tara tried to tell herself, the best thing for Julie. Every girl deserved to know her daddy. Even a daddy like Rhett.

But what if he wanted custody?

Tears clogged Tara's throat. Maybe he wouldn't want the baby. Maybe he would understand he wasn't equipped to care for an infant with ongoing health issues. Maybe he would agree to relinquish his parental rights, so Tara could adopt her.

Please, she prayed silently, *please*.

She'd spent the past three days, since she'd learned of his identity, planning how to lobby her case. She could rally the Alzate and Lockhart clans. Get them to convince Rhett he wasn't in any position to raise a child. He didn't have the skills or, let's face it, the constitution for fatherhood. He was a party hound with wanderlust, a single-minded rodeo cowboy driven to win at all costs. Not the ideal situation for childrearing.

They passed Tara's view from the window, climbed the front steps, and for the first time she saw that Rhett was sporting a black eye, bruised lips, and a stitched cut over his left eyebrow. Bull-riding casualty? Or barroom brawl over a woman? With him, either was highly possible.

Her heart pounded, as weird waves of sensation that felt way too much like sexual attraction undulated through her. No. She was mistaken. This bizarre feeling was *not* sexual attraction. It was a physical manifestation of fear. Fear could cause strange symptoms in the body, and that's exactly what was happening here.

She put Julie in her bassinet and whisked from the living room, down the foyer to the front door. Got there just as they knocked.

Tara took a deep breath. Opened the door. Meant to say hello but couldn't find the words. Terrified that if she spoke, she'd break down.

Ms. Bean stood on the welcome mat, a tight little smile on her face. The caseworker turned to Rhett. "Mr. Lockhart, this is your daughter Julie's foster mother, Tara Alzate."

Behind the caseworker, Rhett's battered eyes met Tara's gaze, and he gifted her with his most rakish grin, which provoked her uterus to do curious things again. "Surprise, sweet cheeks, it's me."

WHY HAD HE said that? Sometimes Rhett thought he should go around with Gorilla Tape plastered over his big mouth.

Tara shot him a glare hot enough to wither daisies. She lowered her shoulders, shifted her center of gravity. "Don't you *ever* call me sweet cheeks."

That was Tara. She'd never been shy about carving out strong boundaries. Probably because she had a loving father. In his experience the women with the weakest personal boundaries were the ones most likely to have daddy issues.

In the past, he'd taken full advantage of that. But now, standing here in the face of Tara's disapproval, he felt a bit ashamed of himself.

Tiny Ms. Bean looked unnerved, glancing from Tara to Rhett and back again. "I know you two have history, but let's keep this civil, shall we?"

"Sweet cheeks is the way he addresses his numerous women because he can't remember their names." Tara's pupils constricted. She was peeved at him. Everything about her was knotted up as wiry as baling twine. Stiff shoulders, disapproving mouth, rigid face.

"Won't happen again."

"See that it does not." Tara's tone dripped venom. If she'd been a snake, she would be a cobra. Flaring nostrils. Wicked tongue. Deadly stare.

He wasn't scared. Not much. "Because clearly your cheeks are pretty darn sour."

Tara snorted, sounding for all the world like a rodeo bull

going after a bullfighter. Goose bumps broke out on his arms the way they did when he was in the arena. Part excitement, part terror, part delight.

He had a striking urge to touch her, taste her. The impulse was so strong and unexpected, he blinked and told himself to ignore it. He felt overly warm, while his fingers and toes went oddly cold, as if all his blood was being funneled straight to his torso.

"Civility," Ms. Bean said in a butterfly voice, light and fluttery.

Tara blew out her breath through clenched teeth, ziplined an exclusive smile to the other woman, leaving him out of it. "I'll try."

"Thank you." Ms. Bean, that little ray of sunshine, gave a that's-the-spirit swing of her arm.

Tara turned her attention back to Rhett. "You look like hell."

"Aw, thanks for noticing. You, on the other hand, look nice."

She snorted again. "Stop giving me compliments. I'm not one of your bimbos." The haughty look she gave him would have dropped green apples off the tree in the Garden of Eden. "What caused that?" She waved a hand at his face. "Irate husband?"

"I don't date married women." Gently, he touched the corner of his eye.

"But apparently you *do* date children. Rhona was barely twenty-one."

"Hey, she was over eighteen; old enough to vote, old enough to serve."

"Oh well then, you are Mr. Honorable. Wanna blue ribbon?"

"How do you two know each other again?" Ms. Bean hoisted up her tote bag stuffed with case files. It had to weigh twenty pounds. He marveled at her ability to shoulder it.

"We're related," Rhett explained.

"By marriage *only*," Tara said.

"In-laws." Ms. Bean nodded as if she were fifty instead of in her mid-twenties. "I get it. Small world."

"And getting smaller by the minute," Tara muttered.

"Your being related should help things along," Ms. Bean chirped. Clearly, she was a keep-on-the-sunny-side-of-life type. His favorite sort of woman. He wondered if she would like to grab a drink after this.

"Or make them worse," Tara muttered so quietly he barely heard her.

"Civility," he said, and offered up a slow wink. His go-to grin designed to win people over. It didn't work on Tara. He should have known. She was a killjoy from way back.

She glowered like a thundercloud and set her lips to "prim."

His smile wavered. Did the black eye mar the effect of his trademark grin? Or was he forever doomed where Tara was concerned?

She waved them over the threshold. "Please, come inside."

Tara stood next to the door. She was the tallest of the Alzate girls. Five-seven. With a sturdy but trim figure appropriate for the physical demands of a nursing job. Full hips and breasts. Curvy waist. Long, straight black hair pulled into a single braid at her back. High cheekbones paid homage to the Mescalero Apache ancestry on her father's side.

Ms. Bean went first, passing Tara in the foyer.

Rhett followed, his shoulder accidentally grazing Tara as he passed. A shot of static electricity snapped between them.

Crack.

She gasped. It was a soft but audible sound. He felt a corresponding underground vibration running through him like a mallet striking a gong.

He jerked his head around and met her gaze.

Her dark eyes were wide and startled. She moistened her lips, and he saw a dash of her pink tongue. For a whisper of a second, their gazes locked, and it felt as if they'd gotten trapped together in some exotic maze without an exit.

Then he scooted away from her as fast as he could, following Ms. Bean into the living room. The duplex was small, but clean and orderly. Still, it was not the palace his little princess deserved to grow up in.

"Please sit down," Tara invited, fastidious and proper. She eased onto the edge of the couch, the baby tucked securely in the crook of her arm.

The room was stiff with awkward silence. A coffee carafe and teapot rested on a serving tray, along with baked goods and his childhood favorite, strawberry wafer cookies. Had she recalled he liked the cookies or was it merely coincidence?

It touched him to think she might have remembered.

Kitschy cookies aside, the elegant spread looked like something from a fancy women's magazine. But that was Tara, hostess to the max.

A lazy memory drifted over him. An outdoor tea party organized by Tara. The four Alzate girls wearing their mother's jewelry and high heels. Sipping grape Kool-Aid from tiny teacups, their pinkie fingers stuck out in the air. Munching on wafer cookies and animal crackers.

Man, but he'd wanted in on that tea party.

Rhett had been hiding out from his brother Remington, lurking on the roof of the well pump house, crouched above them in his secret spot underneath a giant old mesquite tree.

He'd spied on them until he'd gotten bored, dropped down from the roof to land in the middle of the folding table. He'd slipped on the shingles in the descent, hit the table, and rolled off. Ended up on his back on the ground, all the air knocked from his body, lungs spasming, staring up at the squealing girls gathered around him.

"Stupid boy," Ember, the oldest sister, had muttered, scowled, and sank her hands on her hips and shook her head, a motion that sent her Irish red curls bouncing. She was the only one of the Alzates who looked like their mother, Bridgette. "You've ruined everything."

"You killed Walker!" Kaia cried, cradling a squashed walking stick insect in her palm. "Murderer!"

"You got Kool-Aid on my new shirt," Aria wailed. "Punch him, Em, punch him."

"Don't punch him, Em," Tara had pleaded, sinking to her knees beside Rhett. "Can't you see he can't breathe?" She stroked his forehead. "Kaia, put down the dead walking stick and go get Lucy. Aria, hush up. Ember, stand over here to give us some shade."

He remembered staring up into Tara's face and in that split-second thought, *She's an angel.*

The memory loosened its grip, but seeing Tara pick up the baby from the bassinet, *his* baby, the premature baby she'd taken care of in the neonatal unit for four months, he thought again, *She's an angel.*

Ms. Bean took the chair opposite the couch, leaving Rhett to sink down beside Tara.

She stiffened, giving off don't-touch-me vibes.

It made him want to touch her all the more. To make sure that he didn't, Rhett scooted as far away from her as he could get until his hip bumped against the arm of the couch. But he could still smell her scent, the soft, muted fragrance of lavender and lemons.

She kept her eyes trained on Ms. Bean and her arms wrapped around the baby. "Please, help yourselves to some refreshments."

God, but she was a polite one even when she didn't want to be, with that starched spine and those shapely knees pressed tightly together. She wore a sunflower yellow dress, and her tawny legs were bare.

What gorgeous gams.

"You too," she said to Rhett without making eye contact.

While they'd never been buddy-buddy, there had never been this level of animosity between them before. Not even when she threatened his private parts over dating Aria. But hey, this was understandable, right? Considering the circumstances.

"I need to feed Julie." Tara leaned over and reached into the diaper bag positioned at her feet. She took out a small bottle of baby formula.

"Julie?" he whispered. "Is that her name?"

"Julie Elizabeth." Tara rested the bottle's nipple on the baby's tiny pink mouth, and Julie began to suckle.

"Julie Elizabeth Lockhart," he said, testing it out.

It was a sweet, delicate name that stripped him of all his defenses. He had a daughter named Julie Elizabeth. "Who named her? Rhona?"

It didn't seem like a name Rhona would have chosen. Not that he knew Rhona all that well, but she seemed the type to name her baby something offbeat or exotic. Like Jett or Sierra or Trinity.

"I named her," Tara said. "She needed a name, and since I was her primary nurse, the hospital allowed me to name her."

"It's not uncommon," Ms. Bean explained, "in the case of babies abandoned at hospitals for the nurses to name them."

Abandoned.

The word was a knife to his chest. His little girl's mother had abandoned her. Hell, in a sense he'd abandoned her too. Guilt was a sledgehammer, whacking him over the head. He was a lousy-ass father. Julie had been all alone for four months.

Well, not completely alone. Tara had been with her.

His heart opened, and his chest softened, and if Tara hadn't been holding the baby, he might just have given her a hard, impulsive hug. It cut him to the quick that his child did not have a mother. He knew what it was like to lose your mom. His mother had died of breast cancer when he was eight, and Duke had completely checked out. Leaving Rhett and his brothers to be raised by a string of nannies, with help from their housekeeper, Tara's mother, Bridgette.

"Would you like to feed her?" Tara invited.

"Huh?" Rhett blinked.

"Would you like to feed your daughter?"

"Me?" He placed a palm over the right side of his chest.

"You *are* her father." Tara extended the baby toward him.

His hands trembled as, hesitantly, he reached for her. The clock on the mantel gonged the hour. *Dong, dong, dong.*

"Hold her like this." She demonstrated how he was to cradle the baby for the most support, and then showed him how to hold the bottle so Julie wouldn't suck in too much air.

Oh gosh, oh wow. The baby was in his arms, looking up at him. Her big blue eyes wide with curiosity. That little mouth, so fascinated by him, was no longer working the nipple. She stared, watching him.

Their gazes met. Held.

Then she did the most amazing thing. She reached out a little hand, curled it around his pinkie finger, and went back to sucking on the bottle.

Rhett's heart squashed in his chest, flattened by a truckload of emotions. A virtual floodgate of feelings. Who knew?

Lamar was right, damn him. He shouldn't have come. He should have signed that affidavit and relinquished his rights on the spot. Because seeing the baby *did* change everything.

Walking away was no longer an option.

Chapter 5

HONEST BUCKER: A bull that bucks the same way every time out of the chute.

TARA mustered every ounce of courage inside her, placed the baby in Rhett's arms, forced herself to let go, and stepped back.

The sinewy cowboy, whom she'd known all her life, peered down at the baby as if she were a magical unicorn. Rhett looked utterly gobsmacked. His eyes widened and his breath quickened, and his mouth formed a surprised O.

Her heart staggered sideways. He felt something for the child. She could see it in the way his face softened and his eyes glistened.

"Hey," he whispered. "Hey there, little one."

She couldn't bear to watch him watching Julie. Gnawing her bottom lip, Tara dropped her gaze to his feet. Studied his cowboy boots as if they were the most fascinating things she'd ever seen. Black hand-tooled leather, red flames inlaid, special order.

Of course the boots were special order. Everything about Rhett Lockhart was special order.

Her gaze drifted up his faded Wrangler's to that dazzling belt buckle. The showoff. He wore a blue and green plaid shirt with mother-of-pearl snaps instead of buttons. His body was lean and hard in the way of bull riders, full of swagger and gall.

He was colorful, energetic, rash, and extravagant. He was the first person to pick up a restaurant tab or stuff a twenty-dollar bill into a tip jar. A party followed him wherever he went.

His quicksilver mind was both intriguing and exhausting. He'd
dropped out of high school at seventeen, but later he'd gotten
his GED. He was whip-smart but tended toward laziness. Rich.
Spoiled. Alluring.

And now he was a father.

The father of the baby she yearned to adopt with every fiber
of her being. The child she ached to call her own. Tara placed a
palm over her lower abdomen, inhaled deeply.

Rhett cooed to the baby, "I'm your daddy."

Tara cringed. Adorable. The man was freaking adorable. But
it was easy to fall head over heels for Julie. That didn't mean
Rhett had what it took to be a father. Not for the long haul.
Surely, he had to realize that he was in no position to raise a
child on his own. He was constantly on the road. He had a dangerous job . . .

"Hey there, Jules. Can I call you Jules?" He slid a sidelong
glance over at Tara as if asking for her permission.

Fear was a band around Tara's chest, squeezing tight. *He's
given her a nickname. He's going to take her away. You're going
to get left out.*

The teapot rattled.

Tara shifted her gaze to Ms. Bean, who was peering at her
over the rim of her teacup, pinkie out. Observing. Assessing.
That '70s Show meets British high tea.

Tara hid her jealousy with a soft smile. *I'm cool. I'm civil.
Can't you see? I want what's best for Julie. Always. And what's
best for Julie is me.*

But what if she were wrong? What if Rhett *was* best for Julie?
What then?

Everyone, from her colleagues, to her family, to her lawyer,
warned her not to get too attached. So many obstacles stood
between her and the adoption. And the biggest obstacle of all
was sitting right next to her on the couch.

Julie's tiny little fist was curled around Rhett's big pinkie finger. Transfixed, Rhett stared at the baby. "She's a miracle," he murmured, clearly bowled over. "A solid miracle."

Tara's heart was a fist, pummeling against the inside of her chest like a punching bag. Overcome by the sweet sight of father and daughter, she had to look away again. She glanced out the window to the backyard, where she'd already put up a small swing set. The wind gusted and set the empty swing swaying.

Ms. Bean stood up. "Bathroom?"

"Down the hall, first door on your left," Tara directed with a wave.

Ms. Bean's high-top sneakers padded softly against the tile floor. The minute the door clicked closed, Tara whirled to face Rhett. It was on the tip of her tongue to bark, *What in the hell do you think you're doing?* But she managed to control herself. Exploding like an incendiary device would not help her case.

Easy does it.

Rhett was the sort of guy who took demands as challenges. For him, rules were something to break, tradition something to flaunt. She'd get nowhere by throwing shade.

Julie was her goal. Love was her motive. Rhett was the monkey wrench. She had to conduct the situation with a delicate hand.

"Overwhelming, huh?" she said, infusing her tone with a friendly note. *Way to keep things light. Thumbs up, Tea!* Her snarkier inner voice cut her no slack.

Rhett glanced up, his eyes shiny. "I . . . I . . . had no idea."

Ah, crap. Why did he have to look so utterly vulnerable?

"Parenthood is not something to be taken lightly," she whispered.

"No." He nodded as if he had a clue. "It's not."

"Raising a child is a lifelong commitment. It doesn't stop at age eighteen. It's not a whim."

His face paled beneath his tan. His Adam's apple pulled up and down in a massive gulp, moving like a nibbled fishing bobber on a calm lake. "Yeah."

"Pretty tough raising a child for a single man who lives on the road." A tickle of fear feathered through her. Had she pushed too hard?

His eyes narrowed, and his nostrils flared. He was scared, but too tough to admit it. Wasn't that the definition of foolishness?

Or was it courage?

"You want to adopt her." His voice was flat. The muscles in his arms tensed, the veins at his wrists ropy and strong.

The baby was still clinging to his pinkie.

Tara moistened her lips, met his gaze head-on. Heard the theme song from *Brave* rise in her head as she mentally channeled her bold older sister, Ember. "I do."

"Why?"

"I love her." It was an ironclad statement, honest and true. "Long before I learned she was my niece by marriage, I was in love with her."

"Do you want to adopt all the babies you fall in love with?" His tone held the sliver of a blade, razor-sharp and piercing, a quick stabbing wound.

"Only the ones who've been abandoned," she said, her words coming out more tartly than she intended. He'd started it with the tacky tone.

His features hardened, and his cheeks reddened. "I didn't know."

His shame mollified her. Maybe he wasn't a complete lost cause. "Because heaven forbid you would ever check back with any of the women you've bedded and see how they're doing."

"That's harsh."

"Is it untrue?" She softened her voice, not wanting to be a total ball-breaker, especially when he'd gone contrite.

The redness in his cheeks darkened. "No."

She shrugged, her point made.

"You're angry with me."

"I'm angry *for* Julie. This isn't about you."

His lifted the eyebrow with the stitches, winced. "No?"

God, why did he have to look so adorable? "Surprise. Not everything is about you."

"I agree. Not everything is about me. But your attitude? That self-righteous tilt to your head? That *is* about me. You disapprove of my lifestyle and don't even try to deny it."

Purposefully, she relaxed her spine. She *was* mad at him, but she wasn't going to admit it. She wanted to say, *Where were you when Julie needed you most?* But that might goad him into saying, *Well, I'm here now.* And she did not want to say or do anything to encourage him to stick around.

His whiskey-colored curls were mussed from his cowboy hat. His dark eyes plowed into hers over the top of the baby's head. Unabashed and unapologetic.

Tara gulped, and her uterus rippled again. *You're losing it, Alzate.*

A day's growth of scruff ringed his jaw, dusty and stubbled. Compound that with the black eye, bruises and stitches, and, well, he could have been a stunt double for Jesse James. He looked raw, primal, untamed. Except for the baby in his arms. The tender way he held Julie canceled out the outlaw mien. But it did nothing to lessen his sexual appeal.

In fact, if anything, the baby made him more attractive.

She tracked her gaze over him. He sported an outdoorsy tan, and his hands were calloused but clean. He used his body to make his living, and it showed in the way he carried himself. He was a well-oiled, finely tuned machine. As sleek and impressive as a luxury sports car engine.

She hadn't been in a luxury sports car since Kit's Porsche. She missed the feel of how a precision automobile hugged the road's curve. The smell of the expensive leather. The sensation of wind blowing through her hair with the top down.

Tara moistened her lips. Shook off thoughts of revved engines and the smooth ride of sports cars. "It's hard for me," she said. "Thinking of *you* as a dad."

He gave a defenseless laugh, full of nervousness and humility. "I'm still wrapping my head around it too."

There he went again, redeeming himself by showing vulnerability. He was making it hard for her to hate him. "No one I know could ever picture you with a kid."

"Me least of all." He paused, his eyes still on hers. Those steady eyes that had her thinking of rich, dark chocolate.

Her heart knocked like a clunker in dire need of a tune-up. Why?

"I want to thank you, Tara," he said. "For taking such good care of my daughter. You did far more than I ever could have."

Mutely, she nodded. Her muscles—which had tensed when he'd given Julie a nickname and he'd looked at the baby as if he'd stumbled over a secret treasure—started to unwind. He knew he wasn't equipped to take care of a child. He wouldn't be fool enough to file for custody.

To hammer the point home, Tara gave him an earful of what life was like with a preemie. "It's a big responsibility. She has weekly doctors' visits and probably will for her first year. She sleeps on an apnea monitor to alert you in case she stops breathing. She has GER and is prone to spitting up three or four times a day. To avoid that, she needs smaller, more frequent feedings. She takes daily medication for—"

"What's GER?" He blinked.

"Gastroesophageal reflux."

"Is it serious?" He scooted to the edge of the couch, his body language taut and wire-drawn. "Will she be okay?"

Ooh good, he was panicking. She slathered it on thick, giving him way too much information. Going into minute details about GER. Finished with "Her condition is not life-threatening, but it's something we have to keep an eye on. The opening at the entrance to her stomach hasn't fully matured, so the feedings come back up at times. We monitor her weight closely to make sure she's keeping down enough formula to thrive and grow."

"Will she have to have surgery?"

"Her pediatrician is hopeful that she'll outgrow it." Tara paused a beat. "But it could take months."

Sweat popped out on his forehead. "I need a pen and paper to write all this down. You got a pen and paper?"

Maybe it was the nurse in her, but she had an impulse to pluck a tissue from the box on the table, lean over, and dab away his anxiety. *Which you just caused. What's your deal?*

Ms. Bean, who'd come back into the room, thrust out a pen and a piece of paper torn from her yellow legal pad.

He juggled Julie, trying to shift her in his arm so he could reach for the writing instruments. Julie whimpered, and he shot Tara a helpless look.

That got to her. She had a hard time resisting folks in need. "Do you want me to write it down for you?"

"Yeah."

No "please" or "thank you," but what did she expect? He was a Lockhart, accustomed to having his every wish, want, and need catered to by others.

Play nice, Tara. The situation would be difficult for anyone.

"I can do better than that," Tara offered, feeling magnanimous, although maybe she was secretly hoping the information would overwhelm and discourage him. "I'll make you a copy of her care plan."

"Care plan?" His question trailed after her as she headed for the nursery.

"It's an action plan for Julie's medical team," she called over her shoulder, as she entered the nursery and took the care plan off the wall where she kept it posted, and she trotted back to the living room. She sat beside him again, held out her palm. "Your phone."

He jiggled Julie to his other arm as he fished in his pocket for his smart phone.

The baby made a mewling sound.

Rhett looked terrified. "What is it? What's wrong?"

"She's just expressing herself." Tara used his cell phone to take a snapshot of the care plan, front and back.

"Are you sure?"

"I've been with her four months. I've come to know all her little sounds intimately," she said. If he felt guilty, it was on him.

Shamefaced, Rhett eyed the care plan on his phone screen. "That looks extensive."

"Par for the course. She's an extreme preemie. She'll have lingering health issues for many years to come."

The sweat on his brow trickled down his temple. His color turned ashen. He didn't look so good. "Um . . . okay . . . I didn't know."

Triumphant, Tara murmured, "You don't have to be involved in any of this. I'm taking great care of her. That can continue."

"I can see that."

"Caring for a baby with these kinds of health issues is a lot to dump on anyone. Much less a guy like you."

He bristled. "What's that supposed to mean?"

"It's not an insult." She backtracked, realizing too late she'd said the wrong thing. "I didn't mean to imply that you were incapable of taking care of your child. I'm just saying I'm here to lighten your burden. There is no shame in allowing me to adopt your daughter. In fact, some might say it is the more noble thing to do."

He looked conflicted, his gaze going from Julie to his phone screen to Tara.

She gave him a practiced, perfect C-shaped smile. "No shame at all."

"You want me to sign my daughter over to you? Just like that?" He leaned forward with the baby in his lap. He wasn't holding her nearly secure enough to suit Tara. It was all she could do not to correct him.

Easy does it. Tread lightly.

"Allowing me to adopt her doesn't mean you won't get to see her," Tara said, talking desperately fast. "You could come see her any time your busy schedule allowed. But you wouldn't have to deal with the daily grind of child care. And who better to adopt Julie than a relative? You'll have the best of both worlds."

She could see the tug-of-war playing out on his face. His lofty goals and devil-may-care values on one side; the sweet little baby, with her hand wrapped around his finger, on the other.

"I know it's complicated," she said. "You have a lot to think about. I'm sure you'll want to discuss this with the family and your lawyer."

He ran a finger around his collar. "What if I want her?"

"You're willing to quit the rodeo circuit?"

He puffed out his cheeks. "I could still ride."

"How?" she said. "Who would care for Julie while you're focused on besting bulls?"

"I could hire a nanny?" His voice wobbled, uncertainty turning the statement into a question.

"To live in your tiny horse trailer while you're on the road?"

"Well, no . . ." He plowed his free hand through his hair.

"Oh, so you would have the nanny live at the Silver Feather with Julie while you are on the road for weeks at a time?"

Rhett blew out his breath in two forceful huffs. "Okay, okay, I haven't really thought this through."

"Clearly."

He looked as if he'd been double-barrel gut-kicked by a mule. "I just came to see her."

"And so you have."

"I didn't expect to . . ." He peered down at the baby, smiled like he had a secret crush. "*Want* her."

Tara clamped her knees and her teeth together. "Are you planning on filing for custody?"

"I don't know."

Argh! What kind of answer was that? She needed something solid, something she could count on. "One thing is for sure, if you get custody, you're going to have to quit the rodeo. You can't keep flinging yourself on the backs of bulls if you're a single parent. Not if you want to be a *good* parent. She deserves a good parent."

"Yeah." His voice was thin as an old T-shirt.

"How will you make a living?" she asked, heaping it on. "You don't know how to do anything else but hold on to the back of a bull for eight seconds."

His mouth flattened out as if he'd taken a bite of something bitter. Outside on the patio the wind chimes rang merrily, as if all was well with the world.

"Face facts, Lockhart. You're ill-equipped for parenthood."

"If I do decide to file, I'll figure it out."

Tara's heart jumped. He sounded more and more like he might file for custody. "At Julie's expense?"

"Isn't that how all parents do it?" he asked.

"Not me. I'm already a trained nurse."

"With no children of your own."

Ouch. The hard edge of his statement sliced her on a subterranean level. She wasn't childless by choice.

"Rhett," she murmured, battling the tightening of her throat. She felt breathless and helpless, and she *hated* feeling helpless. "You'd make a terrible father. You'd be worse than Duke."

Silence settled over the room.

"Low blow." Glowering, Rhett jumped to his feet. In his quick shift of position, he startled the baby awake. Julie's little face scrunched, and she let out a wail.

"Look what you did," Tara scolded, leaping up from the couch.

Rhett shifted the baby in his arms, ineptly. The blanket Tara had bundled around her came loose and drifted to the floor. Julie's tiny butt was cupped in his palm, her head balanced on his fingertips, and her legs dangled from either side of his hand as if he were holding a football.

"Give her to me." Tara held out her arms.

"She's fine." He brought Julie to his shoulder, supporting her bottom with one hand, the back of her neck with the other.

"She's *not* fine. She's crying."

"It doesn't hurt for a baby to cry."

"Oh yes, like you know so much about babies."

"Excuse me," Ms. Bean said. "Civility, please."

"No problem." Tara stabbed her fingernails into her palms. It was all she could do not to snatch Julie from Rhett's arms. "None at all."

"Mr. Lockhart?" Ms. Bean's voice turned to steel. "Do you have a problem with Ms. Alzate?"

"No problems here." He kept his gaze locked on Tara.

Ms. Bean pushed her open palms toward the ground, twice. "Sit back down. Both of you."

Tara eased back against the couch.

"Mr. Lockhart." Ms. Bean indicated the spot beside Tara. "Please join us."

Julie was still whimpering.

"I can quiet her," Tara whispered, reaching for the baby.

"So can I." Rhett sat down beside Tara, but he had eyes only for his daughter. "Hey, baby girl. Shh." He began humming, then slipped into song. *"Hush little baby, don't say a word. Papa's gonna buy you a mockingbird."*

Julie stopped crying at once, grinned, and flailed her tiny arms at him.

Rhett shot Tara a triumphant look. "You can just call me the baby whisperer."

Yeah, well, one time did not a baby whisperer make. "Here's a revolutionary idea," she snapped. "Let's not."

Loudly, Ms. Bean cleared her throat.

They both turned to the social worker.

"Mr. Lockhart, I know you just recently learned of Julie's existence and that your emotions are running high. But Tara is right. Julie has unique health care needs. That said, I'm aware you have the resources to hire someone to care for her if you choose to do so."

"Damn right I do."

"Language." Tara inclined her head toward the baby.

"What if I did decide to file for custody?" Rhett asked Ms. Bean. "What would be my first steps?"

"First think it over. Talk to your family. Consult a lawyer. And a counselor."

Rhett nodded. "Will do."

"Just to let you know, if you did decide to file for custody, it's not as easy as waltzing in and staking your claim. Because she was abandoned by her mother, Julie is currently under the auspices of Child Protective Services. In order to get custody, there has to be a court hearing. You have to prove you're worthy of raising a child."

"That's not fair," Rhett protested. "Why do I have to prove I have a right to my own child?"

"For Julie's protection. It's the law."

"If Rhona had given her to me directly then none of this would be necessary, right?"

"Alas, Rhona did not. In fact, Miss White couldn't even say for sure which man had fathered her baby. In the future, Mr. Lockhart, might I suggest you use more discretion when choosing a bed partner?"

Tara bit back a laugh, but it came out like a snort. *Zing.* She wanted to high-five Ms. Bean.

Rhett shot her a look dirty enough to singe her hair off.

"Sorry," Tara said. "But Ms. Bean makes a solid point. If you were more selective about where you spread your seed . . ."

"Hey!" Rhett said sharply. "My love life is none of your damn business."

"Ah," Tara said, "but it is. I'm the one raising your daughter."

"Not if I file for custody." He shifted to Ms. Bean. "What would be my next step *if* I decide to go for it?"

"For starters?" Ms. Bean's eyebrows flattened out. "You need a permanent residence."

"Done. I already own a house in Cupid."

Ms. Bean took out a stack of papers from her tote, leafed

through them. "Which you haven't lived in since you built it seven years ago."

"How do you know that?"

"I do my research, Mr. Lockhart." Ms. Bean leveled him a stern look. "It's my job."

Tara *so* wanted to high-five her.

"Noted," he said. "What else?"

"Are you truly serious about filing?" Ms. Bean asked.

"Just information gathering for now. I need to know what I'm up against."

Ms. Bean gestured at his black eye and battered face. "I advise you stop doing whatever caused that."

"This?" Rhett touched his face. "Rare occurrence. Won't happen again."

Ms. Bean sent him a skeptical look. Tara really, really liked the woman. "Take parenting classes."

"Parenting classes?"

"Parenting classes," Ms. Bean confirmed. "There are several kinds, and some of them will be court mandated. But the more you take, the better it will look to the court. You'll learn about child development, how to discipline your child, how to recognize your strengths and weaknesses as a parent . . ."

Rhett's face paled beneath his tan. "Um, how does that work?"

"You can take the classes online, but because Julie is an infant and she has special needs, I suggest you take the infant parenting classes in person. You'll learn how to properly care for your baby with hands-on demonstrations."

He blew out his breath, looked longingly at the door as if he ached to bolt. "That's a lot."

"Yes. That's why you need to take your time before deciding that assuming custody of Julie is the right step for you."

"Still, it won't hurt to have a parenting class under my belt, right?"

"Tara, what do you think?" Ms. Bean asked her, and to Rhett

she said, "Tara teaches an infant parenting class one weekend a month at El Paso Children's Hospital."

"No need to take parenting classes until you're ready to be a parent," Tara said. Then again, maybe she should encourage him to take a class. That ought to send him running for the hills. "But I do have an opening in the class."

"Great," he said. "I'll sign up."

"Won't you be on the road?" Tara knitted her fingers together in her lap. Holding herself in.

"I will, but I can ride on Friday and fly home that same night. I'd only have to miss Saturday's event. When's the next class?"

"The eighteenth," Tara said. "But there really is no rush. You could take the course in June or July—"

"Sooner would be better. Right, Ms. Bean?" Rhett asked the caseworker.

Ms. Bean toyed with her peace sign necklace. The cell phone in her lap buzzed with the ringtone of Lynyrd Skynyrd's "Was I Right or Wrong." What was with the young woman's love affair with the 1970s?

Ms. Bean held up an index finger. "I need to take this. Will you excuse me for a minute?" Pressing the cell phone to her ear, she hurried into the nursery and shut the door behind her.

Leaving Tara alone with Rhett and the baby.

"Why are you doing this?" she hissed.

"Doing what?"

"Pretending you are going to take parenting classes."

"I might take parenting classes; if I decide to file for custody I'd have to take them anyway."

"You don't want a baby. You just want to gig me."

"Get over yourself, woman. Who are you to tell me what I do and don't want?"

"I know you, Rhett Lockhart. The last thing you need is a baby."

"No," he corrected. "You know the kid I used to be. Stop judging me by my seventeen-year-old self. I've changed."

"*Riight*. Changed into a guy who has slept with almost all the eligible women in Cupid, including my sister."

"Jealous?" He smirked.

A gust of wind blew desert dirt at the windowpane, rasping grit against the glass. Irritation gripped Tara. "Of you? Why in heaven's name would I be jealous of *you*?"

His gaze drifted over her body, lingering at the swell of her breasts, interest sparking in his eyes. Who was the man trying to kid? He hadn't changed a bit. "Maybe because it's been a long time since you've had sex."

"Excuse me? That is absolutely none of your business."

"It kind of is. You're in charge of my child. A sexually satisfied foster mom is a happy foster mom. I could help with that, you know."

"What?" she screeched. "You . . . you . . . you . . ." She put as much loathing into her voice as she could gather. "You . . . *Lothario*."

"Lothario?"

If she could have turned him to stone with her glare, she would have. Tara crossed her arms over her chest, hiding her breasts from his cocklebur gaze. "God! You are hopeless."

"Wait, did you think I was offering my sexual services?" He placed his free palm to his chest. "Oh no, no, no. I was just thinking of buying you a vibrator." He met her stare, not backing down. A twinkle of mischief sparking his brown eyes. He gave her a leisurely wink that said, *Gotcha*.

"Grr." She literally growled at him and bared her teeth. "It's time for you to give me the baby and go." She pointed at the front door. "*Now!*"

Chapter 6

FREIGHT TRAINED: What happens to a rodeo contestant who gets run over by a bull traveling at top speed.

RHETT was still trying to wrap his head around the fact that his sister-in-law was Julie's foster mother, and she wanted to adopt his baby.

He sat in a bar in downtown El Paso, an hour after he left Tara's place, nursing a beer and staring at a basketball game that he wasn't really watching. The waitress had recognized him and made several unsuccessful attempts at flirting. Rhett simply wasn't in the mood.

His mind was ablaze.

A kid.

A baby.

A daughter.

His.

He circled the rim of his beer mug with an index finger, watched the bubbles dissipate. Reality sank in like a stone. He felt a million different things. Guilt. Shame. Worry. Doubt. But at the bottom of the mix was one emotion, unmoving as granite.

Love.

He loved that baby girl.

Rhett didn't know how it was possible to feel so much for a tiny little thing he'd just met. But it was a big, huge, overwhelming thing. Solid and certain. This feeling wasn't going to go away. Not ever.

Love at first sight was as real as water.

It was a new kind of feeling, something he'd not ever experienced before. The baby changed everything. Problem was, Rhett had no idea what he was doing, and didn't Julie deserve a parent who could take care of her the way she deserved to be cared for?

He could love her all he wanted, but if he didn't have the skills to care for her, wasn't it selfish not to let Tara adopt her?

No matter how much people believed otherwise, love was not always enough. His own mother had loved him fiercely, but her love for her sons hadn't been enough to save her. And Tara loved Julie just as much as he did, and she had the skills to be an awesome parent.

You could learn.

Yeah? When was that? The PBR schedule ran from January to November. He was always on the road. Roaming from town to town, event to event, and he *loved* it.

As much as you love Julie?

God, this was so hard. He'd been on the PBR circuit since he was nineteen. He barely knew Julie. But he loved them both with equal vigor.

Aw shit.

Something his father said to him when he was learning how to ride bucking bulls stuck in his head. *Take it one second at a time.*

If he thought about parenthood too much, he was going to freak out.

So don't think.

He was pretty darn good at compartmentalizing and blocking off his feelings. It made him an excellent cowboy. But wouldn't those same talents make him a crappy father?

One second at a time.

Just like the quirky Mariah Bean had said. Establish a permanent residence. Take parenting classes. Get to know his daughter. That was enough for the immediate future. He didn't have to decide right now. Julie was safe with Tara. There was no rush to file for custody if that's what he wanted to do.

He'd worry about the next step after that. Rhett groaned and gently rubbed his bruised eye.

"Another beer, cowboy?" asked the waitress, her smile eager as a new puppy. She'd already recognized him, and they'd had a long talk about the PBR before she'd gone off to fill more orders.

"I'm good." He placed a hand over the top of his mug.

"Yes, you are." She slanted him the same hot, buttery look he often saw in the eyes of women.

She was pretty enough, petite, skinny, blond. Tara's polar opposite. Her nametag said her name was Shay. Her shapely calves said she spent a lot of time on her feet. The sultry look in her green eyes said she wouldn't mind sharing her bed with him.

"I don't have to be Mrs. Right," she said. "I'd be happy with Miss Right Now."

Once upon a time, that would have been music to his ears. Any other night, he'd be squiring her back to his place after she got off work, but not now.

Not tonight.

Not ever.

It occurred to him that any number of women he'd been with could have been the "right" one, and he'd let them slip through his fingers. But he'd never let himself consider marriage or long-term commitment. The women hadn't been the problem. They weren't the reason he was alone. He'd made that choice. He'd been too self-absorbed, too focused on his career to pay the women in his life the kind of attention they craved.

Dammit, but he had a lot of baggage to unpack. Julie, and unexpected paternity, had thrown his future into turmoil. Fast-tracked the unpacking. The mistakes of the past were rushing at him with warp speed, and he'd better start learning the lessons or he was going to end up forfeiting everything that mattered.

He couldn't act like a randy young buck anymore—following his fancy into whatever warm body welcomed him. He was a father now. The father of a daughter who could one day work in a bar, and the last thing he wanted was for some tricky dick cowboy to hustle her into bed.

"You got any kids?" he asked Shay, taking a slug off the beer that had gone lukewarm.

She seemed surprised, cocked her head back, peered at him from underneath thick false eyelashes as if assessing him for potential father-of-her-children material. "I do."

"Boys or girls?"

"One of each."

"How old are they?"

"Three and five."

"Fun ages."

"Those little rug rats run me ragged." She smiled softly, affection for her kids easy to see on her face.

"You married?" he asked.

"Not anymore." Shay winked and touched his wrist with her fingertips.

Slowly, he inched his hand away from hers. "What's it like?"

"What's what like?" She lowered her lashes, polished the bar between them with a cleaning towel.

"Being a single parent."

She pressed her palms to the seat of her jeans. "It's exhausting and demanding. Your life is never your own. Something as insignificant as a long, hot shower becomes a moment to treasure. And if you don't have a community of family and friends to help pitch in, you're really screwed."

Rhett winced. "But you don't mind. You've got more patience. You're more understanding. Right?"

Shay tossed her head, laughed. "Having kids doesn't make you a different person. Sometimes I wish it did. It would be so much easier if I didn't have a sarcastic, selfish streak."

He felt a noose tightening around his neck. He coughed, put a hand to his throat. *You don't have to be a parent. You can let Tara adopt her.*

"You about to have a kid or something?" Shay asked.

"Just found out I've already got one. She's four months old."

"Oh shit," she said. "That's heavy."

Heavy, yeah. As a grand piano.

"Do you get along with the baby mama?" she asked.

Tara wasn't the baby's mama, but he didn't want to get into all of that with Shay, so he simply said, "She doesn't like me very much."

"You done her dirty?"

He shook his head. "We just don't see eye-to-eye."

"It can be rough." Shay shrugged. "My ex and I try to be respectful for the kids' sake, but sometimes I just want to strangle the sonofabitch."

Rhett laughed because she seemed to expect it. "How do you make the coparenting thing work?"

"Best you can. One day at a time."

One day at a time was an upgrade from one second at a time. He wasn't sure which was better. "Sounds like a prison sentence."

"Sometimes parenthood feels like that."

"But it's all worth it in the end . . . right?"

"Sure," she said as if by rote, and Rhett wasn't the least bit comforted. "Sure, it is. There's nothing like being a parent. When they wrap those sweet arms around you and give you sloppy kisses, it's the best feeling in the world."

"Would you do it all over again if you could go back in time?"

Shay paused, and her face took on a faraway expression. "I love my kids more than life itself. And I wouldn't give them up for all the money in the world. But if I could go back in time?"

He waited. At the back of the bar, someone punched a tune into the jukebox. Kenny Chesney. "There Goes My Life."

Rhett rolled his eyes to the sky. Seriously? *This* song? Right now?

"Would I have kids if I had it to do all over again?" Slowly, Shay shook her head.

Rhett gulped twice. Felt a twist of heat start in the base of his spine and corkscrew all the way up to his head. "Why not?"

"Because it makes you too damn vulnerable," she whispered.

"It's like wearing your heart outside your body. Anything happens to them, and you're annihilated." She took a breath so deep her breasts shot up. "You sure you don't want a fresh beer?"

"Naw."

"You got a picture of her?" Shay asked, leaning over the bar so that he got a whiff of her scent, popcorn and beer.

Rhett pulled his phone from his back pocket, called up the photo he'd taken of Julie just before he'd left, passed it to Shay. In the photo, his daughter was cradled in Tara's arms.

"Oh my goodness!" Shay exclaimed. "Isn't she adorbs?"

Rhett felt his chest puff with seam-busting pride, and that surprised him.

"Who is the woman? The baby mama?"

"Foster mom."

"Your daughter is in foster care?" Shay's eyes widened. "Oh, well that changes things. I'm sorry for your troubles."

"It is what it is." He held out his hand for his phone.

Shay didn't immediately give the phone back. Instead, she punched in her number, shot him a coy expression. "Just in case you ever want to talk . . . you know . . . about what life is like as a single parent."

"Thanks," he mumbled, pulled out a twenty to pay for his four-dollar beer, pushed back from the bar stool, and got up. "Keep the change, Shay."

"Hey, thanks." She pocketed the twenty. "You leavin' so soon?"

"Got a call to make." He settled his Stetson on his head.

"Good luck on the circuit."

He gave her a rueful smile. "Night."

"Come back real soon . . ." Shay invited. "Or call me."

Surreptitiously, Rhett deleted Shay's number from his phone and headed outside. He knew if he called the bartender, the last thing they'd end up talking about was single parenthood. His best guess, they wouldn't do much talking at all.

He walked out to his pickup, his thoughts on Julie. In his mind's eye, he saw his daughter's tiny baby hand curled around his pinkie finger. Remembered how she smelled like heaven in a blanket, and what it felt like to hold her in his arms.

Letting out his breath through clenched teeth, Rhett punched in a number on his phone. It rang once. Twice. Three times.

"Yes?" said a familiar voice.

Rhett's gut clenched tight. This was a big step, and part of him was praying the man on the other end of the line would talk him out of it.

"Rhett? You there?"

He hesitated.

"Hello, hello?"

He took in a deep breath and asked his manager, "How long can I reasonably stay off the circuit, and still have a chance to make Vegas?"

AFTER RHETT AND Ms. Bean left, Tara put Julie down for a nap. Then the first thing she did was phone Aria.

Quickly, she filled her youngest sister in on what had happened with Rhett.

"Can you believe he said that vibrator thing to me?" She was still quivering with anger. "What gives him the right to comment on my sex life?"

"Or lack thereof." Aria giggled.

"Unlike some people, I don't easily swing from bed to bed."

"Low blow, sister."

"I was talking about Rhett."

"Oh."

"He thinks he knows everything there is to know about sex."

"Well . . ." Aria cleared her throat.

"Well what?"

"He is pretty skilled in the bedroom. Practice makes perfect, I suppose."

"I don't need to know this."

"He's also rather gifted in the nature department, if you know what I mean."

"Nature?"

"He's got a big di—"

"Shh, I get it, I get it." Tara put a palm over the ear not pressed to the phone.

"Just saying, you could do worse than a night with Rhett Lockhart."

"Oh dear God. No way in hell."

"Kit has been gone for over two years, Tea. It's time to move on."

"Not with Rhett!"

"No, but there's nothing wrong with having a good time in bed."

"You don't get it. I'm a mom now. I can't run around having random sex."

"I'm available to babysit. Even moms need a little sumptin', sumptin' once in a while."

Tara sank down on the couch, picked up one of the strawberry wafer cookies that was still sitting on the tray on the coffee table. Munched it. Hmm, the cookies were pretty tasty in a childhood nostalgia kind of way.

"You're crunching in my ear," Aria said.

"Oops, sorry." Tara finished off the cookie.

"How did he look?"

"Who?"

"Rhett, who else?"

"Like he'd been in a barroom brawl. Black eye, stitches, busted lip, the works."

"Ooh." Aria breathed heavily. "Sounds sexy."

"The things you consider sexy," Tara muttered.

"You need to get out more. Have more fun. I know you're the savior of children, but—"

"I have fun," she said, feeling defensive.

"Reading does not constitute fun."

"It does to me."

"Neither does eating ice cream alone in the bathtub."

"So what do you think is a lively time? Wait, forget I asked."

Aria did not forget. "Shopping, swimming, getting soused at Chantilly's, dancing, going out with hot guys . . ."

"I'm not twenty-one anymore, Aria."

"Mentally, you've never been twenty-one, Tara. You were born forty."

"I just don't see the point in trivial pursuits." Tara switched on the baby monitor perched on the end table, kicked off her shoes, and stretched out on the couch.

"That's probably one reason you and Rhett clash like cats and dogs. You don't know how to have fun and he's party central."

"That's one reason."

"Invite him dancing. He's a great dancer. I'll babysit."

"Are you nuts? Why in God's name would I take him dancing?"

"To smooth things over between you two."

"Things don't have to be smooth. Wrinkled is fine with me."

"Dancing with Rhett is like dancing on a cloud." Aria sighed dreamily.

"So go dance with him."

"Been there, done that. It was fun while it lasted."

"Why did you two break up?" Tara asked.

"We both knew our thing had an expiration date. Neither one of us were in a place to get serious."

"Do you think Rhett could ever be serious about anyone?" Good grief, why had she asked that? What did she care?

"Probably not."

Tara let out a sigh of relief. "Thank heavens for that."

"You're worried he wants custody of Julie?"

"You should have seen the way he looked at her, Aria." Tara tightened her grip on the phone.

"Did he say he *wanted* custody?"

"He said he was going to take a parenting class. Why would he take a parenting class if he wasn't considering it?"

"Rhett's got a good heart, but unless it has something to do with bull riding, he doesn't have much stick-to-it-ness. I wouldn't worry too much."

"Easy for you to say. You don't have anything at stake."

"Think of it this way. Do you ever see him willingly giving up the PBR? That man will ride until he's so busted up he can't walk."

"That's what I thought, but Aria, you didn't see his face when he looked at Julie." Tara reached for another wafer cookie and nibbled it softly to avoid crunching in Aria's ear.

"Trust me on this. Once he brushes up against a few dirty diapers and a colicky baby, he'll backpedal."

"I'm not so sure about that."

"I get it. Fretting is your thing. Fret away, and when he signs over his parental rights to you, I'll say, 'I told you so,' and you can take me out to eat at MacClain's," Aria said, naming one of the priciest restaurants in El Paso.

"If you're right, gladly. You can even order the most expensive thing on the menu."

"Wanna know Rhett's kryptonite?" Aria asked.

"Duh, yes!" She'd take any advantage she could get.

"Daisy Dukes."

"What?"

"You know, blue jeans cut off so short you're falling out of them, like Daisy Duke on the old *Dukes of Hazzard* show."

"I know what they are," Tara said. "How are Daisy Dukes Rhett's kryptonite?"

"Wear a pair in front of him and find out."

"Oh, good grief, I'm not wearing Daisy Dukes."

"Okay, just saying, if you want to bend that man to your will, put on a pair of Daisy Dukes. He'll be putty in your hand. He's a leg and butt man, and boy do you qualify on both scores."

"Thanks for the tip, but I don't use feminine wiles to get men to do what I want."

"Now see, that's your first mistake. Men secretly want to be controlled, and you love to be in control. Use it. Wanna know what he likes in bed?"

"I do not." An image of Rhett in bed, his naked body casually draped by a thin cotton sheet, cowboy hat on his head, a come-hither smile on his face, one finger beckoning her to join him, popped into her head.

What the hell?

She shook her head but could not shake the vision.

"He's a sucker for—"

"I'm hanging up now." Tara sprang to a sitting position and switched off her phone. Horrified to find she was sweating and her breath was coming in rapid little pants.

Aria and Rhett were both right about one thing. She had gone without sex for too long. And apparently hormone overload was poisoning her brain.

Chapter 7

ARM JERKER: A bull that bucks with the power to cause a great amount of pull on the contestant's arm.

On Saturday morning, May 18, Tara checked her roster for the weekend attendees, and learned she had eighteen students enrolled. It was her first time going back to work since she'd brought Julie home from the NICU two weeks earlier. She'd left the baby in the hospital day care for the six-hour class, but she'd already texted twice in twenty minutes to see how Julie was doing.

"Still asleep," the day care worker assured her, barely able to keep the exasperation from her voice. "I promise to let you know if she has any issues."

"Thanks," Tara said, but she couldn't quell her worry.

The one thing she was not worried about, however, was Rhett. She hadn't heard a peep out of him since he'd come to her house to see Julie. She'd contacted Ms. Bean and learned that the caseworker hadn't heard from either him or his lawyer. Hopeful that Rhett had been scared away by the thought of fatherhood, Tara relaxed enough to start daydreaming about her future with Julie.

Once inside the classroom, she went over the roster and took attendance. Underprivileged pregnant girls made up the bulk of the low-cost parenting classes offered by the hospital. Mothers, sisters, or friends accompanied the majority of the unwed teens, although there were three eager baby daddies in attendance.

And one married couple.

She'd taught the two-day course many times and knew the material by heart. It was a no-brainer. She turned to the whiteboard to write down the outline for the course, even though she'd already distributed handouts. It was important to keep the salient information front and center.

The door creaked open.

Cowboy boots scraped against the tile floor.

A murmur ran through the class.

She turned to see what was causing the commotion and came eye-to-eye with Rhett Lockhart. Looking hot as liquid sin. Strutting into the classroom as if he owned it.

Her stomach quivered. Seriously? He was showing up *now*? Taking *her* parenting class? Of all the parenting classes in all the world, he had to walk into hers?

But that wasn't the worst thing.

The worst thing was how her silly pulse accelerated and her mouth went dry and she was strangely happy to see him. What was that about?

"OMG," one starstruck mother exclaimed, fanning herself with her hand. "You're Rhett Lockhart!"

Rhett doffed his Stetson, gave the woman an aw-shucks grin. "I am, ma'am."

"How come you're not riding tonight?" asked one of the baby daddies.

"Got something more important to do," Rhett drawled and winked at Tara.

She felt herself blush furiously. What the frigging hell was wrong with her? Mentally, she shook herself.

"Parenting class is more important than kicking Claudio Limon's ass?" another father-to-be asked.

"You're gonna be a daddy?" said the starstruck mom. "That is so awesome."

"Mr. Lockhart," Tara said. "You're not on my roster."

"Just registered." Rhett winked. He strolled to the front of the room, handed her his registration form, and plunked down in the front row. He locked eyes with her and stared at her as if she was wearing a G-string and pasties instead of scrubs and a lab jacket.

His sultry smile caused sweat to pool between her breasts. Holy flipping cow. She was losing her marbles.

"Sptt." The starstruck mom had gotten out of her seat and crept over to Rhett, notebook and pen extended. "May I have your autograph?"

"Me too!" said one of the baby daddies.

And the next thing Tara knew the entire class was gathered around him collecting his signature and pumping him with questions about his chances of winning the PBR World Championship.

"Let's get back on topic," Tara said.

No one paid her a lick of attention.

She cleared her throat, clapped her hands. "Class, please take your seats."

But Rhett was in the middle of a story about the worst wreck of his career on the back of a beast named Bushwhacker. It was a story she'd heard many times before when the Lockharts and Alzates got together. He'd ended up with a compound fracture of his right leg that knocked him out of that season.

Tara rolled her eyes, even as her pulse skipped. She'd heard about his injury secondhand. Had no idea it had been so serious. He could have been killed. "There's time for tall tales during the break. Please return to your seats."

No one moved.

Tara marched over and squeezed between the fans gathered around him, positioning herself squarely in his line of vision. "Mr. Lockhart, may I see you in the corridor?"

"You can call me Rhett, sweet—" He caught himself just before he called her sweet cheeks. "Er . . . Teach."

She didn't comment. Simply pointed at the door, pivoted on her heel, and left the room. Crossing her arms over her chest, she waited for him to stroll outside looking pleased as punch with himself. She bit down on her bottom lip and counted to ten, reining in her irritation.

The corridor, which smelled like powdered eggs and oatmeal since the cafeteria was at the end of the hall, lay empty.

"Am I in trouble?" he asked, insouciantly slouching against the wall.

"You are not a freshman, and this is not high school."

"Um, okay." He shot her that grin of his, which had coaxed many a young woman out of her panties, including Rhona White.

Tara was not falling for it, no matter how her body simmered in a completely inappropriate way. She took a step back.

"Why did you call me out in the hall?"

Tara planted her fists on her hips. "Why are you here?"

"To take a parenting class." The words were innocent enough, but his tone held a smart-aleck note.

"I haven't heard a peep out of you in two weeks. I assumed you'd decided not to take the class."

"Assumed?" He lifted his eyebrow. The stitches were gone, the wound healing. "As in: Ass. U. Me."

"Why didn't you call? Or at least text?"

"I had a lot of thinking to do."

"And you've decided you want to file for custody?" She held her breath, her heart tripping over itself in a crazed sprint.

He raised both palms. "Whoa, whoa. Not yet. That's a Grand Canyon of a step. I'm just here to take the parenting class. It won't hurt to take a class."

"And then?"

He shrugged, a quick uplift and downdraft of his shoulders. Looked confused. "I dunno."

She pressed her palms together in front of her throat. She didn't like the way he was yanking her emotions around, giving her first hope, then despair, then hope again. "Please don't ruin the class for the rest of the students. I know you're not taking this seriously, but—"

His eyes narrowed. "Who says I'm not taking this seriously?"

"For one, you show up late. For another you waste my time grandstanding over your rodeo exploits." She drew her arms more tightly around her. Whenever she looked at him she felt a bit light-headed and giddy. Dammit. Why couldn't she stop thinking about what Aria had told her about how good Rhett was in bed and how well-endowed he was?

"I was not grandstanding. People are interested."

"Because you created a diversion." She would not look at his crotch. No, no, not going to do it.

"They need a diversion. Their lives are about to change forever. They're about to become shackled. Chained for the next eighteen years."

"A bit dramatic, don't you think?" She dropped her gaze to his belt buckle . . . and then lower. His tight jeans cupped his man parts in a thoroughly appealing way. Argh! Quickly, she zoomed her gaze back to his face.

"I'm just trying to provide some levity in a time of upheaval." He lowered his lashes, his voice, and her resistance.

"Reality needs to be faced, not avoided at all costs," she said.

"That's your opinion."

"And the only one that counts since I'm running the class."

"Whatever you say, *Teach*." His dark eyes were firecrackers of mischief, sparkly and hot.

God, the man was infuriating. Even more infuriating, she couldn't stop staring at his lips, which were healing up nicely from his brawl. They were wide and angular and . . .

Jesus, Tara, stop it.

She sank her hands on her hips. Dug in. Set her boundaries. "Not everyone considers having a baby a bad thing. You're projecting your fears onto your classmates."

"Can we begin again?" He inclined his head. A rakish move designed to showcase his shaggy curls and give him an endearing look.

"Begin again? From where? Childhood?"

"Yes. I think you've made your mind up that I'm—"

"A shallow, irresponsible jackhole with a short attention span and poor follow-through?"

"Judgmental much?"

Adrenaline shot through her. Part anger and part some kind of weird sexual attraction that she didn't want to think about too much. "We're done here."

"You do know you're cute when you're mad. Your cheeks get all red and you get an adorable little frown line right between your eyebrows—"

She had a petulant urge to stick out her tongue at him. But they weren't kids on the Silver Feather anymore. Tossing her head, she took the high road, stepped into the classroom, and shut the door firmly behind her.

It didn't deter him. He followed. Took his seat in the front row.

Had she really thought he might leave? But why would he? He was enjoying needling her too much. *You're just giving him fodder. Stop feeding his need for attention and he'll get bored and drift off.*

That was the idea anyway.

She went to the front of the class and reintroduced herself. Asked them to go around the room and tell a bit about themselves.

When it was Rhett's turn, Tara cringed, and braced herself for whatever cocky thing he might say. Fearful he'd spill some childhood incident about her that she'd prefer to keep quiet. But he was humble, courteous, and didn't mention a word about his relationship to Tara.

She breathed easier. At least he had some sense of decorum.

He met her eyes, nodded, and winked, ruining the humbleness. She felt her ears turn hot with embarrassment. Really, what did she expect? A tiger couldn't completely change its stripes.

"Welcome to the class." Tara gazed out at the expectant faces. "I'm happy to see so many of you eager to become better parents. You'll find the topics to be discussed over the next two days in your syllabus. We'll also go over the unexpected things that no one tells you about parenthood."

Rhett studied her with an expectant expression in his brown eyes.

Unnerved, Tara averted her gaze and started the course with the basics of infant care—safety, nutrition, hygiene.

Rhett took copious notes. His long legs stretched out in front of him. When he wasn't jotting something down, his full attention was on her. Whenever she made a point, he nodded. When she asked questions to test if they were learning what she'd covered, he was the first one with his hand up.

Head tilted, ears tuned, he was serious about this.

Or at least pretending to be.

"Now that we've gone over the basics of hygiene, let's each take a turn diapering Little Manny." Tara loaded a sticky concoction of flour paste and chocolate syrup into a cloth diaper and put it on the infant medical mannequin.

"Eww!" said one of the girls.

"It's only fake poop, Pumpkin," commented her mother, who'd been the one starstruck with Rhett. "Wait until you have to change the real thing."

"Eww! Eww!"

"You made your bed," her mother said. "Now lie in it."

Pumpkin blew a raspberry at Mom.

"I can't wait for you to get a dose of your own medicine," Mom told her daughter. "Payback is a you-know-what."

"How come we're learning how to put on cloth diapers?" Pumpkin complained. "I'm using disposable."

"Cloth diapers are more economical," Tara said. "And better for the environment."

Pumpkin crossed her arms, hardened her chin. "I am *not* using cloth diapers. My sister used them, and her entire house smelled like pee."

Tara let that pass. She took wet wipes from a drawer and sat it on the conference table beside the mannequin. "I want you all to come up and practice diapering Manny here. Who's first?"

"My baby daddy is scared of changing a diaper," another teen piped up. She was so pregnant her belly pushed flush against the back of the chair in front of her.

"I ain't scared of no diapers, Charlene," said a lavishly inked young man, named Jaime, sitting beside her. He hopped from his chair, swaggered to the front of the room in baggy jeans and a backward baseball cap with "Pit Bull" embroidered on the panel above the strap.

Tara showed Jaime how to use the safety pins, and where to place his fingers so the pins would poke him instead of the baby in case he slipped.

"I don't wanna get poked," Jaime complained, which was ironic considering his multiple tats and piercings. "Charlene, we're getting disposables."

"You could use Snappis," Pumpkin's mom said. "We used them on my other daughter's baby."

"Snappis are an option." Tara picked up the brand of plastic diaper fasteners that were lying on the table arrayed with supplies. "We're going to practice with those too. We're covering all the options."

Jaime was struggling with pinning the cloth diaper. He muttered a few choice curse words.

"Slow down," Tara soothed. "Take your time. And don't forget to wipe the baby's bottom thoroughly. He can get diaper rash if he's not kept clean."

Jaime furrowed his brow. Grabbed a handful of wet wipes, smeared the fake baby poop everywhere. "I suck at this."

"You're doing fine," Tara encouraged. "It just takes practice. You'll be a champ in no time."

Jaime, however, was not doing fine. He'd managed to poke the safety pin clean through Little Manny's thigh.

"Undo the safety pin and try again," Tara guided him.

Jaime's shoulders slumped. "I'm screwing it all up."

"You're not."

"Yes, he is! He jammed a safety pin through our baby's thigh!" Charlene wailed.

"I don't deserve no baby!" Jaime's voice rose to join his girlfriend's panicky pitch.

"Calm down, calm down." Tara kept her tone low. She was accustomed to expectant parents having meltdowns. Welcoming a new baby was a stressful event, even for the most well-prepared. And generally, her students were not the least bit ready for parenthood. "Everyone, please take a deep breath. Inhale, two, three, four."

They obeyed.

"Hold." She counted to seven aloud. "Now let it out slowly to the count of eight."

The room breathed a long, slow sigh.

"Good job. Let's do it again. Deep breath. In, two, three, four." She glanced at Rhett.

He hadn't been watching Jaime and Charlene, he'd been studying her. Tingles of awareness lifted the hairs on her arm. There was a gleam in his eyes that unsettled her. As if he'd been imagining what she looked like without any clothes on.

Tara buttoned her lab jacket, a shield to ward off his gaze.

"As a new parent," she said to the class, "you might often find yourself in a situation where you're losing control over your emotions. This is normal. It happens to everyone. The key is to not judge yourself for having the emotion. Just become aware that the emotion is running you, and then take a deep breath. Hold it. Then let it go."

She led the class through several rounds of deep breathing exercises. In the end, the energy shift in the room was palpable as people calmed.

"It's like Lamaze," Pumpkin's mother said.

"Same idea, yes." Tara nodded. "The breath slows the mind."

"Did you use these techniques when you had your kids?" Pumpkin's mother asked.

"I've not been fortunate enough to give birth," Tara said.

"You don't have no kids?" Jaime, who was still standing at the front of the room with the badly diapered Manny, stared at her. "How come you're teaching this course?"

Her muscles tensed, defensive and guarded. Her chest was a

vise, squeezing tight. Yes, okay, she was sensitive about being childless.

"For one thing," she said, her tone brooking no argument, "I'm a registered nurse with a specialty in neonatal care. I've worked with infants for eight years, and in the NICU for almost two, I've—"

"It's not the same thing as being a parent." Jaime snorted.

"I'm also a foster mother—"

"Still not the same thing." Pumpkin's mother shook her head so vigorously that Tara feared the woman and her daughter would get up and walk out.

The woman's judgment played into Tara's insecurities. No, most likely she would never know the joys of giving birth to a child of her own, but that didn't invalidate her knowledge and experience in pediatrics. It didn't mean she was less than the women who had given birth.

Don't take it personally, she reminded herself. But that was easier said than done.

"You can't teach us what no one tells you about parenthood, because you don't know a thing about it," chimed in another mother of one of the teenagers.

"Yeah, why should we listen to anything you have to say about raising children?" asked Charlene.

Things had taken an ugly turn. How had she lost control of the classroom? The group was mumbling mutinous noises, muttering stings and barbs.

Tara took the hit. Struggled to conceal her feelings. Swallowed their opinions along with a lungful of air. *Take your own advice. Breathe through the emotions.* She closed her eyes.

Inhaled.

A chair scraped across the floor. Someone was leaving.

Tara's eyes flew open. She put a hand to her mouth, smelled the scent of chocolate syrup and flour paste. Who was the first defector?

Rhett.

He was leading the charge against her? Her stomach turned sour, and she wished she hadn't had that egg burrito for breakfast.

Rhett was on his feet, standing in the middle of the room. All eyes locked on him as if he were their spokesman.

The fluorescent lighting over her head was too bright. Sweat broke out on her brow. She moved her hand from her mouth to her stomach. Rhett had his faults, but he'd never been the kind of person to kick someone when they were down.

"People, people." Rhett made a chill-out gesture with his hands. "I don't believe this."

"We don't either," said Charlene. "Can you imagine someone teaching parenting classes who doesn't have children of her own? What was the hospital thinking hiring *her* as an instructor?"

"Preach it, Brother Lockhart," Pumpkin's mother said. "Just 'cause we're poor don't mean we want their cast-off instructors."

Rhett growled at Pumpkin's mother. "*You're* what I don't believe."

The woman pressed her mouth into a thin line. Looked offended . . . and a little scared.

Rhett didn't care. He came to stand beside Tara. "Jaime, sit down."

Obediently, Jaime trotted back to his seat.

Rhett slung an arm around Tara's shoulder. The weight of it was warm, reassuring. His touch pulled her back into her body, grounded her. Her spirits—which had been squirming around in the gutter—lifted. He smelled so good. Like spray starch and leather.

"The rest of you, listen up! You know nothing about Ms. Alzate. What her life is like, what's in her heart. She's giving up her weekend and time with her foster daughter so that she can help you people become better parents. And this is how you act?" He glowered at first one person and then another, his eyes going all around the room until he'd met and held every gaze. "You should be ashamed of yourselves."

"Hey," some man in the back row said. "I never dissed her."

"No, but you didn't come to her defense either, did you?" Rhett said.

The man ducked his head.

"You seem like good people who let the heat of the moment get away from you. But that's exactly what Ms. Alzate is trying to teach you. You're going to feel things as parents, and it isn't always going to be sweetness and light. That's normal. But you can't allow your feelings to cause you to treat someone else badly. Next time, it will be your kid. And I know none of you wants to treat those sweet babies with anything but love and kindness."

He was on a roll, and swimming upstream from his usual anything-goes personality. Challenging the other students, drawing a proverbial line in the sand. Tara loved him for it.

The room went totally silent.

Tara's heart felt as if it had been sliced wide open. *My hero.*

"Am I right?" Rhett trod back and forth, pacing the length of the room.

Eighteen heads bobbed in agreement.

"You all owe Ms. Alzate an apology."

In unison, the class apologized.

Tara smiled and smoothed things over. All was forgiven. She told them to take a short break. Watched her students file from the classroom, her legs weak as boiled rubber bands.

"You okay?" Rhett murmured. His arm went to her shoulder again.

The disturbing thing was, she was in no hurry to step away. "I'm fine. But I could have handled that on my own."

"I know you could have." He bobbed his head, tipping his chin down and sliding a sidelong glance at her. "But what kind of man would I be if I'd just sat there and let them gang up on you?"

"It's not your place to rescue me."

"Ah, c'mon." He chucked her chin in an affectionate gesture. "Course it is. You rescued me plenty when we were kids. Remember that time I got lost in the desert?"

"Because you disobeyed me. You were supposed to be taking a nap."

"I was ten."

"And I was in charge."

"Tara knows best?" Humor crinkled his eyes.

"Most of the time, yes," she said, disarmed.

"You haven't changed a bit." He gave her his most beguiling grin, winked.

"What's that supposed to mean?"

He said nothing, just shrugged and kept grinning.

"What?" Edginess crept into her voice.

He pantomimed cracking a bullwhip.

"Smartass."

"You were the strictest babysitter I ever had."

"And you were the most mischievous kid I ever babysat."

"But you never told on me," he said. "I do owe you for that."

"I don't keep score."

"Not even a little?" He measured off an inch with his thumb and forefinger.

She wriggled her eyebrows at him. "You *did* break one of my collectible porcelain dolls."

"I was practicing my lassoing skills."

"On my doll?"

"I paid you back out of my allowance," he said.

"It took you four months."

"I got really good at lassoing that headless doll," he mused, stroking his chin.

"Good with a rope, are you?" she asked, and then realized belatedly how suggestive that sounded.

He lowered his lashes, sent a hot glance roving over her body. "Uh-huh."

Heat tickled her spine. Why did she feel so effervescent?

"Honestly." His voice lowered. "I'll never be able to repay you. You're taking such good care of my daughter. I'll owe you forever."

"Okay then. Thank you for the white-knight number."

"Why, Tara." His eyes twinkled like stardust. "It was my pleasure."

They stared at each other. Forging a connection. Bonding in a completely new way. It was a bit bizarre, this strange moment of unity.

"Listen," she said. "I know you're busy on the circuit, but just in case you want to see Julie again, we'll be at the Silver Feather for Kaia and Ridge's Memorial Day weekend bash."

"I'm riding that Friday and Saturday."

"I see," she said, relieved. She'd felt obligated to offer the invitation, but she was super-glad he hadn't accepted. The less time he spent with Julie, the more likely it was that he would terminate his parental rights and allow her to adopt his daughter.

"But the event is in Austin. I can leave right after the rodeo and be home before dawn on Sunday morning. The party runs through Monday night."

"Is that safe, driving straight through?"

"I'll sleep in on Saturday and drink plenty of coffee. I do lots of night driving."

Of course he did. Impulsive, reckless, original. Rhett had never been one to play by the rules of normal society.

"See you then," he said, turned, and walked away.

Leaving Tara wishing she'd just kept her big fat mouth shut.

Chapter 8

FIRST GO: The preliminary round of a competition.

RHETT aced the PBR event in Austin, leading a fuming Claudio by five points, and leaving the other riders completely in the dust. He was on the hottest hot streak of his life with no letup in sight. His manager was over the moon, and Rhett should have been too.

But an odd uneasiness nibbled at the back of his mind. When he should have been concentrating on Vegas, his thoughts kept creeping back to Julie . . .

And Tara.

For the last few weeks, he'd been unable to think of little else but Julie and the woman who was caring for her.

Ever since he found out Tara was Julie's foster mother, he'd linked the two of them in his mind. He couldn't think of Julie without seeing her in Tara's arms. He owed Tara a debt of gratitude he could never repay. Because of Tara, his daughter was alive.

He thought about how Tara had looked in the classroom, controlled and in charge. Her dark hair arranged in a no-nonsense bun. But things had changed when she'd ordered him into the corridor and they'd been alone. She'd tried hard to cover her vulnerability with crossed arms and a chiding stare, but he saw her yearning underneath the sternness. Understood that by showing up in the parenting class he'd signaled to her that he was interested in filing for custody of the baby.

But was he?

He was no closer to a decision than he'd been that day Lamar had shown up at his trailer. His mind had boggled from the moment his lawyer tossed those paternity test papers on his kitchen table.

He was a dad.

He was also a professional bull rider on target to win the greatest award a bull rider could receive and earn a bucketload of money in the process.

Problem was, he couldn't make peace with either path. If he went for custody of Julie, he'd have to give up the PBR, and he just wasn't prepared to do that. But neither could he bring himself to sign away all parental rights.

His hope was to string things along until he could figure it out. He had time. His daughter was an infant, she wouldn't know if he was around or not for the next few weeks. But was that fair to Tara?

No, it wasn't.

On the Sunday before Memorial Day, he arrived at the Silver Feather at five a.m. and grabbed a four-hour nap in the house he'd built on a hundred-acre tract on the south part of the Silver Feather Ranch.

His paternal grandfather, Cyril Lockhart, had left such plots of land to each of his four grandsons when they turned twenty-one, along with enough money to build houses on the acreage. Not a bad inheritance for a twenty-one-year-old kid.

The catch?

And there was always a catch where Lockhart generosity was concerned. None of the brothers could sell their part of the Silver Feather without written permission from their father and siblings. Considering that their father, Duke Lockhart, was an ornery cuss, and darn near impossible to please, they'd all built their houses and then promptly left the Silver Feather.

Except for Ridge, who had come home three years ago, made

peace with Duke, and married Kaia Alzate, and now he ran the Silver Feather after Duke's heart attack.

Ridge was Rhett's oldest half brother, born to a honky-tonk dancer who'd died in a one-car collision on the same night she'd abandoned a three-year-old Ridge on their father's doorstep. That was six years before Rhett had been born to Duke and his second wife, Lucy Hurd. As the illegitimate Lockhart brother, Ridge had had a tough row to hoe growing up. But in the end, things turned out great for him. He'd left home right after college when he caught Duke in bed with Ridge's girlfriend, Vivi. The irony of that was that Duke and Vivi were married now, and they had twin eighteen-month-old boys named Reed and Rory.

Between the twins; Ridge's kids, Ingrid and Cody; Archer Alzate's sons, Tyler and Dylan; and now Julie, the Silver Feather was baby-palooza. The ranch was starting to resemble the old days when the four Lockhart boys ran wild and free across the desert with the five Alzate siblings. The nine of them had been pretty close back then.

But now there was a whole new generation, and his daughter was going to be part of it.

If he filed for custody.

The idea of Julie growing up on the Silver Feather charmed him, even though life on the ranch hadn't always been idyllic. The Trans-Pecos was a tough, hardscrabble land, but there was an undeniable beauty in the rugged wilderness, and the desert toughened a kid up to life's barbs and bumps. And the sense of community and camaraderie softened and stabilized the environment.

There was something about the notion of legacy that touched Rhett. His great-great-grandfather Levi Lockhart had come to Texas from North Carolina, survived and thrived here. Building the largest ranch in the Trans-Pecos that sprawled across Jeff Davis and Presidio counties.

Julie was part of the Lockhart lineage.

Growing up, he'd spent his summers milking cows, haying,

shoveling manure, and mending fences. Work became a pleasurable thing. There was something special about family labor, done in service to the collective.

He'd almost forgotten what that was like.

The house Rhett erected was the smallest of the four brothers' homes. Mainly because he spent only half the money Gramps left him on the house. The rest went to horses, bulls, and his first travel trailer. It was a simple three-bedroom, two-bath, ranch-style house. Seventeen hundred square feet.

Currently, Rhett and Ridge were in the main barn at the family mansion, checking out the horses Kaia had rescued from an old cowhand who'd gotten Alzheimer's and had to go into a facility. Rhett, who was bent over shoeing one of the gaunt mare's back legs, glanced up at his older brother.

"Your wife's animals are going to end up eating you out of house and home." Rhett laughed. "How many horses are you supporting now?"

"With this new lot?" Ridge looked happily sheepish. "Sixteen, but two of the mares are pregnant."

Gak! More babies.

"You're making that face again," Ridge said.

"What face?"

"Like you're gonna throw up. Are you all right?"

"Just thinking about Julie."

"It's a big deal."

"Hell, man, a month ago my life was perfect. Everything I ever dreamed of was within reach. The world championship was mine to win. And now . . ."

Ridge nodded. "It's upside down."

"Topsy-turvy."

"Exciting—"

"Terrifying—"

"Fatherhood is—"

"Crazy—"

"Fun crazy—"

"Scary crazy—"

"Like bull riding?"

"Scarier."

They stared at each other. He saw in his brother's eyes a sense of contentment he'd never felt. Was it fatherhood that made Ridge look so happy?

Ridge rested a hand on his shoulder. "Brother, the best things in life scare the living hell out of you."

"Shit." Rhett exhaled, swept off his Stetson, and jammed a hand through his hair. "If fear is any indication, then Julie is the best thing ever."

"Yep, she is."

"How do you get ready to be a father?"

"You don't. You just do it."

"I'm trying to wrap my head around it, but it's too much for me. I—"

"Do or do not. There is no try."

"Quoting Yoda to me, man?"

"He *was* a Jedi Master."

"He was also a fictional nonhuman character."

Ridge gave a smug shrug. "Wise words are wise words no matter who utters them."

"Meaning?"

"It's time to do your business or get off the pot."

"Excuse me?"

"Either file for custody of your daughter or let her go."

Ridge was right. Dragging this decision out was eating him up inside. But he wasn't about to admit that to his oldest brother. Rhett had perfected his easygoing reputation and he was sticking by it.

"Hand me that rasp." Ridge extended his palm. "And I'll shoe her front hooves. You look as if you need to sit."

Rhett slapped the tool into his brother's hand and sank onto a nearby milk crate turned upside down, feeling as if he'd had the wind knocked out of him.

Ridge worked in silence for a few minutes, the steady *whisk-whisk* of his rasp against the horse's hoof the only sound in the barn.

Ridge straightened and met Rhett's eyes. "You'll regret it."

"Regret what?"

"Signing over your parental rights."

"You think?"

"Yeah."

"But if Tara gets to adopt her, I'd still see her."

"And what will you tell Julie when she's old enough to ask why you walked away? That you picked bull riding over her?"

His brother's words were a stone in the pit of his stomach. Rhett hadn't thought that far ahead.

"Your career will last, what . . . five years more at best? Ten at the absolute max. Julie is here forever."

"But the championship is within reach. It's all I've ever wanted. I've lived and breathed rodeo for over a decade."

"You've got something more important now."

A truculent stubbornness grabbed hold of him. "Why can't I have both?"

"Your job is damn dangerous. Every time you climb on the back of a bull, you're rolling the dice with your life."

"Not that many people die riding."

"Tell that to Lane Frost's family," Ridge said, referring to one of the greatest bull riders of all time, who'd died in the arena from injuries sustained by a bull. "And it's not just death. Brain injury is not uncommon."

He couldn't argue that point. Chronic traumatic encephalopathy from head trauma was a very real threat. He dealt with the risk by taking the necessary precautions and then not giving it a second thought. "Most jobs have some kind of risk," he mumbled.

"Bull riding is one of the most dangerous sports in the world."

Not a newsflash to Rhett. Danger was part of the appeal.

"You have to decide," Ridge went on. "What's more important? Julie or your ego?"

"My ego?"

"That's all this is. Your drive to be number one at any cost. Big, fat ego stroke."

"And money. Lots of money."

"You've got plenty of money without the win."

Anger flared through him, hot and aggressive, and Rhett didn't anger easily. He glowered. Felt blindsided and betrayed. "Oh, and you competing against Dad to become richer than he is and flying your own private plane isn't all about *your* ego?"

"I'm not denying my ego got the better of me, little brother. That's how I know what's driving you. If you let it, pride and ego will lead you down the wrong road fast."

"You say that as if you know everything there is to know about me. You have no idea what I've been through. What life is like on the road."

"Simmer down, kid. I'm not judging you."

"No?"

"I'm merely pointing out that it's time to grow up and realize what's truly important. It took Kaia and Ingrid to do that for me." Ridge shot him a meaningful look. "Julie can do that for you if you let her."

"I'm not ready to be a dad."

"So get ready." Ridge's stern tone brooked no argument.

Fear played up and down his spine. "I have no idea how to take care of a baby."

"Learn."

His brother made it sound so simple. "Tara wants Julie more than anything, and she's prepared to be a parent."

"Sounds like you want to take the easy way out," Ridge scoffed.

Did he? That question had been bouncing around in his head for the past three weeks.

"With Tara as Julie's mom you get to have your cake and eat it too, but is that fair to Tara? Or Julie?" Ridge didn't meet Rhett's glare. He'd finished up with the first horseshoe and was reaching for the mare's other leg.

"Why are we shoeing horses?" Rhett asked. "You've got cow-hands for this."

"You too good to shoe horses?"

"That's not what I'm saying."

Ridge's head shot up. "What *are* you saying, little brother?"

"Why are we out here, Ridge?"

"Is it wrong to want to spend time with my brother?"

Suspicion was a cold knife blade underneath his shoulders. He'd forgotten how manipulative his family could be. "Duke put you up to this, didn't he?"

Ridge had the good grace to look abashed. "Duke wants to see all his grandchildren grow up here on the Silver Feather."

"I don't give a shit what he wants. After the childhood he put us through? Narcissistic old sot."

"You're being defensive," Ridge accused.

"The old man is trying to control you," Rhett said. "To control both of us. It's what he does." And it was the reason that Rhett had taken refuge in the PBR.

"He's changed. After the heart attack and the twins. You haven't been around much the last few years to see it." Ridge straightened, put down his tools, and dusted his palms together.

"Unless he's had a personality transplant, I don't see how that's possible." Rhett snorted.

"Just so you know, Vivi and I talked him into going to see a psychologist after the heart attack." Ridge rested his arm on the horse stall gate.

Rhett's jaw dropped. The thought of his domineering father in therapy stretched his imagination to the breaking point. "Why didn't you tell me before?"

"You're always in party mode, working out, or in the arena. Whenever I tried to bring up the old man, you'd wave me off."

True enough. But he still didn't trust his father. Too many times the old man had pitted him and his brothers against each other. Making first one, then the other, either the scapegoat or the golden child. "Dad is reason enough to let Tara have the baby," Rhett said. "She's always stood up to him. It's why he doesn't like her."

"He doesn't dislike Tara. He just believes Lockharts belong on the Silver Feather."

Rhett's body buzzed as if he'd barely dodged a highway collision. The barn seemed airless, claustrophobic. Tightening his lungs, making it hard to breathe. Or maybe it was the judgmental smirk on his older brother's face. He knotted his hands into rock fists. Chunked out the words as if he were spewing gravel. "See? Right now, he's got you acting like his flying monkey. Controlling."

"You're being overly dramatic." Ridge's tone was even, reasonable. "I know this is a touchy topic, and Duke is a complicated man, but don't walk away from your daughter simply to spite him."

Rhett let loose with a string of curse words. "I can't believe you're lobbying his case. You of all people. The one he mistreated the most."

"That's the thing. If *I'm* willing to forgive him, you should be too. We can put this family back together again. We can stop the legacy of abuse."

"Not by letting Duke get his way."

"This isn't about him and you know it."

Rhett jutted out his chin, felt contrary. "Whose side are you on anyway?"

"I'm on Julie's side."

Rhett's heart slid up and down his chest as old emotion churned. He remembered the beatings meted out as punishment. The verbal abuse that their father had dished up on a daily basis. Belittling him and his brothers for not being tough enough. Was that where his anxiety over being a father was coming from? Fear of being like Duke?

Ridge seemed to read his thoughts. "You're not going to be

like him. Look at me with Ingrid and Cody. They completely changed my life in all the best ways. I love them to the moon and back, and no matter how I was raised, or maybe even because of the way I was raised, I would never ever abuse them the way we were abused. And neither will you."

"Can you look me in the face and tell me honestly that I'm the best thing for her?"

Ridge's steely gaze slammed into Rhett's. "Brother, a girl needs her daddy. Don't turn away from her." He paused for a measured beat, added, "Please."

Rhett's pulse was a drum, beating against his ears. Could he actually be a decent father? But how? He was self-centered and shallow. He didn't deny it. He'd built his life around his own needs and desires without thought of anyone else.

Ridge's phone dinged. He pulled it from his pocket, checked the text message. "Tara and the baby will be at our house at one. Bridgette and Armand," he said, referring to Tara and Kaia's parents, "are already there with Granny Blue."

Rhett let out a groan. He was not the elderly Apache woman's favorite person. Granny Blue had given him a rash of crap the brief few weeks that he and Aria had dated. She'd called him a scallywag and said he needed to grow up and stop acting like a boy. What would she have to say about Julie?

He was not looking forward to making conversation with Tara's paternal grandmother. Or Tara, for that matter. She got her moxie from her granny; that much was evident.

Truth was, he hadn't been able to get Tara out of his mind all week. He thought about her in odd moments. The fuzz of early morning, in between sleeping and wakefulness. How she'd bought strawberry wafer cookies to serve when she knew he was coming. One day, as he stood in line in the grocery store, he'd spied a pack of Juicy Fruit gum. He remembered that when they were kids, she'd loved Juicy Fruit. He'd bought a pack and stuck it in his back pocket. He'd planned on giving it to her as a peace offering. But now it just seemed stupid and weird.

"Rhett?" His brother's voice brought him back into the room.
"Huh?"

"You gonna stay here and pout or you gonna go to the party?"

He was still ticked at Ridge, but it seemed less attention-getting
to show up with his brother than to come in alone. Although
neither would be fun. He'd already gotten a heap of ribbing from
his father, brothers, and friends about the baby. That morning,
he'd found a box of condoms on the dashboard of his truck.

Ha-ha. Everyone was a joker.

"Hey," Ridge said. "All testing and teasing aside. You know
when it comes down to brass tacks, whatever you decide, Kaia
and I always have your back, right?"

"I know *you* do. But Kaia is Tara's sister."

"Doesn't matter what we think. I'll support you in your bid
for custody. I'll speak up for you at the hearing. We'll help you."

"What about Tara?"

"Julie isn't Tara's biological child. Much as Kaia loves her
sister, right is right. And it's right for a girl to be with her biological dad."

"But Tara loves Julie as if she were her own."

Ridge ducked his head, shuffled his boots. "There'll be other
babies for Tara. Babies who don't have a father who wants them."

It was too much. He was split right in two. Rhett walked to
the barn door, banged his head repeatedly on the wall.

"You okay?" Ridge's voice was thick and cottony, tinged with
concern.

Rhett turned to his brother once more. "Not really."

"Is there anything I can do?"

"Invent a time machine so I can go back and *not* sleep with
Rhona."

"Do you want to talk about it? I might be able to help."

"No."

"Okay, I can respect that." Ridge bobbed his head.

Rhett didn't intend on spilling his guts. No sir. Not in the
least.

But his eyes met Ridge's and he just started babbling. "I feel like there is a giant detonation button dangling in front of me, and if I push it, I'll blow everything up. But if I don't push it, the ground will crack open and swallow me whole."

"Do you *want* to blow it up?" Ridge asked.

Acid burned its way up Rhett's throat, and when he spoke, he said the truest thing he knew. "I think I already did."

Chapter 9

RAG DOLL: What a rider looks like when he's hung up and dragged around.

Tara walked into Kaia's kitchen on the east side of Silver Feather Ranch, dreading seeing Rhett again. She hadn't seen him or heard from him since the parenting class, and she'd gotten her hopes up again that he was backtracking on the notion of filing for custody.

The silent treatment was a bit maddening and left her in limbo. Although she realized he was probably in limbo too, still debating on whether he was ready to give up the PBR and become a full-time father.

She'd thought about texting him, just to check in, but thought better of it and let things lie. But radio silence escalated her anxiety. What exactly was the man up to?

Kaia was sitting in the corner breakfast nook nursing Cody, a baby blanket discreetly covering her. Her sister's son was the same age as Julie, and Tara couldn't help comparing her tiny little foster daughter to her robust nephew. At four months old, the differences between a preemie and a baby born at term were significant.

Granny Blue and her mother were looking after the rest of the children in the big den, baby gates set up at the doors. The minute Tara had walked into the house, Mom had confiscated Julie, plopped down in a rocking chair, and shooed Tara into the kitchen. "Go spend time with your sisters."

Tara's sister-in-law, Casey, was bustling between the stove and the kitchen island, taking cocktail sausages, wrapped in crescent roll dough, out of the oven.

"Thanks for rescuing the pigs in a blanket," Kaia called to her sister-in-law.

"No prob." Casey got mustard and ketchup from the fridge. "I know what it's like to wish for a clone."

The kitchen smelled of memories. A feast was spread out on the sideboard, a blend of Texas cowboy cuisine and Mescalero Apache fare—barbecue brisket, fried green tomato and okra rolled in cornmeal, potato casserole, green beans, venison steaks, cornbread, acorn squash stew, and peach cobbler for dessert.

Aria was manning the Vitamix, whipping up banana daiquiris for the party. Aria worked as a wedding planner for Vivi Lockhart, Rhett's stepmother. The Silver Feather was a popular wedding venue in Cupid and the surrounding towns of Fort Davis, Marfa, and Alpine.

"Anything I can do to help?" Tara asked.

"Drink this." Aria pressed a daiquiri in Tara's hand. At twenty-five, Aria was still single and carefree.

"Thanks." Tara took a sip.

"Where's Julie?" Aria asked. "I haven't met that little love button yet."

"Mom insisted on stealing her." Tara cast a glance over her shoulder toward the den.

"I still can't believe Rhett has a baby daughter." Aria shook her head, sending her fall of dark straight hair swinging about her shoulders. "Such craziness!"

"Why can't you believe it?" Kaia asked, rearranging herself and draping a well-fed Cody across her shoulder to burp him. "It was bound to happen eventually. Play with fire, you're gonna get burned."

"Despite his fast and loose reputation, Rhett was always careful to use condoms," Aria said.

All eyes swiveled to Aria.

"What?" A nonchalant shrug rolled off her shoulders. "We had a good time together. That's all."

"I've got a question for you," Kaia said. "Did you hear the hum when you kissed him?"

"What?" Aria pulled back her chin, shook her head, looked at Kaia as if she'd lost her ever-loving marbles. "With Rhett? No way. Why would you even ask that?"

"Kaia heard the hum with Ridge. Ember with Ranger . . ." Casey supplied.

"So, you think all the Alzate women are soul mates for the Lockhart men?" Aria laughed and sank her hands on her tiny waist. "That idea is as nutty as the humming thing itself. Rhett wasn't The One."

"The legend is truth."

They all turned to see Granny Blue standing in the doorway. Her braided gray hair looped into a neat crown atop her head. She headed for the coffeepot, poured herself a half cup, and turned to face her granddaughters.

"Ember and Kaia know what's real," Granny Blue said.

"Absolutely." Kaia got up, wrapped her arm about their tiny grandmother's waist, and leaned against her. Kaia wasn't much taller than Granny Blue's five-foot-one. Aria was a bit taller at five-three. Ember was five-five. At five-foot-seven, Tara felt like a tree among her diminutive family members.

From the time they were small children, Granny Blue had been telling the four Alzate sisters a fantastical story about true love. According to the legend, when the women from Granny Blue's lineage kissed their soul mates, they heard an indisputable humming in their heads and knew immediately they'd found their One and Only.

Kaia vowed it had happened to her when she kissed Ridge. Ember backed her up, saying the same thing happened when she'd kissed Ranger.

Tara didn't believe in the legend. She was a nurse, for crying out loud. Her education was grounded in science. She was practical, and down-to-earth. She had always been the sensible one.

When they were kids and their mother read *Little Women* to

them, Ember pronounced that she was Jo, except for the writing thing, Kaia was Beth, Aria was Amy, and Tara was Meg. Aria had gotten miffed at that and thrown an Amy-style fit. Tara might have been offended except it was true. Like Meg March, she *was* responsible, motherly, and kind. Kaia had been the most upset, saying, "I am not Beth. I don't intend on dying young."

"It's just a book," Tara had comforted her younger sister at the time. "And Ember is being silly."

Still, there was a grain of truth in Ember's equating the traits of the four Alzate girls with the March siblings.

"When you hear the hum . . ." Kaia sighed dreamily. "*Everything* changes."

As far as Tara was concerned, the humming story was simply a self-fulfilling prophecy. Her sisters wanted the legend to be true. They *wanted* to believe in it, so when they kissed the men they were falling in love with, through the power of suggestion, their brains produced the humming sound. Suggestible. The placebo effect. The humming myth, while romantic, was nothing more than that.

Besides, Tara had been in love before. And she hadn't heard a thing when she kissed Kit. Not humming. Not ringing. Not a whisper. The lack of love music hadn't changed her feelings for him one whit.

Granny Blue had told her that the missing hum meant Kit had not been her soul mate. Tara had kept quiet. Kit was a good man. But she hadn't wanted to get into an argument with her grandmother.

Tara was a team player who could readily put the needs of others first when need be, which was why nursing had been such a perfect fit. Granny Blue claimed Tara's personality stemmed from the earth element in her sign. Tara was too sensible to buy into something as unscientific as astrology. Which, Granny Blue claimed with delight, was exactly something an earthy Taurus would say.

As a natural historian, Tara was fascinated by Native American lore. She was the one who bought a yearly subscription to Ancestry.com, plotted their family tree, and compiled the myths, legends, and tall tales. She credited her Grandfather Alzate for her love of history. She'd been his favorite grandchild, and everyone knew it. Although she couldn't say for sure if she'd been the favorite because she loved listening to his stories of the Wild West days in the Trans-Pecos and their Mescalero Apache heritage, or if she'd loved the stories because he'd favored her.

Grandfather Alzate had been educated at Sul Ross University in Alpine, sent by his employer, Cyril Lockhart, back in the 1950s, to learn animal husbandry and natural resource management. He spoke fluent English, but with Tara, he would utter the Apache words he didn't use with anyone other than Granny Blue and her father, Armand.

Her grandfather had once said to her, "If you children were school subjects, Archer would be math, Ember would be science, Kaia would be social studies, Aria would be art, and you would be history, Shindálé."

She loved when he would call her by the Mescalero name for a paternal grandchild. In his native tongue, when a grandfather called his grandchild Shindálé, the child called him Shindálé in return. It was only later she learned the complicated language rules for Mescalero Apache kinship that differed so greatly from English, but it seemed like their secret code.

Shindálé.

The term of endearment had made her feel special and she set out to learn the language of her ancestors from her grandparents. She was the only one of her brother and sisters who spoke Mescalero Apache. She'd also, as part of her job in the NICU of a border town, learned Spanish.

When Tara was fourteen, Grandfather was diagnosed with lung cancer. She was the only grandchild who spent hours at his bedside, fetching him glasses of cold buttermilk, holding his hand, reading to him from the history books he loved to debunk. She would fluff his pillows and smooth the covers and put a cool cloth to his forehead when he felt feverish and offer him ice chips.

"You are a born nurse," he told her in the end, his eyes burning bright with gratitude. "It is your sacred calling, Shindálé."

The minute he said it, she knew he was right, and from then on, her career in medicine had been set in stone. He'd even left a modest sum for her education in an envelope he'd given to Granny Blue, with the strictest instructions not to let any of the other grandchildren find out about the gift. The money had paid for her first year's tuition at Sul Ross. To this day, her siblings were clueless, and Tara would never tell. No point stirring up hurt feelings.

She missed her grandfather something terrible.

"Tara will find her soul mate," Granny Blue was saying, and it was only then that Tara realized a whole conversation had been going on without her.

"Huh?" She blinked.

"You'll find him," Granny Blue reiterated. "I know you've given up hope, and that's why you were prepared to adopt Julie on your own and become a single parent, but he's out there. I promise you."

"How do you know?" Tara said, feeling rankled and defensive. "Maybe it's my lot to walk this world alone."

"There's a lid for every pot." Granny Blue's smug smile was armor against Tara's scowl. "He's out there."

"Maybe it's Remington," Casey said, referring to the third Lockhart brother, who was deployed in the Middle East. "Do you think it could be Remington?"

"Oh good Lord," Tara scoffed. "I am *not* getting involved with a Lockhart."

"I'd say you're already inextricably hooked up with one." Aria nodded out the kitchen window. Tara turned to see Rhett's truck pulling up to the house, and her fool heart skipped a beat. "At least as long as Julie is your foster child."

Rhett got out of the truck.

At the sight of his long, lanky body, Tara's stomach churned. She ducked her head and slipped into the den, leaving her daiquiri behind. Maybe she should have downed the thing. She almost went back after it. Liquid courage for facing Rhett.

But no, she needed her wits about her.

She held out her arms to her mother, who was rocking Julie while Casey's youngest, Dylan, napped in a Pack 'n Play. Tyler and Ingrid pushed toy cars around on the rug in front of the fireplace.

"I can take her now," Tara said, anxious to have Julie in her arms again.

"I've got her," Mom said. "Go enjoy yourself."

"She was colicky last night."

"She seems fine now." Mom held Julie closer to her chest.

"Mom." Tara put steel into her voice. "Please."

"All right." Her mother's eyebrows tugged downward. Slowly, she eased the sleeping baby from her shoulder and slid her into Tara's waiting arms.

Tara hugged Julie tight, felt her sweet baby breath warm the hollow of her neck, inhaled her magical scent. Instantly, her muscles relaxed.

"I wanna hold her," Aria said from the doorway.

"Maybe later."

"Baby hog."

"Hold Cody. Kaia won't mind."

"Possessive much?" Aria gave her a you-selfish-wench stare.

"Julie is a preemie. She's delicate. Fragile."

"You don't think I'm competent enough to hold an infant?" Aria snorted and sank her hands on her hips.

"It's not that . . ." It was that exactly. Aria was such a flibbertigibbet.

"No? I think you're still holding a grudge from when I gave Rhett your porcelain doll to practice his roping on."

"You had no business coming into my room and giving away my things."

"I was six."

"And I told you to leave my stuff alone." Even as she said it, Tara could hear the shrillness in her voice, knew this had nothing to do with the long-forgotten porcelain doll and everything to do with the man making his way up to the house.

"Girls, girls," Mom chided. "You're upsetting the children."

Indeed, the kids had stopped playing and were watching Tara and Aria with wide eyes.

"I'm sorry," Tara apologized. "I didn't get much sleep last night."

"So, can I hold her?" Aria raised her hands and wriggled her fingers in a "gimme" gesture.

"Yes." Tara clung to Julie.

Aria's hands went around the baby. "You gotta let her go."

"She needs changing."

"I can do it."

Reluctantly, Tara loosened her grip.

"Oops." Aria pretended to bobble the baby.

"Don't!" Tara grabbed for Julie.

Aria danced away. "Relax, jeez, I was just kidding."

"You don't kid about something like that." Tara put a hand to her chest to still her leaping heart.

"Ooh," Aria whispered, tucking the baby into the crook of her arm and gazing down at Julie. "She's so tiny."

"Support her head." Tara fluttered around her sister.

"I've held a baby before. Right, Kaia?" Aria hollered over her shoulder.

"She's a good babysitter," Kaia called from the kitchen.

"Aria keeps Vivi's twins all the time," Mom chimed in.

Tara could feel herself winding up. Not good. They were her family. They meant well. They wanted to help. She loved them to pieces, quirks and all.

Breathe.

She gathered a smile, hung it up to dry on her face. To prove she trusted her sister, she left Aria holding Julie and went back to the kitchen for the daiquiri. All the while, her ears were tuned for the sound of Rhett coming through the door.

She peeked out the window. Ridge's pickup truck had pulled up beside Rhett's, and the two brothers were standing in the front yard talking.

Tara felt Kaia's hand on her shoulder. Jumped at her unexpected touch.

"It's all going to work out," Kaia said.

But what if Rhett had decided to take the baby away from her?

As if reading her mind, Kaia whispered, "Julie will always be a part of this family, no matter what happens with custody. Even if you don't get to be her mother, you'll always be her auntie."

Tara nodded, unable to trust her voice. Being an aunt-in-law was all well and good, but it wasn't the same as being a mom. Kaia should know that. But then again, Kaia had two beautiful, healthy kids. Motherhood was a breeze for Kaia. Her sister could afford to be glib.

They mean well, they mean well, she reminded herself. But none of them knew what it was like to desperately long for a child of her own and be unable to achieve what came so readily to most women.

God, why was she here? She should have blown off the Memorial Day weekend shindig and stayed home. Then she looked down at the baby, who was gazing at her from Aria's arms with trusting eyes. No, everything she did was for the love of this child. It was the right thing to let Rhett see her. She could not regret anything. Tara nibbled a thumbnail, trying to vent some tension.

The men had come around the back of the house and were on the steps now. She could hear the sound of their deep voices, the scrape of their boots on the welcome mat.

She stared at the round gold doorknob shining in the sunlight. Saw it turn.

The back door opened, and Ridge walked in, followed by his younger brother. On their heels came Tara's brother, Archer.

Ridge went straight for his wife, pulled her into his arms for a long, searing kiss. Archer did the same with Casey.

Kaia giggled like a teenager.

"Still hear the humming?" Ridge murmured, nuzzling his wife's neck.

"Always," Kaia whispered. "Forever."

All this lovey-dovey stuff was annoying. She'd never been a fan of PDAs. Tara glanced away, locked eyes with Rhett. The king of PDAs.

His stare bored into her.

No matter how hard she tried to look away, she simply couldn't unchain her gaze from his. The bruising on his face was almost gone. The faded discoloration lent him the air of a rakish rogue.

"Where's Julie?" he asked right off the bat.

"I've got her." Aria appeared in the kitchen, cradling Julie in the correct way. Tara could find nothing to criticize.

Rhett's face lit up like sunshine at the sight of his daughter. "Can I hold her?"

"She's yours." Aria transferred Julie into his waiting arms.

Tara knotted her hands into fists, and tendrils of tension twisted her stomach. She had to get over this possessiveness when it came to Julie. It didn't serve either of them. But for the past five months, she'd put her heart and soul into keeping the baby alive. Fighting through one medical crisis after another until Julie finally stabilized. Tara couldn't turn her feelings off and on like a switch.

The doorbell rang. More Lockharts arriving for the party—Duke, Vivi, their twins. The living room got more crowded as greetings and hugs were exchanged. But Tara barely noticed. She had eyes only for Julie.

And Rhett. She couldn't stop staring at him.

Rhett grinned at his daughter and she gurgled happily.

"Aw!" Casey said, clasping her hands against her chin. "That is so adorable."

Tara tried not to be obvious, but even when she wasn't meeting Rhett's gaze head-on, she cut her eyes to the side, observing him from her peripheral vision. Taking measure of the man. There was something in the way he moved, as if the world was his oyster, and he didn't even have to shuck it himself.

The man got away with murder. Things just fell into his lap.

Including babies.

Of course, he was a privileged Lockhart, heir to one of the richest families in the Trans-Pecos. He possessed all the flounce and flair that went with it. True West Texas royalty. But there was more to him than wealth and legacy and his larger-than-life bravado. He was a man comfortable in his own skin. He knew who he was, and Tara, who tended to second-guess herself, found his self-assurance sexy and alluring.

Dear God, had she seriously just thought that?

Sexy?

Alluring?

Rhett Lockhart?

Censor yourself, Tea.

She cocked her head and angled him a look from beneath her eyelashes. He was the most handsome of the Lockhart brothers, no doubt about it. And that was saying a lot, considering all four of them were drop-dead gorgeous.

Rhett had the most hair. Thick and wavy, light brown streaked with golden highlights. He was the leanest too, and muscular in a wiry way she found appealing. He possessed lightning-quick reflexes and a come-sit-by-me smile that charmed females from nineteen to ninety. His butt looked cover-model fine in a pair of Wrangler's, and she could see the muscles of his thighs taut against the denim.

The kitchen grew unbearably hot.

"I need some air," she mumbled and slipped outside.

Chapter 10

SLINGER: A bull that tries to hit the cowboy with its horns while the contestant is on its back.

CONFUSED and panting slightly, she staggered over to the lawn furniture underneath a wide awning. Sank down on a cushion warmed from the sun. The breeze was light. Balmy. A perfect spring day in the Trans-Pecos.

Resolutely, she blacklisted any thoughts that didn't have something to do with peace, quiet, and tranquility. She needed a few moments before attempting to slay the dragon that was Rhett Lockhart.

"Hey."

Inwardly, she groaned at the sound of his voice. So much for serenity. She turned to see Rhett standing beside her, holding Julie the way she'd taught him in parenting class. Whiskey-colored hair curling sexily around the tops of his ears. White cotton T-shirt. Starched jeans. Dammit, why did he have to look so good?

"She shouldn't be in the direct sun," Tara said.

Rhett heaved in an audible breath. "I get that I've got a lot to learn about raising a baby, but do you have to criticize every single thing I do?"

"It's not all about you, sunshine. Surprise, surprise. My only concern is for Julie."

"Mine too." He sounded so sincere, she softened.

"Sit down here in the shade," she said, scooting over so he could take the seat beside her.

"Thanks." He eased down, and immediately she regretted

inviting him. His masculine scent—soap, hay, leather—dizzied her. She inhaled deeply, but that only made things worse, his fragrance filling her head.

She smoothed down the hem of her shorts. His gaze tracked her movements. She remembered what Aria had told her about his kryptonite. Thank God she wasn't wearing Daisy Dukes. Not that she even owned a pair.

He shifted, closer.

Her heart thundered inexplicably, and she slanted him a sideways glance.

His eyes were inscrutable, curtained by sultry lids and thick black lashes. A dusky growth of stubble covered his firm jaw, making him look altogether daring and yet . . . vulnerable?

Hmm, she'd never thought of him as vulnerable. It touched her. That unexpected susceptibility. Was Julie the cause of the changes in him?

She glanced out across the patio to the lavish pool Ridge had installed for Kaia because she was such a water nymph. It boasted a waterfall, slide, and diving board. Sweat rolled down the back of her neck, not so much from the heat but rather her nearness to Rhett, and she had a crazy urge to strip off her clothes and dive naked into the cool, welcoming water.

Instead, she kicked off her sandals and curled her feet up underneath her.

Rhett watched her every move. "I can't thank you enough for taking care of Julie," he said. "I think about you all the time."

He'd thought of her? Tara's heart did a strange swoopy thing like taking a tight curve in a racecar. Okay, this really had to stop. She could not keep reacting to him this way.

"And all the hard work that goes into being a parent."

"Hard work, yes," she said. "But it's a labor of love."

They sat in silence for several minutes. She was hyperaware of everything about him—his breathing pattern, the sexy dark hairs on his forearms, the sight of his broad hands gently cradling the baby.

Tara felt a flutter of emotion she couldn't quite put her finger on. Admiration? Appreciation? No, it felt more delicious than that. A sweet burrowing deep inside her. Attraction?

Briefly, she closed her eyes. Dear God, she was attracted to Rhett Lockhart. Her heart punched into her rib cage like a boxer's fist.

He shifted his knees toward her and settled Julie onto his lap, the wicker lawn furniture creaking beneath them in a way that made her feel nervous. "Tara," he said. "We have to talk."

His voice lowered, turned deeper, darker, plucking some primal chord inside her. She raised her chin. "I'm listening."

But she did not want to hear what he had to say.

"I need to warn you . . ." His voice tightened.

A shiver shook her spine. Warn her? What about?

He leaned in even closer, his arm lightly brushing against hers.

She inhaled sharply at the contact. Felt her entire body tense. Was the touch accidental or on purpose? Was he trying to confuse her? Or throw her off balance?

But no, he looked as unnerved as she was, and he quickly redirected his arm. "Um . . . um," he stammered. "That is, you need to know that . . ."

From the sheepishly determined expression on his face, she knew what he was going to say before he said it. Tara's blood ran cold.

"Yes?" Her voice lifted like a helium balloon floating to the clouds.

"I've made up my mind. I'm filing for custody of Julie."

She dropped her feet back to the ground, scooted away from him, stiffened her spine, tried not to let fear and disappointment overtake her. "I see."

"It's not my intention to hurt you—"

"So you're giving up the PBR and your chance at the world championship?"

"No," he said. "I've talked to my lawyer, and until Rhona's

parental rights have been revoked, the most I can hope for is temporary custody. My lawyer is hoping to clog things up in court so that I wouldn't even have to take possession of her until after November."

Take possession. As if Julie were an object. Anger spread over her like a rash. Tara couldn't believe that for a few minutes there she'd thought Rhett had changed. Stupid, stupid woman. He was as selfish as ever. "Oh well then, that makes it okay."

"Huh?"

"Lucky you. You get to stay on the circuit while I take care of your daughter, and then once everything has fallen into place, you're going to swoop in and take her away from me." Tara fisted her hands on her knees. "What a prince."

Rhett looked surprised and then ashamed. "I hadn't thought about it from your point of view."

"Of course not. All you're thinking about is how to get your own way. Just like always. You spare no thought for how your behavior impacts other people."

His jaw muscle jumped. "That's not fair."

"Fair? No, it's not fair. You're a privileged jerk. You have no idea what it's like for normal people. What it's like to make a *real* living."

"I can see I've upset you."

"Damn straight. You're a spoiled, entitled man-child. You don't deserve custody of your daughter." Tara couldn't hold back her opinion one second longer. Yes, okay, she was upset. And perhaps she was being a bit harsh. But it was time someone called Rhett on the carpet for his thoughtless behavior. He'd been skating through life for far too long. "Reality check, buckaroo. You're not the only one with something invested here."

He didn't shoot back with a knee-jerk reaction to *her* knee-jerk reaction. He didn't get defensive, nor did he try and turn her criticism around on her. He didn't accuse her of being an uptight, judgmental harpy, which she halfway expected.

Instead, he met her eyes and said in a calm, steady voice, "Why do you dislike me so much?"

That honest question knocked a dent in her armor. That, and the fact that Julie was staring up at him with owl-eyed wonder.

She sighed and interlaced her fingers. "I don't dislike you."

"No?"

"'Dislike' means I have some kind of feelings for you." She extended her foot, toed a crack in the patio concrete. "I don't."

"No?" His knee was dangerously close to hers.

She angled her legs in the opposite direction. The last thing she wanted was to touch him again.

"If you don't dislike me, then why are you so hard on me?"

"Somebody has to be."

He laughed then, a hearty, lively sound that both pleased and pissed her off. "You are a tough nut to crack, Tara Alzate."

"So why bother cracking?"

"Because I need you on my side. I'm mishandling this. I didn't consider how getting my lawyer to delay the court hearing would sound from your point of view."

"Of course not. You're a Lockhart. Your point of view is the only one that matters, right?"

"No," he said. "You're taking it personally. This isn't personal."

It certainly *felt* personal. "Isn't it?"

"I'm sorry you're getting caught in the crossfire, Tara, but I'm ready, willing, and able to assume care of my daughter."

She drummed her fingers on the arm of the settee. "But not enough to quit the PBR."

He looked unapologetic. "I've been working for this goal since I was a kid."

"Then go for your dreams and leave Julie to me." She heard the desperation in her voice. Disappointment and sadness brought heat to her face.

"I'm sorry, Tea. I can't do that. I wish I could just walk away, but I can't." He lifted his baby daughter in his arms and kissed her on the cheek.

Tara blinked and glanced away. Rhett was going to get everything he ever wanted. A shot at the PBR World Championship. Money. Fame. Adulation. A beautiful baby daughter.

While she was left with nothing.

"Tara," he said. "I have to make a living in order to provide for my daughter. Would you expect a doctor to give up his career for custody of his child?"

"Being a doctor is not one of the most dangerous careers in the world."

"I'm sorry. I hate that you're hurting." He reached over and touched her fingers, and for one insane moment, she could have sworn he was about to kiss her.

But why would he do that?

Instantly, she stilled. Waiting.

His dark eyes turned murky and he covered her entire hand with his.

Every atom in her body quivered. *Holy guacamole.* Something was melting, and she was almost certain it was she. She felt as if she were caught on camera in a slow-motion sequence, time stretching out like pulled taffy.

She stopped breathing.

So did he. His eyes took a leisurely stroll from her red tank top to her white denim shorts to her tanned feet and toes painted pearlescent white.

His hand lightly squeezed hers.

Too much contact!

She pulled away from him, emotions pressing hot against her eyelids. Her hand tingled from his touch. She closed her eyes, willing back tears. She'd been so stupid. Falling in love with Julie, believing she had a real chance at adopting her. Everyone had tried to warn her that she was going to get her heart broken. She'd been stubborn, certain that Julie was fated to be her daughter, and she hadn't listened.

"My goal is to provide for my daughter, and if I don't ride, I can't do that."

"Lie to yourself enough and eventually it becomes reality."

His eyes went soft. Meeting her fierce gaze with a tender one. "I wish things could be different. I—"

"Please," she said, her heart clogging her throat. "Please, just stop talking."

They sat there a moment, listening to the wind chimes clinking lightly in a whisper breeze. The tension thick as a cheese wheel.

"Are you absolutely sure you want her?" Tara ventured.

"The thought of being a dad is damn scary," he admitted. "I'm not going to lie. But yes, yes I want her."

An idea popped into her head. Grasping at straws, but she'd take what she could get. "All right, then put your money where your mouth is."

"Huh?"

"Prove you've got what it takes to care for a preemie infant."

"Meaning?"

"Assume care for Julie overnight." Hope was a skittish little bird flitting around in Tara's chest. Her plan seemed crazy, but it just might be the thing to convince him this was nuts. It was easy for him to claim he wanted the baby, but the reality of two a.m. feedings, numerous diaper changes, and dealing with Julie's health issues was another thing entirely. This was Tara's opportunity to show him the day-to-day rigors of infant care, exaggerate the difficulties to the max, and scare him off parenthood.

He looked utterly panicked. "You . . . you want me to keep her overnight?"

"She *is* your daughter."

"Wh-wh-when?" he stammered.

"I'm here, you're here, Julie's here. Let's do it tonight."

"But . . . but . . . what if I can't handle it?" His face blanched white.

Feeling triumphant, Tara went in for the kill. "Then before

you file those papers, you'll know that single parenthood isn't for you."

UNTIL HE'D HELD Julie again, Rhett had not known for certain that he was going to file for custody. He'd been thinking about it for weeks, mulling over the pros and cons. Then his conversation with his older brother, and the realization that he was hung up about having kids because subconsciously he was afraid he'd be just like Duke, altered his perspective.

He didn't *have* to be like his father. He could do better. Ridge had done it, so could he. Awareness was all it took, and a strong intention not to make the same mistakes. He could end the legacy of crappy parenting passed down through his paternal lineage.

When he'd felt the slight weight of his daughter in his arms, smelled her sweet baby fragrance, peered into those darling blue eyes, all doubt fled, and he just knew. He could not turn his back on her. No matter how much he had to change in order to be a good father.

Even if it meant quitting the PBR.

That sent a raft of panic sailing through his bloodstream. His mind was still scrambling for a way to be both father and bull rider. He had no idea how he was going to swing it, but he couldn't let that stop him from filing for custody. He would figure it out. One second at a time.

"I'll do it. But you have to spend the night with us. I can't do it by myself. Not the first time."

"Oh absolutely," Tara said. "There was no way I was going to leave her all alone with you for a whole night. Julie is my foster daughter. She's my legal responsibility."

That sort of ticked him off, but at the same time, he was grateful for her honesty. He wiped the back of his hand over his sweaty forehead.

She raised a finger. "Under one condition."

"What is that?"

"You provide one hundred percent of her care throughout the night. I'll merely be there to supervise."

This was a big step, taking sole care of his daughter. Could he handle it? "Um . . . um . . ."

"No shame in admitting you are in over your head," she goaded.

"I've got this." He growled, putting on his best PBR face. "Bring it."

Tara clamped her jaw shut tight as if biting back a string of words she'd thought better of uttering. Paused. Inhaled. Snorted delicately. "I mean it," she went on, as if expecting an argument and not happy without one. "You get up for the round-the-clock feedings every hour and a half."

"Natch."

"You change every diaper."

"Aye, aye, Nurse Ratched."

"You walk the floor with her if she gets colicky." Tara might seem all thorns and stinging nettles, but that was only because she had a gooey marshmallow center and she was desperate to hide her vulnerability. He found that incredibly endearing.

"Got it," he said.

She took her phone from her purse, typed in a text message.

"Who are you texting?"

"Mariah Bean. I want to make sure she's on board with this."

"That's ridiculous. I'm her father. I shouldn't have to ask permission to keep her overnight." He cradled Julie closer. She'd fallen asleep, and he marveled at how beautiful she was.

"Doesn't matter. Julie was turned over to CPS."

"Through no fault of my own."

The second he said it, Rhett realized how that sounded. As if he was blaming others for the situation he was in. He wasn't, was he? Uneasiness perched in his stomach. He had been skimming through life on a wide streak of luck and family fortune.

Rhett shoved the thought aside, focused on Tara. She looked

quite regal—shoulders straight as a ruler, defiant chin lifted slightly.

Tara laughed, a thick, humorless sound. "Let me get this straight. Rhona getting pregnant was a complete accident? You tripped and fell into her?"

"Ha-ha. Witty."

"Sarcasm," she corrected.

"Either way, I like it."

"Don't do that."

"Do what?"

"Try to charm me."

"Why not?"

"Don't waste your breath. I'm immune to you."

That sounded like a challenge, and for a guy who spent his life trying to last eight seconds on the back of a bucking bull, with both precision and finesse, it intrigued him.

"Are you?" Goose bumps popped up on his arms, and he felt a strange tingling sensation deep in the core of his body. "Are you sure?"

Before she could answer, her phone dinged. She glanced down at the screen. "Ms. Bean says it's okay as long as I stay with you and the baby."

"Yay," he said.

"Now you're getting the hang of sarcasm." She clicked off her phone.

"I wasn't being sarcastic." He noticed she tucked the cell into a side pocket with practiced ease instead of just tossing it willy-nilly into the middle of her purse. She was the kind of woman who neatly hung up her clothes, organized her closets alphabetically, and bought storage containers in bulk.

"No?"

Rhett pulled up his spine, ironing out his casual slouch. "Are you always this suspicious?"

"Cautious is the word you're looking for."

"Mistrustful."

"You haven't *merited* my trust," she said, holding out her arms for Julie. "Why should I give it to you?"

Rhett shifted the baby to the crook of his other arm, farther away from Tara. "It's Ms. Bean's trust I need to win, not yours."

"Can't win it without me." She lowered her eyelids, slanted him a sideways glance that was one part anger, one part curiosity, and one part amusement. "I've got custody of your daughter. When it comes to Julie, you need my permission for *everything*."

That fact seemed to bring her much joy. Smirking, Tara kept her arms extended for the baby.

He ignored her outstretched hands. "*Temporary* custody," he corrected.

Tara hardened her jaw, the pulse in her throat jumping like a jackrabbit. She snapped the fingers of both hands. Twice. "Give me the baby."

Julie woke, snuggled in his arm. He peered down at his daughter and she grinned at him, and his heart chugged sideways.

That soft smile set his goal in concrete. This was *his* daughter. *His* girl. Come hell or high water, he would get custody of Julie. Tara Alzate, and anyone else standing in his way, be damned.

"She needs changing," Tara said.

"I can do it. Where are the diapers?"

Tara glared. In her expression he saw her Mescalero Apache heritage, fierce and proud, and he liked her all the more because of her ferocious sense of honor and righteousness. Too bad she did not really like him.

They sat staring at each other, breathing hard as if they'd just run a tandem sack race and lost.

She slapped her hands against her thighs, the muscles in her arms spring-loaded as if she would jump up without a moment's notice, jack-in-the-box style.

He could feel the tension radiating off her. Felt corresponding tension coil inside him. "Diapers?"

"Still in the car, I think. Give her to me and go check my backseat."

Backseat.

Immediately an immature, sexual comeback popped into his head, but he resisted making the joke. "I don't believe that," he said. "You're just trying to get me to surrender Julie to you. You know exactly where the diapers are, and I bet you a hundred dollars they are not in the back of your car."

Her cheeks colored. "How do you know that?"

"You were in the Girl Scouts until you were eighteen. You are always prepared."

"I was seventeen. By eighteen I'd already graduated high school."

"You have an annoying habit of correcting people," he said.

"Only when they're wrong."

"I can see why you've never been married."

"Don't even . . ." Her tone turned tart. "You have no place to talk about the way others lead their lives."

Touché. "You—"

"Are you trying to piss me off?" she asked before he had time to apologize. "Dumb move from a man who needs my help."

"I was trying to compliment you. If you'd listen instead of biting my head off. You're *always* prepared. That's a good thing."

"No one is *always* anything," she said, purposely being contrary.

He stared into her eyes and saw fear lurking beneath her disagreeability. If things went well during the overnight stay, he'd get more visits, and, eventually, the courts *would* grant him custody of his daughter.

And Tara would lose her.

For the first time it fully dawned on him that Tara loved Julie as much as he did, maybe even more so, and a big old pile of regret stacked up inside him. He fumbled in his pocket for the pack of Juicy Fruit and presented it to her.

An involuntary smile fluttered across her lips. "What's this?"

"Peace offering."

"It's my favorite gum." She wrapped her hand around the end of the pack.

He held on to the other end. "I know."

"You bought it for me?"

He shrugged as if it didn't mean anything. "I was standing in line at the grocery store, saw the gum, thought of you, bought it . . ."

"That was thoughtful." She palmed the gum, stuck it in her pocket, and ducked her head, but before she hid her face, he swore he saw the ghost of a grin.

Aha! He'd gotten to her.

Rhett softened his voice. "Remember that time you were baby-sitting Remington and me, and I cut my leg on barbed wire?"

"What a crazy daredevil stunt. Making a catapult to shoot yourselves over the pasture fence."

"What can I say? I was ten and restless."

"You were supposed to be doing homework and you two sneaked out while I was in the bathroom. You were always trying to sneak out."

"No one is *always* anything," he tossed her quote back at her.

She rolled her eyes. But smiled. A tight little I-don't-want-to-but-I-can't-help-it sort of smile.

"You had Band-Aids in your pocket," he said. "Who goes around carrying Band-Aids in their pockets?"

She sniffed, but it was a humorous sound. She was entertained, not offended. "Conscientious babysitters, and nurses-to-be?"

"You were both."

"Are you trying to flatter me?"

He lifted an eyebrow and gave a chuckle. "Is it working?"

"No."

"Rats."

Tara held out her arms again. "May I please have the baby, please?"

Her hair was pinned up in a prim bun and anchored with a

tortoiseshell barrette. He wanted to unsnap that clip and watch her hair fall to her shoulders like a sable curtain. She looked so sexy sitting there that he felt an instant response in his body. A startling response he had not anticipated.

The stirrings of an erection.

He was spending the night with Tara Alzate, and suddenly the last thing on his mind was child care.

At that inopportune moment, Aria popped her head out of the back door. "Get in here, you two. It's time to eat."

Chapter 11

ARENA: The area in which the bull-riding action takes place.

AFTER the meal was over and the dishes washed and put away, the guests gathered outside for a pool party. The kids splashed in the shallow end. Aria, Vivi, Casey, and Archer went in swimming with them. Kaia and Ridge slipped off to the barn near their father's mansion, under the guise of checking on the horses she'd rescued. Tara sat in the shade with Julie, holding a conversation with her parents and Granny Blue.

Leaving Rhett the odd man out with his father. They sat away from the main group under a striped umbrella eating cold watermelon.

"Your kid's pretty cute," the old man said. "For a baby."

"Thanks."

"You gonna do the right thing by her?"

"I texted my lawyer an hour ago and asked him to file the papers on Tuesday."

"Tell me you're yanking my chain." Duke spit watermelon seeds into the grass.

"What?"

"Getting custody of that baby ain't the right thing for you."

Rhett bristled. "What do you mean? I thought you expected me to cowboy up and take responsibility for my actions."

"Yeah, well, not this time. This time you need to do what's right for the kid. Cancel those custody papers and sign your rights over to Tara."

Rhett felt like he was getting whiplash. Ridge had led him to believe the old man wanted him to file for custody. What kind of manipulative game was the old coot playing?

"You've got no business being a father." Duke used a pock-etknife to cut a slice out of the heart of the melon on the table between them.

"Neither did you," Rhett said.

"I'm trying to do better by those two." Duke nodded at Reed and Rory, his eighteen-month-old twin sons, who were splashing in the pool with their cousins.

"I hope for their sakes you are. Thank God for Vivi. A good mom can make up for a lot," Rhett sassed. "I should know."

"Here we go again. When are you gonna stop whining? I was a shit dad for you and your older brothers. Yeah, I got it. But that's the reason I can say that *you* shouldn't be one. We're too much alike, you and me."

Rhett clenched his jaw, knotted his fists, felt as if he'd been gut-kicked. "We're *nothing* alike."

"Keep telling yourself that. We're both selfish as the day is long. Two peas in a pod."

Rhett bit down on his tongue. Sprawled back in the chair, showing he wasn't getting perturbed. Acting like he didn't care.

"You've got more finesse than I do." Duke shrugged. "I'll grant you that, and you're a damn fine bull rider. Better stick with the rodeo."

"Hey, if you can change and become a halfway decent father to Reed and Rory, then anyone can."

Duke snorted. "I'm trying to help you out here, kid."

"Sounds to me like you're just trying to control me. Like always."

"If I hadn't been a controlling sonofabitch, you wouldn't be where you are today. Who pushed you into bull riding?"

"You did." And not just because Duke first sat him on the back of a steer when he was three and laughed when he got dumped off. Bull riding had been Rhett's escape from his domineering father, especially after his mother died.

"You're my favorite, you know," Duke said. "Always have
been."

"Lucky me."

Duke ignored his sarcasm. "That's why I'm giving you this bit
of advice. Don't burden yourself with kids. They'll ruin everything."

"Good talk, Duke." Rhett slapped his hands on his knees and
jumped to his feet.

"You sleep with her yet?"

Rhett swung his head around, met the old man's crafty gaze.
"Who?"

"Tara."

"What is wrong with you?"

"It's not an unreasonable question. She's hot, and you sleep
with anything that moves."

"No," Rhett said. "That was *you*."

Duke let out a loud guffaw. "Told you we were peas in a pod."

"Rhett?"

He looked over to see Tara standing there with concerned
eyes. "Yes?"

"May I speak with you?"

In that moment, Rhett wanted to swing her into his arms
and give her a big hug for getting him off the hot seat.

"You never did answer my question about her." Duke nodded
at Tara.

"It's none of your damn business."

"Peas in pod." Duke laughed again.

Tara slipped her arm through Rhett's and drew him to her.
Instantly, he felt soothed. "Sorry to interrupt, Mr. Lockhart, but
I need to borrow your son."

Rhett latched on tight to Tara's arm. "Get me out of here," he
murmured near her ear.

"Working on it." Tara motioned to Vivi, who moved to settle
in beside her husband. Prying him away from Duke took a tag
team.

"See you later, Mr. Lockhart," Tara sang out, grabbed Rhett's wrist, and tugged him around the side of the house.

"You're a lifesaver." He chuffed out a breath. "If you hadn't come along when you did, I might have belted him."

"I could tell you were drowning. I know your father is a piece of work." Her smile lifted his spirits. "Besides, I really do need you. If Julie and I are going to spend the night at your house, it's time to get this show on the road."

IT WAS JUST after seven-thirty p.m. and even though it was daylight saving time, the Davis Mountains cast long shadows across the valley, bringing cooling temperatures with the encroaching dusk.

Excitement didn't begin to cover what Rhett was feeling as Tara followed him down the dusty ranch road that led the twelve miles from Ridge and Kaia's expansive home on the east side of the Silver Feather, to his more modest bungalow to the south.

He told himself that his jittery belly and wild heart rate were due to spending the night with his daughter, but his anxiety ran far deeper than that. Rhett was thrilled about Tara too. He'd been thinking about her almost nonstop for the past three weeks. The only time his mind had been off her and Julie was when he'd been in the arena.

It was slowly starting to sink in that he really, truly had a child. He hadn't had nine months to prepare like most dads, and the jolt of learning that he was a father was still fresh. What he had not expected was the fierce protectiveness he felt for the baby.

And by association, Tara.

Because Tara so loved his daughter, he wanted to protect her too.

These emotions were new and unexpected. He'd believed he was wired differently from other men. That he'd missed out on some paternal gene. He had not ever dreamed of having a family. A wife and kids hadn't been a blip on his radar.

His lack of nurturing instincts probably had something to do with his old man. Not that Rhett had given it much thought. He was neither prone to introspection like Ranger nor a planner like Ridge. Rhett breezed through life on his looks and his charm and the family name. He liked it that way.

Until Julie.

And Tara.

Seeing Tara again today, dressed in white denim shorts, sexy sandals, and that sleeveless red tank top, his body had responded in classically masculine ways.

She was sexy.

She was strong.

She was beautiful.

And she was spending the night at his house.

"Don't get cocky, Lockhart. She's here for the baby, not you," he muttered as he bumped over the cattle guard leading to his spread. Yes, he was attracted to Tara. Yes, he couldn't stop conjuring up images of the two of them naked in bed together.

But would he act on his desires?

Hell no.

Getting custody of Julie was far too important. Besides, from Tara's side there was no love lost. She didn't like him the way he liked her. He wouldn't make a move. But that didn't mean he couldn't enjoy being around her.

Before they'd left Ridge's house, four members of her family—count 'em, four—had pulled him aside and had a serious talk about treating Tara with kid gloves. She might be fierce and proud and strong, but she was vulnerable too.

Granny Blue had promised to strangle him if he hurt her granddaughter. Tara's father, Armand, had clamped him on the shoulder and stared into his eyes and said, "No funny business." Kaia had clucked her tongue and reminded him that Tara was doing him a big favor. And Aria cornered him by the back door on his way out and said, "Tara does not need to know any of the details of our time together. Keep your lips zipped."

Alzate overwhelm.

They looked out for each other and he admired the one-for-all-and-all-for-one philosophy. He dug how they supported and lifted each other up. Unlike his messed-up family. The Alzates had been the glue that held the Lockharts together. Without them, the Silver Feather would have been infinitely less than.

This was what he longed for without ever really knowing it. To be part of a clan who good-naturedly badgered and bantered, who shared and cared, who loved hard and deep and forever. It was the foreverness that got him the most. The promise that no matter what happened, you did not have to face the bad stuff alone.

The only thing he'd come across that was remotely close to what the Alzates had was being in the PBR. But while he had found belonging on the circuit, competition underscored everything. Either you were up or you were down.

That wasn't the case with the Alzates. No one kept score. They understood that life had a natural ebb and flow. That what looked good could later turn out bad, and vice versa. Building each other up instead of looking for ways to tear each other down to size.

The second he pulled into the driveway, he killed the engine and hopped out of the truck. Jogged to where Tara was parked on the far side of the drive, flung open the car door for her before she could do it herself.

"I had forgotten how far and gone your place is back here," she said.

"Southernmost part of the ranch." He waved at the fence in the distance. "Last section of Lockhart land."

"Pretty isolated."

He held out his arm to help her out. "How long have you had the minivan? What happened to your Corolla?"

"I traded it in when I decided to become a foster parent."

"You bought a new car for Julie's sake?"

She met his eyes, and as soon as her sandals hit the dirt, she let go of his hand and didn't say a word. Just turned to open the back door.

"Let me help." He leaped to her side.

"I've got the baby," she said brusquely, and leaned over the car seat to undo the infant carrier portion from the rest of the apparatus. Giving him a fine view of her shapely rump.

He tried not to notice, but that was like trying not to notice the sun. Her heart-shaped butt was out-of-this-world sexy. He didn't know what it said about him that he couldn't look away. Or that he imagined cupping those luscious cheeks in his palms.

Grow up, Lockhart.

"You can unload Julie's things," she told him.

Pulled back to earth, he startled. "Yes, ma'am."

She jerked her head up, glared. "Are you being a smartass? Remember, I'm doing you a favor. Julie and I can leave right now."

He tipped his Stetson. "I was not being a smartass. You're in charge. You tell me what to do and I'll do it."

She sank her top teeth into her bottom lip.

The urge to kiss her bowled him right over. Of course he wouldn't. But damn if he didn't ache to do so. She was standing there, the baby carrier with a sleeping Julie in it looped over her elbow.

Nope. He wouldn't kiss her no matter how hot her butt looked in those shorts. For one thing, he wouldn't do anything to ruin his chances for getting custody of Julie. For another, he had a feeling if he tried anything hinky, Tara would belt him.

And there were those warnings from her family . . .

She must have seen something in his eyes, because she ducked her head, hoisted the carrier up higher on her arm, and said, "Let's get this thing over with before I change my mind. I could kick my own bum for even suggesting it."

Bum.

A cute word pickup from her Irish mother and oddly more provocative than if she'd said "ass" or "butt."

His body got hard.

Even though she was thirty-two and a nurse and had many life experiences, there was still an innocence about her that drew him. He had an irresistible urge to merge with her in the hopes some of that sweetness would rub off on him.

Ha! Fat chance.

How did she do it? How did she stay so grounded and practical while at the same time exuding this wide-eyed, the-world-is-a-beautiful-place quality that drew him in? God, but he *wanted* her!

Resolutely, Rhett tamped down the urge. He might not be able to control his penis, but he could control his thoughts and actions.

The infant carrier tugged against the material of her tank top, pulling the V-neck down to reveal a heart-shaped gold locket resting on her light brown skin above a generous spill of cleavage.

Call him a scoundrel, but he couldn't tear his gaze away. She looked like an earth goddess, a woman unto her own. So different from the needy buckle bunnies who followed him around the circuit—a priceless work of art in a stack of hobby store posters.

And the proud flounce of her fanny as she moved past him for the front door had his unruly body standing at attention. Toned and rounded, her feminine form was substantial, solid, and made for sin.

He'd known her since he was a kid, but as adults, they hardly came in contact beyond the Alzate/Lockhart gatherings, and even then, she was usually huddled with her family in the kitchen while he hung out with his brothers in a barn or corral.

A mosaic of memories came back to him, Tara at the center of them all. The time at Archer and Casey's wedding rehearsal dinner when he'd walked up on the porch at the mansion to find Tara and her sisters dancing around the room, bananas in their hands using them like microphones, singing "You Can't Hurry Love" in off-key joy. Tara had been leading the conga line of sisters-turned-doo-wop-girls, her face alight with happiness.

The time, on the ten-year anniversary of his mother's death, he'd gotten drunk and stumbled to the cemetery. Found Tara there putting red roses on the graves of family members, only to discover she'd left a single bud on his mother's grave as well. The sight of that rose had brought him to maudlin tears. She'd taken him home, made him drink three big glasses of water and down two aspirins, took off his boots, and put him to bed. She'd never spoken of it again.

The time, five years ago, he'd been out riding Golden Boy at sunrise and spotted her in the distance near the stock tank, wearing a hooded poncho, arms outstretched, eyes focused on the horizon, welcoming the day.

"What are you doing out in the middle of the desert all by yourself at dawn?" he'd asked.

"I was out for a run. I stopped by the tank to remember my grandfather and give thanks for having known him. He used to bring me fishing here. Out here, I see him everywhere," she had said, a mysterious twinkle in her dark eyes. She'd awarded him with a luminous, droll grin.

That moment had forever altered the way he looked at sunrise.

"Later, dork," she'd said affectionately. Then without another word, she sprinted away. Long legs skimming over scrub brush and sand, lush straight hair flying out behind her, running like a wild thing. Leaving him feeling raw and exposed in a fundamental way. Aching for a woman who viewed him as nothing but an annoying kid brother.

Confounded by the sudden flood of unexpected emotions, Rhett rushed past Tara. He was her humble servant, and keyed open the front door just as she hit the top step behind him. He could hear the soft scrape of her sandals on the wooden porch, the calming sound of her even breathing.

"Ta-da," he announced inanely, flinging the door open, moving aside, feeling like an idiot and having no excuse for it except she scrambled his brain six ways to Sunday.

Rhett cast a nervous glance at her, saw amusement tipping up her lips. Oh, this was a good thing.

She tossed her head and breezed past him into the house, her long dark hair swishing over her shoulders. On the drive over, she'd released it from the tight bun.

What would it feel like to gather those straight, thick locks into his hands like reins? To press his mouth to the underside of her chin? To taste the sweet-salty flavor of her skin?

Cool it, cowboy. Tara is off-limits.

To get control of his libido, he darted back out to the minivan, unloaded an insane amount of equipment—two diaper bags, a Pack 'n Play, and a stroller. Juggled the stuff up the steps. Staggered off-balance into the house. Kicked the door closed.

The smell of talc and baby formula and spit-up surrounded him. Rhett dropped the baby supplies onto the foyer floor. Panic washed over him.

Get used to it, buddy, this is what your life is going to be like from now on.

For one deer-in-the-headlights moment, he almost told Tara he'd changed his mind. He had no idea what he was doing. He had no business raising a baby. It was all ego to think he could do this on his own.

And then she peeked her head around the corner and smiled at him, and he was reassured.

Chapter 12

CHUTE FIGHTER: A bull that will not stand still and tries to fight the cowboy before leaving the chute.

EVEN though the whole spend-the-night thing had initially been her idea, Tara was thrown off-kilter by the reality of sleeping over at Rhett's house. She swept into the living room and settled Julie, who was asleep in her infant carrier, onto the coffee table. Her plan was to overwhelm him with the details of child care so that he'd back off filing for custody.

But she was the one feeling overwhelmed.

"Let's get started," she announced crisply. "There's so much you need to know about Julie."

"Slow down, Tea." Her childhood nickname slipped off his tongue like a caress. "We've got all night."

Good grief! He made this sound like a seduction.

"There's a lot to learn. No time to waste." She kept her tone low and urgent, and her eyes off his face.

He removed his Stetson and hung it on the hat rack by the door, his hair disarmingly messy. He unsnapped the cuffs of his shirt and one at a time, slowly rolled the sleeves up to his elbow. Getting down to business and showing off tanned, strong forearms roped with veins and muscles.

Her heart shifted gears, slipping like a transmission going bad. The nurse in her wondered idly what her heart rhythm would look like if she were hooked up to a cardiac monitor. Would the pattern look as crazy as it felt?

Knock it off. There's nothing wrong with your heart.

Other than that the sight of this sexy slab of man sent her pulse jumping. Understandable. She hadn't had sex in over two years. He was hot. They were all alone except for the sleeping baby, far away from anyone . . .

But it was *Rhett*, of all people.

She eyed his biceps bulging beneath the material of his shirt. Her stomach clenched in a happy way, a thrill buzzing through her veins. Good God, but he was handsome.

He's the one taking Julie away from you.

That did it. She snapped clear. Whew. Now that was better. No more sexy fantasies about *this* guy.

She stuck her hands in her pockets, felt the pack of Juicy Fruit he'd given her. Smiled. She opened the gum and offered him a piece. "Want a stick?"

"Sure."

He took the gum. In unintentional unison, they unwrapped their gum, curled the stick in their mouths, and chewed.

Their gazes linked.

He grinned.

She giggled. Which wasn't like her. Not at all.

"This is fun," he said.

Strangely, it was. The moment felt too intimate, and Tara quickly looked away, shifting her attention to the baby.

"While she's still sleeping, let's get to work." Tara folded her gum into the paper it had been wrapped in and tossed it in the wastebasket next to the computer desk in the corner of the room. "First, I'll teach you how to prepare her formula. After that, we'll move on to the apnea monitor and her nighttime meds."

"Is it like whipping up formula for baby calves? I'm already pretty good at it."

"Julie is not a baby calf," she said. "Best to remember that."

"Yes, ma'am."

"Kitchen." She gathered up the diaper bag he'd brought in, which included formula and supplies. She'd been inside his house for a housewarming party when he'd built it seven years ago, but she hadn't set foot in the place since. She breezed into the kitchen, Rhett on her heels.

She emphasized the importance of washing his hands and cleaning off the prep surface, showed him how to prepare the formula and store the bottles.

"Contrary to the opinion you seem to have of me, I am not a complete slob," he said.

His place was very tidy, but she suspected it was the result of a housekeeper and not his innate cleaning skills.

"Because she's a preemie, Julie's immune system is more compromised than a normal baby's. Please pay close attention."

He "yes ma'amed" her again.

"Shouldn't you be writing this down?"

He held up his phone. "I've been filming you."

"Oh," she said.

"You want a beer?" he asked, pocketing the phone and opening the fridge. He grabbed one for himself, glanced over his shoulder at her.

She was about to refuse, then decided, why not? She wasn't driving home and she did feel pretty keyed up. "Yes."

"Lime?"

"You remembered." After her first broken heart when she was in college, she'd climbed up in the barn loft behind the mansion for a good cry. Only to be interrupted by Rhett, carrying a six-pack of warm beer he'd stolen from his father's garage.

He too was going through his first breakup.

When Tara told him that she liked lime in her beer, he'd sneaked back into the house to fetch one. They'd split the six-pack and spent the next few hours talking, listening to breakup songs on his iPod, each taking one side of his ear buds, getting drunk and shouting out loud, "Love Stinks," along with the J. Geils Band. Their racket brought Duke out of the house, and he yelled at them for drinking his beer.

"You're a hard woman to forget," Rhett murmured.

What did he mean by that? "I would have thought you'd have

gotten my beer preference mixed up with your endless parade of women."

"My womanizing is exaggerated. I'm not as wild as everyone makes me out to be." He twisted off the cap and handed her a long-neck Corona. Palmed a chilled lime and sliced it into wedges on a wooden cutting board.

"No? Julie's existence seems to suggest otherwise."

"I never said I was a choirboy."

She squeezed a lime wedge into her beer, pushed her back against the door leading into the dining room, drew one knee up, and propped her heel against the wall behind her. Maybe tonight wouldn't be as bad as she feared. With Rhett looking after the baby, she could relax a little, and she hadn't had a chance to kick back since she'd brought Julie home from the hospital.

He picked up his beer and stepped over to her. Raised his bottle. "A toast?"

"To what?"

"Julie."

"I can drink to that." She clinked the neck of her beer bottle against his, and they both knocked back a long swallow.

"Thank you," he said. "For being there for her."

"It was my privilege."

"When I think about Rhona running out on her . . ." His voice caught and his eyes misted, and his vulnerability punched her square in the solar plexus. "Well . . ." He raised his bottle in her direction. "You're both a miracle worker and a saint in my book, Tara Alzate."

A warm, buzzy feeling rolled through her body. She blamed the beer. She lowered her knee, rested her foot on the floor, grounding herself.

"Tell me, what do you do when you're not taking care of babies?" he asked.

"I volunteer on the Letters to Cupid Committee," she said, referring to the local custom of answering the letters from the lovelorn that tourists and townsfolk alike left for the giant stalagmite in the Cupid Caverns that bore an uncanny resemblance to the Roman god of love. It was a fun way to increase tourism to Cupid.

"How often do you do that?"

"Once a month . . . or at least I used to before I became a foster mom."

"That leaves you with a lot of time on your hands."

"There's Julie . . ."

"Before Julie," he said. "What did you do for fun?"

"We don't have to make small talk."

"No," he said. "I'm really interested."

"Really?"

"Really."

"I enjoy reading."

"And that's it?"

"I used to hang out with my friends until they all got married and started having children. Now every time we set something up it seems to get canceled. A baby gets sick. Someone gets pregnant again . . ."

"You feel left out."

"That makes me sound pathetic." She took a pensive sip of beer.

"Not pathetic," he said. "Human."

"I used to like to go dancing. Until I met Kit, who had two left feet."

"Oh, really," he practically purred. "I'm a pretty good dancer if I do say so myself."

"I recall."

"You do?"

"I've seen you cut a rug plenty of times at Chantilly's."

"May I ask you a personal question?"

She hesitated. Not sure if she was up for personal questions. "If I can reserve the right not to answer."

"Okay."

"All right, shoot."

He was absolutely motionless, staring at her, fascinated. "Why did you stay at Kit's side the whole time he was hospitalized?"

"Where did you hear that?"

"Kaia. She was worried about you."

Tara folded her arms over her chest. "Why do you want to know?"

"I'm just trying to get to the bottom of why you have this need to take care of everyone you love. Kit had a mother and sisters to help. Why did you stay at the hospital 24/7?"

That pissed her off and she glowered at him. "Kit was my *fiancé*."

"Many women would have cut bait when he got meningitis."

"Maybe the women you've been tangled up with would run, but not the women in my world. I'm a nurse. If you can't depend on a nurse to help you when you're sick, who can you depend on?"

"Nursing is your job," he said. "Not your identity."

She clamped her lips shut, stared at him as if she could reduce him to a speck of dust with her glare. "You're all about Rhett Lockhart. You don't get what it's like to live for someone else."

"Isn't that kind of codependent?"

Was it? Tara paused, rattled by his question. "No. I'm a caregiver. That means I make a conscious choice to help someone. I do not *need* to take care of them. I do it because I see it as the right thing to do. Taking care of people is not my raison d'être."

"You sure?"

She lifted her chin. "I am."

"So, your way is best, huh?"

"It's best for *me*. Satisfied?" she asked.

"Not yet."

He pulled out his cell phone again, thumbed through it, found the music of his choice. Propped the phone against his beer bottle, which he rested on the top of the refrigerator. Hit play. The sound of Tim McGraw's "I Like It, I Love It" poured into the room.

"The music," she protested. "It'll wake Julie."

Ignoring that, he moved with breathtakingly sexy grace, swaying toward her, rolling his shoulder, shuffling his boots over the hand-scraped wood floor, and closing the gap between them. He took her beer, set it on the fridge beside his.

Turned back, extended his hand.

Her brain shied, cringing against the door to the dining room, but her body started swaying in time to the music.

He took her hand, pulled her into his arms for a spin around the room. Her head felt dizzy and giddy. Her body stiff, rusty, and unfamiliar.

"Relax." His voice was dangerously husky.

Tara took a deep breath, let the music carry her away, her feet acting of their own accord, happily following his lead. She liked dancing with him. Liked being in his arms. It was fun, exciting . . .

"That's right, sweet cheeks. Let go."

Sweet cheeks? The generic term of endearment he used on his buckle bunnies. Starch shot up her spine, and she pulled away.

"I warned you once. Don't you dare call me that again," she said. Hell, she deserved being called sweet cheeks. Letting herself get sucked in by a man as slick as Rhett Lockhart. What was wrong with her?

His face reddened. "I'm sorry, you didn't deserve that. Bad habit."

Tara's heart whipped up tumult. "Damn straight."

He took a step toward her. She backed up.

"A bad habit . . ." he said, still moving forward, "I intend on breaking."

She backpedaled until her butt bumped against the door again. There was nowhere else to go, unless she opened the door and fled, and doing that would give him too much power. "Is it? Or are you lumping me in with your other conquests?"

"You're not a conquest, Tara." His voice was quiet, his tone melancholy. "I just wanted to dance with you."

"Why?"

"You looked like you could use some fun."

"I'll take care of my own fun, thank you very much."

"Can you?"

"Yes."

"But you don't."

"By choice."

"All right."

"Good. Glad we got that settled."

He took another step, then another. They were as close as PB&J on bread. He was the peanut butter, all smooth and creamy. She was the jelly—messy, sticky, shaky.

Her breath lodged in her throat. Her lips—the disloyal things— pursed of their own accord. She was both hot and cold. Her pulse sped through her veins, heated her insides. Goose bumps chilled her outsides.

Yep, she was a gooey, feeble mess.

And yet she did not walk away.

Why not?

Rhett's eyes drilled into her, dark and sultry. His mouth crooked up in the sexiest of smiles. Energy and eagerness radiated off his body as if he were back in the rodeo arena, cocked and ready for a thrill ride.

As if she were something special.

You're not special, she scolded herself, *not to him*. To Rhett Lockhart, women were nothing more than a pleasant way to kill time. *That was the old Rhett*, something loony inside her whispered. *He's grown up.*

But had he? Had he really?

"Tara," he whispered, his deep voice mesmerizing her like a hypnotist's watch.

"Rhett," she said, intending for it to come out crisp and no-nonsense. But good gosh if she didn't sound like Scarlett O'Hara, flirtatious and sassy.

He rested his arm on the door frame above her head. The door solid against her back. He leaned down, his eyes pinning her to the spot. His mouth widened, and his eyes softened. He touched the tip of his tongue to his upper lip.

A quick, hungry gesture.

She was trembling. Waiting for the kiss she prayed was coming.

He dropped his arm from the door frame, slipped it around her waist, pulled her flush up against him as if they were about to dance the tango.

Tara sucked in her breath, an audible gasp in the quiet room. She wanted this. Wanted *him*. The longing inside her was acute. She hadn't wanted anything so overtly sexual since high school when she'd done Cole Nielson's math homework in hopes he'd ask her to the prom. He had not. He'd gotten a B on the assignment and told her that wasn't prom-worthy work.

But this wasn't high school, and the man in front of her was not Cole Nielson. This was Rhett Lockhart. His hair fell rakishly over his forehead and his breath smelled of Juicy Fruit and Corona.

Tingles raced up and down her spine.

It bothered her that she was so easily losing her head. She was known for her ability to stay calm when those around her were losing their shit. Rhett's older brother Remington had once told her that she'd missed her calling. That with her single-minded focus, attention to detail, and ability to know her place in the grand scheme of things, she should have been a soldier. She'd pointed out those qualities fit nurses just as well.

Rhett reached out and traced her bottom lip with the pad of his thumb.

Brazenly, she snagged his thumb between her teeth, and gently bit down.

A low, rough groan tumbled from his lips.

Spooked, she gulped. Was this happening? Their first kiss? She didn't raise a hand to resist. *Why not? Snap out of it!*

"Rhett," she whispered again, in what she thought was protest, but it sounded far more like entreaty.

His lips hovered above hers. He held her by her shoulders, his warm fingers sinking into her skin. The room was darkened, lit only by the light from the Vent-A-Hood and his phone, which was now playing Faith Hill's "This Kiss." The sun had set while they'd been in the kitchen.

Her knees wobbled, buoyant and bouncy. She felt as if she were a tumbleweed, blown willy-nilly across the desert floor, flowing with the wind, unable to control her own destiny. It was concerning . . . and oddly freeing.

Here she was, at the whim of fate. Trembling on the verge of something monumental, *if* she but dared. Great no-strings-attached sex.

Audaciousness was not her strong suit. Well-thought-out, calculated risk was more her thing. Weighed. Studied. Researched to the nth degree.

Sleeping with him would be the worst move *ev*-er. She knew it in her heart, blood, soul. But her body, oh, her stupid body, had other ideas. Her toes tingled, nipples tightened, womb warmed.

She would not be one of his casual conquests, no, no, no.

The curtain blew in the breeze, the night air coming inside through the open window, carrying with it the scent of sand and hummingbird mint. Her mouth watered—from the aroma, his nearness, her anticipation, she couldn't rightly say. Maybe all three.

Julie whimpered from the living room.

Grateful, oh so grateful, for the interruption, she ducked underneath his arm. Grabbed for the formula they'd prepared for the baby and thrust the bottle into his hand. Said breathlessly, "Chow time. You're up, *Daddy*."

Chapter 13

INTO HIS HAND: When a bull is spinning in the same direction of a rider's riding hand.

Rhett fed Julie while Tara supervised and sipped her beer.

The room was masculine with a Texas cowboy motif. The walls behind the couch and the fireplace were both limestone. The other two walls were paneled with dark mahogany wood. Hand-scraped hardwood floors. Hat rack in the corner. Thickly padded leather furniture. Plush sheepskin rug. French doors led out onto a luxurious composite deck, and a wide cathedral window let in the yellow glow of a full moon.

She studied him in the muted lighting from the bronze floor lamp with an Edison bulb on the lowest wattage. Shadows fell across his handsome face as he leaned over Julie, his concentration fully on his task.

For the first time, Tara saw in him the dedication he brought to his sport. The determined set of his mouth, the ability to sit in the moment without losing focus, how his entire body said he was all in.

A tiny circular bite, like the quick snick of a hole punch, perforated her heart.

She was going to lose Julie to him. The way he looked at his daughter, with awe and tenderness, told the story she did not want to hear.

He was hooked.

But so was she.

Although she was sitting across the room from him, it was

still dangerously close. She could feel the enigmatic pull squarely in the center of her stomach.

The man was flat-out beautiful, and she was alone with him in the middle of nowhere. If she strained her ears, she could hear the far-off howl of coyotes. She'd grown up on the ranch, so coyotes didn't scare her, but other things about this situation alarmed her.

The isolation.

Her unexpected and unwanted attraction to Rhett.

The crazy rise of sexual desire she'd feared long buried with Kit.

Julie finished her bottle. He lifted her to his shoulder, gently patted her back to burp her. "There, there, sweetheart—"

Tara was just about to tell him to put a blanket over his shoulder, but before she could get the words out, Julie spit up all down the back of his shirt.

"Oopsy," he said, taking it in stride. Such a light, child-friendly word she doubted he'd ever used before.

Tara started to get up and take Julie from him, so he could get cleaned up, but Rhett raised a stop-sign hand.

"I've got this." He reached for a wet wipe from the box Tara had arranged on the table before he'd started feeding Julie. He cleaned off her little face and eased her into her baby carrier sitting on the floor beside him.

Then Rhett stood, straightened, and stripped off his shirt. Right there in front of her. Giving her a full-frontal view of his exquisite bare chest.

Tara gulped and her lungs spasmed.

He wadded up the shirt and tossed it onto the floor, his honed muscles bunching and broadening under sleek, burnished skin as he moved.

Her jaw dropped. Mesmerized, she could not have looked away if a herd of wild bulls had come charging through the door.

Completely at ease, he raised his arms over his head, interlocked his fingers, and stretched. Revealing super-sexy armpits and even more hot muscles. Arching his back, he leaned to first one side and then the other, working out kinks. Every muscle in his chest and abdomen clearly delineated. Lean. Toned. Six-pack. The coveted V. Seven percent body fat.

Yummy, yum, yum.

Her breathing slowed.

Her ears flushed hot.

Her stomach quivered.

Rhett Lockhart should be classified as a Schedule 1 drug. Dangerous and highly addictive. No wonder women fell for him. He was the perfect specimen of physical manhood.

Dazzled and dazed, she felt as if she'd floated outside her body and was seeing herself sitting there from a great distance. A lonely woman desperate for the tender touch of a man. Her senses scrambled. She smelled colors, tasted music, heard textures. A mad conglomeration of synesthesia.

What was going on? It had to be the beer. She didn't drink much, and surely it had gone to her head. This man's body was the stuff of romantic fantasies.

She closed her eyes. *Pipe dreams. Come back down to earth, Tara.* She felt a solid jolt as she reconnected with herself, settled back into her body. Her eyes flew open.

He was staring at her, and immediately something intangible hit like a thunder crash between them. "Is it just my imagination?" he asked, his voice gruff. "Or is there chemistry bubbling here?"

Tara stopped breathing, and the hairs on her nape lifted while goose bumps spread up her arms the way they did when she experienced something particularly moving, like when a NICU baby suddenly took a turn for the better. "Cheesy, Lockhart. Super cheesy."

"I'm not—"

"Do us both a favor and save your pickup lines for the buckle bunnies. I've got no time for your silliness."

His eyes narrowed, and his mouth flattened out. "Too bad you feel that way. Because I was definitely feeling something brewing."

So was she. But she would cut out her own tongue before she admitted it. "Nope. Nothing brewing. No brew here. I'm brewless."

He lowered his lashes, assessing her. "Well, except for the beer in your hand."

Her hand seemed welded to the neck of her beer, and she couldn't have moved if the house had been afire.

Then that bad-boy grin of his lit up his face, and helplessly she flashed him a smile in return.

Mischief widened his eyes and deepened his smile, and he looked at her as if he was aching to throw his lasso around her and haul her close to his chest. He looked as if he was about to say something highly inappropriate.

Flustered, Tara jumped up and turned to the baby. "JuJu, honey, it's time for your bath."

She scooped Julie out of her carrier, cuddled the baby close, and forced herself not to glance back as she headed for the bathroom.

Under Tara's tutelage, Rhett bathed the baby, gave Julie her medication, set up the Pack 'n Play in the guest room, dressed Julie for bed, and hooked up the apnea monitor. By the time he finished, it was just after ten o'clock, but Tara was already yawning.

Rhett insisted that Tara sleep in his bed while he stayed on a futon in the guest-bedroom-turned-makeshift-nursery.

She argued.

He countered. Pointing out she was the one who insisted he had to take full charge of Julie's care, using her words against her like a weapon.

Sometimes, Tara wished she could kick her own ass. She fretted at the notion of not sleeping beside Julie. Worried about what could go wrong.

Except she managed to get a full eight hours' sleep, something that hadn't happened since she'd brought Julie home from the hospital.

The morning sun peeking through the curtains woke her well after dawn.

Stretching opulently on the big king-sized mattress, she reached her arms and legs out to the four corners of the Western-style bedposts, spread eagle on her back. Wondered idly what it might feel like to be tied up to those posts with soft restraints. Shocked herself, particularly because in her bondage fantasy, Rhett was the one doing the tying.

Those wayward thoughts shot her upright in bed, hair tumbling into her face, heart pounding. What the fudge?

To distract herself, she picked up her cell phone, which she'd left charging on the bedside dresser. Checked for texts. There were several.

From Mom: Hope all went well last night.

From Kaia: A picture of her kids snoozing soundly in her and Ridge's king-sized bed. Little angels.

From Aria: A snapshot of blueberry pancakes and bacon. Yum.

She texted them all back with a gif of a cartoon cow blowing kisses and a selfie of her looking sheet-mussed, well-rested, and flashing a thumbs up. Best sleep N months.

Aria shot back: Ooh La La. What does Rhett look like?

Tara wrote: Is your mind always in the gutter?

Pretty much. Aria confirmed. Rhett?

TARA: We R not hooking up.
ARIA: Two words for you. Daisy Dukes.
TARA: Over my dead body.
ARIA: Really? Not even a kiss?
TARA: Nothing happened!!!
ARIA: Dammit. I lost a bet with Kaia.
TARA: U 2 R incorrigible.
ARIA: I know.
TARA: Goodbye.
ARIA: Tell Rhett I said hi.

TARA: No.
ARIA: Fair enough.

Just as she finished sending the texts, another message came through for her. This time from Rhett. Her stomach did a funny little twisty thing.

U up yet?

Grinning, she slid out of bed, put her bra on underneath the T-shirt she'd slept in, and wriggled into her jeans. She padded to the bathroom, splashed water on her face, brushed her teeth and her hair. Caught herself humming "Walking on Sunshine" as she strolled across the hall to the nursery.

She paused at the door. She could almost feel the room yanking her forward as she raised her fist to knock. Her goal was singular. Check on the baby. Make sure all was well. *Don't bother knocking, just open the door and walk on in.*

But would Rhett appreciate that?

Did it really matter what he appreciated?

As a compromise, she lightly ran her fingers over the door like a keyboard, a short riff of hi-I'm-here, before she turned the knob and stepped inside.

Julie was sound asleep in the Pack 'n Play. An empty bottle of formula sat on the bedside table. Rhett lounged on the futon, head thrown back, mouth open, snoring softly, baby blanket wrapped around his shoulders. His cell phone rested loosely in his hand.

Aw. He looked so adorable. He was making such an effort. She had no choice but to give Ms. Bean a good report.

Julie gurgled.

Alarmed that the baby might be choking, she spun around to see Julie smiling and waving her little fists. Julie made an I'm-happy-to-see-you noise that filled her with joy.

"Shh, let Daddy sleep," she whispered, leaning over the crib to change Julie's diaper, only to discover it was already dry. Rhett must have changed it when he texted Tara, and then they both had fallen back asleep.

Julie looked up at her with big eyes. Her mother's eyes, Tara thought, and felt a quick stab of anger at Rhona deep in the center of her chest. No, no. She couldn't be mad at Rhona. It wasn't her place to judge Rhona. All she could do was love this sweet little button.

She scooped Julie from the crib and carried her to the kitchen. Prepared a bottle, and then went outside to sit on the front porch rocking chair to feed her. Julie ate, staring up at Tara as if she was the most magical person in the world.

They peered into each other's eyes, transfixed.

"I love you," Tara whispered to the baby. "So, so very much."

"Cup of coffee?"

Tara startled, turned to see Rhett standing in the doorway, holding two mugs of coffee. He had an odd look on his face that she couldn't quite decipher. It was part wistfulness, part regret, part worry.

"Just the way you like it," he enticed, treading barefoot across the porch toward her.

"No creamer, two sugars?"

"Yep."

Julie had stopped eating and had fallen asleep again. Tara set the bottle down on the side table, readjusted Julie so she was stretched out over the top of Tara's thighs, and accepted the coffee mug Rhett passed to her.

"Thank you. Since Julie came along, I've been mainlining this stuff."

"After last night, I can see why. My daughter takes after me, she's a night owl."

"Didn't get much sleep?" Tara asked, not feeling the least bit sorry for him. It was all she could do not to say, *Suck it up, buttercup.*

"Couple of hours, tops."

They both paused to gaze down at the sleeping baby. Neither one of them mentioned what had almost transpired between them last night. Thank God, they had not kissed. It would have been a disaster. But the feelings he'd stirred in her were stronger than ever, and that was problematic enough.

To take her mind off the kiss-that-almost-happened-but-didn't, Tara took a sip of coffee. "Oh wow, this is a perfect cup. How is it you take note of the things I like and remember them?"

He squatted beside the rocking chair, stroked the baby's cheek with a calloused finger. "I'm doing my damnedest to impress you. Is it working?"

It was, but she wasn't about to admit that. "Why are you trying so hard to impress me?"

"I want you to think well of me."

"Why do you care what I think?"

"I value your opinion."

He did? She eyed him. He aimed that stunning smile at her. Something was up.

"And because I really need you on my side."

Selfish man. It wasn't enough that he'd come to take Julie away from her, he expected her to be happy about it too. "And why is that?"

He held up his phone, his face long and solemn. "My lawyer just called. Since you, me, and Rhona are all from Jeff Davis County, he's suggesting I petition the court for a change of venue in Julie's custody hearing. And Ms. Bean has agreed to start the paperwork with CPS so you can move back home to Cupid while you're fostering Julie."

Tara stared at him blankly, as if he were speaking gibberish.

Had she not heard him? Should he repeat himself?

Rhett watched her closely, trying to figure out what to say next. She set down her coffee and moved Julie from her lap to her shoulder and started humming a sweet lullaby. Tara's hair fell gently over the curve of her cheek, her face luminous in the morning sunlight.

"Tea?" he ventured.

"I'm not going to yell at you in front of the baby," she said, her tone measured and calm.

He got a sick feeling in the pit of his stomach. What had he done wrong?

Tara stood up from the rocking chair and, with Julie in her arms, breezed past him into the house. He followed on her heels, every muscle in his body tensed.

She took Julie into the guest room, settled her into the Pack 'n Play, then grabbed his wrist and led him to the living room. Once there, she whirled around to face him, hands planted on her hips. "You've already filed for custody? You lied to me about only making your decision yesterday."

"No, no." He shook his head, gave her a friendly smile that only deepened her scowl. "I just texted Lamar yesterday that I wanted to file for custody. He jumped right on it."

"Over the Memorial Day weekend?"

"He's a very efficient lawyer. I have him on retainer."

Tara smacked her forehead with a palm and pivoted a full three-sixty on her heel. "And he wants to take the hearing out of El Paso?"

"It makes the most sense since everyone involved is from Jeff Davis County."

She pounded her right fist into the open palm of her left hand. "You're forgetting I have a job in El Paso. Unless you just don't give a damn."

"It's not like that."

"No? It's a three-hour drive to El Paso. I'm caring for a premature infant. How easy do you think it is to make that trek for the court hearings?"

"That's the reason Lamar suggested the venue change. So that you could be near your family."

"Don't feed me that line of bull. You're doing it because you think your chances of getting custody are better in Cupid where your family casts a long shadow."

"I'm not going to lie, that's part of it."

"You're a jackass, you know that?" She looked shattered and her voice trembled. With anger? he wondered. Or fear?

"I was just trying to help."

"Either you're a liar or delusional."

"I understand you're upset, but will you just listen to me for a minute?"

Her arms were a straitjacket laced around her body. Hands clutching her opposite shoulders, elbows stacked over her breasts. "Speak."

"I approached the administration at your hospital about you taking a leave of absence—"

"You did what!"

"I called—"

"When?"

"Last week. Before I'd even decided for sure I was filing for custody. I told them I wanted to pay Julie's medical bills and that I wanted to hire you to be her personal nurse. They thought it was a good idea."

She was livid, steam practically coming out of her ears. Rhett knew he'd screwed up big-time. "You can't mess around in people's lives like that."

"Aw, c'mon, Tea. Don't be upset."

Her eyes were razor blades, slicing him like sushi. "Oh, I'm not supposed to be unhappy that you're wrecking my life?"

"I was trying not to wreck your life." Misery crawled over him, a slow slug of nastiness. He'd offended her, and that was not what he'd intended. "At least not long-term."

"Explain."

"I'm going to get custody of Julie eventually," he said. "You know that."

She squeezed her eyes closed, heaved a heavy sigh. When she opened them, he saw tears swimming there, and it tore him apart. He wanted to reach out to her, take her into his arms, and promise that everything was going to be all right.

"Tara," he said. "Listen to me. My hope is to give you as much time with Julie as I can. And yes, it does help me stay on the circuit. I'm not going to deny that or apologize for it. I talked with my lawyer and I gave this a lot of thought. If you take a leave of absence, I will pay you double your salary to move in here and take care of Julie while I'm on the road."

"You expect me to live in your house?"

"I'm offering you the opportunity—"

"You're controlling and manipulating me."

"You don't have to take leave. You can stay at your job in El Paso. I'll even get Ridge to fly you to Cupid for the custody hearings so that you don't have that long drive. But we *are* filing for a change of venue. It makes sense legally. Whether you take leave from your job or not, that is up to you. But here's the bottom line. Julie is my daughter, not yours. And I have a right to do what I think is best."

"You're forgetting *I* have legal custody of her."

"For now."

She began to pace, knees locked, walking on wooden legs in short stabbing steps. "You damn Lockharts are so high-handed. You think all Alzates are your servants. You believe just because you're rich you're entitled to get your way."

"I understand you're upset. This is a lot to process. I'm going to give you some time to think." He could see it from her point of view, but she couldn't see his.

She stopped mid-pace to throw daggers at him with her eyes, aiming straight for the center of his brain. "You know *nothing*. You're as selfish as ever. I can't believe I thought you had changed."

"I *have* changed."

Her laugh was a bark, astringent and rude. "You haven't changed a bit. I admit, you had me hoodwinked for a bit. But you're still the same old Rhett Lockhart through and through. The guy who expects to have his cake and eat it too."

He tried the charming smile, unrolling it like a red carpet. "I've always been a fan of cake."

Grunting, Tara picked up a couch cushion and smacked him in the shoulder with it.

"Hey!"

"You deserved that." She tossed the pillow aside.

"Does this mean you're softening to the idea?"

She stared a hole through him, but she didn't look quite as angry as she had a few minutes ago.

"What do you say?" he wheedled. "Move in here, take care of Julie while I'm on the road. Be near your mom and dad, granny and sisters. I won't even be around."

Tara leaned her back against the wall, folded her arms over her chest, this time looking like a sullen gangster in a 1940s movie. "That's your plan. I stay out here in the middle of no-where, taking care of your daughter, while you gallivant around on bulls, living the high life. That doesn't seem fair, even if you're paying me double. I'll be working twenty-four hours a day, seven days a week."

She made a strong case. In good conscience, how could he expect her to do all the work while he got off scot-free? "How about this. I'll hire someone else to come in for a few hours twice a week so that you can get a break."

"My mother and Kaia can spell me when I need it, that's not the point."

"What is the point?"

"You sure you want to hear this?" She sliced him again with the hard edge of her gaze.

"Lay it on me."

"You say you've changed."

"I have." He came toward her, heart pounding. She'd put her own back against the wall. He stopped in front of her, the tips of his boots touching her socks.

She didn't blink. Didn't back down. "You claim that Julie means the world to you, but yet you still want to ride."

"What would you have me do? It's my job."

"Either be all in or all out. Quit the rodeo. Or . . ."

"Or what?" He could feel the warmth of her breath on his skin. He wondered what she would do if he kissed her right now. Probably slap him, and he would deserve it. Or maybe, just maybe, she would kiss him back.

"Drop your bid for custody."

"And let you have my daughter?" That rankled. All she wanted was the baby. Why had he imagined she had any interest in him? Yes, they'd had a deep conversation, danced, and almost kissed last night, but they'd both had a couple of beers. It had just been the alcohol.

"I've got her already. Make it official, Rhett." Her eyes were begging. "For my sake and Julie's. Relinquish your parental rights. Walk away."

Slowly, he shook his head. "No can do."

She looked crushed.

He had her over a barrel and she knew it, but he took no satisfaction in it.

Tara met his stare, wrinkled her nose as if smelling rotten eggs, surrendered. "If I do this, we need to get one thing absolutely straight."

"What's that?"

"I am never, ever sleeping with you."

"I never asked you to."

"Good."

"Fine."

"Great."

But it didn't feel great. Not the least little bit.

Chapter 14

DOWN IN THE WELL: A situation in which a bull is spinning in one direction and the force pulls the rider down the side of the bull into the motion's whirlpool in the direction it is spinning.

R HETT was right.

If he filed for custody, he was going to get Julie. And if he got the venue moved to Jeff Davis County and CPS granted her permission to leave El Paso with her foster daughter, there was no reason not to take a leave of absence from her job. If she wanted to spend as much time with Julie as possible before she lost her, Tara really had no other choice. Otherwise, she'd be working and leaving the baby in child care.

The thing she'd feared most had come upon her. She did not get to adopt the beautiful little girl who'd been in her care for the past five months. The baby she loved with all her heart and soul.

It was a bitter pill.

She'd known what she was getting into when she'd become Julie's foster mom, and she couldn't regret trying, but shaking off the sadness and resentment was not easy.

Especially when Rhett was using his money and influence to control her.

She called her family. They were supportive but agreed that she hadn't much recourse. They urged her to take comfort in the fact that she was Julie's aunt by marriage, and even when Rhett assumed custody, she'd still be able to watch her niece grow up.

But what if Rhett married someone who didn't want to live

on the Silver Feather? What if he took Julie out of state and Tara only got to see her on rare occasions at family gatherings?

Tara's heart wrenched.

Her mom told her to stop living in the land of *what if* and just be in the moment. Sound advice but so hard to do.

With her mind made up to do the lemons-to-lemonade thing, Tara called her boss. The hospital administrator, thrilled to have recouped the expense for Julie's four-month stay in the NICU, eagerly encouraged Tara to take a six-month leave of absence with the promise that her job was waiting for her when she was ready to return.

The tough part was deciding to stay at Rhett's house while he was on the road. On the one hand, it made perfect sense. If he was getting custody of Julie, why not take care of her in the house where she would be living? On the other hand, it put him in a position of power over Tara. It was his place. His rules. Her life in his hands.

But where else would she stay? She could move in with her parents, but they'd downsized with Dad's retirement and they were in their sixties. Was it fair to bring an infant into their house?

She could rent something in Cupid, but why waste the money? Especially since she still had to pay the lease on the duplex.

In the end, she caved and agreed to move into his place. She comforted herself with the thought he wouldn't be there.

On Tuesday, Rhett drove her to El Paso to get her things, leaving Julie with Kaia and Ridge. The three-hour car trip was tense, with them disagreeing on just about everything. What music to listen to—he wanted heavy metal, she wanted country. Which route to take—he wanted to hit the freeway, she wanted back roads. Where to stop for lunch—he wanted fast-food tacos, she wanted to zip into a market for fruit and cheese. They didn't have anything in common, but they did manage to hammer out compromises—an hour and a half of heavy metal, then an hour and a half of country. They took the freeway part of the distance, then switched to back roads. Instead of fast food or a market, they stopped at a little roadside diner for salads.

Rhett's lawyer, Lamar Johnston, called him on the drive to let him know that the change of venue had been approved, and the temporary custody hearing had been set for June 24, almost a month away.

Once they were at the duplex, he helped her box up her clothes and personal items, then he rented a small U-Haul trailer and, separately, they drove back to Cupid. Tara stopped at Kaia's house to pick up Julie. The minute she saw the baby, pure joy washed over her.

By midnight on Tuesday, Tara was unpacked and all moved in.

She stood in the guest-room-turned-nursery, hands on her hips, seeing where she would be living for the next several months. Tara bit her lip. Each step she took was drawing her closer to her deepest fears. Losing Julie to Rhett. Not having anyone to take care of. Not having anyone to love. Not having a husband or child to love *her*.

She'd already lost Kit and their unborn baby. Now she was losing Julie too. Why couldn't she have a family of her own? Why was life so unfair? Why was it so hard to let go?

Hush! No pity party allowed.

"You okay?"

She turned to see Rhett standing in the doorway, the sleeping baby in his arms, his hot eyes pinned on her. "Fine."

"You sure?"

She nodded. "It's an adjustment."

"I just fed Julie and rocked her to sleep."

"Thanks."

"Hey, even though I'm paying you, this is a team effort. I don't expect you to do everything for her. I have to learn."

"You're doing great." She smiled grudgingly. She had to concede that. He was a quick study and he was determined to do a good job. He was great in the short haul, but could he keep it up?

He moved to settle Julie into the crib they'd brought from

Tara's house. They both gazed down at the sleeping baby. He leaned over and kissed the top of her little head. It was a special moment, the three of them together. As if they were a family.

But you aren't. Stop thinking like that.

Rhett stepped back, and his eyes met Tara's. "Thank you for everything. You have no idea what an amazing gift you've given me."

"Ditto," she whispered.

They stared at each other for a long moment. Bonding. Appreciating and admiring each other. Each time he stepped up to the plate and accepted responsibility, Tara liked him just a little bit more. It was starting to get scary, how much she liked him.

"Good night," he murmured.

"Good night." As she watched him walk away, Tara had the wildest urge to chase after him and beg for a good-night kiss.

On Wednesday, they went shopping in Pecos for baby supplies and decorations for the nursery. The tension of the previous day dropped away in the fun of planning Julie's room. And when Tara suggested painting the room a muted rose pink, Rhett agreed with a dopey grin.

"Who knew Home Depot could be such fun?" Tara said as they walked through the parking lot with their purchases.

"Who knew the baby store could be fun?" Rhett laughed, moving aside the boxed baby supplies in the back of his truck so that they had room to stash the paint cans, brushes, and drop cloths.

He stretched long as he leaned over, giving her a spectacular view of his backside.

Good gravy, but the man was gorgeous. Her stomach tightened in an unholy way, filled with excitement that spread through her bloodstream like molten lava.

Wrangler's cupped his firm, toned butt. She imagined that glorious butt totally naked. Imagined sinking her fingers into it. Imagined how it would feel beneath her hot palms.

He stretched deeper into the truck, reaching to grab the jar of spackle that had fallen on its side and rolled down the bed.

Oh man, he was making things worse. Giving her a glimpse of his taut belly as the tail of his untucked shirt lifted. Excellent body. If she could just use him for sex and then toss him aside, he'd be perfect.

Cool it, Tara.

She closed her eyes. But that only accentuated her wild imagination, and she saw herself licking a hot trail down his flat, hard abs.

Something bumped into her hip.

Her eyes flew open and she lost her balance. As she fell, she had just enough time to register that a shopping cart had rolled across the parking lot to smack into her. She braced herself to hit the asphalt.

But Rhett was there. His strong arms going around her waist, catching her before she tumbled to the ground. His body was right against hers.

She looked up at him. "Thanks," she whispered breathlessly.

His eyes met hers. She could feel his warm breath on her cheek. Could hear his labored breathing. Could feel an erection pressing against the zipper of his jeans.

She flushed from the inside out.

And here was the worst part: she was just as charged up by being held in his arms as he was. The burning heat of raw desire blazed inside her. Sizzled. Smoldered. She should be ashamed of her involuntary response . . .

But she wasn't.

A soft moan escaped her lips.

"Are you okay?" he asked, tightening his grip.

"Fine," she said, wriggling out of his arms. "Let's get this show on the road."

Panting, she turned and raced for the passenger side of the truck. Heard the tailgate slam behind her. Wondered how in the world she thought she was going to live in the same house with him when her treacherous body overreacted to his simple touch.

He had a hard-on. You're not the only one with body problems. "Yoo-hoo."

Tara glanced around and spied an RN she used to work with in the newborn nursery at Cupid General. She rolled the window down. Waved. "Merylene Renfro! How in the world are you?"

Merylene was four years older than Tara, and she'd been in the same grade as Archer and Ridge at Cupid High. She stood over six feet tall and was greyhound-thin. She wore short bangs and long earrings and spoke in a quick, up-tempo voice surprisingly squeaky for her height. "Fancy seeing you here. You look amazing."

"Thanks, so do you."

Merylene squinted against the sun, held the flat of her palm over her brow, and followed Rhett with her eyes as he returned the shopping cart to the cart corral several yards away. "I heard about Rhett's baby and that you are moving into his home to take care of her as a full-time nanny."

Damn, but gossip traveled fast in the Trans-Pecos. "That's true."

"Gotta say, I wouldn't mind that gig," Merylene said.

Merylene was almost a decade older than Rhett and happily married with three kids. Tara knew Merylene wasn't really interested in Rhett, but the gleam in the woman's eyes as she watched Rhett putting away the cart punched Tara right in the throat. Dear Lord, she was *jealous.*

"It's not as glamorous as it sounds," Tara said.

Rhett waved at Merylene as he sauntered toward the pickup.

Her face brightened, and she waved back madly. "Are you kidding? He's handsome as the day is long. Worth it strictly for the eye candy. Mmm."

Get, Tara thought uncharitably. "He's not worth the trouble."

Merylene's eyes widened. "You two aren't hooking up?"

"God, no! I'm taking care of his daughter. That's it. End of story."

"When I heard you were living at his house I thought maybe—"

"No, no. Nothing like that. He'll be on the road most of the time. That's why I'm there."

"That's good because he's a heartbreaker and you've been through enough heartache." Merylene dropped her smile, placed a sympathetic hand to her chest.

"Tell me about it," Tara mumbled. "Well, it's been good seeing you again—"

"Wait, wait," Merylene said. "I came over for a reason besides just to say hi." She straightened, and her gaze zeroed in on Rhett, who'd reached Tara's side of the truck.

Tara thought, *Did she come over here to hover over Rhett?*

"Hi, Merylene." He tipped his Stetson.

"Hey, Rhett." Merylene giggled.

Tara barely restrained herself from rolling her eyes.

"You're looking good," he said. "You still running marathons?"

"That I am." Merylene swatted him playfully on the shoulder. "Ran the Cupid Marathon in three hours, forty minutes, a personal best."

"Good for you."

Tara cleared her throat. "How's Hank?" she asked, referring to Merylene's husband.

Both Merylene and Rhett turned to look at her. "Hank's fine," Merylene said.

Tara met Rhett's gaze and inclined her head toward the steering wheel. "Chop, chop, Mr. Lockhart. We've got a lot of things to get done before you hit the road tomorrow."

"She's just as bossy as ever, isn't she?" Merylene joked, and elbowed Rhett in the ribs.

Rhett raised an eyebrow, his mouth pulling up in amusement. "That she is."

"She'd be perfect for the RN job at the WIC clinic. We need someone organized, disciplined, practical . . ."

"That's our Tea in a nutshell," Rhett said. "But she's already got a job."

"I know that," Merylene went on. "But we are also in desperate need of someone who can speak Mescalero Apache *and* Spanish. Not too many people around with those particular language skills. I saw you guys over here and I had to come ask. What do I have to lose by asking?"

Tara perked up. She loved using her language skills to help out.

Merylene rested her elbows on the doorsill, peered into the truck. "Tara, I know you've got a job taking care of Rhett's daughter, but would you consider volunteering at the clinic one day a week as a translator? We could arrange for the clients who don't speak English to show up on the day of your choice." Merylene pressed her palms together in front of her heart, beseeching. "You would be such a godsend."

"Why don't you do it?" Rhett encouraged. "I can pay your mom to watch Julie one day a week."

"Oh my gosh, that would be so wonderful." Merylene looked relieved. "What do you say, Tara? Could you spare a day out of your schedule?"

Tara was a big believer in giving back to her community. When she was getting her master's degree, she'd interned on the Apache reservation in Mescalero, New Mexico. Family heritage and culture were important to her.

"Of course, I'd be honored to, Merylene." She offered a genuine smile. "Give me a call tomorrow when Rhett's on the road and we'll work out the details."

WHEN THEY GOT back to his house on the Silver Feather and unloaded their purchases, Rhett rolled up his sleeves and headed for the kitchen.

"Where are you going?" Tara asked. "We have the nursery to paint while Mom's watching Julie. No time to waste."

"I'm going to start a pot of chili, so we'll have supper ready when we finish putting together the furniture and painting the room."

Tara looked skeptical. "You can cook?"

"I can cook chili. It's the single dish in my culinary arsenal, but it's a good one. I won a blue ribbon at the county fair one year."

"No kidding?"

"I have hidden depths."

"Seduce a lot of women with your chili, do you?" she asked dryly.

"Don't you know it." He winked, exaggerated and outrageous.

She rolled her eyes, but he caught the hint of a smile beneath it. She was looking extra hot today in a short denim skirt and a snug-fitting sage green top that complemented her tawny coloring. Her long hair was tied up in a high ponytail, and she wore pink lip gloss and little other makeup. She didn't need makeup. She was a natural beauty.

"Seems counterproductive to serve chili before a seduction."

He laughed. God, he loved her dry wit. "Trust me, the seduction comes first. The chili is the reward."

"For having slept with you? Chili is the best you can do?"

He lowered his voice. "Clearly, you've never had *my* chili."

"What's so special about your chili?"

His gaze dipped quickly to her cleavage and he tried hard not to ogle, but she was just so damn sexy. "It's hot and spicy and has a little something extra."

"What's the secret ingredient?"

"Besides the quarter cup of good-quality tequila? It's a labor of love," he said. "I make everything from scratch. Roast my own chiles, toast and grind the cumin and coriander seeds . . ."

"Do you need any help?"

The idea of them working side by side at the kitchen counter brought a smile to his lips. "Sure."

"Where do you keep your aprons?"

"Aprons?"

"You know, those things you tie around your waist to protect your clothes while you're cooking?"

"I don't need no stinking aprons."

"Maybe not, but not everyone is as loosey-goosey as you are. I need an apron."

"Hang on." He dashed to the bathroom and got a towel. Came back to the kitchen. Dug around in a kitchen drawer for industrial-sized zip ties. Knotted and tied two corners of the towel with the big zip ties. "C'mere."

She eyed his makeshift apron suspiciously. "That's not going to work."

"Are you always so negative?"

"Fine." She came over, and her wonderful scent lit him up inside. "I'll give it a chance."

"Turn around."

She put her back to him.

Rhett was surprised to find his hands were trembling as he reached around her waist to cover her with the towel and cinch it in place with a third zip tie that connected the other two. His thumbs brushed her curvy hips and he felt himself start to unspool.

Quickly, he stepped away. "How's that?"

She tested the makeshift apron, tugging on it slightly. The zip ties held. "Hmm," she said. "It'll do."

"Would it kill you to give me a compliment?"

She turned and gave him a saucy grin. "Quite possibly."

"I'm getting a beer," he said. "You want one?"

"I'll get it." She cracked open the fridge and pulled out two Coronas. Handed him one. "Limes?"

"Crisper," he said, trying hard not to stare at her ass.

"Who taught you how to make chili?" She brought the lime to the counter and took the wooden cutting board in the shape of Texas off the wall.

He watched her long fingers gracefully slice the lime. "A girl I dated who worked for *Texas Monthly*. But I adapted her recipe. Made it my own."

"But of course. I should have known one of your buckle bunnies taught you to make chili." Her voice dragged down in judgment.

"I have an active dating life. Why do you find that so offensive?"

"I think 'indiscriminate' is the correct word."

"I like to have a good time. What's wrong with that?"

"Um, you end up having children you don't want."

Ouch. Out came the claws. "Look at it this way: if I hadn't been indiscriminate, I wouldn't have Julie."

"A happy accident." Her tone softened.

He took a pair of rubber gloves from a box in the pantry, stemmed and seeded the ancho and pasilla peppers he'd brought in from his travel trailer that morning with chili-making on his mind.

"What can I do?"

"Mince two onions and fifteen cloves of garlic."

"Wow, that's a lot of garlic."

"Eat my chili and you never have to worry about vampires," he bragged, taking a porcelain-enameled cast-iron Dutch oven skillet from the copper rack hanging over the kitchen island, switching on the gas burner to medium high, and adding a layer of chili peppers.

"Vampires were never a big concern for me." She straightened from peeling an onion, her ponytail swinging against her swan-like neck. "Zombies or werewolves either."

"You're not the least bit whimsical, are you?"

"Nope." She looked proud of herself.

"Down-to-earth as they come," he said.

"You say it like it's a bad thing."

"No, not at all." He shrugged. "I just don't get it. I mean, what is life if not a grand dream?"

"I feel like life is about helping people," she said. "It's about relationships, not chasing fantasies."

"You can't have both?"

"Not when you make people and relationships a priority."

"You mean put other people's needs ahead of your own?"

"Not exactly—"

"You give to get. It's why you're here with me right now."

She ducked her head, hiding her face from him. "Maybe."

"It's all about maintaining control."

Her head jerked up and she stared at him as if he'd guessed her dirtiest secret. "What? Are you saying I'm controlling?"

"No, I'm saying you use giving as a way to be in control of your life. Ultimately, that's why you give. Because you're afraid of being out of control. The giver has all the power in a relationship."

She looked pensive. "You think so?"

"Oh yeah. Believe me, I'm usually the taker, and the only place I have control is on the back of a bull. That's why I do what I do. In the arena, I'm in charge."

"Or the bull is."

He grinned. "Can't let me have one illusion, huh?"

"Sorry, that's not how I roll."

"Now that's not a people-pleaser trait. You're supposed to support my high sense of self-regard," he teased.

"Quite enough people polish your ego. I'm not getting aboard that train."

"That's because you're scared of me."

"Say what?" She stopped mincing the onions and garlic and tossed down the chef's knife. "I am not the least bit scared of you."

"Oh yes, you are."

A frown cleaved her brow. "Support your claim."

"Because I can see through you. You get mad at me whenever things get real."

"I don't."

"You do. Just like now."

"Wow." She snorted, and her body stiffened. "Dinner *and* psychoanalysis. How lucky can one girl get?"

Dammit, why had he said all that stuff? Over the past couple of days things had been really good between them and now he couldn't help feeling that, because of his big mouth, their relationship had just taken two steps back.

Chapter 15

HONKER: A really rank and hard bull to ride.

FOR the next three weeks, as June barreled toward the temporary custody hearing, Tara and Rhett kept in touch through texts and Skype sessions. Each morning, Tara would start her day by sending him pictures of Julie, showcasing how she was growing. Each night when he was finished with his day, Rhett would call in.

On Wednesdays, Mom kept Julie while Tara volunteered at the WIC clinic in Pecos, using her language and nursing skills to help the underserved Mescalero Apache population that visited the clinic. The side job reminded her of how much she'd been neglecting one half of her heritage, and it put her back in touch with her culture. Strengthening ties to her tribal community. Plus getting out of the house for a few hours a week helped balance the demands of caring for an infant. Each time she came away from the clinic, Tara felt renewed and invigorated.

Rhett's last check-in with her was on Friday night, June 21, after another high-scoring ride in Billings, Montana, which put him three points ahead of Claudio Limon.

"I'll leave Sunday morning after I've rested up after tomorrow's ride," he said. "But it's a seventeen-hour trip. I'm worried I might not make it back to the Silver Feather in time to pick you up."

"Don't rush. Take plenty of breaks. You'll be exhausted after riding." Tara propped her feet on the coffee table, the computer in her lap, Julie on the couch beside her, swaddled in a blanket.

"Instead of you driving thirty miles out of the way to the ranch, let's just meet at the courthouse at nine a.m. on Monday."

"All right," he agreed.

She leaned over to put a sock back on Julie that she'd kicked off.

"Tea?" he said.

"Yes?"

"Are you okay?"

"Fine." She straightened. "Why shouldn't I be?"

"You could lose custody of Julie on Monday."

Tara gulped; she'd been trying not to think too much about that. "But nothing will change. You're going to stay on the road and I'll keep watching Julie until the PBR season is over, right?"

"That's the plan."

Tara chuffed out a breath. See, nothing had to change until November. She had plenty of time to prepare for losing Julie. Her chest tightened, and she had to remind herself to inhale.

"You look good," Rhett murmured, his eyelids lowering on the computer screen.

"Not so bad yourself, cowboy." She kept her tone light.

"Have you been getting any sleep?"

"No." Tara laughed. "The little munchkin of yours wakes up every hour and a half like clockwork. If I look wide awake it's because I'm on a coffee high."

"I can't wait to get home and take over, so you can get some rest." His gaze latched on to hers. "I miss you guys."

Tara's heart skipped a beat at the wistfulness in his voice. She missed him too. "We'll be waiting."

AT NINE A.M. on Monday, June 24, Rhett met Lamar Johnston on the steps of the Jeff Davis County Courthouse.

Lamar eyed Rhett in his suit jacket, tie, and starched blue jeans. "You don't have any dress pants to match the suit jacket? Image matters. You're a Lockhart, you should look the part."

"I'm also a cowboy. I feel weird in anything but jeans."

Lamar sighed an it-is-what-it-is sound. Leaned over to straighten

Rhett's tie. Stood back to admire his handiwork. Lamar's curly black hair was clipped short close to his scalp. He sported a single diamond stud in his left ear, a tolerant smile on his russet-brown face, and a Barbie Band-Aid on his little finger.

"Domestic injury?" Rhett nodded at the Band-Aid.

"Paper cut." Lamar let out a deep bass chuckle. "Zoya insisted on playing nursemaid." He held up his pinkie. "She kissed it and made it all better. Just wait until your girl is five. It's a whole new level of fun."

"*If* I get custody."

Lamar waved a dismissive hand. "You'll get it. You've just got to jump through a few hoops first. Mere formality."

"I love your confident front."

"No front, man." Lamar swept an arm up and down his body. "This package is the real deal. I've got your back."

"You sure I'm going to win custody?"

"There's nothing standing in your way." Lamar ticked off the advantages on his long, muscular fingers. "Your family is a pillar of the community. You're solid financially. You assumed responsibility and paid for Julie's hospital bills when you didn't really have to. Baby mama out of the picture. No maternal relatives wanting your daughter. Piece of cake."

"But what if Rhona comes back?"

"That's a problem for the permanent hearing. Right now, we're just determining temporary custody. One step at a time. You're a shoo-in."

"So, there's no way I can lose her?" Rhett fretted, which wasn't like him. Usually, he was the type to latch on to good news with both hands and run with it. Why was he not accepting Lamar's optimism at face value?

"Not if you jump through the legal hoops."

"Just tell me how high."

Lamar winked, poked him with his elbow. "Now that's the attitude I'm talkin' 'bout."

"I'll do everything the court asks of me."

"No sense sweating it out here on the steps." Lamar clasped a hand on Rhett's shoulder. "Let's head inside."

He and Lamar pushed through the glass double doors into the court building. Simultaneously, he and his lawyer pulled off their sunglasses as they passed through the security screening. Once inside the cool of the lobby, Rhett spied Tara sitting on a bench.

Aria was with her, holding Julie.

Tara stood up. She was wearing a print green, short-sleeved dress that nipped in at the waist and showed off her shapely figure. Her legs, the tawny color of desert earth, drew his attention.

"Hey," he said, meeting her gaze.

"Hey," she said back.

He had an overwhelming urge to tug Tara into his arms and plant a big kiss on her lips. The impulse both alarmed and electrified him. He'd missed her so much.

"How are you doing?" he asked, realizing she was probably as nervous as he was. She had as much on the line as he did. More so, really. She was losing Julie. His stomach hitched.

"I'm taking Julie to the park across the street," Aria said.

Tara's eyes locked tight on his and she didn't spare a glance for her sister. "If it gets too hot, take her to Stormy's," she said, referring to the nearby ice cream parlor.

"Can I give her ice cream?" Aria asked.

"No," Rhett and Tara said in unison. He'd learned a few things in her parenting class.

Lamar tapped the face of his expensive watch. "Tick tock."

"I'll come get you when this is over, sis." Tara finally dropped his gaze and walked over to Aria, who was holding the baby in her arms. Tara bent to kiss Julie's cheek.

Should he do that too? Rhett started toward the stroller, but Lamar was already holding the door open to the courtroom and nodding him inside.

Rhett turned and joined Lamar, who escorted him to the front of the courtroom. Ms. Bean was already seated in the witness section. She gave him a smile and a small wave. He waved back, heartened by her kooky friendliness.

Everything was going his way. Just formalities. Hoop jumping, as Lamar said.

He thought of Tara, wondered how she was doing. He glanced over his shoulder to find her. She was slipping into the pew behind the bench where he sat with Lamar.

Tara raised her hand, her eyes steady and calm. He waved back, felt a trickle of fear shift through him like hourglass sand.

"All rise," said the bailiff. Not that there were many people to obey his command. It was just him, Lamar, Ms. Bean, and Tara. "The honorable Judge Helena Brando presiding."

An iron-jawed, gray-haired, robed woman swept into the room and settled herself on the bench, looked out across the group, spied Rhett, and immediately crinkled her nose in distaste. She cleared her throat, slipped on the reading glasses that hung from a chain around her neck, picked up the papers in front of her.

The room hushed. No one spoke a word as the judge perused the documents. The only sound came from the ticking of the courtroom clock.

Finally, Judge Brando glanced up, shot Rhett a scalding scowl. "This is an initial hearing to review the status of the minor child, Julie Elizabeth Lockhart, for the possibility of permanent placement with her father."

Rhett's scalp felt itchy, as if he had a persistent heat rash, but he didn't dare scratch it.

The judge held up the results of his paternity test for the courtroom to see. "Rhett Winston Lockhart, you have petitioned the court for custody of the daughter who was abandoned by her mother, Rhona White, at El Paso Children's Hospital in El Paso County."

"Yes, Your Honor," he said.

"Please stand when you address the court." Her voice was steely.

He sprang up, not wanting to tick her off any more than she already seemed to be, but he accidentally knocked Lamar's pen and yellow legal notepad off the desk. He leaned down, fumbling for the pen as it rolled away from him.

"Leave that for now," she snapped. "Sit back down."

He sat.

She leafed through the documents again. "I see you have paid the child's extensive medical bills."

"I have," he said, popping up again. She gave him such a piercing stare, he quickly added, "Your Honor."

"That gesture has bought you some goodwill with the court."

Whew. Good. Great.

"Don't look so relieved. You're not off the hook. Not by a long shot." The judge raised her arm, and the sleeve of her robe caught on a loose nail. She snorted like a PBR bull and yanked herself loose. "Bailiff, make sure to get a hammer and nail this sucker down."

"Yes, Your Honor."

"Now back to you, Mr. Lockhart. You are a professional rodeo cowboy?"

He was still standing. "Yes, ma'am . . . um . . . er . . . Your Honor."

"You want custody of this baby?"

"I do."

"Then I suggest you find another line of work." If her tone was a dagger, it would have slit his gut wide open. "I'm not going to give you the baby until I am certain the environment is safe. She is a preemie and has special needs. I want to be sure you're equipped for that."

He shot Lamar a helpless look. His attorney shrugged.

"It's a dangerous job," the judge went on. "And since you'll be a single parent, who would raise the child if you were to get seriously injured or killed?"

"Um . . . um . . ." He had no idea what to say. "But . . . but . . . Your Honor." Fear was a boa constrictor squeezing his chest. "I'm ahead in the standings. This is *my* season. The world championship is mine to win. If we could delay the permanency hearing until after November, I—"

"Mr. Lockhart." Her eyes were firehoses now, dousing him in high-pressure water. "The state of Texas is not your piggy bank, nor your personal babysitter."

"But—"

"Mr. Lockhart?"

"Yes?" Shit, his knees were barely holding him up. He had to grab hold of the table to steady himself.

"Shut up."

He rested his knuckles over his mouth.

"I know who you are. Who your family is. You are a spoiled, rich, arrogant, young man. You are used to getting your way. Accustomed to people waiting on you hand and foot. For too long you have thought only of yourself. That must change."

"Yes, ma'am, but—"

"Here's what's going to happen. If you want custody of this child, when you return for the permanency hearing, you will have a contingency plan. You will have chosen a guardian for the baby in case something happens to you. You will show proof your environment is safe."

"Yes, ma'am." He could do that.

"She is not to be taken on the road with you. She is a preemie and her health is of primary concern."

He bobbed his head, his mind whirling.

"And, this is only a suggestion, since I can't *force* you to quit your highly dangerous job, I hope you will give some serious thought to a new line of work. That would go a long way toward proving you truly want this child."

What? Rhett's stomach bottomed out. To prove he was a good father, the judge was essentially forcing him out of the PBR. But how could he give it up? It was his life, his love, his everything.

Not everything. Not anymore. You have Julie now.

"Judge—"

She pointed a condemning finger at him. "You stop right there."

He nodded mutely, feeling a bit like he'd been hit by a tractor and dragged through a field of rocks.

"Listen to me." With pronounced exaggeration, she said, "Do. You. Want. Your. Daughter?"

"I—"

"Yes or no, Mr. Lockhart. Those are the only two options I want to hear come out of your mouth."

Did he want Julie badly enough to hang up his spurs for good?

Behind him, Tara made a noise of dismay. It was an aborted sound, sharp and halfway as if she was trying her best to stifle it.

He threw a glance over his shoulder, saw Tara's eyes filled with pity. He winced. She knew things were going south and she felt sorry for him.

"Mr. Lockhart." Judge Brando lightly rapped her gavel. "Eyes on me. Right now, I should be the center of your universe."

He whipped his head around to face the judge once more.

"Yes or no, Mr. Lockhart. Do you want custody of your daughter?"

He found his voice, said loudly, clearly, "Yes."

"Then by the next hearing date, you will have done the things I've outlined."

"Yes, ma'am."

"Good. I'm glad we understand each other." Judge Brando raised her gavel. "Review hearing will be set for September 26. Please see the county clerk for details. If Mr. Lockhart has complied with the court's conditions, we will then establish a date and time for the permanency hearing pending termination of the biological mother Rhona White's parental rights. Until that time, the minor child shall remain in the custody of her foster mother, Tara Alzate."

"MAY I SPEAK to you a moment?" Tara had lingered in an alcove of the courthouse, waiting for Rhett to leave so she could approach his attorney. She'd gone to high school with Lamar, knew him to be a square shooter.

Lamar jumped, and slapped a hand to his chest. "Shoot fire, girl! You scared me spitless. Tie a bell around your neck if you're gonna sneak up on people."

"Sorry," she apologized. "I didn't mean to startle you. I just wanted to talk about Rhett's situation."

Lamar glanced at his watch. "I have a deposition in fifteen minutes . . ."

"This won't take five."

"Okay, if you make it quick."

"Is this normal for a judge to recommend that someone quit their job in order to get custody of their child?"

Lamar stroked his jaw, looked pensive. "Normal? No. But Rhett has a dangerous career and Julie is a preemie and it seems Judge Brando sees something in Rhett that causes her to doubt his commitment to the child."

"What if Rhett were married? Do you think the judge would have recommended he quit his job if he were married?"

"But he's *not* married."

"What if he were?"

"Does Rhett have a girlfriend?"

"Not that I know of."

"Wait . . ." Lamar's eyes widened, and he let out a little *hoot-hoot* sound. "Are *you* offering to marry him?"

"I didn't say that. I was just wondering, since I'm legally Julie's temporary guardian, if Rhett and I were to get married—"

"I knew it!" Lamar slapped his thigh. "I could feel sparks shooting around the courtroom whenever you two looked at each other."

"No." Tara shook her head. "No sparks." But it came out sounding as if she were trying to convince herself as much as the lawyer. "But if we were to marry, I would be there to take care of Julie when he's on the road or if something happened to him. I would be her stepmother."

He blew out his breath, Big-Bad-Wolf style. "Whew, girl, that's a big step. I know you love that baby, but c'mon. A marriage of convenience?"

"There's another solid reason for us getting married," Tara said, thinking about the gnawing question that had been eating at the back of her mind from the very beginning.

"What's that?"

"In case Rhona comes back. Wouldn't she have a harder time getting custody if Rhett and I were married?"

"The courts do tend to favor the biological mom, but you're right. If the two of you were married and providing Julie with a stable home environment, as a single parent who abandoned her baby, Rhona would have a harder time against you."

"That's what I thought," Tara said. "Thanks, Lamar."

"Listen, I gotta get to that deposition, and I know you're just taking the idea for a test drive, but marriage isn't easy. It's hard enough when people are madly in love, but a marriage of convenience?" He shook his head. "That's a tall order."

Chapter 16

FOULED: If a rider is fouled, it means something happened during the eight-second ride that gave the bull an unfair advantage over the rider.

AFTER the hearing, Rhett searched the courthouse for Tara, but she'd disappeared. Disappointed, he'd texted her to see if she wanted to grab lunch, but she hadn't answered him back.

Feeling raw and wrung out, he'd headed home.

If he wanted his daughter, he needed to give up the PBR in the middle of a red-hot year that could lead him to the one thing he'd spent his entire life working for. It was a punch in the belly for sure.

He paced his living room, gut tightening, heart lurching. He felt mighty claustrophobic in the house. Empty now without his daughter or Tara in it.

Needing to clear his head and move his body, he jammed his feet into his worn riding boots. Went to the stables, filled with tack—bits, bridles, blankets, braided ropes—pulled a saddle down off the wall and strapped it onto Golden Boy.

The palomino was over twenty years old, but he still had a lot of spunk left in him. Golden Boy preferred male riders. Tara had been the only woman who'd ever been able to ride him with any consistency. Which had irritated her sister Kaia to no end, since she was the biggest animal lover in the family. Rhett supposed Golden Boy's affinity for Tara came from her calm, sensible approach. Horses could sense when people were anxious or stressed, and Tara had a natural, soothing way about her.

Loosening the reins on the stallion, Rhett tried not to think of Tara.

He and Golden Boy jetted across the pasture, flying over tumbleweeds, tarbush, cacti, and yucca. Sand kicked up beneath the horse's hooves, and the sun was halfway down the afternoon sky. The air was arid and warm, but not uncomfortable. At this altitude, even in the desert terrain, the temperatures rarely shot out of the eighties. Riding salved him, particularly at the Silver Feather. Wide expanse of open land, no one around, no distractions, just Rhett and his horse and nature.

Lightly, he nudged Golden Boy with his heels, sending the palomino into a full gallop. No plan to where he was headed. Simply riding, wild and free. Letting his mind wander to find an answer to his problem.

He should have seen something like this coming. Life rarely went as planned. He should have been on guard. Tara would have been on guard. He should be more like Tara. Less go with the flow, more circumspect.

Dammit.

Could a fella change his entire personality?

Thoughts swirling, he leaned in tighter, lowering his head over Golden Boy, urging the stallion into his top speed. The ground blurred beneath pounding hooves.

Even though Judge Brando said she couldn't force him to quit, did he really have a choice if he wanted to be the best father he could be? He *had* to quit the PBR. For Julie's sake.

He eased up on the reins, sat up higher in the saddle. Golden Boy slowed, breath heaving from the full-out run. He wheeled the stallion around, headed in the opposite direction, toward the stock tank.

Within a few minutes he arrived at the tank, located beneath an old wooden windmill he and his brothers and the Alzate kids had climbed a thousand times. Remembered that time he'd come across Tara when she'd been out for a run. While the horse drank from the pond, he pulled his canteen from the saddlebag, and gulped back several long swallows of lukewarm water.

And there, in the middle of the desert, two piercing dark eyes met his, and cut straight to his soul.

Tara.

Standing a few yards away from his old farm truck. He'd been so lost in thought he hadn't even heard her drive up. What was she doing here? And why? She sank her hands on her hips, her lush silhouette startling against the barren landscape. It was as if he'd conjured her with his thoughts. What an eerie notion. Unless she was a mirage.

He stopped breathing, didn't dare blink in case she vanished.

"Afternoon, Rhett. How are you doing?" Her voice was smooth and even like always. She'd changed from the dress she'd worn in court, trading it in for tight-fitting jeans, a white peasant blouse, and red Old Gringo boots.

He much preferred this outfit. How it molded and complemented every sensuous curve. The woman was flat-out killing him.

He skirted the stallion around a clump of prickly pear cactus, struggling to keep his mind centered as he maneuvered the craggy terrain. Stopped beside her.

She straightened her back, and the movement lifted her glorious breasts, widened her stance.

Sweat broke out on his forehead.

All he could think about was how her jeans clung to her gas-flame-hot body and the fact she had no panty line, and did that mean she went commando, or was she wearing a thong?

Cripes, Lockhart. Tara was strictly hands-off. Forbidden. Banned. Taboo. That was clear enough. He would never know what lurked beneath those skin-tight jeans.

"How did you find me?" Perplexed, he lifted his Stetson, scratched his head.

"I came home from the hearing just in time to see you galloping away. You'd left me the keys to your truck, so I just followed you."

"So . . ." He jammed his hands in his front pockets, feeling more than a little unsettled by her unexpected appearance in the desert. Did they share some kooky telepathy? "Why were you following me?"

Her inky brown eyes were starlight bright. "I've been thinking."

"About what?"

"How to save your career *and* get you custody of your daughter," she said, her voice thick with conviction.

THEY WENT BACK to his house. Her driving the truck, him riding beside her on Golden Boy.

"Where's Julie?" Rhett asked after Tara parked in the driveway and came over while he led the stallion into the stables.

"Aria's still got her. I'll go pick her up after we talk."

He unsaddled the horse and turned to Tara. "Even if I quit the PBR, there's a possibility I could still lose her. Judge Brando is not a fan of mine."

"You won't." Her steely resolve bolstered his spirits. "The courts favor biological parents. The judge is just making you jump through hoops to prove your commitment. She wants you to think about the magnitude of fatherhood. That's the downside of having the trial in Jeff Davis County—Judge Brando knows you and your family. Your reputation preceded, but she can't withhold your child based on your reputation."

"I wish I shared your confidence."

"Let's go into the house," she said. "Sit down with a cold drink. We need to talk."

"All right." He texted one of his father's ranch hands to come curry out Golden Boy, led the way inside. They went in through the back door. A pink Strawberry Shortcake pacifier he'd bought for Julie lay on the table. Tara picked it up, traced a finger over the ring, her eyes filled with wistful longing.

"Ice tea?" he asked.

"Coffee."

Slinky as a mountain lion, she slid into a kitchen chair. Her peasant blouse rose up as she settled, revealing a brief flash of her taut, flat, tanned belly.

He focused on leveling out the right amount of coffee, and slowly exhaled. "I bought a box of animal crackers for Jules while I was on the road if you'd like some."

"She's too young for cookies—" Tara broke off. "Sorry, there I go again, trying to tell you how to raise your child."

"You're right. She is too young for them. I know that. They just looked so cute on the shelf I bought them anyway." He opened the crackers, pushed the box toward her.

Tara fished out an elephant and nibbled on its ear.

At the sight of her pink tongue, his body hardened, and he wondered what it would feel like to have those straight white teeth nibbling on *his* ear.

Oh, that he were that elephant. Thrown by the heat rushing through his body, he grabbed two cups from the cabinet. Poured the coffee, carried the drinks to the kitchen table. Sat across from her.

Their eyes met, and they watched each other in the space of a long minute, neither speaking. She looped the white string attached to the cookie box around her slender wrist like a bracelet.

"When we were kids, my sisters and I used to pretend the animal cracker boxes were our purses," she mused.

"I remember," he said. "I was there. I kept checking your 'purses' for leftover cookies."

"You were a little scoundrel, even back then." Her laughter was rich and full, and the sound aroused him.

He lifted one shoulder, trying for casual nonchalance, despite the sudden sweat ringing his collar. "What can I say? I like animal crackers."

She took a giraffe from the box, slid it across the table to him. "Stingy."

She removed two more cookies, a camel and a lion, pushed those at him as well, slanted a glance at him from beneath lowered lashes. Did she have any idea how sexy she looked right at that moment?

He bit the giraffe's head off. It made a satisfying *crunch*.

Tara munched her own cookie, her eyes never leaving his face. "I'm sorry Judge Brando is urging you to quit the PBR."

"That's big of you," he said. "Considering I'm the one taking Julie away from you."

"She's your biological daughter." Tara dusted cookie crumbs from her hands. "I'm just the foster mother."

"Who wants to adopt her."

Tara nodded. "But I knew when I got into this what the risks were. Until all parental rights had been terminated, I knew I could lose her. Then they found you and you wanted her . . ." Tara's eyes misted, and she gazed over his head. Gulped. "It was my fault. I got too attached."

"You love her."

She met his gaze boldly. "I couldn't love her more if I'd given birth to her."

"Little wonder. You were there fighting for her life when her own mother walked out." Rhett felt a hard yank on his heartstrings, and his admiration for Tara bloomed.

"I'm glad you turned out to be her father." Tara ran a thumb along her bottom lip. Her fingernails were clipped short, clear polished, professional. Strangely, it was more erotic than if she'd had long, glossy red nails.

"You are?" He was barely breathing, his lungs so full of her healthy, fresh Tara scent.

"If it had turned out to be one of the other men Rhona had been with and they wanted her . . . well . . . I'd never get to see Julie again."

He deflated a little. Had he been expecting that she was happy about *him* and not just because she was related to him by marriage?

"But you . . ." She swept her hand broadly, a wide, expansive gesture that indicated the whole of the Silver Feather. "You're family. I'll still get to watch Julie grow up. Maybe I can still take care of her sometimes."

"Unless Judge Brando doesn't give me custody after all. Then you get to keep Julie."

"I can't adopt her if you don't terminate your parental rights. You'd have to do something heinous not to get custody."

"That's not the way the judge made it sound."

"Like I said, she's just testing your resolve. The only way I get Julie is if you voluntarily give her up."

Her words were a hard slap, knocking him back to reality. "Is that what you came here to ask?" He hardened his chin. No matter how much he liked and admired Tara, he was *not* giving up his parental rights. In a short amount of time, that baby had become his world, and if it meant quitting the PBR on the hottest hot streak of his life, then so be it.

"I have a better plan." Tara pressed her palms. "An answer to both our prayers."

"What's that?"

She took a deep breath. Held it. Crashed her gaze into his.

A moment passed between them, charged and full of meaning. He could see she was all in. "Tara?"

Her gaze locked him to his seat. Serious. No nonsense. "Let's get married."

TARA COULDN'T BELIEVE what she was saying. Marry Rhett Lockhart? Had she lost her ever-loving mind?

But then she looked at the animal crackers and the sweet Strawberry Shortcake pacifier and thought of Julie, and her heart melted away any fears.

There was nothing wrong with a marriage of convenience. Lots of people did it. Had done it for millennia. Not people she knew personally, but some people, somewhere. It happened. No, it wasn't romantic. No, it wasn't how she'd envisioned her life unfolding.

But Julie was worth it.

And let's face it, Rhett Lockhart was pretty darn easy on the eyes.

"You . . . you really want to do this?" Excitement filled Rhett's face and he looked the way he did when he was on the back of a bull in the chute, waiting for the gate to open and the adventure to begin.

"Being married, especially to a neonatal nurse, is an optimal scenario at gaining custody. I talked to Lamar. He's on board."

"When did you talk to him?"

"After you left the courthouse."

"So that's where you went."

She nodded, bit her bottom lip. "Are you upset that I interfered?"

"Hell, no." His laugh was jovial. "But we have a lot to discuss."

She shifted to the edge of her chair, jiggled her leg, exhilarated. One marriage license and Julie would be hers. But so would Rhett, and that thought was scary.

Rhett Lockhart, her *husband*? Talk about complicated.

"Like what?" she asked.

"Compensation."

"You're offering me money to marry you?"

"If we get married, you'll have to give up your job in El Paso for good. You can't live here and work there."

"Oh," Tara said, realizing she'd gotten so caught up in the idea of becoming Julie's mother she hadn't thought this through. "Or you could move to El Paso."

He shook his head. "I want Julie to grow up on the Silver Feather. The same way we did."

Tara folded her hands in her lap. It had been an idyllic way to grow up. He was right. She would have to quit her job.

"We'll need a prenup that builds in money based on how long we stay married."

Prenup.

It sounded so clinical. So cold. But what did she expect? This wasn't romance. This wasn't love.

"I'll have Lamar draw up a contract." He looked at her with those impossible eyes.

Her hormones did a swirly little jig, all tingly and breathless. Her attraction to him worried her. Rhett wasn't her type. He was younger than her by four years. He was too charming, too expressive, just too darn much. Truth be told, Rhett scared the hell out of her.

She needed to know that she and Julie were protected from the drama that followed him around. Buckle bunnies and fistfights. Partying hearty and busted bones. The highs and lows of rodeo life.

No wonder Judge Brando urged him to quit the PBR.

She could fall for him if she wasn't careful. She could feel it in her bones. Living with him as man and wife. Day in and day out. Taking their meals together. Caring for Julie.

And at night—

Dear God, he was right. There were so many details they needed to iron out before they took the plunge.

And yet, despite all her fears and concerns, on a gut-deep level, she trusted him. He was tender with Julie, so kind and gentle. His love for his little girl was written all over his face. He would move heaven and earth for the child, and Tara found that utterly irresistible.

His eyes were on her face. Her cheeks heated. She cleared her throat. "There's something else we need to get straight right off the bat."

"What's that?"

"This will be a marriage in name only."

One eyebrow went up. "Meaning?"

"Are you going to make me spell it out?"

"Yes, for the prenup."

"You're *not* putting this in the contract."

"It's your condition, it goes in."

"This is not something Lamar needs to know about." She crossed her arms and petted herself on the elbows.

"What's not?" He lowered his tone and his eyes to a sultry half-mast that undid her in ninety different ways.

"A no-sex clause."

He leaned forward. "We're going to be celibate?"

"Not celibate, no."

"So, we *are* going to have sex?" Humor rumbled through his voice with childlike enthusiasm.

"We're not going to have sex with each other." Tara's breathing quickened, and her heart rate, oh, that was a freaking lightning bolt, zipping through her veins like a runaway train. She moistened her lips, couldn't quite meet his eyes. She *so* should have thought this through before coming here.

"Let me get this straight. We won't be celibate, but we won't have sex with each other."

"I . . ." she said. "You . . ."

He leaned forward, so closely she could smell his masculine scent and see the pulse at the hollow of his throat tick rapidly. "We'll have an open marriage?"

"Yes . . ." She pointed a finger at him. "That."

"Should we talk about the rules?"

"There's only one."

"And that is?" His eyebrows arched like twin question marks on his forehead.

"You don't bring your women around Julie. *Ever.*"

He snorted, scowled. "Of course not."

"Be discreet. Don't flaunt your affairs. For Julie's sake. You're a public figure. If the gossip rags get wind of this—"

"I get it."

"It's—"

"Tara." His voice was stern.

"Yes?"

"Are you going to be a nagging wife?"

Tara raised her chin. "If you need nagging, then yes, yes I am."

He drummed his fingers on the table. The vein in his throat ticked faster. Finally, he laughed. "All right. Fair enough. What about you?"

"What about me?"

"You're a sexy woman . . ." His gaze traveled over her, hot and leisurely.

Goose bumps cooled her skin, as a lava flow of desire bubbled over inside her. Oh no.

This was not good. Not good at all.

"In the prime of life. You have needs too."

"Julie is my only need."

"Uh-huh." He eyed the front of her blouse, and that's when Tara realized her nipples had beaded so tightly that he could see the outline through her bra. She cleared her throat. Shot him a pointed glance.

"I'm just saying, if you need to take a lover . . ." His eyes darkened, and his jaw muscles tensed, and his hands knotted up into fists.

Hmm, was he jealous? That idea sparked a thrill inside her. *Seriously, Tara?*

"I can live without sex." She'd already gone without for two years.

His eyes went back to her chest. "You're responsive as hell, Tara Alzate. You shouldn't have to live without sex. You need a man who appreciates how hot-blooded you are and puts your pleasure first."

Prickly heat burned her nape. "My pleasure is none of your business."

He was a handsome man. No denying it, and when she studied his face, met those piercing eyes as dark as her own, she felt an irresistible pull in the center of her solar plexus. A soft whispering deep in her brain, *What if?* Begging the question, could she stick to her own no-sex rule?

"We need to talk about a time limit," he murmured.

"A what?" She blinked.

"How long does this marriage last?"

"Oh." Something else she had not thought through. In her mind, she was Julie's mom until the end of time.

"How long will we stay together? Until I get permanent custody of Julie?" He scratched his chin, screwed up his mouth in thought. "That could take months. Rhona's parental rights have to be terminated first. Let's say we stay married a year for good measure."

He was right. They couldn't have a marriage of convenience for eighteen years. Could they? There had to be some kind of time limit. But only a year to be Julie's mom? It wasn't nearly enough. "I . . . um . . . I could stay longer. Get you through her toddler phase and the terrible twos? Although the threes aren't any picnic either."

He shook his head, his hair falling adorably over his forehead. "That's a tempting offer, but I can't do that to you. As long as you're hitched up to me, you can't be out there finding your true love and having babies of your own." He didn't point out that she was thirty-two, which she appreciated, and the clock was ticking, but she got it.

"Um . . ." She gulped. "That's not a concern. I can't have children of my own."

"Huh?"

"I can't have kids."

"Oh, Tara." He gave her the saddest look, which pierced her chest like an arrow. "I didn't know. No wonder you're so invested in Julie."

His kind tone stirred her tears, but she refused to cry in front of him.

Silence. Long and awkward.

He cleared his throat. "If you don't mind my asking, what happened?"

She *did* mind him asking, but he deserved an answer. She gave him the pat version, left out the part that wrung her soul.

The lost baby. She placed a palm to her abdomen. "I had severe endometriosis."

"Oh." He looked uncomfortable, and she realized she might as well have been speaking Greek.

"It's a medical condition some women get that scars their uterus. That's why Julie means so much to me," she said.

He leaned back in his chair, stroked his chin with a thumb and index finger. "In that case, do you think a marriage of convenience between us is wise?"

Her heart stuttered. She was invested in Julie up to her eyebrows; if he backed out now, she'd be devastated. "Why not? You need help, I want to help . . ."

"The more you're around Julie, the harder it will be for you to let go when the time comes." He reached across the table and took her hand in a gesture so tender she could scarcely staunch the tears. "The last thing I want is to hurt you."

She traced his knuckles. "Too late. I'm already in love with her. I'm going to get hurt. I know that. But she's worth it."

His eyes grew wide and solemn. "Julie and I are both lucky to have you."

"And don't you forget it," she joked with a smile, ignoring her jackrabbit pulse and the lonesome feeling dug into the pit of her stomach. She was playing with fire and she was going to get burned. No way around it.

He steepled his fingers. "If we do this, no one can know we're planning to split up eventually."

Tara nodded. Couldn't speak. Moved by the catch in his throat, the fear in his eyes. The changes in him since he'd discovered he'd had a daughter were unequivocal. The playboy rodeo star had finally grown up. His only concern was for his daughter. Tara admired him more than she could express.

"Let's not do this," he said. "I'll just quit the PBR. It's the smartest thing. I have to quit sometime. It might as well be now."

"You *need* this win, Rhett. The PBR means everything to you. You've worked your entire life for this."

"Julie means more."

"You need the money for Julie's future, and if you think you can win the championship, you have to take that chance. I'm on your side and I'm prepared to help you win. Besides, there's Rhona. She's the wild card in all this. She could show up out of the blue and want Julie back, but she'll have a harder time convincing Judge Brando she deserves custody against the two of us."

He bobbed his head. "All right."

"All right what?"

"I accept your proposal. When do we do this?"

This part she had thought through. The sooner the better. "Fourth of July weekend?"

He frowned. "There's a big rodeo that day."

She gave him a pointed look.

"Oh yeah, right, priorities."

"Is there anything else we need to discuss?"

This was not the marriage of her dreams, but then again, Rhett was not her dream man. It wasn't a *real* wedding. She was sensible about this. No stars in her eyes. No hope for anything more. Why, then, did she get a catch in her side and a clutch in her chest?

A fearful little voice in her head panicked. *Back out. This isn't going to work. Get up and walk out that door. Marrying him will damage you in ways you can't possibly imagine. Get out. Get out while you can.*

But she overrode the fear, held steady, and waited for his answer.

Chapter 17

HUNG UP: A rider who is off the bull but is still stuck in the rope.

SWEET heavens, when did Tara get so gorgeous?

He'd always found her attractive, but right now she looked positively dazzling. Maybe it was because he was seeing her through the lens of a husband. She would be his wife.

Wife.

What an alien word. He'd never imagined himself with a wife or family. But then Julie had come along and turned his world upside down. Now, all he could think about was creating a happy, stable environment for his daughter. It was his duty to give Julie the best life possible, and that started with marrying Tara . . .

It would work.

It *had* to work.

Tara was still sitting at the table, coffee cup and a box of animal crackers in front of her. The blouse had dipped low, revealing a hint of cleavage that sent every masculine nerve inside him into overdrive.

He must have been staring because she straightened her shoulder. A move that pulled the pucker from her blouse and hid that glorious valley.

Rhett ducked his head so that she couldn't see him grin.

She plucked a hair tie from her pocket and pulled her long, dark hair into a ponytail, a tidy, efficient do. Sending him a message? But a few unruly strands escaped and trailed down her nape in wispy tendrils.

Her high cheekbones had sharpened as she'd grown older, giving her a sleek, elegant appearance—a woman fully in charge of her destiny. One side of her mouth crooked up in a knowing smile. And he got a quick flash of straight white teeth.

Her entire family had the most amazingly white teeth. Something gained by great genetics and not professional teeth-whitening solutions. Her enigmatic chestnut eyes glimmered as if she was keeping a mysterious secret she would never share.

She'd always been lithe and graceful, but when she shifted and crossed her legs at the knee, the supple fabric of her skinny jeans outlined the curve of her shapely calves and thighs. She was voluptuous and fit. A radiant specimen of womanhood in full bloom.

His eyes, unable to resist temptation, tracked up the length of those thighs to where her jeans formed a sexy V. He shouldn't be ogling, but he could not seem to control himself. She was a sight to behold. From the golden glow of her tawny skin to her perfectly arched eyebrows, he was spellbound. She was perfection.

How unfortunate that she could not have children of her own. They would have been so beautiful.

His heart ached for her.

Their gazes locked. Her eyes were steely and smooth. She was unaffected by him. Not the least bit ruffled. At least not that he could tell. If she felt anything for him beyond lifelong familiarity, she did not show it. Just noncommittal friendliness, the kind she might dish out to anyone.

Eyes back in your head, Lockhart. He'd be damned if he'd drool over her like a hound dog. He was better than that. *She* deserved better than that.

"Well?" she said.

Had she asked him a question and he'd been too busy eyeballing her to notice? "Mmm?"

"Is there anything else we need to cover to pull off this arrangement? Skeletons in the closet? Old girlfriends I need to know about beyond Rhona?"

"Rhona was never my girlfriend."

"A one-night stand?" A disapproving look lit her eyes.

He wasn't proud of himself, but neither was he ashamed. He was a grown-ass man, free and single. He could have sex with whomever he wanted. "It was a weekend thing."

"Oh well then." Her tone was snide. "That makes all the difference."

"Who are you to judge me?" he asked.

She raised both palms. "I think you're projecting."

"Huh?"

"Don't pull that redneck cowboy stuff with me. You're sharp as a tack, Rhett Lockhart. *You're* judging you. Not me."

Yeah, probably. He threaded a hand through his hair, paced the kitchen. Impatient. Jumpy. And fully aware of her sitting so still and unperturbed, watching him like he was a patient on a psych ward observation unit.

"Go easy on yourself," she murmured. "Your life has done a complete one-eighty, and it wasn't by choice. It's okay to feel ungrounded."

Her sultry voice triggered smoky images in his head—Tara doing a striptease, rolling slowly out of her clothes, showing off that magnificent body of hers.

Holy shit, he needed to stop this. He clenched his hands.

But he could not stop the thoughts from tumbling in on him. What kind of men did she like? What kind of things did she like in bed? What would her lips taste like if he leaned over and kissed her right now?

"Rhett?"

"Huh?"

"Are you all right?"

"Fine, why?"

"You've got the weirdest look on your face. Almost as if you were—" She broke off, shook her head. Hopped to her feet.

Intrigued, he stepped closer. "Almost as if I were what?"

"Nothing." She glanced away, and her cheeks pinked as if her mind had been stirring up sexy thoughts too. Had it?

"Are you having second thoughts about this?" he asked.

She tilted her chin up, swung her gaze back to meet his again. "Aren't you? It's a big step even if it is a fake marriage, and you *are* allergic to commitment."

Friction sparked between them. Hot. Electric. Scary as hell. He wanted to turn tail and run, dying for breathing room. *Better get used to it.* They were going to be sharing a house . . . and a bed?

"Sleeping arrangements?" he asked.

"What?"

"Where will you be sleeping when we're married?"

Tara sank her hands on her hips. "Certainly not in your bed."

"Won't your family think it's weird if we have separate bedrooms?"

"They'll know it's a marriage of convenience. I won't have to prove anything to them. I'll continue to sleep on the futon in the nursery as I've been doing."

"No. *I'll* sleep in the nursery. You'll take the master."

"And you'll wake up at night to take care of Julie?"

"She *is* my daughter."

"And I'm the nurse."

He drew himself up tall. "You don't think I can handle it?"

She eyed him up and down, taking his measure. "You'll be on the road most of the time anyway."

"Which is why you should sleep in my bed."

"I'm not doing that."

"What are you getting out of this deal?" he asked, narrowing his eyes.

"I love Julie." Her eyes were bright and clear, her body language earnest. She meant it. "I spent four arduous months at her side making sure that little girl had a fighting chance at life. You've got grit and heart, but you'll most likely have to quit the PBR without me."

"And you need to be needed," he said. "It's the reason you're a nurse."

She frowned. "That's utter bullshit."

"Is it?"

"Yes."

"Why were you the one who babysat us younger kids when we were all growing up and not Ember? She was the oldest girl."

"You know Ember. She's not the warm and fuzzy type. Her babysitting style would have been to lock you in your rooms."

"My point exactly. Why were you the one to bake us cookies and play checkers with us and tell ghost stories around the campfire?"

"I enjoyed it."

"Why?"

She looked puzzled, as if no one had ever questioned her motives before. "Because it was fun."

"Why was it fun?"

"You're annoying as hell, you know that?"

"And you're avoiding the question."

"Why does it matter? I'm willing to marry you to help you get custody of your child and keep your PBR dreams alive."

"Why?"

"Why are you looking a gift horse in the mouth?" she cried, exasperated.

"Maybe I'm afraid it's a Trojan horse."

That silenced her. She sat down abruptly.

"Listen," he said, settling down, shifting gears, trying to get his mind off that sweet mouth of hers. "It *is* my business. You're putting your own life on hold for me. Why? As much as I need you, before I step into this arrangement, I have to drill down to the truth. What are you getting out of this besides being near Julie? You're her aunt-in-law. She'll always be in your life. Wouldn't your time be better spent moving on and finding a real husband?"

Doubt flicked across her face. Worry lowered her eyelids. She bit her lip, shifted her weight. Uncomfortable. He got it. He was uneasy too. Caught between a rock and a soft place that would be far too easy to sink into.

Those soft places, he'd discovered, were far more dangerous than the rocks.

Soft places lulled you to sleep. Relaxed your guard. Lured you into a false sense of security. Robbed you of your will to fight.

"I love Julie. My intentions are pure," she whispered. "I just want to help."

"We're back to why," he said. "Why me? Why Julie? Why now? What do you hope to gain?"

She shrugged, her face reddening. "Nothing."

"No expectation?"

"None."

"I don't believe that. Everyone has expectations."

"Why are you badgering me?"

He hitched in a breath and spoke the truth as he saw it. "I like you, Tara. I admire and respect you and I don't want to see you get hurt. I believe you *do* have expectations."

"Since you think you know me so well, please . . ." She waved with an exaggerated flourish. ". . . enlighten me."

"Forget me. Forget Julie. What do *you* want?" He lowered his voice, kept his eyes trained on her. They were getting somewhere. Finally. "What do you *need*?"

WHAT DID SHE need?

It was a simple enough question. Why did she find it so difficult to answer? And why was he beleaguering her to provide it?

No one had ever held her feet to the fire like this.

She danced away from the question, away from him. Picked up their coffee cups, took them to the sink, washed them out.

Rhett would not be dismissed. He followed, hovered over her as she hunched her shoulders and squirted liquid soap into the cups. "Tara?"

What did he want from her? She swished the soap with water and a kitchen cloth, cleaning as if her life depended on it.

"Tea." He had a hand on her forearm. "What do *you* need?"

The heat of his hand stilled her movements and she hitched in a jagged breath. "I don't know what you mean."

"What do you need from this relationship?"

"I told you. To be with Julie. To help you stay in the PBR—"

Gently, he removed the soapy cup from her hand, set it in the sink, took her by the shoulders, and turned her to face him. "Tara." He said her name in a kindly chiding way.

"I love taking care of people. I really do. It's what I really love." She stood there, her hands dripping soapy water, her heart beating like crazy.

He handed her a towel. She busied herself with drying off her hands, one finger at a time, avoided looking at him.

With a click of his tongue, he tilted her chin up, forcing her to meet his gaze. "I'm not going to take advantage of your goodness, Tara. I've watched people do that to you your whole life. They usually didn't do it consciously. They were clueless as to how they were abusing your giving nature, or selfishly didn't reciprocate your gifts, but I see you. I understand you."

I understand you.

Wonderful words she wanted so badly to believe in. "And what is it that you understand?"

"You think if you just do enough for people they'll recognize how lovable you are and do stuff for you in return."

His insight was a sword straight through her gut. How did he know?

"But people don't always return your love the way you expect them to."

A sudden rush of emotion pushed up her throat, tasted salty. He'd nailed it and rendered her speechless. Rhett Lockhart was much more than a kick-ass bull rider with a handsome face. He possessed unexplored depths. It made her itch to don a wet suit and do some diving.

He took her hand in his, rubbed his thumb along her knuckles. "I promise you, Tara Lynn Alzate, I won't take advantage of you.

I appreciate everything you are doing for me and Julie. For the sacrifices you are making, and I swear to be the best husband I can be."

Yes, but will you love me?

The thought was blinding, and it dropped from nowhere and scared Tara to her roots. Unnerved, she gently pulled her hand away, painted on a can-do smile, and said, "Cowboy, I think you just wrote your wedding vows."

Chapter 18

FREE HAND: The hand a bull rider does not use to grip the bull rope during a ride.

Pumped with enthusiasm, Aria put the wedding together in ten days. At this late date they weren't able to reserve either the family church or the wedding chapel Duke had built on the Silver Feather for Vivi's wedding venue business.

Instead, they held the wedding at Duke and Vivi's sprawling mansion. Father Dubanowski was willing to rearrange his schedule to officiate; after all, he'd known both Tara and Rhett from birth. The ceremony was in the garden grotto near the elaborate backyard pool, with just their families and closest friends in attendance.

They stood in front of the altar Archer had built, listening to the rock waterfall burbling in the background. It felt close-knit, communal, and slightly claustrophobic.

Standing beside Tara, Rhett looked so breathtakingly handsome, she felt drab in comparison. No matter where they went, he would attract attention like a rooster, cock-of-the-walk.

His smile was shaky, but so were Tara's hands. This was it. She was about to get married. This man would soon be her husband.

It's not real. Don't romanticize this.

But it felt real when Father Dubanowski prompted her to look into Rhett's eyes and vow to honor and cherish him to the end of her days.

"Do you have the rings?" Father Dubanowski asked.

They'd bought plain matching gold bands—no point spending a lot of money on a marriage that wouldn't last—and Tara forwent an engagement ring. Which had caused a murmur of disappointment in her family, but whatever. She wasn't doing any of this for them. Julie was her sole concern. Besides, Rhett couldn't wear the ring when he was on the circuit. He could get his finger ripped off if the ring caught on anything during a ride.

Tara darted a quick gaze toward her mother, who was holding a parasol over Julie's baby carriage situated next to her and Dad. Mom was going to keep Julie for the evening. At their families' insistence, they would spend the night at the nicest hotel in Marfa. Tara wanted to skip the wedding night plans, but Mom and Dad had paid for the honeymoon suite at the Sebastian as a surprise wedding gift.

"I know you're marrying him just to be Julie's mom," her mother had said when she'd given Tara the greeting card with the hotel reservations inside. "But you both deserve a night to remember."

Tara mumbled thanks and told her mother she appreciated the gesture, but it meant a night alone with Rhett in a swanky hotel room. She was not looking forward to it.

Ridge, who was standing behind Rhett as his best man, pulled out the golden band meant for Tara and handed it to him, while Kaia passed Rhett's wedding band to Tara.

"Rhett, repeat after me," Father Dubanowski said. "With this ring, I do thee wed."

Rhett took Tara's hand. His palm was as sweaty as her own. Together, the two of them could double as a Slip 'N Slide.

"With this ring, I do thee wed." His eyes latched on to hers, hooked her in like a cross stitch. He eased the ring onto her finger. The sunlight caught it, sent a golden shimmer over her skin.

Tara's heart slammed into her chest. This was no joke. Marriage of convenience it might be, but it was a legally binding union. Her knees wobbled, and she might have turned and bolted if not for the look on Rhett's face.

His smile beamed bright as a red helium balloon against a gloomy gray sky, looking all googly-eyed and happy, and she thought of puppies and birthday cake and Fourth of July fireworks, and her doubts just exploded.

Poof!

"With this ring, I do thee wed," she whispered, and took his hand, slipped on the ring. Now they were holding opposite hands, arms crossed in front of each other.

"By the power invested in me," Father Dubanowski said, "I now pronounce you man and wife." He closed his Bible. "Rhett, you may now kiss your bride."

Here it was. The moment Tara had been dreading since she'd cooked up this farcical idea. She'd made him promise to dole out nothing but a mere hint of a kiss, the barest brushing, the smallest increment of lip touching that they could get away with.

He'd promised.

She trusted him.

He leaned in.

She braced herself, locking her knees. *Hang on. It'll be over in an instant.*

His head dipped.

She tipped her chin up.

Rhett's mouth came down on hers, and for a second, he was playing by the rules and she sighed with relief, and thought, *Wow, this is nice . . .*

But the thought was premature.

Her lips parted involuntarily, and she closed her eyes and sank against him. Well and completely lost.

Rhett did not hesitate to take full advantage of the opening. He pushed straight for the edge. His lips soft, but firm. A deep, rumbling laugh of delight slipped from his throat.

His mouth was so sweet that Tara thought of honey, thick like treacle, and in that dizzying suspension of time and place, she completely forgot where she was and what she was doing.

Her breathing shortened, quickening against the electrical charge pulsating from him to her and back again.

She simmered inside, her body a cauldron of sensation. The kiss was an instant combustion of glitter and glory. Spiking crucial sexual pointers down her body. Hardening her nipples and softening her tender flesh. Igniting a rapid trail of rolling wildfire.

Her head whirred.

At first it was a teeny-tiny vibration, low and deep in the center of her brain. Gradually it gathered in speed, growing in intensity. A noise quite unlike anything she'd ever heard before. A vibrant drone of a million honeybees all humming at once.

Hum. Hum. Hum.

High-voltage and mind-boggling. Snappy and smart. The sound seemed to emanate from deep within the center of her head and spread throughout her body. All of it stirred and fed by Rhett's amazing mouth and tongue. Which, at the moment, were doing strange and wondrous things to her.

Overwhelmed, she sucked in her breath, trying to pull in more air, but all she got was more *him*.

Rhett. His flavor. His smell. His body heat.

Oh, this was a mistake. She knew it as surely as she knew her own name, but she would not stop him.

Instead, she pressed closer, her hips ironed against his. And the buzzing in her head grew louder still. A riotous, joyful noise.

It was true! All true!

Granny Blue's legendary humming. No denying the escalating crescendo. The noise engulfed her. Swarmed her. Along with the heat of his lips, the taste of his mouth. Kissing him was far more disorienting than she could ever have imagined.

And satisfying.

So damn satisfying.

She opened her eyes, stared into his pupils gone gigantic with lust. She curled her fingers around his biceps, bulky beneath his tuxedo. Everything about him glowed shiny and magnificent.

His kiss certainly lived up to his reputation. Mind blown.

Kablewy!

He lightened the kiss and started to straighten.

Terrified that he was going to break contact, Tara grabbed him by the collar and tugged him back down. She could feel him smiling against her mouth. She sighed and parted her teeth. He slipped his tongue right in as if it belonged there. As if it had *always* belonged there.

Tara craved him. Ached for more.

The humming in her head was a sweet hallelujah. She couldn't explain it. Didn't want to explain. All she wanted was to keep on kissing him forever and ever and ever.

Crooked thoughts. Wild and dangerous as the Chihuahuan Desert at midnight.

Starved for his vibrant touch, she drank him in like fine wine, tipsy with possibilities. He smelled so good, earthy and rich. His hazy heat seeped into her. He was hard and lean and magnificent. His hair sunlight-bleached, a beachy buckwheat brown.

A dull, relentless ache urged her to run her fingers through those silky locks. Hammered at her to pull him into the shadowy depths of poolside foliage, kiss him until both their lips were raw.

The humming in her head spurred her murky, wayward thoughts. A hubbub of sound. Turbulent and tingly.

She wanted to put on ballet shoes and pirouette around the guests on knotty toes, singing along with the intoxicating tune like some frenzied actor in a Broadway musical.

His hand moved to her nape, his fingers threading up through her hair pinned in a crisp updo. He held her close and plundered her mouth so thoroughly, their audience broke out in catcalls.

Ripped to her senses, Tara tumbled away from him. The humming faded the second his lips were gone, settling into a slow, hissing sizzle. *Hummmmmmmmm*. Until it was nothing more than a faint whisper.

She stared at his lips, gasping, her fingers pressed to her mouth. Her eyes drilling into him as he drilled into her.

People were up out of their seats, coming toward them. Clapping their backs. Shaking their hands. Offering heartfelt congratulations.

Stunned, Tara stood there, unmoving, trying to figure out what had happened to her.

Aria took her elbow, bustled her aside, while Rhett's three brothers, Ridge, Ranger, and Remington, tugged him in the opposite direction.

His gaze linked with hers again and he offered an apologetic smile across the distance and her hopes just leaped . . . *him*.

He was THE ONE.

The mate fated just for her. So said Granny's legend. So said the humming in her head. So said the riotous song in her heart.

She *loved* him.

Loved Rhett Lockhart with unbounded zeal. Had, in fact, loved him from the moment she saw him cradle his baby girl in her living room in El Paso.

This new knowledge swept through her, a brushfire of realization, burning up everything she thought she knew to be true about life and the world. Leaving her with one trembling, cockeyed thought. She'd sewed herself into marriage with a man who simply wanted someone to take care of his child while he chased the rodeo. She could have been anyone. She wasn't special to him beyond her nursing skills, her family, and her desire to help.

And that was the cross Tara seemed doomed to bear. In love with a man who'd not ever shown the slightest capacity for happily-ever-after.

TWO HOURS LATER, following the reception at Rhett and Kaia's house, Tara sat far to the opposite side of the limo, staring out her window, tension undulating off her like heat waves.

Rhett studied the back of her head. She'd yanked off the wedding veil and knotted it in her fist, clutched the fluffy lace tightly in her lap.

Her dark hair was swept up, revealing her long neck and her straight, graceful shoulders. Between them a bottle of champagne rested in a silver bucket filled with ice. Neither of them was inclined to pop the cork.

There was nothing to celebrate. Not yet. Not until he . . . er . . . they . . . got full custody of Julie. That's what this was about, after all.

Rhett's gaze dropped to Tara's left hand, which was holding on to the wedding veil with a death grip. The plain gold band looked cheap and dull against her bronze skin. She deserved a big diamond. A honking sparkler to show off to her friends. A ring that said, *I* belong *to my man.*

He'd wanted to give her such a ring, had almost bought a three-carat marquis-cut diamond behind her back. But she'd told him that was silly and impractical. He needed to save his money for things that mattered.

As if she didn't matter.

That got to him. Her practicality. Her selflessness. He wished he was more like her.

She turned her head slightly, giving him a splendid view of her profile. Straight slender nose, cheekbones cut high, smooth unlined forehead. No one would guess she was thirty-two. In fact, she looked four years younger than he, not four years older. Such good genes. What a shame that she could not have children of her own.

His heart ached for her. He imagined her pregnant, belly rounded with child, and he got the strangest feeling inside him. An intense kind of yearning he'd never experienced. It threw him more than the meanest bulls on the circuit.

Watching her, reality sank in with a weird kind of leery joy. She was his wife.

They were married.

Wife. Married. Alien words when applied to him.

Her legs were crossed at the ankle, the hem of her wedding dress rode up to reveal those smooth, shapely calves. Her delicate feet encased in bling-studded shoes that would have sent Cinderella dissolving into fits of happiness.

Except this was no fairy tale, and he was no Prince Charming.

Tara cut such a beautiful image. Any man would have been proud. *He* should have been proud. And happy. Today was his wedding day, and yet he felt as isolated as if he were stranded on a deserted island. Lonely.

Why? This was a business arrangement, efficient and uncomplicated. No emotions. No fuss. No long-term commitment. Just a mutual agreement and a binding contract, with an easy-out clause. Lamar had suggested a one-year time period and then it would be over if they wanted to end it then.

They could walk away unscathed by romance and expectations.

So why wasn't he happy?

His mind went back to the moment when Father Dubanowski had pronounced them man and wife and he'd kissed her. Her eyes had widened, and she'd pulled away roughly, as if she'd been shocked by a bolt of electricity. Granny Blue had been watching them with eagle eyes, no doubt assessing the kiss for soul mate potential.

He didn't blame Tara for distancing herself from him after the kiss. Huddling with her family, avoiding him. There was a lot of pressure. Honestly, he'd been relieved she'd put space between them. Because being that close to her stirred him in ways that he didn't fully understand. Not smart at all for a man in a sham marriage.

The limo pulled up at the Hotel Saint Sebastian in Marfa. The driver lowered the partition. Announcing the obvious to the silent backseat, he said, "We have arrived at your destination."

For the first time since they'd slid into the limousine at the Silver Feather, Tara turned to face fully forward. "Thank you."

Rhett passed the driver a tip large enough to raise Tara's eyebrows.

"Thank *you*," the man enthused.

Rhett sprang from the limo before the driver had a chance to unbuckle his seat belt, and he opened the door for his new bride. "Welcome to your honeymoon, Tara Alzate."

"*Fake* honeymoon," she mumbled under her breath as both the doorman and the valet hovered behind him, anxious to get in on the extravagant tips.

"We can still have a good time." He held his hand out for her, and she looked reluctant to take it.

"I bet you'd love that." She let go of his hand as soon as she was out of the limo.

"I didn't mean it like *that*."

"Didn't you?" Her tone was barbed. "I saw the way you were staring at me in the limo."

"How? You never once looked at me. You got eyes in the back of your head?" Playfully, he moved to examine her fancy hairdo as if searching for a second set of eyes.

She swatted him away. "Stop it," she hissed.

"Image, image," he chided. "Don't forget you're a bride on her wedding day."

She forced a smile then, but she came off looking a bit like a shark bearing down on chum. "You're working the hell out of this."

"Getting married was your idea," he reminded her.

"To help you get your daughter. *That's* it. No side benefits for you."

"Hey," he said as she swept up the sidewalk in front of him. "You can't blame a guy for trying."

She tossed her head in an I-can-and-I-do-blame-you tilt.

Whew, okay. Tonight was gonna be icy. No fun. No games. Message received. He'd had no intention of violating their agreement, but what was wrong with a little flirting? They *were* newlyweds, for crying out loud.

The valet grabbed their bags from the limo driver, and the doorman ran to hold the door open. Tara swept inside, haughty as a queen, leaving him to dole out more tips and bumble along after her. She was an expert at putting him in his place. The one woman who did not pull any punches with him.

He liked her all the more because of it. No twisting her around his pinkie. She was her own person.

Inside the building, she paused to glance around. The hotel was a new incarnation of the first Hotel Saint Sebastian built in 1886. Most everything inside the sleek architecture had been re-purposed from reclaimed materials. The original concrete floors had been burnished to a high sheen, the walls constructed from salvaged brick; the interior featured rescued marble surfaces, overhauled steel doors and counters. The old mingling with the new—paintings, sculptures, and design from world-class local artists. Marfa was vibrant with a rich and varied artistic en-clave, and it showed.

"Have you ever been here before?" Rhett asked.

"I grew up twenty miles from here. What do you think?"

Okay, dumb question. He'd asked because she was frugal and rarely splurged on herself, and the Saint Sebastian was one of the nicest hotels in the Trans-Pecos. Plus she didn't seem like the type to have rendezvous in expensive resorts.

"With a lover?" The question popped out. Damn his impul-sive tongue.

"That," she said, "is none of your business."

"I've been here too," he said. *Stop talking!*

"I have no doubts about that. I'm sure you've been here nu-merous times with numerous women."

Guilty. "Not all at the same time," he teased.

Her mouth gaped. "What?"

"The women. I didn't come here with more than one at a time. I'm not like that. I don't sleep with more than one woman

at a time. Not that I'm judging someone who does. I mean . . ."
Shut the hell up, Lockhart.

"Oh, you paragon of virtue." Her voice dripped sarcasm.

Crap. Rhett dragged a palm down his face. He was digging himself deeper with every word that he spoke. "I . . . um . . . er . . . I just meant that when I'm with a woman she has my full attention. One hundred percent."

"Is it heavy?"

Puzzled, he studied her deadpan face. "What?"

"Lugging your ego around."

Quick as a whip, he shot back. "No more than that chip on your shoulder."

Humph. She snorted.

Rhett grinned. "You can dish it out, but you can't take it, huh?"

"Mr. Lockhart, welcome back." The desk clerk looked up from where she'd been checking in another guest and beamed at him. "No need to check in. We have your credit card on file for incidentals. Silas will show you to your room."

"Your home away from home," Tara muttered.

"Snide isn't a good color on you."

Tara rolled her eyes, and when Silas, a rangy young man in a morbid black suit, appeared with a room key in his hand, she swept after him. Leaving Rhett to cock his head, smile, and watch her walk away.

"Stop staring at my butt," she called over her shoulder, garnering giggles from three women sitting in the lobby.

"We're newlyweds," he explained to the guests as he went by.

"We assumed," said one of the women with a that's-too-bad look in her eyes. "What with the wedding dress and tux and all."

"Honey." Another one of the women raised her voice to Tara as she stood waiting at the elevator beside Silas. "You're married to him now, appreciate the fact that he enjoys looking at you while you can. The honeymoon phase doesn't last all that long."

"Hey," finished the third. "If you get tired of him, you can always throw him my way. I like it when handsome men stare at my ass."

Tara, that bold and unexpected woman, raised a middle finger over the top of her head and climbed into the elevator.

Leaving Rhett to hustle fast in order to catch up.

Chapter 19

KISSING THE BULL: When a cowboy's face meets the back of the bull's head.

SERIOUSLY? Was being married to Rhett always going to be like this? Random women feeling free to ogle her husband and comment on his hotness while she was within earshot?

Tara gritted her teeth. The marriage wouldn't last for long. Why did she even care?

Why?

They'd agreed that they were free to have outside love interests as long as it was discreet. But that display in the lobby had been anything but discreet. They were on their honeymoon, for crying out loud. Not that it was a *real* honeymoon, but those voracious women didn't know that. Plus, Tara wasn't interested in anyone else.

Ouch. There it was, the pathetic truth.

She *wanted* him.

Especially after that kiss at the altar. She wanted him as her for-real husband. Dear God, why? What was wrong with her?

The hum.

She'd heard the hum.

Silliness. A legend. A fable. A fairy tale. It meant *nothing*.

Except all she had to do was just glance at his mouth and she'd hear the faint buzz of it starting in the center of her brain—the sweet, dizzying hum of love.

His kiss had completely blown her socks off. What would happen if . . . ? No way. Not going there.

You're losing it, Alzate, she scolded herself. *Get a grip.*

Silas opened the door and announced, "The honeymoon suite."

Without preamble, Rhett bent and scooped Tara into his arms.

"Ooh!" she cried, not expecting it and grabbing on to his shoulders for stability. "What are you doing?"

"Threshold, wedding night, newlyweds. It's a thing."

"But we're not—" Silas was watching, so she shut up.

Rhett carried her over the threshold, and the bellhop followed.

"Champagne." Silas motioned to the bucket of iced Dom Pérignon. "Compliments of your brothers. Shall I open it?"

Rhett, still holding on to her, cocked his eyebrows. "Should he?"

"You can do it."

"I can do it," Rhett told Silas, and set Tara on the ground. He handed a twenty-dollar tip to the bellhop. Silas thanked him profusely and scooted from the room. The door shut behind him.

Click.

Alone.

Just the two of them. There was no one else around to act as a buffer.

Their eyes met. Her heart took a running jump into her throat. "You gotta stop overtipping," Tara said. "You need to be putting money aside for Julie."

"It's our honeymoon."

Tara tapped her foot. "It's not real, and I'm trying to make a point here."

"So am I."

She curled her fingers into her hips. "And what is that?"

"You only live once."

"That attitude is what got you into a marriage of convenience."

"Tara." His voice was gravel. "You gotta stop lecturing me. I have my own way of doing things. They might not be your methods, but they work for me." He slammed his gaze into hers. "Got it?"

In the moment of his manly forcefulness, she wanted nothing

more than to rip his clothes off his body and ravish him. Gak! What was wrong with her?

You heard the hum. He's yours!

Her heart took a roller-coaster loop. "I'm—"

He stepped closer, his walk loose but calculated, intentionally encroaching on her personal space. "Time and again I've proven to you that I've changed, and yet you keep seeing me as the doofus kid I was and not the man I've become. You need to stop talking down to me."

"I don't—"

"It's your default mode, I get it, but it's time to stop that behavior."

She felt her jaw drop. "I . . . I . . ."

"What do you want to say, woman?"

She gulped, forced a smile, and swept a hand at her dress. "I'm going to change out of this pouf."

"I see." He nodded, jammed his hands into his pockets, and lifted his shoulders to his ears.

Tara escaped to the bathroom before she did something she couldn't undo. "Real mature," she muttered at her reflection in the mirror, her heart still beating faster than it should. What on planet Earth was happening to her?

It's the hum, darling, she heard Granny Blue's voice in her head. *When it grabs you, you're gone and there's nothing you can do to change it.*

Oh, that couldn't be right. She was a progressive modern woman. She did not have to believe in fables and superstitions.

She stared down at her fingernails, manicured bright red. She rarely polished her nails, usually kept them cut short. That worked best in her job as a NICU nurse. But Aria had insisted on treating her to the manicure, complete with artificial nails. She couldn't have felt less like herself.

There was a knock on the bathroom door.

"What is it?" she asked.

"I've got your suitcase here. I thought you might need something to change into, unless you've decided to make this into a real wedding night. Just wanted to let you know I'm game if you are."

She flung open the door, snatched the small suitcase out of his hands, and slammed the door again. Heard him chuckle.

Trying her best to look anything but sexy, she scrubbed her face clean of makeup and unpinned her hair. The only thing remaining of her glamorous new self was the fingernails. She planned on putting on the unsexiest pajamas she could find, which she'd bought just for tonight. That ought to dampen his ardor.

But when she opened the suitcase, instead of the clothes she'd packed, Tara found pair after pair of Daisy Duke shorts. She dug deeper, pushing aside the Daisy Dukes in a myriad of denim colors—blue, purple, green, red, white.

Immediately, she knew who was behind this.

Aria.

Tara grabbed her phone, texted her sister. What did U do?

No answer.

"Argh." Tara stabbed her fingers through her hair. Aria was so going to pay for this. She went through the suitcase again. G-string panties that she had *not* brought. Teeny crop tops that matched the Daisy Dukes. And absolutely nothing else. What was she supposed to sleep in?

Except, wait . . . there, something in the outside pocket.

She held her breath and unzipped the side pocket, rummaged around, felt silk. Yes! She pulled out the lingerie equivalent of Daisy Dukes. Black lace baby-doll pajamas.

"You are so dead, little sister." She seethed.

"Did you say something?" Rhett called from the bedroom suite.

Crap! She had no choice. She had to either put the wedding dress back on, wear a pair of the Daisy Dukes and a crop top, or don the baby-doll pajamas. Maybe there were bathrobes in the closet and she could put one on when she got out of here.

Why hadn't she changed for the reception? Oh yeah, Aria had kept going on and on about how beautiful she looked, and it would be the only time she'd get to wear the wedding dress, yada, yada . . .

Tara picked up the phone again. Get over here with my clothes, right now!!!

Nothing.

Dammit. She could text her parents, but they were looking after Julie. Kaia and Ridge were putting their kids to bed, and she couldn't expect them to drive the forty-five minutes from the Silver Feather to Marfa.

She was stuck, and Aria knew that when she'd repacked Tara's suitcase.

Disgruntled, she texted Aria a gif of a fox squeezing a goose by the neck. The goose's eyes were popping out.

A gentle knock at the door. "Tara? You okay?"

"I'm fine."

"You sure? You've been in there a long time."

Huffing, Tara picked up a pair of Daisy Dukes and a matching crop top, dressed quickly, and yanked the door open. "Do I look okay to you?"

"Holy smokes!" Rhett took a step back, his eyes lit like a roaring forest fire. He was still in his tuxedo, but his tie was loosened, and the top button of his shirt was undone.

"I did not bring these." She reached for the suitcase, grasped a handful of Daisy Dukes. "This is all the clothes I have in my suitcase."

He wasn't looking at the short-shorts in her hands. His gaze was fixed on her thighs at the level of the skimpy hem.

She dropped the clothes, snapped her fingers at her temple. "Excuse me? My eyes are up here."

Like a man coming out of a fog, he blinked and met her gaze, but slid another quick glance down at her legs, before bouncing back up to her eyes again. "Aria?"

"She repacked my bag."

He grinned.

"It's not funny."

He was looking at her as if she were an ice cream sundae with a cherry on top. "It's kind of funny."

"I can't go around like this."

His grin widened. "Why not?"

"It's embarrassing."

"Tea, you've got *nothing* to be embarrassed about."

"Mothers shouldn't go around looking like this. I'm officially Julie's stepmom now." That brought a thrill and reminded Tara of why she was here in the first place.

"It's behind closed doors. Just me and you." His voice deepened on *you*.

Tara gulped. "You'll be staring at me all night."

"Is that so bad?"

"I'm putting the wedding dress back on." She started to shut the door, but he quickly jammed his foot between the door and the wall. If he kept staring at her as if she were the Hope Diamond, she might end up doing something she'd regret.

"C'mon. I have the champagne poured." He motioned to the coffee table, where two glasses of champagne bubbled effervescently. "I want to toast those legs." He cast another wolfish grin at her thighs. "The best legs in the Trans-Pecos."

"You have to stop flirting with me."

"Why?" he asked, looking genuinely confused. One corner of his mouth quirked up in a playboy grin that set her heart pounding erratically. What would her cardiac rhythm look like on an ECG? Could too much sexy cause a myocardial infarction? Because right now, it felt as if her heart was about to pop out of her chest.

"Because we have an understanding. A rule," she said, curt and to the point. "A no-sex clause."

"Tea," he drawled, his gaze bearing down on her. "You

should know by now that I'm not the kind of guy who plays by the rules."

"WE . . . WE HAD a deal." Sweat pearled at the cute little scoop between her nose and upper lip, and he had a powerful urge to lick it off.

But he'd promised to keep his hands to himself. Never mind those little short-shorts were driving him bonkers. It wasn't her doing. The only way he would take his new bride to bed was if she initiated it. She'd set those rules, and he'd agreed to them. She was the only one who could break them.

"There's always room for negotiations." He reached up and pulled his tie off, watched her track his movements. Saw her gulp.

Twice.

Oh yeah, she wanted him. He hid his smile.

"Have some champagne," he said, nodding at the flute on the dresser beside him. "It *is* our wedding night."

"No, thank you." She hugged herself. Shivered.

"All right." He settled down on the couch, crossed his legs at the ankle, and picked up his glass of champagne. Noticed her nipples beaded up tight beneath her shirt and bra. "More for me."

"I trust you'll sleep on the chaise." She moved to stare out the window, just as she'd done in the limo, turning her back to him. Giving him a fantastic view of her cute ass.

"Nope."

Her shoulders marshaled up to her ears and she let out an exasperated sigh. Swiveled her head to glare at him. "You can't go changing everything on me now. We had an agreement. No sex between us."

"I'm not going to do anything to you that you don't want me to do."

The muscle at her jaw twitched.

"But I'm not sleeping on this hard chaise"—he put emphasis

on the word "hard," watched her jaw flicker again—"when there is a soft king-sized bed we can share."

"I—"

"Don't worry," he said. "I won't touch you." *Unless you ask me to.*

"You're being unreasonable."

"No, my dear Tea, you are."

"Don't do that," she said.

"What?"

"Use terms of endearment."

"Why not?"

She nibbled a thumbnail. "I like it too much, and I know you don't mean anything by it. We're not a forever couple."

"Aw," he said. "Tea, you worry too much."

She folded her arms, and he wondered if she knew the gesture brought her breasts up higher. He was enjoying the view, so he decided not to tell her.

"In your laid-back way," she said, "you're never braced for the fall when it comes. My way, if I worry about things that don't come true, I'm relieved and don't get blindsided."

"And you never fully enjoy the here and now." He held out the second glass of champagne toward her. "Enjoy the moment, Tea."

"Bull-rider wisdom?"

"Rhett wisdom."

"That sounds like an oxymoron to me."

"Barb me all you want. I love that tart tongue." He waggled the glass at her.

"I should have known that anyone dumb enough to crawl onto the back of a bull would be in love with my greatest flaw." She snatched the champagne from his hand and downed half of it in one swallow.

Rhett was impressed. "Snippiness is not your greatest flaw."

She leveled him a go-to-hell look.

He laughed. He knew this crusty exterior was a ruse to hide her vulnerable heart.

"So, enlighten me. What is my greatest flaw?"

"Pretzel girl."

"What?"

"You twist and bend and change yourself to please whoever you're with."

She looked chagrined. "And that's a bad thing?"

"We don't need to label things as good or bad. I'm just pointing out that you tend to live your life for other people instead of for yourself."

"That's called altruism."

"It's called not looking out for your own best interest."

She downed the rest of the champagne. He cleared his throat, lifted his eyebrows at her.

"What?" she said. "It's my wedding night. I'm allowed to get a little tipsy. That champagne is damn good, by the way."

"Should be. It cost a hundred dollars a bottle."

"What!" Her eyes flew wide. "Your brothers are insane."

"Welcome to the Lockhart family. We don't play by anyone's rules."

"What have I gotten myself into?" she muttered, but she smiled a soft little smile that told him she was secretly pleased to be part of his gang of rabble-rousers.

"I'm ordering room service," he said. "What would you like?"

"I'll have whatever you're having."

"No, no. You don't get to do that."

"Do what?"

"Change yourself to please me. I'm ordering a steak. What do you want?"

"Do they have tacos?"

He leafed through the room service menu. "Chicken or beef?"

"Chicken," she said.

"Good for you." He picked up the phone.

"While you do that, I'll FaceTime with Mom and see how Julie is."

He called for food. She called her mother. When he finished

ordering, he came to sit beside Tara and waved to Julie as his mother-in-law—*mother-in-law*, now that felt weird to say— held the baby up for them to see her.

Pure happiness washed over him, and Rhett felt like he was the luckiest man alive.

The food arrived, and they ended the call. They ate and watched an animated movie, Pixar's latest, just to have something to do. The tension between them was palpable.

When the movie was over, he said, "I have a feeling many more movies like this are in our future."

"The baby in the show made me miss Julie."

"Me too. You wanna go home and get her?" he asked.

"I'd like nothing more." She sighed. "But it's already ten o'clock. By the time we got to Mom's and picked her up and made it back home, it would be after midnight. Too late to be dragging Julie out in the night air."

"Good point."

"Plus we've been drinking."

"We had one glass before dinner and a movie. The alcohol has worn off."

"You want some more champagne?" she asked.

"Why not?"

She got up from the couch and refilled their champagne flutes, brought them back, handed one to him. "We didn't toast before."

He held up his glass. "To Julie, the best thing that ever happened to us."

She clinked her rim against his, echoed, "To Julie."

"She is awesome." Rhett heard his voice turn sappy and he didn't feel the least bit guilty for it.

"The sweetest little thing."

"I wonder what her personality is going to be like," he mused.

"I hope she's laid-back like you," Tara said. "Life is easier when you don't take it too seriously."

"Happy-go-lucky has its downside."

She lowered her lashes. "And what is that?"

"People never take you seriously."

She turned to kneel on the couch cushions facing him. Her eyes shiny. The champagne was getting to her already. "*I take you seriously.*"

"You do not." He hooted.

"Yes, I do." She bobbed her head. "Why do you think I asked you to marry me? I couldn't risk you taking Julie away from me."

"You really do love her, don't you?"

Her dark eyes drilled straight into his. "You have no idea."

"Thank God for you," he said, emotions sprouting everywhere. "I'm so glad you were there for her when I couldn't be."

"Me too."

"I can never make that up to you, Tea."

Tara yawned, stretched. "It's been a big day and I'm exhausted. You take the bed. I'll stay on the chaise."

"Tara," he said. "I promise if we share the bed, nothing untoward will happen. Trust me."

"Oh," she said. "It's not you I don't trust. It's me."

That pulled him up straight. "You *want* something to happen?"

"I'm so hot for you I can't stand it," she whispered.

"It's just the champagne talking."

She shook her head. "No, it's not."

"So . . ." His hopes flickered like a flame. "Do you wanna . . . ?"

"More than anything." She hitched in a big breath. "But we can't."

"Because . . . ?"

"I can't handle it. If I ever . . . if we ever, well, I know there would be no going back."

"Meaning?"

"I'm a one-man woman and you're a whatever-woman-is-in-my-bed-for-the-night kind of man."

"I never had a woman worth being faithful to before," he said, surprised by his admission and the tight clutch of his chest.

"And you think I'm the one woman for whom you can change your ways?"

He held her gaze, didn't blink. "I do."

"Why?" she whispered. "Because I love your daughter?"

"That's part of it."

"What's the other part?" she whispered.

"You're gorgeous as hell."

"Pfft." She swatted the air as if she were waving off flies. "You've had hundreds of beautiful women."

"Not hundreds."

"Okay, dozens."

"Forget them. You're all that matters now."

"But why me?"

"You hold my feet to the fire and make me a better man."

"No one ever did that for you before?"

"My mom." He shrugged. "But I lost that when I was eight."

"Is that why you go through women like carnival rides? You lost your mom, and now you can't trust anyone to have your back?"

"No one's ever had my back before, Tara. Women just want to be with me because I'm fun, have money, and grandstand on the back of a bull. But none of that stuff impresses you. Why not?"

"Because that's all surface stuff, Rhett. I want a man I can count on."

"And I can't be that guy?"

"This isn't a love match."

"Maybe not at first, but that doesn't mean it can't grow into one. It's definitely a like match," he said, too afraid to tell her his feelings ran far deeper than that. What if she didn't feel the same way? "I like you. A lot. And I admire you more than I can say."

She laughed. "That's quite eloquent. Being a husband suits you."

"Tara," he said. "*You're* what suits me."

She inclined her head, her hair falling softly against her cheek. "What are we doing here, Rhett?"

"You mean at this hotel or—"

"Our goal is to get permanent custody of Julie. That's where our focus needs to be."

"Shouldn't it be on creating a loving family for Julie?"

"Custody comes first."

"Unless Rhona comes back, we're going to get custody."

"But that's why we're doing this. To make sure we get custody whether Rhona comes back or not."

"And that's why you and I need to make sure we're on solid ground."

"What are you saying?" Tara whispered.

He met her gaze, held it. "I don't want to have any secrets from you."

Chapter 20

BOOT THE BULL: A term used to mean a particular bull can be spurred.

TARA bit her bottom lip. Secrets? What secrets was he keeping from her?

Rhett got up and poured another glass of champagne. Nodded at her. "Another?"

She shook her head, put her palm over the top of her glass.

He was still in his tuxedo slacks and dress shirt, the sleeves rolled up to his elbow. Such a sexy look. "Scooch over."

She scooched, and he sat down beside her. Rested his hand on her bare knee. It felt warm and heavy. She liked it. "What secrets?" she asked.

Pausing, he met her gaze, his eyes sincere. "Don't panic. It's nothing terrible. It's just something I've never told anyone, but I feel like I need to get it off my chest."

"Not even your brothers?"

"Especially not them. They're all so accomplished. Ridge is the rich ambitious one. Ranger's the smart one. Remington is the brave one, and I was the screw-up."

"That's not true."

"Yeah, it is. I was the clown. The one who would do anything on a dare. The joker . . . the joke."

She reached out and touched his forearm, offering moral support. "That's not the way I see you."

He rewarded her with the most grateful look. "No?"

She smiled at him, reached up to tuck a strand of shaggy curl behind his ear. "In my eyes, you are the bold one. The quick one. The charming, confident one. The one who doesn't let life eat up his soul. If I had to marry a Lockhart, I'm so happy it was you."

"Considering two of your sisters are married to my brothers, I'm not sure that's a huge compliment." He laughed, a self-effacing sound.

"Thank you for trusting me enough to tell me what you're about to tell me."

His face sobered, and he set down his champagne. "Now I'm rethinking my true confessions. I'm afraid you'll think less of me."

"We all have things we're ashamed of," she murmured.

"Woman," he said, "you're a breath of fresh air."

"Even with my tart tongue?"

"Oh yes. I *love* that tongue."

Love. If only he loved her the way she loved him. Was it too much to hope that he could fall in love with her? Too much to wish for? But she wished it anyway.

Feet planted solidly on the floor, he spread his legs, dropped his elbows on his knees, interlaced his fingers, and rested his chin on his joined hands. He stared at the champagne glass on the coffee table in front of him.

Rhett looked so sad that Tara wanted to gather him to her chest, rock him in her arms, and tell him that everything was going to be all right. Instead, she sat quietly, waiting for him to continue. Feeling like it was something monumental he was about to reveal.

"Rhona wasn't the only woman I got pregnant."

The news was not startling. She'd already suspected this was the direction where his story was headed. "Your high school sweetheart?" she guessed, remembering that long-ago night in the Lockharts' barn where they'd shared beers and broken hearts.

"Yes. I was seventeen. Brittany was sixteen. We were each other's firsts."

"Really?"

"You sound surprised."

"I figured you'd lost your virginity in middle school."

"Nope. Seventeen. Brittany Fant. And Tea, I was *happy* when she told me she was preggers. Scared, sure, but happy. I thought finally something that belongs to me."

She placed two fingers over her mouth, her thumb resting against her jaw, the last two fingers curled underneath her chin. From the way he was seated, she couldn't see his face, but she heard the pain in his voice. Saw his shoulders knot beneath his crisp white shirt.

"I wanted to marry her, have the baby. It was a stupid idea. I know that now, but at the time?" His head shook vigorously. "I couldn't forgive her for not fighting back when her mother took her to the abortion clinic."

"Oh, Rhett." Tara leaned over to massage his shoulders. Her breast brushed up against his hard, sinewy muscles. "I am so sorry. You must have been devastated."

"That's why I dropped out of high school and went on the circuit. Those bulls kept me from losing my ever-loving mind. I pushed myself hard, probably my teenage way of punishing myself. But it paid off." His laugh was hollow. "If I'd married Brittany, I'd probably be working as a ranch hand for my family on the Silver Feather."

"Did you love her?"

"I thought I did." He shrugged, turned his head, met her eyes. "But now . . . I realize it was just infatuation."

She swallowed hard. What had that look meant? She pressed her thumbs into the knots under his skin, kneaded with the right amount of pressure.

He groaned, a feels-so-good sound that turned her on. "Tara."

"Rhett."

"I feel like we're in *Gone with the Wind*." He laughed.

"Frankly, my dear, I *do* give a damn," she quipped. "Maybe

I should have named Julie Scarlett instead. If I'd but known you were her father maybe I would have."

"God," he said. "You are amazing."

"Not too shabby yourself, mister. You've been through the wringer and survived. You should be proud of yourself."

"I'm just proud that you're proud of me." He paused, said, "Wife."

Wife. The word so delicious and hopeful.

They stared into each other's eyes, longing surging between them, strong as an electrical current.

"I want a real marriage," Rhett said. "I don't want to sleep with anyone else, and I sure as hell don't want you to either. I want sex with *you*. I don't want out of this marriage after a year. I want this to last, *us* to last. I want us to build a real family with Julie."

Tara gasped. She wanted the same things but had been too afraid to voice her wishes in case he wasn't on the same page. "What about the prenup?"

"We tear it up." He gulped. "That is, if you feel the same way."

"Are you sure?"

"I've never been more certain of anything."

"When the buckle bunnies come knocking at your door—"

"I've had that life. I don't want it anymore. I mean it. Once this season is over, whether I win the championship or not, I'm quitting the PBR."

"What will you do for a living?"

"I've been giving that some thought and it occurred to me to start a bull-riding school. I think I'd be pretty good at it."

"You'd be brilliant at it," she said. "You should do it."

"Does that mean you'll come along for the ride?" His smile was tight, fearful. She could read his expression. He'd gone out on a limb and was terrified she'd saw it off.

"It would be the greatest honor of my life."

The next thing she knew, she was in his arms, and he was

kissing her like happily-ever-after in some romantic movie, and her head was filled with the sound of a million bees humming.

The One. The One. The One.

"Rhett." Tara murmured his name low and sultry, her thick, dark hair falling straight to the middle of her back, shimmering in the light from wall sconces on either side of the bed. Her lashes lowered seductively over those alluring chestnut eyes, so sophisticated, and yet simultaneously so winningly naive.

Was this the right time? They'd had a lot of champagne. Emotions were running high. Maybe he should give her some time to think about this before they did something that could not be erased.

Tilting her head, she examined him in that clinical way of hers, a hint of a smile brushing the corners of her mouth.

Sonofagun, but he was a lucky man.

She unstitched him in a way no other woman had, and he'd been with a lot of women. She could completely dismantle him with one of her long, lingering looks.

He burned for her. In every corner of his body, every nook, every cranny, he ached for her. But his blazing sex drive was not what scared him.

Lust, he could deal with. But these feelings blistering through him? They were much bigger than simple desire. This woman, above all others, possessed the ability to hurl him over the cliff of madness. He was that hot for her.

That much in love with her.

He was terrified that she did not feel the same way. That she was agreeing to this because she loved Julie, not him so much.

Her scent was in the air. A womanly fragrance that drove him wild. Her body heat. She could have doubled as a radiant heater.

Tara touched him. One fingertip. On his chin.

That was all it took for Rhett to get harder than he had in his entire life. His erection throbbed painfully against his zipper.

A groan tore from his mouth, so rough and feral, it shocked him. *Please don't let her change her mind now.* He didn't think he could survive another night without being inside her.

"Are you sure?" His voice was a raspy croak. "Are you sure this is what you want?"

In answer, she leaned in and flicked her hot, wet tongue over his lips.

He inhaled so sharply that he couldn't immediately exhale. His breath was trapped in a nether land of hope and suspense. What was coming next?

For weeks he'd been dreaming of a moment just like this. The two of them all alone and eager for each other. He hadn't been with anyone since he'd walked into her duplex. He'd told himself it was because of Julie. But he'd been lying. Tara was the reason he hadn't invited any of those eager buckle bunnies back to his trailer. He hadn't been the slightest bit interested. Those girls all seemed vapid and silly now. Immature and impulsive. Just like he'd been.

He was ready for something more. Something bigger. Something long-term and meaningful. He was ready to be a husband. And that realization made him laugh.

"What's so funny?" she whispered. "Let me in on the joke."

"No joke," he said. "I'm just so damn happy to be here with you that I can't contain myself. I want to laugh and laugh and laugh."

"Me too." Her eyes were soft, but her fingers were quick. Working the buttons of his shirt, nimble as a spider. One second his shirt was buttoned to the top, the next second it was drifting to the floor behind him.

One of her hands cupped his jaw, the other slipped to the snap of his trousers.

He grabbed the wrist of her hand at his zipper. "Whoa, slow down. We have all night."

"I haven't . . ." She panted. "Had sex since Kit died."

That stilled him. "That was over two years ago."

She looked a bit embarrassed. "Sex has never been a big deal for me . . ." She eyed him. "Until now. Until you."

"Wow," he said.

"Don't get me wrong, I *like* sex. I've just never been particularly driven by my urges."

"Putting the needs of others first again," he said, thrilling to all the things he wanted to show her, teach her about having fun in bed. "We're changing that tonight."

"Meaning . . ."

"Tea." He leaned in to press his mouth against her ear and whispered, "You're gonna *come* first."

The hum filled her head, filled every part of her as Rhett's mouth claimed hers. She reeled with lust for him. She'd not had much luck with oral sex. Kit had been clumsy and sloppy, and she'd found it more of an irritation than a turn-on, but at the thought of Rhett going down on her, she shivered.

The man knew his way around the female body; she had little doubt that he knew what he was doing. Maybe she would discover what all the fuss was about.

Already she was moist in all the right places, blood throbbing low in her belly, heat spreading between her legs.

She was fascinated by the pressure of his body flattened against hers and his sexy brown eyes that seemed to peek directly into her soul. His mouth moved from her lips to her chin, his fingers stroking her skin.

His lips kissed the column of her throat. His hands slipped her top off, dropped it to the floor on top of his shirt. She felt it rather than saw it. She was too busy reveling in his hot, wet kisses. She wanted him so badly that her entire body shook like lava. She was alarmed by the scale of her desire, but her fear blanched in comparison to the terror she felt at the risk of doing anything that would cause him to stop.

He stroked her breast with soft fingertips, his tongue at the hollow of her throat. "It's okay," he said. "Just let me take care of your pleasure."

Tara squeezed her eyes so tight that she saw little flares of white light, felt herself go limp against him. Let go in a way she'd never been able to let go before. Trusting him.

"That's right, Tea." He breathed and waltzed her to the bed.

Slowly, he slipped her Daisy Dukes off, along with her white cotton panties. She wished like hell she'd gone to Victoria's Secret, bought something red, skimpy, and lacy for his enjoyment.

"I'm sorry about the panties," she said. "I wore them with the no-sex clause in mind."

"You think the granny panties put me off you? You could wear a tow sack, Tara, and still be the most beautiful woman I've ever seen."

She knew she was pretty enough, but she certainly wasn't a beauty. But the way he said it, the way he looked at her, she believed that *he* found her beautiful, and that was all she needed.

Still in his trousers, he sat down on the bed. She felt exposed in her nakedness; she moved her hands to cover her breasts.

"Don't be embarrassed with me," he said, and gently moved her hands away. "I'm your husband."

Husband. Was that the sweetest word in the English language or what?

He wrapped his knee around her leg, used it to lug the lower half of her body over his. She lifted slightly so he could scoot them both closer to the center of the bed. Kissed her again and set off a fresh round of humming.

"You are so beautiful," he repeated.

Her heart skipped a beat. His face filled with wonder, fascination, love and sex and her. He was so strong, so masculine, so male. His hair was tousled, and his lips were wet from kissing her. He loved her. That was clear. He was in love with her. He hadn't said it, but she could see it in him.

"Oh . . . Rhett . . ." she whispered. She closed her eyes, unable to bear the intensity of his gaze.

He burned kisses between her breasts. Suckled her nipples, first one and then the other. His hands were doing sensual things to her body; there was magic in his fingertips.

He stopped for a moment and she opened her eyes, saw the raw insanity of his need flashing in his dark eyes just before he kissed her in the sweet, moist place between her legs.

She spread herself wider for him, felt her pulse quicken and her breath thin.

His lips were fueled by hunger and love. As soon as his mouth was on her heated inner lips, the hum grew to more than just a sound. It was energy—pounding, pulsating, electrical. Vibrating throughout every cell in her body. Jolting her like a shock.

A thrill swooped through her as his big hand slipped to her lower back and pressed her pelvis against his. Their bodies welding them together. She felt his erection through his pants, large and hard and throbbing.

She kept thinking about what he'd said. *I want a real marriage. I want us to build a real family with Julie.* It was the most seductive thing anyone had ever said to her.

Woozy, she felt as if she were being flung out into black space, weightless, airless. *I'm in love with this man* was all she could think, surrendered herself to the power of his magnificent mouth. Melted into the bed, into his palm that still rested at the small of her back, anchoring her.

His mouth was everywhere. Moving, kissing, licking, sucking. Her world narrowed to the triangle between her legs and the miracle of his bold tongue. This man was an adventurer. He didn't hold back. He tackled everything in life with verve and gusto, and she was the lucky, lucky beneficiary of his trailblazing.

He consumed her. The headlong dash of pleasure stunned her senses, ambushed her in every way possible.

"Oh Rhett, oh yes!" She entangled her fingers in his hair, holding him in place right where he was.

He laughed against her skin, his hot mouth devouring her. The feel of his tongue thrusting inside her was beyond ecstasy.

Within minutes she was tingling and quivering and crying out, "Rhett, Rhett, Rhett." And in that exceptional moment when she experienced the biggest orgasm of her life, Tara's mind separated from her body and she was nothing but a giant, pulsating hum of sheer sexual energy.

The encounter was so otherworldly, it was as if she were watching herself from inside a long, dark tunnel and at the end was bright, white light. He was that light. Drawing her into his arms. Holding her close. Kissing her forehead. Tucking her tightly against him. He was so loose and easy. Relaxed and free.

And exactly everything she'd never known she needed.

"God, Tea." He breathed. "That was . . . you are . . . simply amazing."

Her mind, still floating from her body, watched herself wind her arms around his neck and hold on tight as if her very life depended on him.

Chapter 21

BEAR DOWN: To ride with maximum effort, giving it one hundred and ten percent.

RHETT didn't know much, but he knew one thing for certain. He wanted Tara as his forever wife and he wasn't going to stop until he convinced her that this marriage was as real as any other.

What they'd just done was a great start toward cementing their status as man and wife, but he had more tricks up his sleeve and he wasn't planning on slacking up until dawn.

Tara was studying him from the crook of his arm, her head thrown back, her eyes on his face. She was completely naked. He was still wearing his trousers and socks. At some point, he'd kicked off his shoes, although he didn't even recall doing it.

She reached up to stroke the slight crook in the bridge of his nose. "You broke it."

"More than once."

"You've got a dangerous job."

"I know."

"There's a long time between now and November. Who's to say you'll come out unscathed?"

"Are you worried about me?"

"Yes."

"I promise not to get hurt."

"As if you have any control over it. Those bulls are the ones in charge."

"A fella can't always control life. Sometimes you just have to take what comes."

"I do find that sexy, how troubles just roll right off your back."

"Tell me more," he said, playing with her hair. "What else do you find sexy about me?"

"The way you give everything you do one hundred and ten percent."

"That's because I don't do very many things," he drawled. "Bull riding and . . ."

"Sex."

"Well, now that you mention it . . ." He tickled her cheek with his fingertips.

She shivered. "Why don't you get out of those pants, cowboy, and give a hundred and ten percent to your new bride."

"Lordy, woman, you are brazen."

"Don't pretend you don't like it."

"No, ma'am."

"And stop with the 'ma'am' stuff. Just because I'm four years older doesn't mean I want to feel four years older."

"Pfft," he said. "Age is nothing. You're in the prime of your life, Mrs. Lockhart."

"Mrs. Lockhart," she murmured. "I like the sound of that."

"Me too." He kissed the V of her hairline at her forehead. "I love your widow's peak."

She put her fingers over the spot he'd kissed. "So did my grandfather. I inherited it from him. No one else in the family has one."

"You were pretty close with your grandfather."

"I was his favorite."

"Maybe because of the widow's peak?"

"Maybe."

"I love how smooth your skin is. No freckles or blemishes."

"I'm getting crow's-feet."

"You mean these sweet little laugh lines?" He kissed her temple beside the corners of her eyes. "Beauty marks."

"I can see why women fall over you," she said. "You are full of charming baloney."

"It's not baloney," he said. "It's how I see you."

Her cheeks colored, and she seemed embarrassed by that. She trailed her fingers down his abdomen to the waistband of his pants. She'd already unbuttoned them earlier, and the band gaped wide at her touch.

"Are you trying to distract me?" he asked.

"I'm interested to see what's inside there."

"You wanna see me naked?"

"I do."

"Well, why didn't you say so?" He slipped off the end of the mattress, stood. She peered up at him, a mischievous smile lighting up her eyes. He'd never seen anything sexier.

He yanked off his pants and underwear in one swift move, saw both her eyes and her smile widen. He crawled back onto the mattress with her. She opened to him, knees splayed. He ran his hands up the sides of her legs, to her thighs and then her hips. Her soft belly was warm and quivering against his lips. He planted a row of kisses up to her straining nipples.

Her feminine fragrance dazzled his senses. She smelled like wildflowers after a summer shower. Her scent stirred memories of picnics and treehouses, of cold watermelon and homemade ice cream, of family parties, Sunday school socials, and car trips to the springs at Balmorhea.

He swept his hand lower, caressing her silky skin with this thumb, slipping it between her legs. She was slick with desire. He eased his thumb back and forth over her alert womanhood throbbing with heat and energy.

Audibly, Tara inhaled on a gasp and her body went rigid. He'd struck gold.

She was wet and ready for him. So wet.

His erection swelled so big and hard, he thought he might pass out from the pressure. God, he needed release. Needed *her*.

He trembled, starved for her. It was all he could do not to plunge into her without preamble, desperate and deep.

"Condoms?" she whispered, reading his mind.

Stopping the action for a moment, he hopped off the bed, raced to his overnight bag on the floor where Silas had left it. Dug around until he found the packet of condoms he kept in his luggage. He got a complete physical annually, but with Tara, he wasn't about to take any chances. One day, when they were sure they were safe, he would ride bareback with his beloved. Until that time, he was taking all precautions. He wasn't about to pass something dangerous to her.

He returned to the bed. She took the condom from his shaking hand, opened it with her teeth and a low, fierce growl. Then she took him into her hand and rolled the condom on.

She stroked him, slow and firm, with one hand. With the other hand, she cupped his balls in her palm.

He hissed in a hot breath. "That feels so damn good, but you're going to have to stop that if you want me to last more than eight seconds."

She giggled, and the sound sent delight bucking down his spine. "Eight seconds is fine for me—for the first time."

"My, my, someone is desperate."

"From the size of that hard-on, it's you."

"Guilty as charged. Put the cuffs on me, Officer."

"Do you have handcuffs?" She sounded intrigued.

"Alas, not with me. That kind of horseplay will have to wait until we're home."

"Ooh, fun." She clapped. "I've never played cops and robbers. At least not since I've been grown."

"We've got lots of things to explore, you and me."

"I can't wait to see what you've got in store."

"I don't want to oversell myself, but I am pretty good." He winked.

"Put your money where your mouth is, buckaroo."

"You like poking the bull."

Her chin shot up, happy and defiant. "So what if I do?"

"You're asking for a tickling, missy." He wriggled his fingers at her.

She squealed.

He pounced.

They wrestled in the bed. He caught her in a light headlock. Held her down while she squirmed against him. Nibbled her earlobe.

"Oh dear God, what is that? I call foul."

"Am I hurting you?" Immediately, he let go.

"No, no, you play dirty. Distracting me with your advanced sex techniques. Whatever you were doing sent tingles through my entire body."

"Well, c'mere, and I'll do it again." He covered her in ravenous kisses.

She giggled again and inched back. He loved it when she giggled, since she rarely did. His serious wife was feeling carefree tonight, and he loved it.

He went to work on her earlobe again, biting with just the right amount of pressure that had her writhing and panting in no time.

"Please, Rhett," she begged. "Let's just do it."

"You want me?"

"You know I do." She wrapped her hands around his shaft and he was done teasing her.

They were both primed and ready, and he slid into her warm, welcoming home.

She gasped and sank her fingers into his shoulders as he shifted and slipped deeper inside her. She squeezed him tight with her inner muscles, and then he was the one gasping.

He clenched his jaw.

His new bride was frisky, moving and shaking, massaging his backside with strong fingers. His entire body contracted, tension-filled and lucid.

Rhett slipped his palms underneath her lower back, grabbed hold of her lush butt, pulled her closer, diving in as deeply as he could go. She wrapped legs around his waist, her body surrounding his. He cradled her face in his palms, stared into her eyes.

She clasped her hands around his upper arms, dug fingers into his biceps. "Oooh," she cried, and her eyes gawked gauzily as if she were staring into the mysteries of his soul.

He wondered then about her family's strange legend, and if she heard the humming when she kissed him. She hadn't mentioned it, so probably she had not. He felt sadly disappointed, even though he didn't believe in the silly notion of humming heads when an Alzate woman kissed her true love. Aria had assured him she had not heard a peep when she'd kissed him.

Rhett shook his head. Why the hell was his mind wandering when he had the most amazing woman underneath him? *Get your head back in the game, cowboy.*

Tara snaked her arms around his neck and tugged his head down for a ravenous kiss. It didn't matter if she heard the hum or not. They were married and the sex was sizzling, and neither one of them could get enough.

They rocked and grunted, pushed and clung. Learning each other's rhythms, their own special dance. They almost reached completion several times, but each time, he would pull them back from the edge, wanting this, their first time, to last as long as possible.

Finally, worn out and het up, he could stall no longer, and he gave her his all. In the wonder of the moment, he felt something give, a loosening deep inside his core. Something swung open or dissolved or cracked or, hell, he didn't know what, but it happened.

A shift. A correction. An evolution.

And when her inner muscles seized him, and contracted with a mighty squeeze, he knew there was no going back. He was gone and so was she.

One last forceful thrust and they burst. Together. Hot and sweaty and victorious. An implosion of fire and heat and sensation.

She mewled.

He groaned.

They shuddered in unison, ripped open by the same earth-quake.

Breathless, he disintegrated. Became formless, borderless. He was part of her and she was part of him and they were one.

At least in the ebbing flood of the moment. They lay clasped together for a few shallow breaths, then, wanting to give her breathing room, he tried to roll away, but she pinned him in place, her legs clutched around his waist. It felt damn good here. So he stayed.

And he didn't mind the least bit being held down.

He pushed up on his elbows so that he could peer into her face. Normally, missionary position was his least favorite. Too intimate. Too much eye contact.

But with Tara, he loved it.

"You . . ." she whispered, and laughed, and brought her arms between them to hug herself. "That was . . . we were . . . fantastic."

"Terrific." He wriggled his eyebrows.

"Fabulous." She grinned.

"Splendid."

"Amazing."

"Fabtastic.

"Fantabulous."

"Amazballs."

"Amatastic."

"Amagasmic."

"Oh, you're just making up words now."

"There *are* no words." He touched the tip of her nose with his index finger.

She gave a playful snarl and nipped his finger between her teeth.

"Help! I didn't know I married a finger-eating shark."

"Moral of the story?" she mumbled around his finger, which she kept snugged between her teeth. "Be careful where you put your fingers."

"I thought you liked where I put my fingers."

"Hmm, that's right. Good point." She released his finger.

He beamed down at her. "You are the best."

"Best lover ever?"

"Yes," he said. "Unequivocally."

"You're just saying that because you married me. You've been with lots of women. How could I possibly be the best?"

"Because it's you," he said. "Some of the others might know more tricks, but you've got them beat when it comes to passion."

"I do?"

"Absolutely. I've never seen a woman as responsive as you, Tara Alzate Lockhart."

"That's hard to believe. I'm not very adept in bed—"

"Hush that nonsense. I don't want to hear another word about it. I'm the one who's not good enough for you." He lowered his head and kissed her.

She closed her eyes, and a dreamy look came over her face. "Mmm."

Did she hear a humming noise when he kissed her? Rhett was itching to know, but he couldn't come right out and ask her, because what if she said no?

It was just a goofy legend. Forget about it.

And yet, the question burrowed into his brain and wouldn't leave him alone. Was he her soul mate? He didn't believe in soul mates.

So why then was he so eager to be hers?

You can't force someone to be your soul mate. Either she heard humming when she kissed him, or she didn't. He couldn't intentionally cause it. Could he?

"I'm feeling sticky," he said to distract himself from the thoughts going around in his head. "You want a shower?"

"Are you inviting me to shower with you?"

"Um-hm." He lowered his eyelids and sent her his best bedroom gaze. "There's this thing I want to show you . . ."

"Well, what are we waiting for?"

* * *

AFTER EYE-OPENING SHOWER sex, they were lying on the chaise together in white hotel bathrobes that Rhett had gotten Silas to bring up for them from the gift shop. Rhett was brushing Tara's hair. She'd pinned it up in a bun while they were in the shower, and when she'd let it down afterward to run a brush through it, Rhett had taken hold of her wrist, took the brush from her, and said, "Allow me."

Now he was counting the strokes, pulling the brush down the length of her hair to the middle of her back. "Ninety-seven."

It was mesmerizing, the brushing, the counting. How good it felt to have someone else brush her hair for her. No one had done that since she was a kid.

"Ninety-eight."

She sighed, her scalp tingling pleasantly. He was almost done. She wished he could go on brushing her hair all night. She glanced at the clock, saw it was well after two a.m. Correction, all the wee hours of early morning.

"Ninety-nine." He drew out the word and the brushing. Slowly passing the brush from her crown to her back.

"That feels fantastic," she said. "Thank you so much."

"One hundred," he finished. "And it was my distinct pleasure. Let's make it a bedtime ritual. I brush your hair for you every night."

"When you're not on the road," she reminded him.

"You and Julie could come on the road with me," he said, setting the brush on the end table and easing her into the crook of his elbow.

"That's not very practical. Your trailer is small, and Julie has a lot of needs."

"I know." He sighed. "I just hate the thought of leaving you two."

"It's only until November. After the finals we can really start our life as a family."

"*If* we get custody of Julie."

"C'mon, how can we not? You married Julie's foster mother who is a NICU nurse. What's Judge Brando gonna do? Take Julie away from us and give her to a stranger just because we got married?"

"I'm just worried."

"Hey, for once you're the worrywart." She reached up and lightly knocked her fist against his noggin. "Don't borrow trouble. We'll let Lamar handle Judge Brando. For now, it's just me and you in a fancy hotel room . . ."

"You got that right," he said, and kissed her, and she heard that magnificent hum again. "Let's enjoy every second of our wedding night."

He took her back to bed and they made love again.

"I'm beginning to see why all the women are crazy for you."

"I thought we were done discussing other women. My past is behind me. I'm an old married man now."

"You are not the least bit old. Three times in one night? Who can do that?"

"Don't get to thinking it'll be a regular thing," he said. "I've been sitting on a lot of sexual energy."

"How come?"

"I haven't been with a woman since the weekend before I came to your house in El Paso."

"You've been without sex since May? Two months ago? That's forever for a guy like you."

"Believe me, I know."

"Is that the longest you've gone without sex since you've been grown?"

He paused, rolled his eyes to the left. "I'm trying to remember. No, no, I went four months once."

"You're incorrigible." She lightly swatted his arm.

"That's why you like me so much. You're very corrigible." He licked his lips, and she saw he was getting another erection. Holy smokes.

"During the past two months you didn't . . . um . . . take care of yourself?"

"Nope."

"Why not?"

"I was saving myself for you."

"Oh, that's a load of crap."

"No," he said. "It's not. Okay, initially, I was so stunned about Julie that sex was the last thing on my mind, but then I started hanging out with you, and sex was all I could think about."

"So why didn't you just take care of yourself?"

"Because if I did, you'd be the one I'd be fantasizing about and it seemed . . . disrespectful."

A warm little shiver started at the top of her head and shook all the way down her spine. Could it be true? Could she be the one woman to change him?

The hum is never wrong, she heard Granny Blue's voice in her head. *It will change you forever, and nothing will ever be the same again.*

She could certainly vouch for that.

They lay on their backs, staring up at the ceiling. Rhett's arm was stretched out underneath her pillow and she was curled into his side, smelling his manly scent. God, he smelled so good.

A long moment of silence passed. Tara closed her eyes, feeling completely content.

"Tell me," Rhett whispered, close to her ear. "What's your greatest sorrow?"

"Huh?" She blinked, almost asleep.

"What's the worst thing that's ever happened to you?" he asked. "You know my two. Losing Mom, and Brittany Fant getting rid of my baby."

"You're killing the mood, Lockhart. What's this all about? You're supposed to be the glib, happy one."

"I just want to understand you better. Was it losing Kit? Or was it your grandfather?"

"Grandfather had lived a full life," she said. "And he was in so much pain from the cancer. While I grieved him terribly, I was happy when his suffering came to an end."

"So Kit. That was unexpected. You were young. You were in love."

"Losing Kit was horrible, tragic, but his death wasn't the worst part."

"No?"

Tara placed a hand on her belly. She didn't really want to talk about it, but he'd opened up to her about Brittany. If he was letting go of his secrets, it was time for her to let go of hers. "When Kit got meningitis, I was eight weeks pregnant with our child."

"You had a miscarriage?"

She nodded, bit her bottom lip.

"I never knew."

"I don't talk about it much. I . . . had just found out I was pregnant. Even Kit didn't know. The shock of his death hastened the miscarriage, but my doctor said it would have happened eventually. That I can't carry a child to term. That's the biggest sorrow of my life, Rhett. The baby I lost. The children I can't have."

"Sweetheart, I am so sorry." He held her close. "If I could wave a magic wand and give you what you wanted, I would do it."

She wept then. Letting herself go in his arms. Just for a moment. Then she swiped at her eyes and smiled at him through the tears. "But that's life, right? Full of ups and downs, joys and sorrows."

"And there's nothing that can be done?"

"There's a surgery I could have, but insurance doesn't cover the procedure and there's little guarantee it would work . . ."

"But there's hope."

"Small, but yes."

"So have the surgery. I'll pay for it. Even if it doesn't work, you will know that you did everything in your power to make your dream come true."

"And if it doesn't work," she said, "we always have Julie."

"And me," he added. "You have me too." He reached for her left hand with his right, interlaced their fingers, curled toward her, until they were facing each other in the dark, with only the night-light for illumination.

"It doesn't bother you that you might not be able to have more children?"

"Tea, I've got you and Julie. I'm a lucky, lucky man. There's no need to be greedy. If we have more children, great. If not, that's great too." He squeezed her hand.

She squeezed back. They were in this together.

"Now," she said. "We've covered our greatest sorrows. What was your greatest joy?"

"Yesterday. When you said, 'I do,' and made me the happiest man in the world. Made you and me and Julie a real family."

"You say the sweetest things."

"What was your greatest joy?" he asked.

"That moment when you kissed me, and I heard the hum and knew you were The One I had been waiting for all along."

"Really?" His eyes were shiny, and his voice husky. "You heard the hum?"

She nodded, smiled shyly.

"Tea," he said. "I've changed my mind."

"About what?"

"*This* moment is the greatest joy of my life. Because I hear it too."

"What? You hear the hum?" She sat up and peered down at him. "You really hear it too?"

He reached out to cup her chin and smiled as if he'd just learned he'd won the Powerball lottery. "Maybe not in my head, but I hear it right here." He touched his chest. "In my heart."

And if she hadn't been madly in love with him before, she most surely was now.

Chapter 22

BAD WRECK: A seriously painful buck off, commonly followed by getting horned or stomped.

A WEEK after their brief honeymoon, Rhett went back on the road.

During his time off, he gave Tara a brief education about the rules and scoring of the PBR so that she could better understand and follow his progress.

She already knew that a professional bull ride was an eight-second endurance effort between the bull rider and a strong, massive bull determined to buck him off. The rider had to last those eight seconds with one hand in the air the whole time in order to earn a score.

She learned that the clock started the second that the bull's hip or shoulder broke the plane of the gate, and the clock stopped when the rider's hand came out of his rope, involuntarily or intentionally. If the rider touched anything with his free hand—his body, the bull, or the ground—it stopped the clock.

And she learned that each ride was worth up to one hundred points: fifty points awarded to the bull and fifty points to the rider if he managed to last for the full eight seconds. So if the rider scored fifty points and the bull scored fifty points it was credited to the rider as a 100-point ride. The bulls themselves were in competition for points and standings. The bulls received a score anywhere from zero to fifty points after every ride or attempted ride, whether or not the rider was able to make it to the eight-second buzzer.

A panel of PBR judges scored both the bulls and the riders. The bulls received points for how difficult they were to ride. A rider was judged on how much control he exhibited in the ride. What fascinated Tara was that while Rhett wasn't particularly controlled in his personal life, on the back of a bull, his precision, strength, and agility gave him supreme control. This year, all his years of work had culminated in top-notch skill.

At each event leading up to the finals, he scored points and made money.

"So you've already made a lot of money this season," she'd said. "Even if you don't end up winning the world finals, you've still had a great year so far."

"Best year yet. If I'm careful and invest right. I'm trusting you to help me with that," he said. "I've never paid much attention to money."

"That's because you've always had money," she said, pleased to be invited to help him with his finances. "You'll have to trim back on those twenty-dollar tips. I love how generous you are, but Julie comes first."

"Yes, ma'am . . . oops, sorry about the 'ma'am' . . . yes, my queen."

She'd laughed then and ruffled his hair.

The time between their July wedding and the court review hearing at the end of September crawled by.

Time with an infant was a roller coaster of emotions. Tara swung from joy and elation to exhaustion and a feeling of being overwhelmed. Instead of taking his travel trailer on the road, Rhett parked it and flew to each event, giving him more time with Tara and Julie. Ridge would fly his private jet to El Paso to drop him off and pick him up. It was nice to have family help. Without Ridge carting him to El Paso and back, he couldn't have done all that flying.

During the week, when Rhett blew back into town, things were great. He thrilled to the ups and downs of parenthood, knew how to relax and enjoy the ride. Showed Tara a few tricks.

His enthusiasm and fluid personality helped her realize she did not always have to be in total control. It was okay for the house to be messy and for her to spend the day in her pajamas if that's how things turned out. His ability to turn any mundane task into fun was one of the things she admired most about him.

When he was home, he insisted that she indulge in self-care. He would draw her a bubble bath in his big jetted soaker tub. Letting her linger while he rocked Julie in his lap, lightly bouncing her with his knees in a gentle version of giddy-up horsey.

He planned outings. A trip to the stables to introduce Julie to the horses, a stroller ride through the Cupid park, meet-ups with Kaia and Ridge and their kids at the ice cream parlor, giving Julie her first taste of vanilla ice cream.

When they stayed in, Rhett would pump music through the house, playing a variety of tunes from Nat King Cole to George Strait, Arctic Monkeys to Mozart. He had more eclectic tastes than she'd first thought. Digging up Bessie Smith, Buddy Holly, and Cole Porter records from a trunk in the attic and playing them on an old record player that had once belonged to his mother. He'd dance Julie around the room until she chuffed and grinned and flapped her little arms like a baby bird trying to take flight.

Many times, they spent the day burrowed in bed, Julie sandwiched between them. Counting her fingers and toes, playing This Little Piggy Went to Market. They lightly tickled the bottoms of her feet, blew raspberries against her bare belly, and played peek-a-boo.

Yes, when Rhett was home, life was good.

But he left every Thursday morning to catch a plane to his next event, and he did not return until late Sunday evening. Giving her just three short days with him each week.

The rest of the time, the responsibilities of single parenthood pushed her limits. If it hadn't been for her family, she didn't know how she would have managed.

While he was gone, she did her best to stay occupied. Which

wasn't hard to do since Julie required a lot of care. She did things with the baby to stimulate her development—range-of-motion exercises, stretching, massage. And Julie thrived.

Her family was great about getting her out of the house. Kaia invited her and Julie over for lunch on Sundays after church, and her parents came over every Thursday night to watch Julie, insisting she have mommy's night out with her sisters or friends. It helped to ease her loneliness, but she didn't stop missing Rhett. Without him in it, the small bungalow felt empty and oversized.

On Wednesdays, she continued to volunteer at the WIC clinic, and that's when Rhett got to spend his alone time with Julie. Father and daughter bonding. Tara was beloved at the clinic and found the work so rewarding. Being around other Apaches put her back in touch with her heritage and culture. Her grandfather would have been so proud. Merylene told her numerous times that when she was ready for a full-time job at the clinic to just say the word and the job was hers.

It was nice having that option. Maybe when Julie was a little older and Rhett was no longer in the PBR, she'd think about it.

She and Rhett Skyped every night. Texted each other in between the Skype sessions. They discussed everything and nothing. Movies, books, music, pets, medicine, bull riding, religion, politics, food, philosophies on childrearing. No topic was off-limits.

Through their Internet gab sessions, they deepened their connection and discovered they had way more in common than it seemed on the surface.

They both loved *The Voice* and had binge-watched *Breaking Bad* three times. They preferred dogs over cats, Alaska to Hawaii, and their eggs over easy. They hated split pea soup, boiled okra, and marshmallow fluff.

They'd both worn braces at age thirteen. Both lost their virginity at seventeen. Both raised calves in FFA their freshman year in high school and showed them at the Fort Worth Stock Show.

Neither cared for gin, bologna, or any brand of jeans other than Wrangler. They agreed it was important to vote but they were both lax about it. Politically, they were moderates who thought both parties had gone a little mad. They discovered they shared an obsession with the Texas Rangers—the baseball team, not the law enforcement agency—and they enjoyed hiking the Davis Mountains on the search for arrowheads.

And yes, they did a bit of sexting and Skype sex—they were newlyweds, after all. Long-distance romance sucked, but Rhett knew all kinds of innovative ways to spice things up.

Two or three times a week, he sent gifts. Some romantic, others practical. A footbath, which she adored. Long-stemmed red roses that filled the house with a beautiful scent. A gurgling fountain to help her fall more quickly asleep between Julie's frequent feedings. An oversized chocolate chip cookie, iced in chocolate ganache with the words "I Hear the Hum." Then impishly, the next day, a personal vibrator engraved with "You Hear the Hum."

One time a massage therapist showed up on her doorstep and announced Rhett had hired her to give Tara a ninety-minute massage. Kaia was right behind the therapist. Rhett had sent her to watch Julie, so Tara could have uninterrupted self-care.

The next time it was a pedicurist and Aria.

When she told him that while she appreciated the lavish gifts, he needed to save money, he sent her a toy bullwhip with a note that said: *You can crack this over my head when I get home.* A case of Juicy Fruit gum. A box of animal crackers. Cute cards. Silly social media gifs.

He was a helluva romantic, and Tara luxuriated in his attention. She couldn't wait to see what creative surprise he came up with next.

Every Friday and Saturday, she was parked in front of the TV watching the channel that aired the PBR events. Eyes glued to the screen, watching her husband ride. The stakes were high, and every time he got on the back of a bull, her heart was in her throat.

Sometimes Ridge and Kaia would come over to watch the events with her, but mostly, it was just she and Julie. She would sit on the couch, fists clenched, yelling at the bull to leave her man alone. Hopping to her feet to yell, "Yes, yes," every time the timer hit eight seconds. He was on a hot streak. Winning events right and left. The announcers were impressed. Going on and on about the changes in him. How focused he seemed. How he'd matured. They speculated marriage and fatherhood were good for this rodeo cowboy.

When he was home, it was a sexfest as they made up for lost time. They had lots of quickies. With a small infant in the house, long, lingering make-out sessions just didn't happen. There was a rousing encounter on the washing machine as he seduced her in the laundry room during one of Julie's naps.

And a fun time on the backyard swing until the frame broke and they ended up on the ground laughing their asses off. Then there was a frantic, naughty roll in the hay barn one night when her parents dropped by. She'd left them in the living room with Julie and had gone to the barn to call Rhett in for dinner, and one thing just led to another.

He cooked for her and watched Hallmark movies with her and gave Julie her baths. It wasn't easy, but they made the best of it. Laughing together when things didn't go as planned. Working as a team. Appreciating every single moment they had in each other's company.

It was the best two months of Tara's life, and then came the Labor Day weekend rodeo that turned everything upside down.

On Saturday, August 31, Tara sat glued to the TV in the living room, watching the PBR event in Tacoma. Julie was in her bassinet beside the couch, studying the mobile of galloping horses that Rhett had bought her when he'd been in Wyoming.

Rhett was up next, and the two announcers were speculating about why he'd gotten married in the middle of the season. How taking time off had dropped him in the standings.

"Claudio Limon took advantage of Lockhart's absence last month," the first announcer said. "And Lockhart lost his solid lead. They've been neck and neck ever since. Given Claudio's win history, Lockhart's marriage just might have handed the Brazilian the title."

"It's still early in the season, Ray," said the other announcer. "A whole lot can happen between now and November. There's bad blood between Lockhart and Limon. They were dating the same woman. It's turning out to be a world-class grudge match."

"The thing about bull riders is, at the end of the day, these people are a little crazy, Tom," the first announcer said.

"You've got it," Tom said. "It's not a question of *if* these riders will get hurt, but when and how bad."

"Looks like they're having some trouble in the chute with Widow Maker," Ray said. "Lockhart's getting off."

The camera panned down to the chute. Rhett was huddled with his manager, while the bull named Widow Maker was thrashing wildly in the chute.

"Do we know what it's about, Ray?" Tom asked.

"There's some kind of delay," Ray said. "While we're waiting, let's cut to Lacy Manning's behind-the-scenes interview with Lockhart from last night's win."

The screen shifted to a female reporter with a mike in Rhett's face.

Rhett's eyes were shiny from his victory the previous night, his stance deservedly cocky. Tara's heart swooned. She'd been so damn proud of him. Watching him in action was a natural high.

"That was quite a ride, Mr. Lockhart," the reporter said, standing far too close to Rhett for Tara's liking. "Great hip action."

"Well," Rhett drawled, looking straight into the camera, clearly courting America. "You gotta know how to move your hips to ride bulls."

"Oh my." The reporter giggled and batted her false eyelashes.

Tara covered Julie's ears. "Don't listen to this part, button. Your daddy is making a fool of himself."

"Tell our viewers, Rhett—may I call you Rhett?" The reporter simpered. "How you got started in the sport."

"Well, ma'am," he said, giving her his humble cowboy, aw-shucks smile. "You can call me anything you want as long as you call me for dinner."

Tara rolled her eyes. Hard.

"Oh, none of that 'ma'am' stuff. You must call me Lacy." The reporter laughed and showed a mouthful of straight white teeth.

"Veneers," Tara told Julie. "I could have them too if I wanted to spend the money."

"Lacy," Rhett said. "I been riding bulls since I was knee-high to a grasshopper." Rhett stuck his thumbs in the front pockets of his jeans. "When I was three years old, I used to ride on my daddy's back and he'd buck around the living room like a bull. Later, he told me I used to wear him out." Rhett's smile widened. "I treasure those memories. Whenever I climbed on the back of a bull, it was the only time my daddy paid much attention to me, especially after my mother died. I knew when things got bad I could always find a bull to ride and everything would be okay."

The words he spoke were sad, but there was no trace of bitterness in his voice. No residue of disillusionment or blame. His childhood was what it was.

"That's such a touching story," said Lacy, totally missing the point. She turned to the camera. "To all you little cowboys out there, keep riding, and someday you too can be in the PBR."

Tara, however, did not miss the point. She sat up straight, Rhett's baby clutched her in arms.

Whenever I climbed on the back of a bull, it was the only time my daddy paid much attention to me, especially after my mother died.

In that poignant statement, Tara learned everything she needed to know about why Rhett was the way he was. Why the PBR meant so much to him. Why he was an incorrigible flirt.

Why he was hard driven to succeed as a bull rider. Why he really *did* want to be a good dad to Julie.

Her heart broke for him. He was living his life trapped in old childhood patterns, and he didn't even realize it. Trying to please a father who was impossible to please. Trying to replace the love of his mother with a string of women who always fell short of ideal.

He had a fear of going too emotionally deep, terrified of getting chewed up. His attraction to all things pleasurable—sex, a good time, the high of a win—he saw as a positive flow when in fact, his constantly seeking the next emotional high masked a flight away from pain.

It made such sense why he could never pass up an invitation for fun. Why he'd gone back on the circuit. Rodeo and its unpredictability was all he knew.

Yet, in his soul he craved stability, just as he feared it.

But now, Tara knew why. The sudden realization that he was still running away from his mother's death, twenty years later, touched her to the core.

And all she wanted to do was love him back to wholeness.

The camera panned back to the arena. Rhett was back in the chute on Widow Maker.

"Looks like they've got the problem resolved," Ray, the announcer, said.

"Do we know what caused the delay?" asked Tom.

"Oh, this is a funny one. Apparently, Lockhart lost his good luck charm and wouldn't get on the bull without it."

"What is his good luck charm?"

"It's an animal cracker."

"An animal cracker?" Tom cackled. "What kind?"

Ray pressed his fingers against his earpiece. "I'm being told it's a giraffe."

"These riders are a superstitious lot. Did Lockhart find his animal cracker?"

"Afraid not, but he has to get on the bull or forfeit."

The camera focused on Rhett for a close-up in the chute at the Tacoma Dome, geared up and ready to rock. His head was down, and he had a helmet on, so she couldn't see much of his face, but his body was loose, and easy. He was at home here. This was where he belonged.

Even so, she couldn't help wondering what he was thinking. Was he scared? Was he freaked out over losing his lucky charm? And when had he started carrying animal crackers as a good luck symbol? Or was he feeling pure thrill? Was adrenaline spilling through his bloodstream? Or was he as cool as his body language?

The bull beneath him bucked and snorted. He looked very mean. Tara's stomach somersaulted. How in the world did Rhett do this? What drove him to time and again test his mettle against such angry, gigantic beasts?

Tara drew her knees to her chest, wrapped her arms around them. "This is nerve-wracking."

Julie made cooing noises.

"That's your daddy," Tara said, pointing at the screen. "He might not be the smartest man alive, straddling an animal that could kill him, but he's pretty darn brave. You should be proud. Not everyone has the courage to go for their dreams."

Julie flapped her little arms and legs.

The chute opened, and the bull came charging out, snorting and bucking. The time ticked off on the TV screen agonizingly slow. One second, two seconds, three . . .

Her heart slammed into her chest—*ka-bam, ka-bam, ka-bam.* She crossed all her fingers and toes. *Please, please.*

Rhett held on. Looked magnificently in control. A man in his element at the top of his game.

A rush of feeling she couldn't quite name cleaved her. She curled her hands into tight fists, squinted, rocked forward on the cushion as if it were she on the back of the bull. "Hang on, hang on."

Four seconds . . . five . . . six.

Dear God, eight seconds was a lifetime. She chewed a thumb-nail. How did the wives and mothers of bull riders stand the suspense?

Widow Maker was spinning and leaping out of control. Just as the buzzer sounded, indicating that Rhett had managed to hang on for those eight interminable seconds, the bull's back hooves briefly touched the ground, and using the momentum the giant beast sprang straight up into the air.

"Widow Maker's gone vertical!" exclaimed Ray, the an-nouncer, stunned awe in his voice. "And Lockhart is still along for the ride!"

For one breath-stealing moment, man and beast hung sus-pended as if dangling from a giant invisible rope. A seemingly impossible feat.

The announcers gasped in unison as the crowd cheered in-sanely. Terrified, Tara screamed and jumped off the couch. Julie burst into tears.

Widow Maker landed with a teeth-jarring jolt.

Rhett flew off the bull's broad backside. Immediately, Widow Maker spun around and came after him. The bullfighters jumped in, trying to distract Widow Maker. But the bull lowered its head, hooked its horns beneath Rhett's shoulders, and tossed him across the arena like a straw scarecrow.

Rhett landed hard, facedown, dust flying up around him . . .

. . . and he did not move again.

Chapter 23

OUT THE BACKDOOR: When the rider is thrown over the back end of an animal.

Rнетт heard his name being called from a faraway distance, blurry and indistinct, as if he were floating above the earth on a fluffy white cloud.

His face was buried in the dirt and his head buzzed. His vision dimmed, and the voices grew more distant as the cloud he was riding drifted farther away. Everything slowly going black and quiet.

It would be so nice to go to sleep. Nap, just for a little bit. He was so very tired. But he couldn't because some irritating bull-fighter was screaming in his ear.

"Cowboy up, you candy ass!"

Go away.

"C'mon, Rhett, get up. Get up. GET UP!"

Then someone was slapping his back and he gasped, drawing in a lungful of dust. He opened one eye, saw his paternal grandfather squatting in the dirt next to him. He had a cigar clamped in the corner of his mouth and a tumbler of whiskey in one hand.

Huh, this was weird. Grandpa Cyril had been killed in a cattle stampede when Rhett was five. What was he doing here?

Grandpa Cyril glanced at his watch. A raggedy-ass Timex that could take a licking and keep on ticking. "Tock, tick, buckaroo."

Tock, tick? Wasn't that backward?

"They'll be here soon. You better get up or you're going with us," Grandpa Cyril advised.

He tried to lift his head.

"Don't move!" someone commanded.

It wasn't Grandpa Cyril. Through the dust in his eyes, he made out Claudio Limon on his knees beside Rhett's head, as paramedics and the bullfighters rolled him over and loaded him onto a backboard and strapped him down.

"You be okay?" Claudio asked, springing up to follow the crew as they carried Rhett from the hushed arena. His face was drawn with concern, and he commanded, "You *be* okay."

Rhett tried to nod but they'd taped his head to the backboard. Claudio was a great competitor who would do anything to win, but Rhett knew he didn't want to win like this.

Claudio squeezed his hand just before the paramedics whisked him into the ambulance, and the last clear thing Rhett thought before he lost consciousness was *Tara is gonna kill me.*

TARA STOOD PARALYZED in the middle of Rhett's living room, watching the paramedics carry her lifeless husband from the arena. Panic wrapped her lungs in a vise, seized. Her knees rippled like coastal Bermuda grass in a northerly breeze. Both hands plastered against her mouth.

Dear God, no, no, no. This could not be happening. Maybe she'd missed something, and it was another rider who'd gotten injured. Maybe he was spoofing everybody, and he was totally fine. Rhett could be a cutup.

Oh denial, that sweet self-deception.

Face facts. It *had* been Rhett on the ground, and he wasn't joking around. The arena was silent, the announcers solemn. Speaking in hushed, reverent tones reserved for funeral parlors.

Please let him be okay, please let him be okay, she bargained, turned her eyes heavenward.

He couldn't die. Not her strong, vibrant, daredevil cowboy.

Anger ripped through her. At the bull, at the PBR, at Rhett

for being so reckless. He was a father. How could he continue to ride? This was why Judge Brando had ordered him to leave the PBR. This very reason right here. The sport was incredibly dangerous.

But mostly, she was mad at herself. By marrying him, she'd enabled him to stay on the circuit. If she hadn't stepped in and proposed a marriage of convenience, he would have quit.

Pressing a palm against her forehead, she paced the living room, emotions falling in on her. Anger, fear, worry, hurt, sorrow, guilt, regret, sadness, so much sadness.

The PBR program had cut to commercial after they hauled Rhett off. Yes, never mind that a man had been injured, even possibly killed, they had to keep up the advertising to pay for that air time.

Denial, anger, bargaining. She was crashing through the five stages of grief with a sledgehammer.

She had to go to him. She couldn't stay here and do nothing. She had to tell him how much she loved him. Had to be with him.

But she couldn't. She had Julie.

Her world spun, tilted off its axis.

A knock at the door.

Before she could answer, the door opened, and Ridge and Kaia burst in. She stared at her sister and brother-in-law. "Rhett—" She whimpered.

"We know," Kaia said. "We were watching."

A tremor rattled Tara's body as her sister moved to hug her.

"It's okay, Tea," Kaia whispered. "We're here. I've come to get Julie, and Ridge's flying you to Tacoma to be with Rhett."

"She needs—"

"Shh."

"I should—"

"Shh, we'll figure it out. Don't worry about Julie. Rhett needs you now."

Tara broke down, sobbing into her sister's hair, whispering over and over, "Thank you, thank you, thank you."

Kaia produced a tissue from her pocket, pressed it into Tara's hand. "C'mon," she said. "Let's get you packed."

"Where are Cody and Ingrid?"

"Aria's watching them. We'll all pitch in with Julie while you're gone. Me, Mom, Aria, Archer and Casey, even Vivi said she can help. Don't worry about a thing except looking after Rhett."

Fresh tears tracked down Tara's face. She was grateful. So very grateful for her family. What on earth would she ever do without them?

That's when she knew, no matter what happened, she would not be going back to El Paso.

When Rhett came to again he was in a hospital room.

He blinked and stared at the clock on the wall opposite his bed: 12:00. Was that noon or midnight? The blinds were drawn, but he could see sunlight pushing through the slats. So, noon.

And damn, but he had a mother bear of a headache. It felt as if a wire band was twisted tight across his entire scalp. His left shoulder, which he'd dislocated more than once, was in a sling and it throbbed like a sonofabitch. He had an IV in the back of his hand, and there were electrodes hooked to his chest. Somewhere, a heart monitor beeped.

"Rhett?" His name was a soft whisper coming from his right side.

He turned his head, saw Tara, and his heart filled with joy. "Are you real?" he croaked.

She reached for his hand, squeezed it, nodded past a misting of tears in her eyes. "I am."

"How . . ." He swallowed, his throat parched. "How did you get here?"

"Ridge flew me in."

"My brother is here too?"

"He's down in the cafeteria getting some lunch."

He met her gaze. Her smile filled with fear and sorrow. "Hey, hey," he said. "It's okay. I'm okay. Don't cry."

"I thought you'd—" She broke off, shook her head.

"I *am* okay." This time, he squeezed *her* hand.

"You dislocated your shoulder."

"Not the first time. It pops right back in." He smiled, but it made his head hurt worse, and he dropped it.

"You also had a concussion that knocked you out for hours."

"How's Widow Maker?" he asked.

"What?"

"The bull. Is he all right?"

Tara looked exasperated. "The bull is perfectly fine. He almost killed you."

"Wasn't his fault. Nature of the beast."

"And nature of the beast who was dumb enough to crawl on him."

"It was my fault. I lost my lucky charm."

"Seriously? You believe not having an animal cracker in your pocket is what caused you to get tossed by a bull?"

"Not per se," he said. "But when I have the animal cracker in my pocket I think of you and Julie, and when I think of you two I remember why I'm doing this. Not having it in my pocket shifted my energy from happy and confident to anxious. Widow Maker picked up on that."

"Sounds like superstition to me."

"You have your way of controlling life, I have mine." He grinned at her, but she wasn't buying it.

She glowered at him.

"Are you mad at me?" he asked.

"Yes!" she said.

"Why? I was only doing my job."

"Because you're crazy enough to think bull riding is still a good idea."

"Tara," he said. "I know you're upset, but bull riding is all I know."

"Well, it's time you learned something else. You're a father now. Julie is counting on you to be there to see her graduate high school. To dance at her wedding."

"There's no guarantees in life. My mother didn't see me graduate."

"You didn't graduate," she said.

"You know what I mean."

"Not to mention, the review hearing is coming up in three weeks. You're supposed to have another line of work."

"I can always work on the Silver Feather as a ranch hand."

"Don't you think the universe is trying to tell you something?"

"I'll quit after November," he said. "I promise."

"You sound like an addict."

Her words hurt. Rhett bit the inside of his cheek. She cared about his well-being, he needed to remember that.

"I think you're addicted to the adrenaline rush," she said, dropping his hand and standing up. "I don't think you *can* stop."

"I can quit anytime." God, he did sound like an addict.

"Prove it. Let this be your wake-up call. Walk away from the PBR."

"The world championship is less than two months away," he wheedled. "I promise you, I'll quit after that."

In that moment, she looked so sad, as if her heart was breaking. "The doctor said you'll need three weeks of rest before you can return to the circuit. You'll be so behind by then you can't catch up. It's time to let it go, Rhett. Not just for me and Julie, but for your own sake."

She was right. He could see how he was hurting her. He was torn right in two pieces. His lifelong dream of proving he was the best bull rider in the world on one side, Tara and Julie on the other.

He looked into her eyes, and there was only one choice he

could make. He loved her. He was doing this for her and his daughter.

"You win," he said, regret choking him. "I'll quit the PBR."

It didn't feel like a win.

Tara should have been overjoyed that Rhett was leaving the PBR, but she couldn't help feeling responsible for crushing his dreams.

Under strict instructions from the doctor to get lots of rest and avoid physical activity, Rhett was down in the dumps. He was an active guy, always on the move, and it was hard for him to relax. He did his best not to show his disappointment. Spending time with her and Julie, helping her around the house, staying home to watch the baby so Tara could put in more volunteer hours at the WIC clinic.

But he lounged on the couch a lot, watching clips from his old rides, and insomnia kept him awake at night. Several times she woke up in the wee hours of the morning to find him outside in a hammock looking up at the stars.

Was it unfair of her to ask him to quit when he was so close to achieving his dreams? Wasn't that why she'd married him in the first place? To help him stay on the circuit and gain custody of his daughter?

But all that had changed after he'd kissed her, and she'd heard the humming and known to her core that she loved this man with all her heart and soul. And when you love someone, you wanted the best for them, not what was best for you. Who was she to tell Rhett how to live his life?

They kept things light. Their conversations were pleasant enough, but on the surface. Neither one of them talked about what they were really feeling and thinking. And based on doctor's orders to wait three weeks to make sure he was fully over the concussion, they didn't have sex.

The night before the hearing, Rhett pulled her to him in bed, massaged the furrow between her brow with the pad of his thumb, and said, "Stop worrying. We've got this. What could go wrong?"

He kissed her then, and she rested her head on his chest, listened to the strong *lub-dub* of his heart.

His confidence vanquished her fears and they spent the night just snuggling with each other. It was the best night they'd had since his wreck.

On Thursday morning, September 26, Mom came over to watch Julie and they drove to the review hearing together. Holding hands in the car on the way into Cupid.

By the time they reached the courthouse, they were both keyed up and edgy. "Did you bring your good luck charm?" Tara whispered.

Rhett dug a cracker giraffe from his pocket.

She smiled. "Why the giraffe?"

"Because it's got a long, beautiful neck like you," he murmured, and nuzzled her hair. Hand in hand, they parked the car and started up the courthouse steps.

To find Lamar prowling restlessly back and forth, and repeatedly running his hand over his hair. Uh-oh. He looked agitated. Did he have bad news?

Tara's gut clenched. "What's wrong?"

Lamar's mouth set tight. "Unfortunate news."

Rhett slid his arm around Tara's waist. "What is it?"

Lamar met Rhett's eyes first, then Tara's. "I just learned Rhona White Limon has petitioned the court for custody."

"Limon?" Rhett said, his color blanching despite his tan.

"She married Claudio Limon," Lamar said. "They're here with a lawyer and a therapist that's ready to vouch for her as a good mother. CPS has already been to the house and checked everything out and gave her the green light. I should have gotten advance warning but somehow things fell through the cracks and the paperwork never hit my desk."

"What does this mean?" Tara asked, but deep inside she already knew.

Lamar winced. "Getting custody of Julie is no longer the slam dunk we thought it was after you two got married."

Rhett looked at Tara, and she could see the fear in his eyes. She smiled as genuinely as she could, and squeezed his hand again, trying her best not to let him see that she was terrified.

Chapter 24

HEAD THROWER: A bull that tries to hit the cowboy with its head or horns while the contestant is on its back.

RHETT wished Tara could sit beside him, but Lamar said she couldn't because she wasn't the one filing for custody. He glanced over his shoulder. She perched on the edge of her seat in the front row behind him, wringing her hands in her lap.

He took the animal cracker from his pocket, held it up for her to see.

She smiled, and that lifted his spirits. Things had been a little bumpy since his wreck, but they'd make it through this. He felt certain of their love.

Directly across the aisle from Tara sat Claudio Limon. The Brazilian shot him a smug, screw-you smirk. The same self-satisfied smirk he wore every time he scored more points than Rhett staying on the back of a bull.

This was his life in a nutshell. His adversary on one side, but his rock-solid woman on the other. He shifted his gaze back to Tara, caught her in a worried frown. The minute she saw that he was watching her, she dragged out that tepid smile again.

Ah shit, his rock was looking like sandstone. That was okay. He'd be her rock today.

He mouthed, *I love you*, realized it was the first time he'd actually said those words to her since he'd come home. He needed to do better. Tara worked tirelessly to help others; she deserved a million *I love you*s a day.

Her eyes rounded and her smile cracked open, and she mouthed back, *I love you too.*

Reluctantly, he let go of her gaze, craned his neck to see Rhona from around the back of her lawyer.

Their eyes had met when he'd first walked in, and he'd seen fiery determination lurking there. Rhona was dressed in a matronly outfit, looking nothing like the buckle bunny who had shown up at his trailer door over a year ago. She wore a stiff white blouse with a high collar, an ankle-length skirt, and modest lace-up boots. Playing the part of reformed party girl.

Rhett wasn't buying it, but would the judge?

You changed, a thought balloon popped into his head. *She can too.* Great, just what he needed. Empathy for the woman trying to take his daughter away.

"All rise," bellowed the bailiff.

The people assembled got to their feet as Judge Brando swept into the room in her black robe, reading glasses on a gold chain around her neck.

Rhett gulped and pulled at his tie, suddenly swamped with sweat.

He was playing a part too. Really no different from Rhona. The *only* reason he deserved custody of Julie was because of Tara. Because of her, he'd become a better man. Because of her, he'd learned how to be a father. Because of her, for the first time in his life, he felt grounded and anchored and balanced.

All these years, he'd believed that being solid, committed, dependable meant boring. That if he allowed himself to settle down, it meant he'd be settling for a common life. He'd thought a wife and kids meant the end of fun and happiness.

Because of Tara, he'd learned the exact opposite was true. Now he had to convince Judge Brando that he was a changed man.

Across the aisle, Rhona and her legal team would be arguing the same thing. Both of them clamoring to the court, a court naturally inclined toward giving a child back to its mother, *Pick me, pick me, pick me.*

"Mr. Lockhart," Judge Brando said once the fanfare of opening a courtroom session was over.

He looked into the judge's face, and in that instant when her eyes met his, Rhett knew the truth. He didn't have to wait to hear her decision. He saw it in her face. His goose was cooked. He'd lost Julie.

His hopes dropped, shattered. From behind him, he felt Tara rest a hand on his shoulder. Warm and reassuring. She had his back. His heart swelled, and he picked up his hopes. He couldn't give up. For Tara's sake.

"Mrs. Limon." Judge Brando peered at Rhona.

Rhona stood straighter.

"Please have a seat," Judge Brando invited the courtroom.

The congregation lowered in unison.

Time seemed to warp and stretch, simultaneously elongating and compressing. A tick of the courtroom clock and ten minutes had passed. A heartfelt plea from Rhona's attorney dragged on into eternity. He spoke of how his client was deeply ashamed of leaving her baby. How she'd made amends. How she learned that she was bipolar but knew that was not an excuse for abandoning her child. How she was now on medication and under the treatment of a psychiatrist who was there to vouch for her ability to care for her daughter. How she'd married Claudio and they could provide a stable home for the child.

In his head, the voices were coming out deep and distorted as if a recording was being played at a slow rate of speed under water. It felt as if someone had inserted a giant screwdriver into his chest and had twisted it to the right. *Righty tighty*, he thought inanely.

Was it lingering effects from the concussion? Or raw fear?

He understood what was being said, but it was as if he couldn't absorb it. Lamar pointing out how Rhett changed from a rambling rodeo cowboy into a father and husband. Lamar was some kind of spin doctor, laying it on thick how Rhett was a valuable member of his community, how Tara was a NICU nurse with the requisite skills to care for a preemie.

But Rhona's lawyer was just as adept. She'd learned the error of her ways, she was repentant, yada, yada. She had a husband now who desperately wanted her and the baby she'd fathered with another man. Claudio did not care that she'd strayed; he loved her that much. Claudio came from a culture that was all about family. He would love and raise Julie as if she were his own daughter.

At that, Rhett glanced at Claudio again. His rival's handsome face mocked him. Eyes narrowed, chin hardened. He mouthed a silent obscenity.

Anger blasted through him. Not so much at Claudio's cockiness, but at the thought of his daughter being raised by him. Claudio did not love Julie. He might not even love Rhona, although the brawl he'd had with Rhett suggested that maybe he did. Either way, his love for Rhona was not his primary motivation.

Claudio was all about winning. He lived it, breathed it, thought about nothing but winning. On the back of a bull, in bed with a woman, in the courtroom trying to steal another man's daughter.

Rhett knew because once upon a time winning had been *his* end-all, be-all. But right now, he'd give every trophy, every accolade, every penny he would make in prize money to Claudio, if he and Tara could just get custody of Julie.

Finally, after what felt like hours, but was really only about twenty minutes, Lamar and Rhona's lawyer concluded their arguments.

Judge Brando sat stone-faced, unmoved and unmoving. The courtroom was pin-drop silent. She steepled her fingers, turned her cold stare first at Rhett and then at Rhona. "We'll recess for lunch," she said in a sharp clip. "I'll give you my ruling upon our return." She picked up her gavel, smashed it down hard enough to make everyone jump. "Court dismissed. We'll resume at two p.m."

* * *

PACING THE MARBLE hallway outside the courtroom, Rhett ripped off his tie, wadded it in his fist. Tried not to make eye contact with Claudio and Rhona as they scurried toward the exit with their attorney.

He ground his teeth, struggling to get a handle on his fear. Recalled something Tara had told him once. *You can choose courage, or you can choose comfortable, but you can't have both.* It hadn't made sense at the time she'd said it to him, but now he totally got where she was coming from.

She was right. He'd chosen courage, going all in on fatherhood, and he had not been comfortable since. On any other day, he would have been proud of his choice. But today, on the day he'd come to fight for his daughter, he could feel her slipping away from him. And he realized he wasn't merely uncomfortable; he was steeped in raw, aching pain.

Tara touched his arm. "Let's go get something to eat."

He jerked back from her, saw hurt flit across her face, but she quickly schooled her features to a calm, neutral position. "I'm not hungry. You go ahead."

"You skipped breakfast. You need to eat."

"Don't tell me what to do," he snarled, and the second the words were out of his mouth, he regretted them. Tara was only trying to help the only way she knew how, through nurturing. "I'm sorry," he apologized. "You didn't deserve that. I'm just upset."

"I know." She hovered a hand over him. She wanted to touch him, but she was giving him his space.

"I . . . you . . ." He looked her in the eyes. "Thank you for everything you've done. I couldn't have gotten this far without you."

Her dark eyes lit with alarm. "You sound like you're giving up."

He shook his head. "Judge Brando is going to give Julie to Rhona."

"You don't know that."

"I do."

"So you're a mind reader now?"

"I don't know what's in her heart and mind. All I know is that I've got that same feeling I did on the back of Widow Marker just before he went vertical and I knew I wasn't going to stick."

"Gut instinct?"

He nodded, pressed a fist to his belly.

She moved to touch his back but stopped herself before she did. "Try not to project."

"Now you're sounding like a therapist."

Tara cleared her throat, folded her hands over her chest. As a barrier against him? Or an attempt to control her urge to nurture? "How can I support you without upsetting you?"

"Go get yourself something to eat." He threw her the keys to his truck.

"You won't come?" She sounded infinitely sad.

He shook his head. "I'd be miserable company."

"Do you want me to bring you something back? Tacos?"

"I can't eat."

"Are you sure?"

"Go." He hardened his features because he wanted so badly to give in and allow her to comfort him. But he had to stay strong. Had to prepare himself for the verdict he knew was coming. Had to be strong for her, because when Judge Brando gave Julie to Rhona and it fully sank in on Tara what it meant, she was going to need his strength.

She hesitated.

"Go," he insisted, desperate to protect her. "And please don't come back at two."

She gasped, looked as if he'd hauled off and slapped her. Raised a trembling hand to her cheek. "You don't mean that."

"I do."

"How will you get home?"

"I'll get Lamar to bring me by."

"That's out of his way."

"I'll find someone."

"But not me?"

"No."

That came out far harsher than he'd intended. He wasn't upset with her, far from it. That's why he was sending her away. He yearned to fall hopeless into the circle of her arms, stay in that sweet, comfortable spot for the rest of his life. He couldn't afford that luxury. Not today.

A single tear rolled down the side of her nose. He wanted so badly to reach out to her, draw her back to him. Beg her forgiveness.

But if he didn't get Julie, and he knew in his heart of hearts that he'd already lost her—the slight smile Judge Brando had directed at Rhona before the break convinced him—he didn't want Tara to see him fall apart.

"Rhett," she whispered.

"Go," he growled. He had to get her out of here before he collapsed. "Just go, dammit."

She pursed her lips together, blinked hard against the tears now streaming down her face. "As you wish."

Turning, she walked away, leaving him broken and lame in a way no bucking bull ever could.

UNABLE TO ACCEPT Rhett's demand—she knew he was just hurting and lashing out—Tara returned to the trial at two. She understood he was terrified of losing Julie and she tried not to take it personally. She was not going to allow his fear to chase her off.

But she waited until the last minute to slip in, when he was distracted by the proceedings, and took a spot at the back of the courtroom.

The family was assembled. Tara had put out a call to them all after Rhett told her he knew they'd lost. Lockharts and Alzates presenting a united front. Ridge, Duke, Vivi, Kaia. Archer and Casey were there too. Mom and Dad were watching the kids at their place. Rhona had no one but Claudio and her legal team in her corner. Tara and Rhett had a village.

Kaia turned and spied Tara, motioned for her to join them.

Tara shook her head. Rhett had made it clear he didn't want her here. Kaia lifted her shoulders, looked confused. Tara twirled her finger, indicating that her sister should turn back around. Family was a blessing, but sometimes they could really gum up the works.

Judge Brando returned to the bench. Took an extraordinarily long amount of time to sort herself out. Swallowed a glass of water. Cleared her throat. Shuffled through papers.

Tara's nerves frayed. *C'mon, lady, spit it out.* She watched Rhett's back, saw his shoulders drop and his spine stiffen as he prepared himself for Judge Brando's ruling. Tara crossed the fingers of both hands, closed her eyes, sent up a quick little prayer. *Please, please.*

"I've made my decision," Judge Brando announced.

The courtroom inhaled a collective breath.

Judge Brando swept a glance from Rhett to Rhona. Tara wished she could see his face. "Temporary custody of the minor child, Julie Elizabeth Lockhart, shall be transferred to the child's mother, Rhona White Limon. Permanency hearing to be held December 9."

Chapter 25

BAILING OUT: Getting off the bull the best way you can, generally by throwing your weight against the animal.

SHATTERED to the bone over losing custody of Julie, Tara did what she always did in the face of adversity. Shouldered her burden, sucked up her pain, and trudged on. She could not allow the grief to destroy her.

Ms. Bean, who had been involved in the custody hearing and was the one who had green-lighted Rhona, followed her inside the house she shared with Rhett, Rhona and Claudio and their lawyer right behind her. They'd come for Julie.

She still couldn't believe how fast it had happened, and wondered if Claudio had greased some palms to speed up the process.

Rhett was in the wind. She had no idea where he'd gone or when he'd be back. She understood the handoff was too painful for him, but when he didn't respond to her texts or voice mail messages, she started to worry. She didn't think he was the kind of person who would take his own life, but when someone was stressed to the breaking point, it was hard to predict what they might do. Emotionally, she was none too steady herself.

"This way," Tara said, starching her spine with resolve. The court had made its decision. She had no choice but to accept it.

Tara pushed across the threshold into the darkened nursery. Ms. Bean, Rhona, and Claudio crowded in behind her.

She tiptoed to the bed where Julie was sound asleep, the little horse mobile that Rhett had bought for her swaying in the gust of the air conditioning kicking on.

Tara's mother waited off to one side, looking distraught. Her father stood behind her, his hands on Bridgette's shoulders. They gave Tara a tight look of support that was not quite a smile. They were here for her, no matter what.

"She's so beautiful," Rhona exclaimed, clutching her hands to her chest and leaning over the crib.

"Just like her mother," Claudio said in a heavy Portuguese accent.

"I think she looks like Rhett," Tara said. "She's got his dimples and his dark eyes and detached earlobes and the arch of his eyebrows."

"She doesn't look a thing like him." Claudio snorted.

Ms. Bean cocked her head, and studied the baby. "She does look a little like her father."

Claudio glowered.

Rhona bent to scoop the baby into her arms. Julie stirred, whimpered.

"I have a medical binder for you. I know that Judge Brando has made you aware of Julie's health issues, but I want to make sure you fully understand." Tara opened the top drawer of the dresser, took out a three-inch-thick binder. "It's important to use the formula recommended by her pediatrician. It costs more than other formulas but it's essential for a preemie like Julie if you want her to thrive."

Julie's whimpers grew louder and she wriggled in Rhona's arms.

Rhona clutched the baby tighter.

It was all Tara could do not to take the child from her to comfort her. Rhona looked utterly freaked out and unprepared. Pity tugged at Tara's heartstrings, and she softened her tone. "You're going to be fine."

"Thank you." Rhona looked eternally grateful.

Tara flipped the binder to the next tab. "Here's bathing and grooming tips. Here's a list of her medication. Doctor appointments. Physical therapy exercises. Here's a list of supplies you'll need. Diapers and wipes, bottles, clothing, swaddle blankets, thermometer—"

"Can you let us borrow some of this?" Claudio interrupted, sweeping a hand at the well-stocked room. "To get started? I pay you."

"Yeah," Rhona said. "It's not as if you'll need it any longer."

Tara clamped her mouth shut, resisted saying, *Why did you abandon her?* Rhona's immaturity was showing. She was young and acting on emotions, not reality. Tara forgave her everything.

"We'll grab a few things now and I will accompany you to your house. Help you get settled in." She made the offer for Julie's sake. "I'll get Rhett to bag up some things and bring them to you when he comes to pick me up. How does that sound?"

"Oh yes, please," Claudio said at the same time Rhona said, "We don't need you."

Claudio stared pointedly at Rhona. Julie was still wailing. Tara interlaced her fingers to keep herself from taking the baby away from her biological mother.

Ms. Bean cleared her throat.

Everyone turned to look at her.

Tara had forgotten that the CPS worker was in the room.

"Tara has made you a generous offer," Ms. Bean said. "She's an accomplished NICU nurse. It would behoove you to take her up on it."

"It will be okay," Claudio said to Rhona. "She just wants to help."

"We can pack up the stuff," Tara's mother offered. "And follow you over to Rhona's house and bring you back."

"That's sweet of you to offer, Mom." Tara gave her mother a cottony smile. She was doing her best not to break down. "But Rhett needs to be the one to pack up her things. He needs the closure."

"Yes," Rhona said. "Closure. He needs to get used to it because we're getting permanent custody."

Claudio moved behind Rhona, put his hands on either side of

her waist, backing her up. They were a couple. Husband and wife. A unit. A team.

"Where is Rhett?" Rhona asked.

"He'll be along soon," Tara said. Praying it was true, fearing it was not. Her heart was utterly shattered. Where was Rhett when she needed him most?

AFTER HE LEFT the courthouse, Rhett caught a ride back to the Silver Feather with Archer and Casey. The battery on his cell had played out, and in his rush to get to court this morning, he'd forgotten his charger. He knew Tara had to be texting him. He would contact her as soon as he had a chance.

Right now, his goal was to get home and prepare himself for relinquishing his daughter to Rhona and Claudio.

Archer dropped Casey off at their house and then drove Rhett to his place.

Rhett's King Ranch was in the driveway, along with Ms. Bean's little Kia, Bridgette and Armand's white Camry, and Claudio's black Escalade.

His stomach was a rock.

"Want me to come in with you?" Archer offered.

Rhett shook his head. "This is my bull. I'm the only one that can ride it."

Archer nodded and drummed his fingers on the steering wheel. "Let me know if you want to grab a beer or something later."

"Thanks," Rhett said, but the last thing he wanted after this was over would be company. Tara was the only person who could empathize with him right now. The only person he wanted to be with.

As Archer drove away, Tara, Ms. Bean, Claudio, and Rhona carrying Julie stepped out onto the front porch, followed shortly by Bridgette and Armand. Claudio carried a bag of diapers. Tara had Julie's infant seat in her hands.

His eyes met Tara's and relief washed over her face. Guilt spurred him hard. He'd left Tara alone to deal with Claudio and Rhona. He hustled up the front steps. Stopped in front of Tara.

"Hello," she said, her voice giving away nothing. "I'm glad you're here."

"What's going on?"

"Rhona and Claudio weren't prepared to take her home today. They need supplies."

"So you're giving them ours?"

Her eyes were gentle, and he could see unshed tears glistening there. "I'm giving them to *Julie*."

Feeling chastised and deserving it, he plowed a hand through his hair. "What can I do to help?"

Tara rewarded him with a tender smile. "If you could gather some of Julie's things and bring them over to this address." She passed him a piece of paper with Claudio and Rhona's address on it.

"We just bought the house," Rhona said.

He barely gave her a glance. The location was in the most expensive part of Cupid. Rhett winced. From the trees, a mockingbird called, singing a ripping medley of happiness right there at the most sorrowful point of Rhett's life.

"I can do that."

"Great. I'm riding with Claudio and Rhona to help them get settled in with the little one. Pick me up there in an hour or so?"

"I'll be there." He wished he could get Tara aside and see how she was doing, but she was already heading down the driveway to Claudio's Escalade, everyone following after her.

He stood on the front porch watching them go, feeling as if he was on an ice floe in the Arctic and everything that mattered to him was floating away in the cold.

After they disappeared over the cattle guard in a cloud of dust, Rhett went into the silent house. The only sound was the steady hum of the air conditioner. He went into the garage where he stored extra cardboard boxes, selected the biggest one he could find, and went into the nursery.

He grabbed whatever was immediately at hand. Baby blankets. Onesies. Baby lotion. The Strawberry Shortcake pacifier that Tara had toyed with the day they decided to get married. It was Julie's favorite pacifier and the first thing he'd ever bought for her.

Rhett dropped the box, crossed the room to where his baby daughter had slept for the past two months, dropped to his knees in front of the dresser, and started opening drawers. His gaze fell on a box of animal crackers he'd stuck in the drawer, waiting for Julie to be old enough for them.

His daughter had never had a chance to eat animal crackers with him.

He took the cookies out and dropped the box. His hand was trembling so hard that the cuff of his shirt caught on the drawer knob. He yanked to dislodge himself but knocked over the dresser. He jumped out of the way before the furniture hit him. The pacifier flew into the air and the dresser fell on top of the cookies.

Rhett righted the dresser.

Underneath the dresser, the box was flattened. Crushed.

Just like his hopes and dreams.

He snagged the crumpled box from the floor, the cardboard corner poking him in the center of his palm, and he straightened and pried the mauled flap open. The cookies were snapped into dozens of broken pieces.

He slumped against the wall, slid all the way down until his butt touched the floor. Elbows dangling between his knees. The carpet he'd had installed just for Julie was puffy-cloud soft beneath his go-to-court trousers. He swiped a hand across his face, smelled vanilla from the cookies.

I gotta get up, he thought, and sluggishly, with great effort, pressed his palm against the floor and levered himself up. He slipped the string of the damaged box around his wrist, wearing it like a purse just the way Tara had.

The side of the box hit against his wrist and a piece of cookie fell out. It was a giraffe's head, smiling up at him with silent, cookie eyes.

He picked up the bodiless giraffe, rested it in his palm, remembering that long-ago Alzate sisters' tea party he'd crashed. He scooped up the Strawberry Shortcake pacifier too. Thought about the times he'd put it in his daughter's mouth to soothe her fussiness. It hadn't been nearly enough time with her. Not by a long shot.

Rhett brought the pacifier to his nose. It smelled like milk and Julie's sweet baby breath.

Closing his eyes, he waited for the pain to pass. The smashed cookie box dangling from his wrist. A giraffe's cookie head in one hand, Julie's pacifier in the other.

He ate the cookie. Jammed Julie's pacifier into his mouth and went back to packing.

Chapter 26

FADES: A bull that fades during a ride moves backward while simultaneously spinning or bucking in one or more directions.

THEY didn't speak on the drive home from Claudio and Rhona's place. No words were adequate to capture what they were feeling.

Rhett reached across the seat for her hand, but she didn't immediately put hers in his. "Tea? You okay?"

Her back was razor-straight. Her gaze focused out the window. "No," she whispered, her hand on her lower abdomen.

"You're thinking about the other baby you lost," he whispered, reading her body language.

"Losing babies seems to be my fate."

"It's not over until it's over," he said. "The permanency hearing is two and a half months away. A lot can happen between now and then."

"Unless Rhona does something really stupid, I don't see how."

"Hey, hey," he said, taking her hand from her lap. "No more doom and gloom. We'll get through this. I promise. We can still see Julie."

She gave him a smile as weak as skim milk.

When they got home, Tara told him she needed some time alone. Dusk was gathering, so he went out to feed the livestock. Tara wandered into the house without a word. He was worried about her but did not know how to comfort her.

It was almost dark when he went inside, full of nervous energy and mounting dread. The house was silent, and when he stepped inside he could feel the emptiness.

"Tara," he called, hanging his Stetson on the hat rack in the mudroom.

No answer.

He went into the living room, turning on lights. No Tara.

She wasn't in the kitchen. Nor their bedroom.

He found her in the nursery, sitting in the rocking chair. Her knees drawn up to her chest, one of Julie's baby blankets held up to her nose, tears streaming down her cheeks.

"Tara," he whispered, feeling like a right solid jackass for leaving her alone. He wished he could kick his own ass. "Are you all right?"

She looked up at him, rubbed her eyes with both fists, blotting away the tears. "Are you?"

"No." He squatted down in front of her, put his palms on her knees. "Do you want to talk about it?"

She shook her head. "I don't know if I can."

"Look at me."

She met his eyes. Her bottom lip was trembling.

"I love you, Tara."

"I love you too, Rhett, but it hurts too bad without her."

He took her hands in his, squeezed them. "I know."

Tears glistened in her eyes.

Tension strung between them, tight as a cinch rope. They were both broken and in pain. It was all too much. This had been one of the worst days of his life, and he felt like he had when Widow Maker had scooped him up and thrown him across the arena—hot, sweaty, and scared as hell.

"I don't know what's to become of us without her." Her breathing was shallow.

"What do you mean?" Terror took hold of him.

"We married because of her. We would never have come together otherwise."

"We're good together. So damn good."

"But was that just because of Julie?" Her voice came out crippled and small. "What have we got in common without her?"

"Tea, I—"

She put her index finger over his mouth. "Shh, listen to me. I think there's a lesson here for me."

He rocked back on his heels, giving her every drop of his attention. "I'm listening."

"I've had trouble in my life letting go of things. I hold on too tightly. You asked me before why I like helping so much." She paused, closed her eyes, took a deep breath. "I think I've got an answer for you now."

His stomach and throat twisted. He didn't say anything and waited for her to continue.

"Taking care of people makes me feel in control of my destiny. I thought I needed that feeling of control because I was afraid of losing everything. And the more things I lost, the tighter I clung to my caregiving ways. But with you, and Julie, I realized that every day is a beautiful gift. And with this gift came another gift."

"What was that?" he asked, fear beating his heart like a drum.

"The choice to trust that life is good and on my side. I can't do that if I can't let go."

"Are you saying you want to let me go?"

"I'm saying I *have* to let you go. You quit the circuit because I pressured you. You weren't ready to leave. I was operating out of fear. Terrified I was going to lose you the way I lost Kit. But if I trust life, I must trust that I am going in the direction that's best for both of us in the long run. So I can choose to let go of my fears, let go of the past, and trust that life will take us both to where we can be happy and joyful. If I don't, if I keep hanging on and not trusting, I'm going to stay stuck in my suffering."

"I don't understand."

"My Granny Blue says that because I hear a humming noise when you kiss me that we are destined to be together. I didn't believe in the legend before you, but then I heard the humming and knew it was true. I have to let you go. I have to let you grow. And I have to go too."

"But will we ever be together again?"

She cupped his cheek with her palm, her smile filled with love and caring. "If it's the best thing for us, we will be."

"And if it's not?" His voice quaked.

"Then we'll both have to accept that despite Granny Blue's humming, it's not meant to be."

He blew out his breath. She needed time alone, that much was clear. He had to give her space whether he liked it or not. He had to respect her wishes even as it was eating him up inside.

"You should go back on the road."

"What will you do? Will you stay here?"

"I can't." She shook her head. "I couldn't bear it without you and Julie."

"Where will you go?" he asked, completely befuddled by her logic. It didn't make sense to him, but the earnestness on her face told him she was serious.

"I still have the lease on the duplex. I'll go back to El Paso. Back to my job. There's nothing for me here now that Julie's gone. You'll be on the road. I'll have nothing to do but rattle around this house. There are kids in El Paso who need a NICU nurse. I need to be needed, Rhett. You know that about me."

"Tea, I thought we were a family."

"We were." She lifted her shoulders to her ears, let them slump down hard. "And now we're not. Without Julie, what's the point? We married because of her and now that she's gone . . ."

He squatted in front of her, took her hands in his. "You're just feeling blue."

She shook her head. "No."

"Are you saying . . ." He paused, hitched in his breath, braced himself for the answer he dreaded. "Are you saying you don't want to be married to me?"

"We married in haste. We didn't marry for love—"

"But we found love. We love each other, right? I love you."

He heard his voice crack like fragile ice on a winter pond. "Do you love me?"

She touched his cheek with her palm. "More than words can say."

"Do you still hear the hum when I kiss you?"

"Yes," she whispered. "Yes, I do."

"I'm the one you're supposed to be with. I'm your soul mate."

"Soul mates don't always get to spend a life together." Her eyes turned misty again, and she ducked her head.

"Tara." He hooked two fingers under her chin, tilted her head up, forced her to meet his gaze. "I don't want to go back on the circuit. I want to stay here with you."

"No. I can't allow you to do that. The rodeo is *everything* to you."

"You are more important than any damn rodeo."

"It's your life, your dream, your passion."

"You're my passion!"

"I can't allow you to give up your one chance at greatness for me."

"Are you breaking up with me?" He couldn't believe this.

"Rhett, you deserve a woman who can give you children, especially now since you've lost Julie. You know how wonderful it is being a parent. I cannot deprive you of that joy."

"I still have Julie," he said. "*We* can still have Julie."

"Part time. Visitations. She's won't be in your life day in and day out when Rhona gets permanent custody."

He sat down hard on the floor in front of the rocker, feeling devastated, not knowing what to say or do. Nothing could make this better. They'd lost the love of their lives. She was right. What were they without Julie?

He searched her face, saw nothing but sorrow etched there. "We'll sleep on this. Things will look brighter in the morning. No rash decisions."

"Says the king of rash decisions." She laughed, but the sound was as hollow as the hole in his ragtag heart.

She reached out a hand to him. He took it.

He had so many things he wanted to tell her. How he appreciated and respected her. How these past few months with her meant the world to him. How she'd changed him in countless positive ways. But he did not say those things; if he started talking like that, he would start crying too, and she needed him to be strong for her. He would not let her down.

"I miss her already." She brought the baby blanket to her nose and inhaled deeply.

"I miss her too."

"This was even harder than I thought it was going to be. This morning, we were so sure we were home free. And tonight, we're splintered."

"Oh, Tara." He pulled her from the rocking chair and into his lap. He kissed away her tears, then claimed her mouth. He should not be kissing her right now. She was too vulnerable. But so was he. Grief sex. It wouldn't fix anything, but right now, they both needed something to cling to.

She kissed him back with an urgency and desperation born of sorrow and shattered dreams. It was a frantic, hungry kiss. The kiss lovers shared after a funeral to prove they were still alive.

The next thing he knew they were ripping each other's clothes off. Buttons popped. Shirts floated. Boots flew. Pants unzipped.

Instantly, they were ripe and ready for each other. Her body slick and wet, his hard and strong. They grappled for each other, merging mouths and limbs. He took her right there on the carpet. Neither of them thinking of protection. No condoms. No birth control. Just feral grief sex, raw and aching.

He enjoyed her in a whole new way. A deeper, more mature way. Lovemaking filled with regret and sadness, tenderness and tears. And at the back of his mind, this mantra throbbed: *You have to let her go. You have to set her free.*

It would be so easy to be selfish. To hold on to her. Keep her close. He'd been selfish for twenty-eight years. Until Julie. Until Tara.

They'd taught him so much about what it meant to be a man, a father, and a husband. His own needs did not matter. If Rhona was the better parent as deemed by a court of law, he would accept it. He wasn't happy about it, but he would make peace with it. Do his best. Father her as much as he could.

Julie came first, always.

And as for Tara, he was going to set her free to find happiness with someone who wasn't weighed down with so much baggage. He couldn't give her what she wanted more than anything in the world. A baby of her very own.

What a tragedy!

For almost an hour they made love on the floor of the nursery. Finally, in the end, they came together in one final push. Crying out in unison. Clutching each other. Panting and grasping with salty, sweet sorrow.

When it was over, she rested her head on his shoulder, and he wrapped his arm around her. They stared up at the ceiling, winded and worn out.

Neither of them spoke. Was this, then, really the end of them? Hope could be a dangerous thing, but hope he did.

He stroked her hair from her face. She traced her fingertips over his nipple. He shivered. She laughed. They went at it again.

Sometime later, in the darkness of the room, Tara spoke. "Loss is a part of life."

"The bad part."

"Without the rough parts we wouldn't appreciate the good ones."

"How did you get so smart?" he asked.

"With great age comes great wisdom," she teased, and it heartened him to hear the lighter tone in her voice. "Remember, I am four years older than you."

"Maybe when I'm your age I'll be as wise as you are."

"I'll always be ahead of you, buddy, and don't you forget it." She poked him playfully in the side with her elbow, as if they would be together in four years.

"Tara," he said, "this situation sucks."

"I know," she said.

There was a great pause. A chasm of silence neither of them rushed to fill. Rhett rolled away from her, unable to keep this up. The second her body was gone, his chest got tight again.

"For what it's worth, you're an amazing wife and mother. I consider myself lucky to have spent time with you."

"You're not half bad yourself, Lockhart." She chucked him on the shoulder with her little fist, her eyes bright, belying the shakiness of her smile. "Do me a favor, will you?"

"Anything. Everything. Just name it."

"When you get back to the rodeo, beat the pants off Claudio."

"Now that," he drawled, "I absolutely intend on doing." Then he picked her up, took her to bed, and made love to her as if it were the very last time they would ever make love.

When he woke up, it was dawn and Tara was gone.

On her pillow, she'd pinned a note. He unpinned it. Read it.

To my dearest husband,

You have brought so much joy into my life. So much fun and spontaneity. I couldn't have asked for a better partner. Even when we're not together, my heart is always with you. Know that. I hate to slip off without saying good-bye, but one good-bye per day is enough, and losing Julie knocked the wind right out of my sails. I hope you understand. Text me when you get to your next destination.

With all my love,
Your soul mate, Tara

Rhett clutched the note to his chest and smiled and cried and vowed he would bring that big-assed gaudy trophy home for her to polish, and then he'd retire and spend the rest of his days trying to make this up to her.

Chapter 27

SEEING DAYLIGHT: The term used when a cowboy comes loose from a bull far enough for the spectators to see daylight between the cowboy and the animal.

"MAY I join you?" Katy Jones, one of the other NICU nurses, asked Tara on her second day back at the hospital.

Tara was trying to find her way in a post-Julie, post-Rhett world, and she wanted to be alone. She was on her lunch break, eating by herself in a nearly empty cafeteria at midnight, a container of yogurt, an oversized banana, and a box of animal crackers in front of her.

Katy, who had a plate with scrambled eggs and a pile of bacon from the short-order grill, didn't even wait for Tara to invite her. She set down her tray and pulled up a chair. She eyed Tara's food. "That's a lot of carbs."

"CareFlite is bringing in a preemie from Big Bend," Tara said. "The mom went into labor during a weekend camping trip with her family. I need the energy. Thought I'd grab some lunch while I could. They'll be touching down in twenty."

"How early is the preemie?"

"Six weeks."

"Who goes camping in Big Bend when they're seven and a half months pregnant?" The woman asked the rhetorical question. She placed a strip of bacon on Tara's plate. "You need fat and protein too."

"Thanks," Tara said, crunching the bacon and remembering how Rhett made the best bacon. The right amount of crispy.

"When did you start eating animal crackers?"

"Julie."

"Oh." Katy reached a hand across the table, laid it on top of Tara's. "How are you doing?"

"Good, fine," she lied.

"So you and Rhett?" The other nurse looked at her ring finger. Tara didn't wear jewelry beyond a watch at work. "Calling it quits?"

"We're on hold for now," Tara said.

"Limbo land, huh? That sucks."

Tara peeled the banana slowly.

"You love him, right?"

"So much," Tara murmured.

"Then why are you here? Why aren't you on the PBR circuit with him, waiting in his trailer for him every night when he gets finished?"

"I'd go stir-crazy."

"Are you planning on divorcing him?"

Tara nodded again, felt a hot tear hit the back of her hand.

"For God's sake, why?"

"He deserves a woman who can give him children. He's an awesome dad. I can't tie him down when I can't offer him more kids."

"What about surgery?"

"It's no guarantee."

"That was over two years ago when you got your diagnosis. There have been a lot of advances since then. There's a new procedure—"

"I don't want to get my hopes up."

"Tara Alzate," her friend scolded. "That is so unlike you. You're not a quitter and you're the bravest person I know. Doesn't he get a say in any of this? What are you so afraid of? Getting pregnant and riding off into the sunset with the love of your life?"

They were legitimate questions. Tara sat there staring at Katy, pondering it. *Was* she afraid to be happy?

"Omigosh." Katy leaned forward. "I've got it. You're afraid that if you let yourself be happy something bad will befall you or those you love. You were happy with Kit, and then he died. You were happily pregnant, and then you lost the baby. You were happy to be Julie's foster mother, and then the rug got pulled out from under you again. Oh, my dear girl! You poor thing."

Was Katy right? Could it be true? Tara placed a palm over her chest. Was it the reason she'd separated from Rhett? In her distorted fear, did she believe that if she stayed with Rhett something terrible would befall him?

Yes, yes, she did. Mouth agape, she slumped back in her chair, stared at her friend wide-eyed.

"From the look on your face, I'd say I nailed it." Katy buffed her knuckles against her scrub top. "I missed my calling. I should have gone into psych."

Tara's phone pinged a text. It was the NICU telling her Care-Flite had landed. "Gotta go."

The first thing she did when she got home after her shift was call her gynecologist and schedule an appointment.

WITH TARA WORKING night shifts, she slept during the day. There wasn't a good time for Rhett to call her. They did the best they could, but their texts and Skype sessions grew fewer and farther between as the circuit schedule grew more and more intense going into the finals.

After taking off those three weeks for the concussion, Rhett had dropped in the ratings but there was still a possibility he could win if he drew the best bulls and rode his heart out. Claudio was leading the pack.

To keep from getting depressed about losing Julie and not being able to see Tara, Rhett threw himself into a grueling fitness routine. Working out five or six hours a day when he wasn't riding or driving his trailer from event to event.

Then it was November and they were in Vegas. He'd been here before, one of the rare few thirty-five cowboys. The best bull riders in the world. He was currently ranked at number five. It all came down to this. T-Mobile Arena buzzed with excitement on the final day of the five-day event. Media was everywhere. The Vegas Strip was crowded with revelers wearing cowboy boots and Stetsons and PBR merchandised gear.

Tara had called him early that morning after she got off work to wish him good luck. Just hearing her voice infused him with renewed zeal.

Tonight would be the pinnacle of his career. Tonight he was going to take home the championship. He believed it without a shadow of doubt.

But when it came down to it, when it was his turn to ride, and he went to the chutes, he knew that he did not want to be there. No trophy could make up for what he'd lost. No grandstanding could make things better.

"Ready?" his manager asked. "This is your night to shine."

Rhett stood there listening to the roar of the crowd, smelled the pungent aroma of the arena, tasted victory that could be his if he wanted. For twenty-eight years he'd dreamed of this. It was his everything.

But now, that dream seemed silly. Like the dreams of a child. Riding was in his blood. He didn't deny it. But it *was* just riding.

Tara and Julie were what really mattered. They *were* his life.

Before the two of them, he was a shadow of a man, a hollow boy who placated himself with bulls and booze and women. He saw so clearly now what others had seen in him that he'd been blind to—he'd been a smooth, charming, fun-loving man-child.

He'd thought himself clever. Free from the trappings that encumbered most men. Thought marriage and children were manacles and leg irons.

Oh, what a fool!

When he'd lost his mother, it had crumbled his very foundation. He'd come to distrust women. He'd seen the heartache of loving a woman in his father's broken relationships. In what had happened to his brothers, in the loss of his own mother. Women leave. That was the lesson he'd learned. His underlying belief. Women couldn't be trusted. He'd formed a strategy to deal with that belief. Leave them before they can leave you.

He saw now how his whole life philosophy had unconsciously been driven by the circumstances around him. How he'd formed his view of the world that was nothing more than this misguided belief. Not all women left. And unlike Ridge and Ranger's mothers, his mom hadn't intentionally left him behind. It wasn't her fault, but to an eight-year-old kid, it had seemed that way.

He'd been Peter Pan. Refusing to grow up. Thinking he was holding on to something special, his youth, his freedom. In reality, he'd been clinging to a myth.

Life changed.

People got older.

By ignoring the inevitable, he'd missed out. Skimming along on the surface of life when the real reward came from diving in deep.

Funny how the kid who took the pain of being tossed from a bull with a swagger and a grin, and thought that he was better than most because of it, was the same guy who was terrified of emotional pain.

Maybe taking on physical pain was how he avoided dealing with his feelings. Perverse as that sounded, it made sense. *Look, fellas, I can last eight seconds on the back of a bull.*

But eight seconds in a real, honest, open relationship with a woman scared the living hell out of him.

Until Julie.

And Tara.

Now, they'd become his world, and he couldn't imagine another second without them in it.

Tara.

The sexy earth mother. His rock. His heart. His soul.

His world.

At the thought of spending the rest of his life without her, he felt as if someone had shot a cannonball through him. Without her, he was the walking dead. No hope of becoming what he was supposed to be.

No hope at all.

He saw himself at the end of his life. A broken-down old cowboy, more likely an alcoholic than not, making his living off managing other, younger hotshots. Shuffling through women who took him for what they could get, until he finally ended up sick and alone, dying with his trophies as his only solace.

But there was another option.

He could close out his life having really made something of himself. With a loving wife and family surrounding him. Holding his hand, telling him how much he meant to them, how much they loved him.

But in order to get that life, he had to give all of himself. One hundred percent. He couldn't keep running away when the going got tough. He had to stay and fight for what he wanted. He had to give Julie and Tara, his brothers and his father, and all the rest of his extended family, all the love he had inside him.

He had to stop giving in to his fears. Had to stop hiding. Had to face his future with courage and heart. But not with the false bravado that had shoved him onto the backs of bulls.

Climbing onto a two-ton wild bull was easy. Loving—and sticking with his loved ones through the tough times—*that* took real courage.

The wounds that he ignored, hid, denied, ran from—his mother's death, his father's neglect, Brittany rejecting him and his baby—had festered beneath the happy-go-lucky surface, bubbling into a cesspool of poison he refused to see was there.

He'd glossed over the pain with smiles and sex, flirtation and fun. Replacing his losses with the never-ending chase for fleeting fame. Believing bull riding and winning would somehow save him.

It had not.

Would not.

Could not.

Salvation lay not in running away from his sorrow, but in leaning in. That salvation fit with the bull riders' axiom: *Always pick the baddest bull*. No one ever won riding a mediocre bull. No pain, no gain. He'd understood it in the arena, but he'd never applied it to the rest of his life.

And he couldn't wait to tell Tara all this.

"Sorry," he said to his manager as he stripped off his gloves. "I quit."

Chapter 28

CHAMPION: The rodeo champion is traditionally the high-money winner in an event for the given season.

R<small>HETT</small> raced to the Southwest Airlines ticket counter. The line was miserably long. He hadn't even called Tara to tell her he was on the way home. He wanted to surprise her. Dammit. Maybe he shouldn't be so impulsive. What if she was at work or busy?

Tara had rubbed off on him. Making him stop and think.

Don't go off half-cocked.

Confused, he stepped back, letting other people go ahead of him in the security screening line. People were pouring from the exits to reclaim their luggage. He noticed a flight had just arrived from El Paso.

Something stopped him in his tracks.

He turned his head. Saw a dark-haired woman with a single thick braid dangling down her back. Wearing jeans, a white peasant blouse, and red Old Gringo boots.

Did a double take.

His heart thundered like bucking bull hooves. Tara?

Nah, it couldn't be her. She'd told him she was going to watch the finals with his family at the mansion.

The woman flipped her braid over her shoulder in a gesture so familiar that his pulse skipped a beat.

"Tara!" he called, not caring one whit that people were staring at him. "Tara!"

The woman turned.

Chestnut brown eyes met his. A smile broke across her face, and her eyes crinkled, happy. "Rhett?"

Simultaneously, they raced toward each other. Met in the middle of the room surrounded by cranking carousels and people studying them with amused expressions. Stood breathing and staring and smiling. So much damn smiling.

"What are you doing here? How did you know I was coming in to surprise you? Did Aria call you?"

"No." He laughed. "I was coming home to you."

"What? And forgo the final ride?"

"That doesn't matter. I've got the grand prize right here." He drew her into his arms and kissed her.

"No, you have to ride. You've worked so hard. Let's grab my luggage and go. Let's get you back to the arena. It's your time to shine bright, Mr. Lockhart."

"No," he said. "I'm walking away. I'm not taking any more chances. It's too dangerous and I don't want to do anything that could take me away from you and Julie."

"Oh Rhett," she said. "Do you really mean it?"

"With all my heart and soul." Rhett dipped his head and kissed her right there in the Las Vegas airport. "Do you still hear the hum, Mrs. Lockhart?"

"Forever," she said. "Always."

"Let's go to a hotel," he said. "It's been far too long since I've made love to you."

THEY CHECKED IN to the Bellagio and raced to their room. They fell into a laughing heap on the bed. She got up and did a little striptease for him, slowly shimmying out of her clothes, revealed that she was wearing a lacy black garter belt and black silk stockings beneath her jeans.

"That garter belt is killing me," he said. "You do know that, right?"

"Why do you think I wore it?"

"I'm the luckiest cowboy in the world."

"Rhett." She murmured his name low and throaty, her thick black hair falling past her shoulders. She lowered her eyelids over chestnut brown eyes, so experienced and yet at the same time so beguilingly exposed.

"Yes, Tara?"

"It's time you made love to me now." Slanting her head to the right, she scrutinized him, the faintest Mona Lisa smile lifting the corners of her mouth shiny with strawberry gloss.

Their gazes collided and *boom!* They were in each other's arms again, kissing like tomorrow would not come. He cupped her cheeks between his palms, holding her dear face close while they savagely devoured each other.

"Wait," she said. "There's something I need to tell you."

He paused, held his breath. "Wh-what is it?"

"I had surgery at the beginning of October."

He felt the color drain from his face. "What kind of surgery?"

"To repair the damage from the endometriosis. I just went in for my follow-up appointment. It's sort of why I'm here."

"What happened?"

Her beaming smile was the most beautiful thing he'd ever seen. "My doctor said the surgery was a success."

"You mean . . . ?" He scarcely dared hope.

"There's a good chance we can have children of our own."

"Oh, Tara," he said, a thrill arrowing through his heart. "I'm so damn happy!"

"Me too," she said, yanking at the hem of his shirt, popping open all the snaps in one quick pull. She ran her hot little palms over his chest and let out a delighted moan. "You have no idea how long I've been dreaming of doing this to you again."

His plan, if he'd ever had one, was to take things slow, savor the moment. Play and tease and caress. That honorable notion flew straight out the window. He couldn't wait. He'd already waited too long. Without another word, he stripped off his pants and climbed onto the mattress with her.

She wrapped her arms around his neck, rested her head on his shoulder, and sighed the dreamy sigh of a cartoon princess.

Rhett ground his pelvis against hers and she wriggled beneath him, making go-to-it-cowboy noises. Her hands had slipped around to his lower back and she raked her fingers lightly over his skin and let out a hungry little growl.

He had a tigress by the tail and loved every second of it. Her fingers were sizzling hot against his skin, and she playfully nibbled his earlobe. She tasted of summer, sultry and salty, windblown and tanned.

Then his wife straddled him and took him straight to the stars.

AN HOUR LATER they lay in each other's arms, sated and happy. Rhett called for room service, including champagne.

"What are we celebrating?" Tara asked.

"My retirement . . . and now hopes of baby making."

"You're not feeling a little bit sad about not riding tonight?"

"On the contrary," he said. "I feel free as a bird. It's time for me to step aside and make room for the younger guys."

"I'm stunned," she said. "I really can't believe it."

"It's all because of you letting me go that I was able to let the rodeo go. It's so damn lonely on the road. I simply don't care about winning anymore. And if I keep climbing onto the back of a bull, eventually I'm going to get seriously hurt. It's just not worth the risk."

"Oh Rhett." She stroked his cheek with her knuckle and smiled into her husband's eyes. "I'm so happy for you!"

"I'm so happy for *us*."

She kissed him long and hard and deep. This was the reunion she'd been dreaming of for the past two months.

A knock sounded on the door.

"Wow! Room service at the Bellagio is *fast*," Tara said, jumping up for the luxurious bathrobes in the closet and tossing one to him as she slipped into the other.

Another knock.

"Be right there." He shrugged into his robe, cinched it up, and padded to the door. Tara plopped back onto the bed. He opened the door without squinting through the peephole.

Rhona stood there juggling Julie in her arms. She took in Rhett in his bathrobe and Tara on the bed in hers, and her eyes widened. "Oh, I didn't know you were here too."

At the sight of the baby, Tara leaped off the bed and hurried to join them at the door.

Rhona looked bedraggled and worn thin. Her hair a tangled mess. Her color pale, with dark circles under her eyes. A crust of baby spit-up on the shoulder of her T-shirt. She was a far cry from the girl who'd taken Julie away. Things had been rough for her.

The baby, to Tara's relief, looked healthy.

It startled her to realize how much Julie had grown in the weeks since Rhona had gained custody. She was holding her head up on her own, her hair a fuzzy little halo around her head. Thrilled to see the baby, Tara flung the door open wide, motioned Rhona inside. "Come in, come in."

"Have a seat," Rhett invited, throwing their discarded clothes off a nearby chair. He looked nervous and off-balance. He rested his hands at his waist, thumbs facing forward, fingers to his back. "Oh, you've got a diaper bag." He surged forward. "Let me get that for you."

"You always did have good manners," Rhona said wistfully.

He set the diaper bag back down on the floor by the couch. His gaze was fixed on his daughter. Julie was staring at him with curious eyes.

Eyes that had started to shift color from navy blue to brown, Tara noticed, and her pulse quickened. She had missed so much.

Rhona sank down on the chair.

Rhett and Tara perched on the edge of the king-sized bed across from her.

"How did you know we were here?" Rhett said.

"They're throwing a party in the presidential suite for Claudio," Rhona said. "I was going to drop Julie off with a babysitter and go get changed when I saw you in the lobby. It took me awhile to find out what room you were in. I had to bribe a bellhop."

Tara fiddled with the tie on her robe. Why did Rhona have Julie with her, if she'd been taking her to a babysitter so she could party?

"Claudio won?" Rhett said, not sounding the least bit jealous.

"You knew he was going to when you walked away," Rhona said. "You were the only one who could realistically beat him." She speared a quick glance at Tara. "Why did you walk away?"

"I don't care about it anymore."

"Because of her?"

"Because of her," Rhett confirmed.

Rhona met Tara's eyes. "You're lucky, lady. Really lucky. Your man gave up the circuit for you."

Tara let that slide. "How's Julie? How are you?"

"It's so much work." Rhona sniffled. "An impossible amount of work."

"Can I hold her?" Tara asked.

Looking utterly relieved, Rhona got up and put Julie in her arms.

Tara smiled down at the baby. Julie's eyes widened and a smile wreathed her sweet little face, and Tara's heart melted. The baby smelled so good, sweet and innocent. God, how she'd missed this scent. She kissed the top of her head.

"Rhona," Rhett said, his voice kind. "Why are you here?"

"You got visitation rights. I thought you might want to see her."

"What are you doing in Vegas? It's no place for an infant."

"We've joined Claudio on the circuit."

Tara snapped her mouth closed to keep from saying something judgmental.

"I . . . I want you to take her. It's too much for me. I thought

I could handle it, but I can't. You're a much better mom than I'll ever be." Rhona's gaze burned into Tara's.

"Don't be so hard on yourself," Tara soothed. "Motherhood isn't easy, but it'll get better, you'll get into the groove."

"Julie doesn't even feel like mine, you know? Since I wasn't there for her in the beginning. I don't even like her name." Rhona scratched her ear, stared off into space.

"If you felt like this, why did you file for custody in the first place?" Rhett asked. "You put us through hell, Rhona."

"I dunno." She rounded her shoulders. "I got to feeling guilty about running off and leaving her. I do love her and I want to be her mom, but it's complicated."

Tara held Julie close, fearful that Rhona was engaging in risky behaviors. "What do you mean?"

"Claudio's jealous of her, especially now that I'm pregnant with his baby." She touched her belly. "I mean, I still want to see her, but I think it would be better if she could live with you, and I have visitation rights instead. What do you say? Do you want her?"

"Yes!" Rhett and Tara cried in unison.

Rhona looked utterly relieved. She pressed her palms together in front of her chest, bowed her head. "Thank you, thank you, thank you."

"You're sure about this?" Tara said.

"Yes." Rhona bobbed her head. "Can you take her right now?"

"So you can get to your party?" Rhett asked.

Rhona looked shamefaced, but nodded.

"It's all right," Tara said. "We'll happily take her right now. Don't worry. We'll take care of everything."

With a nervous smile, Rhona shook their hands and darted out the door.

Leaving Rhett and Tara staring at each other in wide-eyed wonder.

"We got our girl back," Rhett whispered, gazing down at his daughter.

Tara looked at her husband with tears in her eyes. "We're a family again."

He kissed her then, as she held the baby. A light, gentle kiss of love that sent her head humming in the most magnificent way.

"ALL RISE."

It was December 9, the hearing for permanent placement of Julie Elizabeth Lockhart.

The people amassed in the courtroom stood up. The place packed with Lockharts and Alzates. Ridge and Kaia, Aria and Remington, home on leave for Christmas, Armand and Bridgette, Duke and Vivi, Archer and Casey, Granny Blue, Lamar, Ms. Bean, and most of the Silver Feather employees. Even Ember and Ranger had flown in from Canada with their new baby daughter to be there.

Judge Brando entered the room.

"Be seated," the bailiff called out.

In a rustle, the congregation sat.

The judge took her chair. Put on reading glasses, examined the paperwork in front of her. Peered out over the rims of her glasses, stared first at Rhett and then Tara. Took a sip of water. Said nothing.

Leaving everyone in the courtroom holding their collective breaths.

"In the case of the minor child, Julie Elizabeth Lockhart, the child's biological mother, Rhona White Limon, has asked to turn custodial rights over to the child's father while maintaining visitation rights. In light of her request, permanent custody is awarded to Rhett Lockhart and his wife, Tara Alzate Lockhart."

A cheer went up from the crowd.

"I'm heartened to see so many loving family and friends," Judge Brando went on. "Because it does indeed take a village to raise a child. Julie is a very lucky little girl."

"And I'm a very lucky dad," Rhett whispered to Tara. "And

it's all due to you. If you hadn't loved her with all your heart and soul from the very beginning, we wouldn't be here today."

Tara kissed her husband and hugged her baby, and everyone went back to the Silver Feather Ranch and threw a big party officially welcoming Julie into the loving arms of her clan.

Epilogue

"COWBOY, there's someone knocking on our door."

Rhett opened one eye and studied his dear wife propped up on the pillows beside him.

Sweet pink lips that last night had tasted of the chocolate layer cake she'd made for his birthday. Bright, happy brown eyes that danced with mischief. Full perky breasts and a belly rounded from the baby growing inside her.

His baby.

Their baby.

A son. Due in a few months.

Rhett grinned, and his heart throbbed like a sonofagun. The culprit was this beautiful, sexy woman, who'd changed everything. Joy pushed through him. Overflowed. What a lucky man he was. Oh, so lucky.

He knew exactly where he was. Rooted deep in the soil of the Silver Feather Ranch, and damn grateful for it.

And he had Tara to thank. She had changed him in so many wonderful ways. He'd gone from a lost, good-time Charlie rodeo cowboy to a settled, solid father and husband. He didn't miss his rowdy youth one bit.

With Tara, he had everything he'd never known he wanted. Now, she and Julie and the new baby were his life. He couldn't imagine a world without them in it.

A soft knock sounded on the door again.

"Come in," he called.

The door bumped open and Julie toddled into the room clutching her blanket in one hand, her teddy bear in the other.

"Morning, pudding pop." He smiled at his daughter, felt his heart fill with more love than he ever thought possible. He leaned over the side of the bed, held out his arms to her, and she ran to him, grinning.

"Dada," she said, and snuggled against him. Julie still had developmental delays from being a preemie, but she was quickly catching up to other children her age. The little Houdini had already figured out how to escape from her crib, so for safety's sake, they'd put her in a youth bed last week. Not a dull moment with this little one.

"Are we really ready for another one?" Tara rested her hand on her expanding belly as a tiny frown pinched between her eyebrows. "I know I always dreamed of a house full of children, but are we going to be able to give them both the attention they need?"

"Listen to your mama." Rhett kissed the top of Julie's head. "She's such a worrywart. Tell her there's always enough love to go around." He met Tara's gaze, and instantly her face softened. He loved the way her eyes turned dreamy whenever she looked at him. "Everything is going to be just fine, sweetheart. I've got your back. *Always.*"

He wasn't making false promises. With all his heart and soul, Rhett was fully committed to Tara and their growing family. Nothing could ever tear them apart.

Keep reading for a sneak peek at

THE CHRISTMAS DARE

the next book in Lori Wilde's
Twilight, Texas series

Coming October 2019!

Chapter 1

On a cinnamon-scented Saturday morning in early December, Dallas's newly elected mayor, Filomena James, walked her only surviving daughter, Kelsey, down the pew-packed aisle of the lavishly decorated Highland Park United Methodist Church.

She slipped her arm through her daughter's, and off they went to the instrumental score of "Let Me Tell You About My Boat." Filomena had insisted on music hipper than "The Wedding March" for her child's big day.

Bucking the old guard.

That was how she won her mayoral seat. Never mind that Kelsey was a traditionalist. After all, Filomena was the one shelling out major bucks for this shindig, and *she* was the rebel with a cause.

To quote her campaign buttons.

So as not to conflict with her bid for mayor, she'd insisted on the December wedding date. In mild protest, Kelsey put up a feeble fuss. Her daughter was not a fan of December in general or Christmas in particular. But, as always, Filomena had prevailed. Luckily for Kelsey. Mama knew best.

Everything was going as Filomena had planned. That is, until the groom hightailed it for the exit, elbows locked with his best man.

Fifteen minutes later, back in the bridal room of the church, Kelsey sat as calm as a statue, demure ankles crossed, feet tucked underneath the bench. Her waist-length hair twisted high in an elegant braided chignon. A bouquet of white roses and a crumpled, handwritten Dear Jane letter lay limp in her lap.

Sounds of car doors slamming and hushed voices stirring gossip drifted in through the partially opened window.

The poor thing.

Did you think she suspected Clive was gay?

How does she recover from this?

Breathing deep, Kelsey hid her smile as relief poured through her. Okay, sprinkle in a dab of sadness, a jigger of regret, and a dollop of I-do-not-want-to-face-my-mother, but other than that, Clive's abrupt adios hadn't peeled her back too far.

Hey, it was the most embarrassing thing that happened to her by far. She'd get through this.

As if being struck by a hundred flyswatters all slapping at once, Filomena's cheeks flushed scarlet. Her thick, black, Joan Crawford eyebrows pulled into a hard V as she scowled. Howled. "Do you have any idea how humiliated *I* am?"

"I'm sorry, Mother," Kelsey said by rote.

"It is your fault. If you'd slept with Clive, as I told you to, instead of sticking to that wait-until-the-wedding nonsense, *I* would not be on the hook for this nightmare."

Kelsey's best friend, Tasha Williams, who'd been standing by the door, lifted the hem of the emerald-green charmeuse maid-of-honor dress and strode across the small room to toe off with Filomena.

"Are you frigging kidding me?" Tasha's deep brown eyes narrowed, and she planted her hands onto her hips, head bobbing as she spoke. "Kels got stood up, not *you*."

Yay, you. Grateful, Kelsey sent her a "thank you" glance.

"The media will eat me for dinner over this." Through nasty eyes, Filomena glowered.

Uh-oh. Kelsey knew the look far too well. A clear signal to give her mother a berth as wide as the Grand Canyon.

"Have an inch of compassion, you witch." Tasha glared lasers at Filomena.

Proud that her bestie had not called her mother a bitch when she knew the word was searing the end of Tasha's tongue,

Kelsey cleared her throat. Long ago, she'd learned not to throw emotional gasoline onto her mother's fits of pique. Courting head-to-toe third-degree burns was not her favorite pastime.

"Yes?" A sharp, cutting tone invaded her mother's voice.

Gulping, Tasha couldn't quite meet Filomena's eyes. The woman's icy stare could quell Katniss Everdeen. "Just . . . just . . . have a heart. Dammit. She's your daughter."

"Don't you dare lecture me, you little upstart." Filomena shoved her face in front of Tasha's nose.

In a soothing, even tone, Kelsey pressed her palms downward. "Mom, I'm fine here. Please, go do damage control."

"Excellent idea." With stiff-legged movements, Filomena shifted her attention off Tasha and finger-pinching the ruching at the waist of her snug-fitting, mother-of-the-bride dress. She straightened herself, dusted off her shoulders, and stalked toward the door. "Clive's father owes me big time for this."

Filomena's exit left Kelsey and Tasha exhaling simultaneously.

"Ah," Tasha said.

"Gotta love how she turns every disaster into a political stepping stone," Tasha muttered.

Busy reading Clive's scrawled letter again, Kelsey didn't answer. Before he and Kevin had fled, Clive had pressed the note into the minister's hand.

Dear Kelsey,

Shabby of me to ditch you this way, but please believe me when I say I wanted to marry you. You are the kindest, most loving person I've ever met and my deep affection for you has gotten me this far. But no more cowering in the closet, praying to turn into something I'm not. You deserve better. I deserve better. I've been a coward, and you were safe. Time to stop running. Kevin and I love each other. We have for a long time. Last night after the bachelor party . . . well . . . let's just say everything changed forever. Out there somewhere is the real love

of your life. Please, cash in the honeymoon tickets and spoil
yourself with a trip of your own.

Best wishes,
Your friend—Clive

You were safe.

Floating off the page, those three words stood tall above the others, accusing her of her most glaring shortcoming. Yes, she played it safe.

Without question.

While Clive's betrayal did sting, the loss and embarrassment didn't equal the pain of the truth. If she hadn't been playing it safe, going for the most accommodating, least challenging man around, she wouldn't have ended up here.

Once again, her mother was right, and this was her fault.

Filomena pushed the union because Clive's father was Texas Supreme Court Justice Owen Patterson. But Kelsey had gone for it. Intelligent, witty, urbane, Clive was entertaining and erudite, and he always smelled fantastic.

How easy it had been to slip into a tranquil relationship with him. When he'd told her that he was old-fashioned and wanted to wait until the wedding night before they had sex, his sweetness had charmed her.

A major red flag she'd blown right past.

"'Sweet' is code for boring," Tasha warned when Kelsey broke the news that she and Clive weren't having sex. "Who buys a car without test driving it first?"

Now it made sense why Clive hadn't wanted to have sex with her. Not because she was special as he'd claimed. Nope, she was safe and gullible, and she'd taken him at his word.

What a dumbass she was. Wadding the letter in her fist, Kelsey tossed it into the wicker wastebasket.

"Good start." Rubbing her palms, Tasha gave a gleeful grin. "Let's cash in those tickets and get this party started. You need a wild night with a hot guy. How long has it been since you've had sex?"

Over eighteen months. Since before the last year and a half, when she'd been with Clive. "Don't know if I'm ready for that.

"Will you stop? Because you must get back out there. Time's a-wasting." Tasha reached for her clutch purse, popped it open, and took out a fifth of Fireball whiskey. "I brought this for the wedding reception, but we need it *now*."

"Believe me." Kelsey held up a palm. "I'm mad at myself for letting things get this far. I should have stopped the wedding, but my mother started the steamroller and I just climbed aboard. The way I always do."

"Reason enough to take a shot." After she twisted the top of the bottle, Tasha chugged a mouthful of hooch, let loose with a satisfied burp, and pressed the whiskey into Kelsey's hand.

"I don't—"

"Drink," Tasha commanded.

"Good gravy, I'm not wrecked. Promise."

"But you should get wrecked. Get mad. Howl at the moon. Let loose." Tasha stuck her arms out at her sides as if she was an airplane. "Wing woman at your service. Never fear, Tasha is here."

Sighing, Kelsey wondered if her friend had a point. Who would judge her for getting drunk after being jilted at the altar?

With a toss of her head, she took a short swallow as the cinnamon-flavored whiskey burned and lit a warm liquid fire in the pit of her stomach.

"Take another," Tasha coached.

Opening her mouth to say no, three words flashed vivid neon in Kelsey's mind. *You were safe.*

Clive nailed it. Since her twin sister, Chelsea, drowned on Possum Kingdom Lake when they were ten, she'd been playing it safe. Honestly, even before then. "Safe" was her factory default setting.

With a snort, Kelsey took another drink. Longer this time, and she felt her insides start to unspool.

"Good girl." A pat on Kelsey's shoulder and Tasha offered her an understanding smile.

After the third shot, Kelsey felt warm and woozy and ten times better than she had half an hour ago.

"Okay, okay." With a worried expression, Tasha took the bottle away from her. "All things in moderation. Don't want to hold your hair while you puke before we even get out of the church."

Snapping her fingers, Kelsey reached for the bottle. "Gimme. I'm done playing by the rules."

Quick as a ninja, Tasha hid the whiskey behind her. "I've created a monster. You'll get it back when we're in the limo."

"Bye, bye limo. Clive and Kevin took it."

"How do you know?"

"Peep at the curb."

Poking her head out the window, Tasha said, "Oh well. Uber, here we come."

"Where to?"

"Wherever you want to go. In place of a honeymoon, we'll spend the next three weeks doing something wild and crazy. Impulse, rashness, and spontaneity are our buzzwords." In that loveable, dramatic way of hers, Tasha tossed her chin.

"Don't you have a job?"

Spinning her finger in the air helicopter-blade style, Tasha said, "I quit last week."

"Wait. What? Why?"

"Had a set to with my boss. Because he pinched my ass, and I slapped his face, yada, yada, he wins."

"Oh Tash, I'm so sorry. Did you consult a lawyer?"

"No need. Handled it on social media." Buffing her knuckles against her shirt, Tasha grinned.

"Why didn't I know this?" Kelsey asked. *You are a shitty friend.* "Why didn't you tell me?"

"Wedding prep and getting your mother elected mayor of

Dallas kept you snowed. Whenever did you have time for my drama?"

"What are friends for? Amends are in order."

"Then kick up those heels."

"Shouldn't you be scouting another job instead of holding my hand?"

"No worries. Got a new one."

"When? Where?"

"Take a gander at the new executive chef at La Fonda's, and I start after the New Year. Tony should have pinched my ass a long time ago. I'd gotten too comfy where I was."

"That's awesome! I mean about the executive chef job, not getting your ass pinched. Congrats."

"Let's do this thing." With one palm raised in the air as if she was a waiter balancing a tray, Tasha pumped her hand. "Celebrate my new job and your freedom at the same time. Epic adventure."

"No doubt." She mulled over Tasha's proposition. Why not? Time to break out of her safe little bubble.

"Where should we go? New Orleans? Eat gumbo, drink hurricanes, and get inked?" Tasha wriggled her eyebrows. "What do you think about me getting a spider tattoo on my neck?"

Wincing, Kelsey sucked in her breath through clenched teeth. "Hmm, Cajun food upsets my stomach."

"Vegas? Blow through our mad money, pick up male strippers?"

"Um, I want something more—"

"Kelsey-ish?"

Sedate was the word that had popped into her head. Sedate. Sedative. Comatose long enough. "Where would you prefer to go, Tasha? Whatever you decide, I'm good with it."

An exaggerated roll of her eyes. "Girl, you got dumped on your wedding day, and I can find a party wherever I go, even in your safe, white bread world."

She adored Tasha's spunkiness. Spunk was also the reason

why Filomena wasn't a big Tasha fan. Five years ago, they met when Kelsey was organizing a fundraiser during her mother's bid for a city council seat. In charge of hiring the caterers for the event at the Dallas Museum of Art, Kelsey had gone to interview Tasha's boss.

When Tasha popped a mini quiche into Kelsey's mouth and it was the best damn thing she'd ever eaten, she'd hired the caterer on the spot, based on Tasha's cooking skills alone. After hitting it off, Kelsey stuck around to help Tasha clean up, and the rest belonged in the annals of BFF history.

"Wherever we go, there must be scads of hot *straight* guys," Tasha said. "How does a dude ranch sound?"

"Good heavens, I have no idea how to ride a horse."

"Yeah, me neither."

"Wherever you want, I'll go."

"Don't make me pick. I always pick, this is for *you*. My mind is lassoed onto hot cowboys. Yum. Ropes, spurs, yeehaw."

"Let the sex stuff go, will you? I don't need to have sex."

"Oh, but you do. Sex is exactly what you need."

"If my libido was a car on the freeway, it would take the slow lane."

"Because you've never had great sex." Tasha chuckled. "For eighteen months, you've been in a deep freeze. Tick tock, time to wake up Sleeping Beauty and reclaim your sexuality."

"I dunno . . ." Kelsey fiddled with the hem on the wedding gown that had cost as much as a new compact car.

"C'mon, you gotta have hot fantasies." Tasha's voice took on a sultry quality. "What are they? A little BDSM? Role-playing? Booty call in scandalous places? A park bench, a pool, a carnival carousel?"

"A carousel?"

"Hey, it happens."

"Tasha, did you have sex on a carousel?"

Her friend shot her a sneaky grin. "Once, maybe. I'll never tell."

Through lowered eyelashes, Kelsey tossed the rose bouquet into the trash on top of Clive's crumpled letter.

You were safe.

"Quit playing coy and cough 'em up," Tasha said. "Name your fantasies. Scottish Highlander in a short kilt and no undies? Or football player wearing those skintight pants? Fireman? Doctor? Construction worker?"

"The YMCA players?"

Tasha heehawed. "No more gay guys for you!"

"Hmm, there is one fantasy . . ." Kelsey mumbled.

"Just one?" Waving her hand, Tasha said, "Never mind, not judging. One is plenty. What is it?"

Not what, *who*. "Forget it."

"Is he a real person?" Leaning in, Tasha's breath quickened. "A celebrity? Or . . ." Wickedly, her voice dropped even lower. "Someone you've met?'

Unbidden, Noah MacGregor's face popped into Kelsey's head. In her mind's eye, Noah looked as he had the last time she'd seen him. Seventeen years old, the same age she'd been, and six-foot-five. Linebacker shoulders, narrow waist, lean hips. His muscular chest bare, hard abs taut with her lipstick imprinted on his skin. Unsnapped, unzipped jeans.

Wild hair.

Wilder heart.

Rattled and rocked, her safe little world tilted. Noah was so big, so tall, and he had a wicked glint in his eyes. An honest man, independent and sexy, and one hot look from him had sent her heart scrambling.

That final night, they'd been making out on the dock at Camp Hope, a grief camp for children on Lake Twilight. Both junior counselors that year after having attended the camp every summer since they were eleven.

On the dock, a blanket and candles and flowers. Courtesy of her romantic boyfriend.

Fever pitch kisses.

They were ready to have sex—*finally*—when he'd jumped up, breathing hard. His angular mouth, which tasted of peppermint and something darkly mysterious, pressed into a serious line. Noah's thick, dark chocolate locks curled around his ears, and his deep brown eyes were enigmatic.

In her bikini, she'd blinked up at him, her mind a delicious haze of teenage lust and longing. "What's wrong?"

"Did you hear something?" Noah peered into the shadows.

Propped up on her elbows, Kelsey cocked her head. Heard the croak of bullfrogs and the splash of fish breaking the surface of the water as they jumped up to catch bugs in the moonlight. "No."

Doubled fists, pricked ears, he remained standing, ready for a fight if one came his way. Ready to protect her. Her pulse sprinted. Proud and brave and strong, he looked as if he were a hero from the cover of the romance novels that she loved to read.

She'd fallen deeper in love with him at that moment. Head right over heels. Over banana splits at Rinky-Tink's ice cream parlor, they had shyly said the words to each other. I love you. Then again when he'd carved their names in the Sweetheart Tree in Sweetheart Park near the Twilight town square. Sneaked off that summer for trysts after their campers were asleep.

They'd kissed and hugged and petted but hadn't yet gone to third base. Tonight was the night. On the pill. A box of condoms. They were ready and eager. Kelsey reached for him, grabbed hold of his wrist and tugged him to his knees. Their first time. Both eager virgins dreaming of this for weeks. Souls wide open.

"Come . . ." she'd coaxed. "Don't worry, it's after midnight. Everyone is snug in their cabins."

Allowing her to draw him back beside her, Noah branded her with his mouth and covered her trembling body with his own.

Hot hands.

Electric touch.

Three-dimensional!

The night was sticky. Raw with heat and hunger. Calloused

fingertips stroked cockily against her velvet skin. The boards of the dock creaked and swayed beneath their movements as he untied her bikini top.

Footsteps.

Solid. Quick. Determined.

Filomena!

From nowhere, her mother was on the dock beside them and grabbing a fistful of Kelsey's hair in her hand, her mother yanked her to her feet. Kelsey's bikini top flew into the lake.

Angry shouts.

Ugly accusations.

Threats.

Regular life stuff with her mother when things didn't go Filomena's way. Mom, dragging her to the car parked on the road after she'd driven up with the headlights off. She'd sneaked up, hoping to catch them in the act. How had her mother known they would be here? Blinded by the idea that Filomena had been keeping tabs by tracking her every move via her cell phone, Kelsey's fears ratcheted into her throat.

A hard shove and Filomena stuffed Kelsey into the car's back seat and shook a fierce fist at Noah, who'd followed them. Warned him to stay away. Promised litigation and other dire consequences if he dared to contact Kelsey ever again.

"Noah!" Kelsey had cried as her mother hit the childproof door locks to prevent him from opening the door and springing her free.

Pounding on the car window with a heavy fist, Noah demanded her mother have a rational conversation with him.

Stone-faced, Filomena started the car.

"I'll come after you," Noah yelled to Kelsey. "I'll find you, and we will be together. We won't let her win. Promise."

Kelsey wanted to cling to that flimsy promise. Take it to mean something. Fervent hopes. Girlish dreams. But even then, she knew her mother would ruin it.

"Over my dead body," Filomena yelled.

"Noah, just go," she'd cried, wanting to spare him.

"Kelsey!" His face was ghostly in the night, his eyes silver dollars as he pressed his face to the glass.

"She'll run over you. Get out of the way. Go!"

Filomena floored the car, leaving Noah standing desolately in the middle of the road.

Sobbing and shivering, Kelsey sat half-naked in the Cadillac's back seat, and she never saw Noah again.

Years later, out of curiosity, Kelsey searched for Noah and found him on social media, and learned he was a successful point guard in the NBA and married to a drop-dead gorgeous model. Did not friend him. Far too late to rekindle childhood flames. Lost hopes. Empty dreams. Ancient history. Soon afterward, she'd met Clive, and that was that.

But now, here she was, dumped and half-drunk. Nothing to look forward to but her mother's predictable holiday harangue. Plenty of reason to hate the holidays. This year, she had little choice but to review her life mistakes.

Ho, ho, ho. Merry *freaking* Christmas.